Hello Listener

Lorien Ray

CONTENTS

PLAYLIST

L o v e l y// slowed down-slo-mo sounds (Prologue)

Close Eyes (Slowed+Reverb)-DVRST (Ch. 1.)

The Perfect Girl-Mareux (Ch. 2.)

Paparazzi-Kim Dracula (Ch. 3.)

Desire(Hucci Remix)-MEG MYERS (Ch. 4.)

Sleepless- Dutch Melrose (Ch. 5.)

Like That- Sleep Token (Ch. 6.)

Bad Decisions-Bad Omens (Ch. 7.)

Under the Influence x Renegade- Neo Soundz (Ch. 8.)

Into It- Chase Atlantic (Ch. 9.)

Can't Take My Eyes Off of You (Slowed + Reverb)- Slowed + Reverb
tiktok audios, creamy & 11:11 Music Group (Ch. 10.)

Disdain-CORPSE (Ch. 11.)

Night Vibe- Skyfall Beats (Ch. 12.)

THE DEATH OF PEACE AND MIND-Bad Omens (Ch. 13.)

Are You All Good-Breathe (Ch. 14.)

Savior- Novulent (Ch. 15.)

White Tee (Alternate Bass Boosted Version)- CORPSE (Ch. 16)

Huey Lewis and the News- Hip to Be Square Vaporwave remix
(Slow + Reverb)-idlevbs (Ch. 17.)

Tonight (demo)- Amira Elfeky (Ch. 18.)

Trigger/Content Warnings

There are many topics in this book that may be triggering and not meant for minors. Please make sure you read them before you continue. If any of the following triggers upset you in any way, please do not continue. My triggers are not listed in any specific order. Your mental health matters!

- Kidnapping

- Masturbation: Discussion and practice

- Strong sexual situations

- Serial killers: Discussion and Practice

- Murder

- Dismemberment of body parts

- Decapitation

- Masturbation with a corpse

- Stalking

- Dangerous obsession

- Primal play

- Blood play

- Breaking and entering

- Gore

- Domestic violence

- Infidelity

- Mention of drug abuse

- Stalking on social media

- Talks of mental health

- Knife Play

- Alcohol use

- Praise kink

- Torture

- Vulgarity

- "Playing" with dismembered body parts

- Degradation

- Manipulation

"Murder is not just a crime of lust or violence. It becomes a possession. They are part of you...[the victim] becomes a part of you and you [two] are forever one...and the grounds where you kill them or leave them become sacred to you, and you will always be drawn back to them. -Ted Bundy

Prologue

I stare at you blankly while you sleep on whatever the thread count of these sheets is. Your blonde hair is spread out over your gray pillowcase, perfectly matching our sheets. Your breasts are hidden under the loose cotton fabric while you lie there, fast asleep and spread out on your side of the bed in your own post-sex euphoria.

My life with you started out like any stereotypical high school archetype. The rich football player who got good grades because no parent wanted an idiot for a son; and the blonde cheerleader from the well-off family. Our relationship began as a manipulated picture. A picture with us hand in hand in expensive tuxedos and silk dresses. A vision that was clouded with us walking happily to high school parties—our faces covered in fake plastic smiles.

I thought I loved you then. Your smile, your long blonde hair in loose waves, your tight athletic body.

It was everything I was supposed to like and eventually love one day. My lust for you has always been in full effect. I wish I could say the same for love.

I once looked at you like a prize to be won. A petite, shiny trophy I could put in a large display case. One that was filled with expensive furniture and decor that does nothing but show off our wealth and status and appeals to her every whim—taunting me with its meaningless use.

Do you see the lackluster of our marriage, or are you still trapped in the fantasy money has put us in? Are your eyes still filled with dollar signs when you're lying in this large bed with a man you promised your life?

Mine are long gone, and I'm left with the what ifs. What if I had decided to not give in to the same role as my spoiled parents and their circle of rich friends? What if I had married for love and not for someone who would only look good hanging on my arm as a trophy wife? What if I had chosen a simpler life? Maybe I would be happy in what may be a smaller house with less objects, and I would finally get to do something for myself, not things to please other people. For once, I would be that simple man rather than a man molded to look good for my family name—an abundant amount of money in my account with the expectation to provide for the two of us.

Perhaps you already see it in me. Maybe you can tell while I'm on top of you, only to fulfill our ultimate job of adding to the spoiled and rich population. I see you, as you put on your best show for me. I know you're thinking about someone else. Maybe your tennis instructor, someone you met online, or at the country club during the numerous times you insisted on going alone, or maybe he is a fictitious man from your books.

If you want me to be completely honest with you my dear, it doesn't matter to me, because all I can think about is *her.*

This isn't how it used to be. Our life is just a picture of what you see in shopping catalogs, filled with price tags and gleaming objects. That's all our marriage is. One big shiny picture.

Chapter One

Hello, Listeners

THALIA

R ain falls softly on my black umbrella, the noise faint against the the the splashing of my boots in the puddles on the sidewalk. I put in my wireless earbuds as I move in and out of crowds of people headed toward me. Even in rain, this city never sleeps.

The deep melody of his voice seeps into my ears. "Hello, ladies and gentlemen." The smooth and slightly mysterious tone sends a shiver up my spine. I can't tell if it's the timbre of his voice echoing in my ears or the crisp October air that causes goosebumps on my arms beneath my black leather jacket. Maybe it's a bit of both.

"Yeah, hey fuckers." A wide smile covers my face as the producer and co-host chimes in. I know it's him by the slight Manhattan accent in his voice.

"Ladies and gentlemen, if you're new here, this is the Manhattan Murders Podcast. Thank you so fucking much for tuning in." His voice is like whiskey, warm as it slips through me. It's a sound that ignites a burning in my own veins. If it could be bottled, I would take shots of it all day.

I finally make it to my destination: The Neon Rose Lounge. There are no free Fridays for *this* bartender. The job always demands my weekends. Through the glass double doors, I watch my best friend Jace wipe down the bar and prepare for tonight's crowd. He cleans the black marbled surface down with what's left of the white tattered rags we store under the bar.

Pulling the front doors open, they squeak as I walk inside. He looks up when he hears my boots hit the hard wooden floor. I set my black purse on one of the small, onyx round tables just as always before we officially open for the night. These empty tables and their matching chairs will be full in a matter of hours. Mostly by drunk men trying to pick up the unsuspecting women drinking with their friends.

"Bitch, about time you showed up." His neon pink hair stands out next to the dark paint on the walls. It *almost* matches the hot pink lettering in The Neon Rose sign posted above the door outside. I smile as I remove my ear buds, knowing it will be a new color in a matter of a few days.

"What the hell, Jace. I'm early."

"Girl, I know. I needed some time to talk shit before the men come crowding in thinking they can fit in between those thick thighs of yours." He teases.

"Well, be my guest! Shit talk away, baby." My pale cheeks turn a bright shade of red that matches the vibrant color of my hair. *He always knows just what to say.*

"Shit talking? Who are we shit talking about?" Our boss, and owner of The Neon Rose Lounge joins in. The sound of the heels from her knee length boots comes tapping towards us as she makes her way closer to the bar. Her maroon hair bounces on her purple-sweater-covered shoulders. Her speed picks up as she eagerly walks in our direction.

"Oh honey, the fun has just begun." Jace's voice lightens. His silver nose ring catches my eye as it shines from the glow of the edison bulbs above us.

"Who do you think will grace us with their presence tonight?" My boss' face turns into a small smirk.

"You think the guy with the neck tattoos will be here," I ask, half laughing trying to hide my distaste for the regular patron. *Anyone but him.* He comes in every Friday in hopes he can take me back to his place. He pulls his dark greasy hair into an unkempt pony tail that shows his badly done neck tattoos. Whoever drew on the crooked lines must've had a difficult time drawing through the constant sweat that pours from his tan skin. Just the idea of being alone with him is enough to make my stomach turn.

"Girl, I hope not. Sonofabitch never tips. It's the least I need of him. Maybe he'll take his hair down so I don't have to see those nasty ass neck tattoos of his. Motherfucker thinks he's God's gift to women." Jace's voice raises, with his arms getting more animated. *You good, Jace?* I can't help my mental question as my eyes widen when he talks about the regular creep that comes in. "Janice," Jace continues. His mannerisms completely transform as he changes the subject. "Your man coming in tonight?" My boss jumps at the thought. Her admirer comes in every Friday as well. He orders the same drink, a Manhattan. *How fucking original.* He stares at her and only her from behind his wire-rimmed glasses. He never takes his eyes off her as she patrols the bar. Poor guy probably thinks it's romantic, maybe even a twisted form of admiration, but it's actually just fucking creepy.

"Oh god, I hope so." She lets out a loud sigh. "The tips he gives are what keeps this bar going." She makes her way to the kitchen but not before giving Jace her over exaggerated wink.

There is always a light on in the kitchen. I personally don't spend too much time there. I know there are guys who were hired to cook the food for this place. By that, I mean warm up pre-packaged frozen appetizers, pour some chips in a bowl, and maybe cut up some vegetables. I'm sure the kitchen has its busy moments, but out here is where the action is. Plus it's where I get my tips.

"Thalia," Jace turns his attention to me. "When are you going to get you a man?" He stops me mid adjusting my black mesh shirt.

"If I had a man, I would never have enough time with you here or on the days I have off." He smiles. He can clearly see through my bullshit.

"What you need to do is pull that shirt of yours down and pull those tiddies out to at least get some tips. Maybe even get you someone for the night." I scoff at the thought.

"I'm not really interested in the guys that come in here."

"Who says you need to be interested? You need more than that vibrator in your nightstand and those headphones of yours."

"Jace!" My mouth opens in shock. But honestly, a part of me agrees with him. It would be nice to have more than my hands and an inanimate object on some lonely nights.

"Girl, everyone knows what you do when you get home. There's only so much true crime you can listen to, even if their voices are sexy as hell." Little does he know, I could listen to people talk of gruesome acts of violence all day if it came from the both of them.

Jace and I turn on our bartender charm as the night grows later and the bar gets louder. Janice, being the good little owner she is, does her share, too. The sounds of chatter and glasses clinking fill the dining area. I turn every now and then to face Jace to check on the line of people in front of him. Just as I suspect, he has everyone's glasses lined up. His rehearsed "honey," and customer service smile makes me naturally grin. Even if not genuine, his aura is addicting.

After noticing the line of people in front of me die down, I take a rag and clean the closest dirty glass to keep busy. My Friday night will move faster as long as I keep working.

The night is coming to a standstill. Closing time is getting closer. Just a half hour more and it's time to head home and do what I love to do best: get in my PJs, lie in my bed, and finish up the newest episode from my favorite podcast. Most of the people who were once laughing, taking sips from their glasses, and slinging back shots have left. Probably to go to their penthouses or the other bars on the street. Now that everyone is gone, you can hear the rain drops hitting the windows and glass door.

"No sign of the guy with the neck tattoos," I point out to Jace. Maybe he won't be able to hear the excitement in my voice. *A night without his constant one liners and creepy looks would be a bit of relief.* Unfortunately, however, Jace and I are fooled with the sound of the front door slowly opening. *Fuck.* Jace turns his head and laughs. He isn't too shy about the humor in all of this. Of course, why did I have to be so lucky. *Why the fuck me?*

"Hey stranger, didn't think you'd make it in tonight." My fake smile and rehearsed bartender character are in full swing. My face burns from the strain it gives me. *Why the fuck did you have to come in this close to closing time?! Hell, why did you have to come in at all?*

"I couldn't end my Friday night without seeing you." I cringe at his rehearsed wink. *Yeah. Get fucked, creep.* He pulls his straight, greasy hair away from his face and puts it in his usual ponytail with a black rubber band. *Come on guy, you're going to get your disgusting hair all over the fucking bar after I just wiped it down. Typical.*

"Well, lucky me." *Keep it together, Thalia. One drink, his usual lame ass pickup line, and he's gone. That's his usual routine.* "What can I get you?"

"Your number maybe?" *Lame ass pickup line: check. Line didn't work the first time.*

"Still not on the menu." I add. Giggling at the start of the sentence. *Maybe that would hide my disgust for this guy.*

"Well shit, just an Old Fashion." *That should be easy enough. It's a favorite around here. It seems like everyone orders it.* I grab the whiskey glass, add a couple of ice cubes, and start pouring in the brown liquor. His eyes move from the small tattoos on my hands to my tits under my black mesh shirt as I make the cocktail. *Fucking creep.* I slide him the sweating glass. *A sweating glass to match his clammy hands.* I add a little wink at the end. *A girl needs her tips.*

"Closing time yet?" Jace asks as I walk over to his end of the bar. There is a bit of a whine to his voice as he lays his head against my shoulder. His pink hair slowly disappears into a fade just along the back of his neck.

"Not until that fucker leaves." He laughs as I place my hands on my hips.

"Just give into the man, damn. Maybe he'll leave you alone once he slides in between those legs of yours."

"Ew. No, thanks. He's not my type."

"What? You into girls now?" Jace laughs jokingly.

"No, but his desperation just hangs off of him. Also, his long, unwashed hair makes me cringe."

"Girl, it's more than what you've been getting. When he whispers in your ear, just think of those men you listen to every night." I gag at the thought. Kind of like those videos you see of cats gagging at the smell of broccoli. Just picture that.

"Jace, I can't. I'm not settling. I'm better than that."

"I know, but who said anything about settling? I'm not telling you to marry the guy. I'm just telling you to get some of that…" He pauses his thought, only to finish it off with a few grinding motions. Making me let out a laugh that may or may not have echoed in the room. My loud cackle causes "neck tattoo guy" to look over in our direction.

"Sorry, Thalia's only interested in the men in her headphones," Jace yells over the music coming from the speakers. *Oh, god.* I hide my head in my hands with embarrassment. Luckily, he smiles and waves it off and proceeds to go back to whatever he was doing on his phone.

The night finally comes to an end as soon as that creep leaves after his drink and verbal desperation. Every weekend, he mirrors his routine visits. Janice stands at the end of the bar and counts down the register. My eyes stare up at her while she counts the money in the tip jar. Big tips meant Thai food from my favorite place on the way home. Best thing about the city, everything stays open late.

"Everything looks accounted for. Looks like you two have to keep working for me." She looks up at us with a smirk once again. Her Latina accent peeks out from her snarky tone.

"Shit!" I say jokingly while she gives me a sly look.

"And now the time you've both been waiting for..." She puts on her best announcer voice as Jace and I drum on the freshly cleaned table tops. "Your tips." Janice hands me and Jace both of our shares. Yes! Looks like Thai for dinner tonight. Janice switches off the lights in the building. One by one, sections of the room go dark and we double check around the bar, making sure the place is ready to close before Janice locks up.

Janice fishes out her keys from her purse. Jace and I follow one another out of the bar as she holds open one of the heavy doors for us.

"Be safe, you two," Janice calls out. She tries to play the role of our bigger sister in this dysfunctional little family we have at work. It's sweet, really.

"Oh, you know we'll be safe. Thalia listens to enough true crime to protect us," Jace yells back towards her taxi. She smiles and climbs in. I notice her shaking her head while she quietly laughs. Never a dull moment with our little family.

"What are you about to do?" He asks as he takes my hand and swings it down the sidewalk. "No wait, I already know. Let me guess. Don't tell me. Thai food?"

"Am I that predictable?" I ask, adding a little whine to the tone of the question.

"Girl, yes. Thai food, then let me guess...shower, podcast, buzz and then bed." He moves each finger down, as if counting down my check list.

"Maybe not the 'buzz' part..." I admit while using finger quotes.

"Don't lie to me and don't lie to yourself." Jace states matter of factly. He looks at me with full confidence. *Who am I kidding, he knows me.*

I shrug. I'm not fooling anyone, especially my best friend. Jace climbs into another cab and waves as the car speeds off.

I continue walking in the cold breeze to my destination. First stop noodles, next stop, home.

The smell of the greasy delicacy hits my nose immediately as I open the clear bag, it only makes my craving for takeout worse. I turn the key into the door of my one bedroom apartment with my cat, Artemis, greeting me at the door. The sound of his purrs are like pure serotonin. I carelessly throw my jacket onto my black couch. Every light is off except for a single lamp on an ebony end table close to my window. You could say it sits in what you would call my living room.

I flop myself down on my couch, my bag of takeout crinkling upon impact. I lay the styrofoam box on the small excuse for a coffee table that I have in the middle of the tiny area. Like a feral animal, I begin stuffing my face with the greasy noodles. It should be a sin how good these are.

I scan through Netflix on my TV that is also probably smaller than it should be. I spend about thirty minutes looking for something to mindlessly watch and end up settling on a true crime documentary that I have already seen multiple times. At this point, it's just background noise while I scroll through social media apps on my phone. I switch from different ones after getting bored with the different feeds. In reality, I know how I want to end this night.

The leftovers are shut in the styrofoam box they came in, and the remaining noodles are a focal point in my mostly empty fridge. My small apartment goes dark after I switch off the lamp on my end table and turn off the TV. Artemis follows me into my tiny bathroom that is connected to my bedroom. My eyes squint as bright light fills the small space with one flip of my white plated light switch. Sounds of the shower can be heard throughout my apartment once stepping in under the scalding hot water. I stand under the water for probably longer than needed, rinsing the smell of desperation and alcohol down the drain. While turning off the shower and grabbing for the nearest towel, my stinging eyes beg me for some relief. Only subduing the pain with one wipe of the gray cotton towel across both of my lids.

After stepping out, my towel is wrapped snug around my body, just above my chest. Like a routine, I flip off the switch to the bathroom light, and almost immediately switch on my bedroom light which is only a few steps to the right. It triggers another small lamp on my nightstand next to my bed in the corner of my room. Artemis is already on the end of my full size bed. He stares up at me, waiting for me to tuck myself in. While reaching into my small dresser for a pair of gray cotton shorts and an oversized Ramones tee shirt, the idea of laying in my bed under my heavy comforter puts a smile on my face.

The climb into my bed is better than it should be. I like nothing more than lying down and scrolling through my phone after a tough night of making cocktails and listening to drunk people bitch about their lives. *Well almost nothing.*

I turn over and reach inside my nightstand. The drawer slides out in one smooth motion, as if it's used to the nightly regime. Without looking, my hand glides over the smooth rubber surface, and I grip around the hard, cylinder device. *Don't lie to me and don't lie to yourself.* Jace's words play in my head. I trace my finger over the button that will help end this night with a smile on my exhausted face. I shut the small drawer to the tiny nightstand as his words, "Hello, ladies and gentleman," play in the speakers of my earbuds.

Chapter Two

MANHATTAN MURDERS PODCAST

▪◉▪ALAN

I sit down in my large, leather office chair. It rolls ever so slightly on the plastic covering the carpet under the small wheels and black desk. You know the covering I'm talking about. The ones you only see in offices and they leave small indentations in the carpet.

After a few seconds of assured silence in my office—which doubles as my studio—it's time to start our new episode. With my mic placed just a few inches from my mouth, I look at Lee and silently ask, "You ready?" He gives me his universal signal of a thumbs up and pushes record.

"Hello, listeners," I speak smoothly into the microphone.

"Yeah. Hey fuckers," Lee chimes in. Both of us end the welcome in quiet laughter, but loud enough to be in tonight's episode. The listeners love that. It makes them feel like they're listening to "real people," not just some person doing it for the money. Besides, the two of us already have enough. We do it for the connection we have between other people who love true crime as much as we do. You have to make sure you include our personal characteristics. *Those* are what the people look for. It's the tiny details that matter.

"If you've never tuned in," I continue in the same smooth tone, "you're listening to the Manhattan Murders Podcast. I'm your host and escort through this spine tingling adventure, Alan Jones. And to my left, for you visual viewers, is the talented Lee Reynolds." I end the greeting by leaning back in my chair. My arms instinctively fold across my chest. The creaking sound of the chair echoes in the mic.

"Hey everybody," Lee starts. "What kind of shit show do you have for us today Alan?"

"Well, *every* episode is a shit show I'd say. People don't come here to listen about good times, my friend." I incline in closer to the mic when I talk.

"That's true. Well, in that case what kind of sick fuck will we be talking about then?" He mirrors my actions and moves closer into his mic. Leaning his tattooed covered arms against the desk. "The listeners and I want to know."

"The sick fuck as you speak of, is none other than David Berkowitz." I answer with an ounce of humor added to my voice.

"The Son of Sam himself..." Lee adds, voice trailing off to create suspense.

"That's right my friend. The Son of Sam. Or as some people would call him, the .44 Caliber Killer."

"He *was* a sick fuck." Lee adds matter-of-factly. "Sick in the head, I mean."

We continue bantering which adds a certain finesse to the episode. People seem to eat that shit up.

You have me, more of the smooth talker type and a bit more eloquent if you will. I'm the one with the facts and information on the cases and the serial killers themselves. While Lee, on the other hand, brings his "I don't give a shit" attitude which helps lighten the mood a little. All while talking about what we, *well mostly me*, are interested in. If you haven't gathered, it's the "sick fucks" of Manhattan.

Unfortunately that doesn't *quite* have the ring to it that we needed. So, we decided to stick with Manhattan Murders. We try to stay within the lines of talking about true crime occurring in or around Manhattan. Lee thought we needed to be specific, something that makes us stick out from everyone else. I agreed since he usually knows what he is talking about when it comes to the media and what people gravitate towards.

After a small pause in the discussion of The Son of Sam, I take a large swig of my coffee from my dark charcoal colored mug sitting just a few inches to the left of the mic. It's nothing special, just one of those plain mugs that cost way more money than it should.

"Alan, what are you drinking in that mug of yours?" Lee asks into his mic.

"What the hell do you think it is? It's a coffee mug. I'm drinking coffee."

"Coffee! Who the *fuck* drinks coffee on a Friday night?" Lee, the bastard, makes me laugh. It's not what he says, it's how he delivers it. He has a talent for enunciating specific words in the best comedic timing. The sound of me spitting coffee out through my laughter will *definitely* be on next week's episode. The listeners will love it. *Maybe they'll even laugh along with me.*

"What about you, what are you drinking? You got something good in there?" I tease, already knowing what it is.

"Whiskey, because I'm not a little bitch." He takes his glass and lifts it to his mouth. The little ice cubes clank in the glass as he sets it back down on the coaster on his desk. Another clip of my laughter is added to the episode.

"Not all of us are liquor connoisseurs." I answer again in the mic before taking another drink from my mug.

"For as long as you have known me, you should be by now." The sound of Lee sipping from his glass can be heard once more. "This guy and his *fucking* coffee."

We continue the episode, adding more and more banter and facts about The Son of Sam. Where he lived—right here in New York. What his home life was like—not the best some would say. Whether or not the voices in his head were demons or if he was just insane. I would tell you, that's up to your own beliefs.

We usually add when the killers had their first kill, what drove them to do it, and when they were finally caught. Just your generic timeline of events. What sets us apart from everyone else, is we add our own twist to our version of a true crime podcast. We are real, and we aren't trying to be like every other serial killer documentary. We're true crime enthusiasts and we love diving deeper into the darker parts of New York City. Only, we add in our own charming personalities.

"Well, that's all of the time we have today ladies and gentlemen. We'll see you in next week's episode."

"You got any hints on who we'll be talking about next week?" Lee asks with his glass up to his lips.

"Just know, he was one sick fuck."

"Oh, another one of those?" Lee laughs and plays our show's exit music. It's a tune made up in one of Lee's editing sessions.

"We've got to have our own thing. Something people will re-member." He'd said when we first decided to come up with the idea for The Manhattan Murders Podcast. I'll give it to him, it *is* pretty catchy. A lot of bass and a hint of unsettling Lofi ambiance.

Lee clicks the record button on the computer so it is no longer highlighted in red. We both gently lay our headphones on the black desks.

"What are you doing tonight? What kind of trouble are you and the 'ol lady getting into?" The 'Ol' lady he is referring to is my wife, Ashley. I assume at this point she is sitting in the living room on the couch with her phone or her Kindle. Most likely reading something full of sex and something social media told her to read. She could be lazily lying down while texting her friends from her book club.

"No, it's probably another night in for us." The thought of going outside in the pouring rain and doing anything around people in a crowded restaurant or bar makes my skin crawl.

"You should let me take you out one of these days after we record. Just us guys," he puts an exaggerated *s* on the word guys.

"Yeah. Sure." I nod. *That's the last fucking thing I want to do. The idea of being around drunk people I don't know sounds like a terrible idea.*

"Yeah. Sure," he repeats. His eyes roll in disbelief. "You know, Alan, there *is* more to life than serial killers and the documentaries made about them. I'm sure she won't mind if I take you out." Honestly, I'm sure she wouldn't. Whenever she is home, which is rare might I add, she's glued to her phone, Kindle, or asleep. Her charming husband isn't usually on her list of activities.

"I've got to get ideas for next week's episode, my friend." I politely counter. "I'm sure she wouldn't care if I went out. If she's home and has her phone and that couch, she's set."

"Well, shit. She has all of that. Let's go! We just finished an episode. I'm sure you need a break from all of the psycho research." Lee grabs his black leather coat from the back of his seat which is identical to mine. He swings it around so that his tattooed arms can slide right in the silk lined sleeves.

"Maybe another night." The sound of the rain getting heavier hits the roof just at the right moment.

"I'm going to hold you to that, Alan." He tips his glass back, leaving it empty aside from a few drops. *Looking forward to it.* I give him a small upturned smile that I know he can see right through.

Without another word, he walks out of my studio and makes his way to the front door through my large living room. With nothing else to keep him here, Lee lets the door snick shut behind him.

A few seconds later, I notice Lee getting into his black Mustang. From the large window in my living room, my mind fills with a small twinge of envy, watching how the light reflects from the street lamps and the raindrops enhance its pristine condition. *Lucky son of a bitch.* He lives the single life of a thirty-two year old man. The New York bachelor life, the mirrored image of the life you see in movies. The one that all men say they dream of. A pretty good looking guy, business owner through his father's inheritance, a ladies man by his account, and of course a co-owner of a podcast. I shut my white curtains after I watch him— the feeling of covetousness worming its way into my chest—drive past a few houses.

My wife and I live in a suburb just outside of the city. I'm sure it's in Lee's best interest to get out of here as quickly as possible. He's more of a city person. The idea of spending time in gated communities makes him squirm. Although, the thought of him living in one of these houses makes me silently laugh to myself. After his first marriage, I don't know if he will ever settle down and move into one of these cookie cutter homes again.

With my back towards the front door, I watch my wife on our overstuffed gray couch. The lamp is still on, but it is the only light on in the room. I see Ashley's ereader face down on her chest. She must have fallen asleep reading again.

The life of the thirty four year old married couple.

I wonder what social media told her to read tonight. She's mentioned to me about a few of her books in the past, but I can never get the titles or the characters straight. Frankly, I don't really care. I am happy she has found something to do while Lee and I do our Friday night recordings. I grab the white cashmere blanket from behind her on the back of the gray couch and lay it flat against her light gray lounge suit. Another wild night for the Joneses.

With my wife asleep on the couch and me wide awake, my studio calls my name. I flip on the lights and quietly shut the door. My chair slides out allowing me to slouch back on the firm leather seat. The black wheels slide back underneath the desk and I reach for my laptop, opening it with ease.

My background isn't anything special. Just a generic, dark blue behind a column of icons. My move on my mouse begins by searching through our audio files for episode titles. I'm always looking over serial killers we have already discussed on our show. Kind of like how a coach reviews the film from a football team's performance. There is always more room for improvement.

My eyes dart around my office for some inspiration. Letters from serial killers to pen pals sit framed on my wooden shelves. I've bought those from a few online auctions. Prints of John Wayne

Gacey's artwork hanging on the white walls. Those weren't too difficult to obtain. They were just prints after all.

I have newspaper clippings of various murderers and their victims laminated and tacked on a cork board. There are a few missing persons posters printed out, pinned next to their killer. I don't know, but something tells me that it's not what the next episode needs. *Something is missing.* Time to do some research.

I double click the Google Chrome icon and quickly type *local murders in Manhattan* into the search bar. Let's fix that. Backspace. *Famous Murders in New York City.* The search continues. Scrolling through all of the perspective choices, it seems repetitive and redundant. *Damn, the links shown are highlighted in purple which means we've already done these in previous episodes.* Our available options are getting smaller. Maybe the listeners have some ideas. The laptop makes a small tap sound as it closes shut.

The small clicking sound of the office door shutting echoes in the hallway. Doing my best to remain silent in my house, I join my sleeping wife on the couch. Her soft snores fill the quiet room as she sits at the opposite end. I begin examining and reading through the comments on my phone, scrolling through the different listening options. First, let's check out our listeners on Spotify.

"Nice job guys." Followed by, "Loved it when you said..." and then "Your voice is so sexy." *I told Lee, that voice would get us more listeners. Making my voice just an octave lower really helps bring in the female listeners.*

Thank you subscribers, but you aren't helping. I was really looking for the rare comments of suggestions. Another time I guess. I wonder if Lee has any ideas.

Hey, got any ideas for the next episode?

I send through a quick text. My impatience takes over. Giving into the restlessness, I can't help but look down after a minute of silence. So far, no response. No surprise there. It's a Friday night in New York and he's a single guy. He's most likely at a new club or bar somewhere downtown.

Time to mindlessly scroll through my phone. First up, Facebook. Nothing but people I used to know in high school. Maybe at one point I would have called them friends. They're all busy being parents and going through societal demands. In other words, growing up, becoming who we are supposed to be in our thirties and taking pictures of it while doing so. *Remember, it didn't really happen if you didn't take a picture and tell everyone about it.*

My wife continues to her Friday night in her sleeping state. Her Kindle on her chest rises slowly each time she takes a breath. Gently, I pick it up and place it on the end table right next to the arm of the chair. It's already plugged in its charger, conveniently sitting under the wooden table. With a sleeping wife, no ideas for the next episode, and no one to be entertained by on social media, only one thing left to do.

The small trek to the kitchen is a slow one. The noise of my brown slippers across the floor becomes a loud tapping sound as they hit the tiles on my kitchen floor. The bright light from the refrigerator is the only source of illumination in the large room. The fridge is fairly full but contains nothing that looks appetizing at this time of night, nothing really piques my interest.

The freezer is my next conquest. Frozen meat, ice cubes, and a version of Mint Chocolate Chip my wife has probably seen on Tiktok or some other social media outlet. The kind where they try to convince you it's healthy. Just another fad for the people to aid in capitalistic health schemes. *Congratulations, it's working. Ladies and gentlemen, we have a winner.*

The white cabinets creak open enough for me to reach in and grab one of the gray bowls. The frozen desert is a struggle to dish out with the ice cream scooper, but I manage to keep quiet. The frozen dessert fits in the freezer in its rightful place after I add several scoopfuls to the bowl. The freezer shuts quietly just before I walk back into the living room, once again lightly tapping the soles of my slippers against the tiles. Ashley, still asleep, now on her side, facing the left arm of the couch. Typical Friday night for us.

The cushion on my side of the couch is still warm. It's a nice contrast from the cold bowl in my large hands. My spoon hits the side of the ceramic with one hand while I check my phone with the other. I left the screen face up on the matching ottoman in the middle of the big space. One missed text message from Lee.

Lee:

Put down the phone Jackass, and go fuck your wife

I smirk and swipe away the notification. More soft snores come from Ashley as if it's her way of subconsciously rejecting the idea.

More doom scrolling through my phone occupies my attention span, only this time my boredom and disinterest is suppressed by Mint Chocolate Chip ice cream. The Instagram app flashes on my screen between spoonfuls of the frozen desert. The same time I press the icon on my phone, I bite down on what may or may not be frozen dark chocolate chips, or was it pieces of ice?

First up, let's check the podcast's Instagram page. The Manhattan Murders Podcast page is strictly for gaining more publicity and listeners. Not much to look at really, just clues about the next episodes. *Which is most likely the reason I haven't really checked the page in a while.*

Occasionally, I check out the competition. However, I am proud of the long list of followers we have gained over the years. We have come a long way. The names that I'm used to seeing as I scroll down, pop up through our list of likes and comments in the notifications tab. I'm skimming them really, rushing through the posts.

What's this though? I rub the lenses of my horn rimmed glasses on the soft texture of my cotton shirt. Ladies and gentlemen, it seems as if something else has grabbed my attention. *Healthy Mint Chocolate Chip ice cream, you may have some competition.* We may have a new listener; our numbers are up by another follower.

We get new followers every once in a while, but *she* seems different.

I click on her page for more information while taking glances at my sleeping wife every couple of minutes. Aside from a few snores, her body doesn't stir under the cashmere blanket. I stare down at the profile picture of our new fan. Nothing to see here, Sleeping Beauty. Just your husband stalking his new and highly attractive follower on social media. *Your profile is public. Haven't you learned anything from listening to our episodes, Thalia Smith?*

Her picture is perfectly posed with her hazel eyes staring into the camera. Her bright red hair rivals the many neon signs downtown. The loose waves frame her face perfectly. *Careful Thalia, you never know who is watching.*

Her public profile guides me to more of her well posed pictures. There are a few with friends, some with carefully planned outfit choices with fabric that clings close to her perfect curves. While taking another bite of my ice cream, my eyes trace up her arms and down her exposed thighs at her colorful tattoos.

She posts other pictures of the drinks that I would assume she makes herself. She placed each cocktail strategically on a long black bar in the perfect lighting. Thalia has successfully filled her Instagram page with an illusion of fun nightlife adventures as a single woman in New York City. *You have excited my curiosity, Thalia Smith. Who are you really, new listener?* I continue to scroll her many posts. *I can't wait to find out.*

Chapter Three

NEWEST OBSESSION

The lights are dimmed in his office. Alan gently pulls out his high back office chair. The leather creaks against him as he sits down. He turns back to look at me. "You ready?" he mouths while pushing up his black thick framed glasses. I give him the signal. A classic thumbs up. The episode is officially recording. Episode one hundred and fifty, or fuck, I don't know. It's somewhere in that ballpark.

"Hello, listeners." He says in that voice of his, the one that turns on every episode. *Anything to get the ladies listening.* I roll my eyes at the transition of his voice.

"Yeah. Hey fuckers." I say in response, leaning back in my chair and putting my arms behind my head. I'm sure they can hear the creaking sounds of the chair in the episode but it'll just add to the flavor of it. Not to mention our visual followers will get a kick out of the easy atmosphere we paint. I don't sugar coat who I am, not even for a podcast that I partially own. People love that though. It shows that I'm a real fucking person, and I'll stand by that.

"If you've never tuned in," he continues. "You're listening to The Manhattan Murders Podcast." He says the same shit every episode, his words finding that easy cadence he's known for. "This, to my left, for our visual viewers is the talented Lee Reynolds." I give a short wave to the camera, nothing too serious. You know, more like a flick of the wrist. Maybe every once in a while, I'll flip off the camera and give them a sexy smirk afterwards. *The broads love that shit. Don't ever let them tell you anything fucking different.*

"Hey everybody," My voice is casual in my introduction. "What kind of shit show have you got for us today?" Every episode is fairly similar. An introduction, a discussion on some sick fuck in our city, and his or her crimes. We don't fucking discriminate. We have a bit of our own spice thrown in. It usually lasts about an hour, and then we end with our usual exit music, just something small I came up with while messing around in Alan's studio. I told him we needed something that really stands out, something people will remember, but not too ridiculous.

Alan usually picks our guy, or lady. Like I said, we're not the type to discriminate. If you're a sick bastard, you're a sick bastard. I don't fucking care what you identify as. That's just how it goes. Alan is more of the true crime enthusiast of the show, if you will. I just edit the material and help him out with my charming personality by being the co-host.

After we introduce the show, we tell you who we're discussing, throw in some information, a little banter, and a few jokes here and there before our episode ends.

When we finish our Friday night ritual, I click off the record button icon. The episode covering Dave Berkowitz will be edited and aired early next week. With extreme caution, I lay the expensive pair of headphones down on the black desk.

"What are you doing tonight? What kind of trouble are you and the 'ol lady getting into?" I ask Alan. I already know the answer. It's always the same every week. The guy never leaves his house unless it's to go to work.

"Probably another night in." He answers, shutting his laptop. I could recite this Friday night routine conversation.

"You should let me take you out one of these days, just us guys. " My eyes point toward the direction of his living room. If she isn't out with her friends, his wife sits there when we record our episodes. She's usually on the couch, attached to whatever the hell she reads and her phone. Alan and I hadn't had a night out together since the day my divorce was finalized and that was for celebration of course. It was just a few drinks, nothing special. *Damn, my ex was crazy. Great in bed, but that's what they say about the crazy ones.*

"Yeah. Sure." He finally responds, but I know what he really means.

"You know, Alan, there is more to life than just serial killers and serial killer documentaries. I'm sure she won't mind if I take you out." I look in the direction of the living room again. Ashley isn't one much for leaving the house. Well, she is, just not with Alan. God only knows when the last time was they left somewhere together. They seem like roommates at this point.

"I've got research, my friend." He's always working, whether it's on an episode, work stuff, or whatever shit Ashley has him doing around the house. *All work and no play makes Alan a dull boy.* "I'm sure she wouldn't care," he continues. "If she's got her phone and that couch she's set." I roll my eyes. Ashley hasn't left that spot since we closed the office door and started recording. She's a creature of habit. If I know her, she's only gotten up to piss and get a glass of wine from the kitchen.

"Well, let's go out! It sounds like she's all set." Anything I can say to get him out of this fucking house. He watches me grab my black leather jacket that I had draped around the back of the desk chair.

"Maybe another time?" He looks to the window across the room. We both can hear the rain getting heavier by the second.

"I'm going to hold you to that, Alan." My whiskey glass I have been sipping for the duration of our recording is cold on my lips as I tip back the remainder of the amber liquid. The burning sensation goes down my throat as I set it back down on the desk.

The rain drops hit my leather jacket as I walk out of Alan's house. They feel harsher than they sounded on the window in his studio. While avoiding the large drops, I walk quickly to my black mustang and climb in. Alan watches from his window, a smile stretched across his face as I climb into the driver's seat. *Sometimes he really is a creepy bastard.* His white curtains somehow match everything in his properly cleaned house. I don't think I had ever seen a speck of dust or even a small stain on their light colored carpet in their large home. Nothing is out of place. Not even a fucking dish in the sink when they have company. Everything is a muted color of gray, white or tan. His furniture in his living room almost blends together with the mix of the lack of color. His office however is the exception.

His office and our studio match his obsession for serial killers. He's got articles, art, and memorabilia from a bunch of fucking creeps. He has all of his collectables in specific categories and in pristine condition. I think Alan would have a panic attack if he noticed one of his laminated prints of the fucking serial killer clown wasn't lined up just the right way. He has a fascination for lunatics that's for sure but who am I to judge. We all have our own passions. Mine just happens to be liquor.

As I turn the key in the ignition, the lights on my dash glow blue. My Mustang roars to life, that perfect *purring* sound filling my ears–god I love that. The leather steering wheel molds to my hands, a sense of freedom attached to it as the car rumbles. The vibration against my hands almost makes me hard in my black jeans. She never gets old.

I start to leave the little suburb Alan lives in, and as I pass by every house, even in the rain, they all look the same. *Creepy.* The sooner I get out of here, the sooner I can leave Stepford.

The rain continues to fall harder on my windshield. My wipers squeak with each fall, making my vision clearer with each swipe. I manage to leave the Cleavers just in time. The lights of the city in the far distance are coming into view. Almost home.

New York City is my sanctuary. I love the nightlife. It's the only place where I can get a piece of pizza and a beer at three A.M. Tonight is the exception. As tempting as it is to go out, my leather couch and a bottle of bourbon are calling my name. *Alan may have the right idea.*

Like an automated reflex, I turn my car into the parking garage behind my apartment. I live in one of the tallest buildings in the East Village. Some would say that I'm pretty lucky, but I would say that I worked my ass off and I deserved it. My inheritance didn't hurt either. The sound of the rain is heavy on the roof of the garage when I turn in and park in my designated spot.

My car locking echoes in the parking garage. The uncomfortable feeling of being the only person here never really goes away. The garage is cold and damp from the weather. It would be a perfect scene from one of those horror movies. You know those ones where the creepy fucking guy stalks the hot girl, and she ends up being the only one that's left alive. What do they call them, final girls? The thought makes me pick up the pace, and head for the lobby across the street.

"Mr. Reynolds." The doorman greets me as he opens the see-through glass doors. I have no idea what the fuck his name is, so I nod and give him one of those generic smiles I give everyone. The ones you give when you see someone in public, maybe you knew them in high school and now you just really don't give a fuck about how they are doing these days. You sure as hell don't want to talk to them.

I walk past him bringing my shoulders up to my ears with the collar of my jacket standing straight up. My cheerful mood doesn't change when I make a beeline towards the elevators. Thank fuck, they're empty. I'm not really in the mood to socialize with any other rich pricks in the building. I say "other" because I guess you could say *I*, myself would be in the "prick" category. I wouldn't personally classify myself as the biggest asshole of the city, but I know some broads that sure would think differently. Don't get me wrong, I can turn on the charm when I need to. I *am* a salesman after all. I could sell a ketchup flavored popsicle to a woman with white gloves. Frankly, I'd rather show you my true colors than paint you a pretty picture of bullshit.

My hand fishes my keys out of the pocket of my jacket to unlock the door and the key slides smoothly into the lock. There is something so satisfying about sliding in your key and feeling the lock turn. I still get a feeling of accomplishment when I walk into my large apartment. Casually, I hang my keys on the black metal hook that's nailed next to the door frame. Man, it's good to be home.

While walking in the front door, I hang my jacket on the black metal coat rack next to the door, removing my phone from my pocket beforehand. *Where would I be without this addicting device.* There is one missed text from Alan. I don't even have to read what he sent to know what the message is about. I truly don't think this guy knows how to relax. Blindly, I type the message:

Me:

Put your phone away jack ass and fuck your wife.

My phone slides smoothly in the back pocket of my jeans. *I need another drink.* I head towards the kitchen, flipping on the bright overhead light that doesn't blind my eyes too much as it bounces off of my black cabinets. *You see a pattern here? My house is the epitome of dark masculinity.*

Reaching for the liquor cabinet, I pull out my newly unopened bottle of bourbon. The empty glass in the sink shines under the overhead light fixture as I rinse it out. Perfect. The amber liquid fills the glass until it stops just below the rim. My mouth begins to water. *That'll do it for the night.*

My attention moves from the kitchen to my favorite spot in the house. Another Friday night in with a glass of bourbon in my empty living room. My black leather chair is calling my name. *See, again, black. You'll get used to it.* I grab my phone out of my back pocket before I make my way to the large space and sit down in the recliner. Nothing like scrolling on your phone with a glass of bourbon by your side, while taking a look on our trusty Instagram page. Facebook isn't really doing it for me these days. Nothing going on there except political bullshit and people you used to know back in the day. I'm not really into all of that nonsense.

Sometimes I like to see how our publicity is growing. I check to see if we have gained any new followers, maybe some new listeners. It looks like we're growing, and honestly, it makes me feel proud. We've grown a lot in the past year. Maybe there are more people that want to hear about the psychos of the Big Apple. It looks like me being a producer is paying off.

I'm riding the high of my achievements when something catches my attention.

Hold on, what's this? *I don't think I've seen you before. Let's see who you really are, or who you want us to believe you are.* Public profile, that's not too safe. *Thalia Smith, who are you?* My eyes stare at the screen. She posts pictures of herself the way everyone else poses these days. *You, your friends, coworkers, and the places you've been in the big city.* Just generic Instagram bullshit everyone shows off these days.

Next picture, this must be you. You're a redhead. Nice. You know what they say about redheads. Not natural of course. No one's hair is the same shade as a fucking fire truck.

The waves of her hair are strategically placed around the curve of her tits in her tight black shirt. She's leaning against her elbows on a dark marbled bartop in front of what seems to be a drink she made herself. Her colorful tattoos on her arms are a nice contrast against the black surface. *If you're posing like that, no one gives a fuck about your drink.* Let's see here. *You tagged where you work? It's like you don't even listen to our podcast. Any crazy person can find you. You're lucky, this time it's only me.*

Chapter Four

Pour Decisions

THALIA

The rain is holding off today. It's a beautiful crisp October afternoon with the falling leaves finally turning different shades of reds, oranges, and yellows. The shops and restaurants have begun to bring out their fall and Halloween decor. It feels just like those comforting family Halloween movies that you watch when you're a kid. The ones where the witches, ghosts, and goblins are the good guys. Thinking about the memory of being a kid, sitting in front of the TV in my witch Halloween costume brings a smile to my face.

Busy people in oversized sweaters and dark boots walk past me on the sidewalk in the overcrowded city. Quickly, looking down at my phone and scrolling through the playlist, I walk through the many other groups of people distracted by technology. The music moves through my earbuds like the perfect distraction it is as I continue to walk through the masses.

I've made it to The Neon Rose with a clear plastic cup filled with my favorite pumpkin coffee order in hand. An iced pumpkin chai latte with oat milk and pumpkin cold foam. Everyone deserves to be basic every now and then. The plastic coffee cup looks nicely wrapped in my tattooed fingers and black nail polish. *What a good opportunity for an Instagram story.* While standing in front of The Neon Rose I snap a quick picture of my black ink wrapped around the sweating plastic cup of iced coffee.

A couple of plastic grocery bags hang loosely on the other wrist. *I'm sure Janice wouldn't mind if I stored my groceries in the fridge until my shift is over.*

The closer I get to work, I can see Jace through the tinted glass doors, prepping the bar by chopping lemons diligently and storing them in a metal container. *Such a good little worker he is.*

"Why the hell am I always here before you?" He takes a break from his lemons and looks up at me as I come in through the front doors.

"Because you're such an overachiever." My bright red lips turn into a smirk.

"I have to be to make up for your late ass," he laughs. "How was your night? Did you remember to charge those headphones?" *Damn. Did I?* Oh yeah that's right. I plugged them right after the latest episode ended. Okay, the last few episodes. I am officially caught up. Some nights are lonelier than others and their voices really help. *Maybe I have a problem.*

"You think I would forget?" I slide the wireless earbuds into their black compact case and place it gingerly into my black leather coffin shaped purse. Jace shakes his head, making a *tsk tsk tsk* sound as he moves it back and forward. *Jace, your overwhelming amount of judging is showing.* He cuts another lemon slice and adds it to the metal container. *What a great employee.*

I begin my shift routine as I always do, taking off my leather jacket and hanging it on a spare brass hook behind where I usually stand at the bar.

"How was your night?" I ask, grabbing a glass out of the sink in front of me. It looks spotless minus a few finger prints, which may have been mine now that I think about it.

"Oh you know, nothing special. Just another night out to the club. Then home at sunrise." His hips make a slight sway motion. He moves in a rhythm with his cleaning as he wipes up lemon juice.

"How do you even function? The thought of going anywhere after work sounds like complete hell."

"I have my ways, girl." His eyes make their way to the two now empty clear plastic cups that I assume were once iced coffee. They are neatly tucked away under the glass liquor bottles. Well, that explains it.

"Don't worry bitch, I got you one too." I can always count on him. He sets the full cup next to me on the bar. Like a magnet to the many silver rings on my fingers, my hand grabs around the cold plastic cup. Being the caffeine addict I am, I pick it up and immediately swirl it around listening to the ice cubes hitting each other. What is it with that? Why do we all love that sound? Is it just the satisfaction of getting something that isn't a necessity to live or just bills? Whatever it is, it's fucking good. The full cup sits nicely lined up next to my already half-drunk coffee. This should help speed the day along.

"Aw, Jace. You shouldn't have."

"Mmm hmm, don't act like you didn't expect it." He says while continuing his daily tasks.

"What would I be without you?"

"A bitch without her second cup of coffee." Such sass from a man who's barely slept.

Our conversation is interrupted by the sound of Janice's boots hitting the tile from the kitchen. They sound heavier and faster today. The thumping echoes throughout the bar. That's usually her "determined" walk. I can tell just by the speed and the rhythm of her pace. I'm not sure if I should be excited or worried about what was to come.

"I just got off the phone with a new supplier. His prices aren't cheap, but it wouldn't hurt to have more of a variety in this place. Not to mention, the networking can help spread the word about The Neon Rose." *Okay, I guess we're just getting right to the point.* Her accent is coming in thicker today. *She's excited.* It must be a highly reviewed company. Janice has made this bar her own from the time of her divorce. With the money she received in the settlement, she's built this place from the ground up. It is good to see her like this. I'm happy for her. She deserves this.

"What kind of supply are we talking about?" I ask. The food supply isn't bad here, but it isn't great either. Just your typical bar appetizers you could get from just about anywhere. Nachos are a popular choice along with the spinach and artichoke dip. Occasionally we'll get an order for the boneless wings. People don't usually come here for the food. They come here to get drunk and tell me about their shitty lives. It's almost like I'm their fucking psychologist. I see that a lot though. Bartenders should get paid a lot more than we do.

"Liquor." Janice answers quickly. "It's our best seller. The guy on the phone said he'd guarantee we'd sell out of his stuff. He said people would be begging for more. Sounds pretentious, but he's rich. So my guess is, he knows what he's talking about and to be honest, I'm a bit intrigued." Her eyebrows raise from her assumption. *I hope she's right. She doesn't need someone to scam her out of money with some trash alcohol.*

"What do you get if we don't sell out of his stuff? What happens if no one likes his shit?" I ask.

"You know, I didn't get that far. His confidence really convinced me." She smiles with her hands on her hips. Her red pointed fingernails tap on the material of her dark blue jeans.

"Don't go falling for another asshole." Jace chimes in. He raises his pink eyebrows in her direction. Since her divorce, we've witnessed a fair share of fuck boys. This is his way of saying "Don't get your heart broken," and "We care about you."

"Oh, don't be ridiculous. If there is anything owning this place has taught me, it's don't mix pleasure with business. He said he'll be in later to have a drink and sign some papers."

"He sounds like a real gentleman."I break out of my own pause. I fill the empty awkward silence with my own sarcasm. It's what I am best at. "What is his company called?" I ask.

"Pour Decisions." Janice answers after pulling up the website on her phone.

"Clever." I wonder if she can hear my eyes rolling.

"Isn't it?" Her smile is still widespread across her tan face. *I guess you didn't catch my sarcastic remark.*

"I wonder if his face matches the name?" *I am just full of them today.*

"Why? Are you looking to get some pleasure out of this business?" Janice's pitch goes up slightly in question. I can feel my cheeks flush at the idea.

"Hell, it wouldn't hurt her any." Jace comments. *Thanks Jace.* "Maybe she can save a little on her electric bill. She may not have to charge her earbuds and her vibrator at once." My face has to be red by now. I'm sure it blends in with my hair.

"Awe look Jace, you have her flustered. Don't be embarrassed, chica. You know we love you and your love for those true crime guys."

"You both are lucky I love you too." The smile on my face will only make the red on my cheeks stand out more.

"I think you'll like this guy, Thalia. His picture certainly helped me make my decision." She pulls up the supposed amazing picture and her eyes go wide as if she just opened a suitcase filled with gold bars.

"I thought we said no mixing business with pleasure."

"Girl, not for me. But we need to get you laid. How long has it been?" *Why is everyone so concerned with my sex life?*

"Too damn long," Jace answers. He isn't wrong. Have I been too picky? No. Definitely not. Have you seen the men that come in here? One thing I've learned from the Manhattan Murder's Podcast is never pick up just any strange man from a bar. *I wonder if that still applies if I work at one.*

Jace looks over Janice's shoulder. His eyes now look similar to hers. "Oh damn." He clutches his cheaply made costume pearls hanging around his black tee shirt.

"What is it?" I ask. This time sounding too eager. I can hear my own curiosity rising.

"Honey, this man may be the man of your dreams. Hell, he may make you put away those headphones of yours."

"Bullshit." I laugh a little too hard at the idea.

"Bitch, would I lie to you?!" His voice gets louder and he looks at me like I just drank one of his many iced coffees.

"Maybe." I smirk and I move closer to Janice. I really *am* curious now. Maybe even a bit intrigued. She moves her phone into the pocket of her navy skinny jeans.

"No, ma'am. I want to see your reaction when he comes in."

"Damn Janice," Jace chuckles.

"You guys just like to torture me. This guy better be as hot as you say he is."

"Fuck yeah, he is," Jace cuts in.

"If you don't go for him, I will." Janice laughs as her boots clunk towards the kitchen. *What happened to not mixing business with pleasure?* The echoes of her boots soften the further away she gets. Her hips sway side-to-side as she struts through the double doors.

"Jace. You better not be fucking with me. It sounds like this guy looks like the perfect man for me and perfect guys don't exist. Believe me, I've lived and worked in this city long enough to know that." I turn to face him.

"Thalia, if you don't step up, I will swoop in before Janice gets a chance. Man has the best hair that I have ever seen. Tattoo covered arms and blue eyes that could match the fucking *ocean*." His emphasis lands on the last word.

His eyes gaze up to the ceiling. He looks as if he just pictured a four course meal with cheesecake for dessert. "You got all of that from one picture?" My concentrated face turns into an upturned smile.

"Girl, yes. You will too once his fine ass comes walking in those doors."

The night gets later and more people crawl in from the crisp fall air. The Neon Rose Lounge is busier than last night, which isn't much of a surprise since we get most of our business on Saturdays.

I must look ridiculous. My head turns towards the doors every time I hear the *swoosh* of it opening. With curious eyes, I look to Jace. Their tease earlier has me questioning if every one of the bar patrons is this mystery man. Only to find out, it is not the "Pour Decisions" guy. Each look he pairs with a shake of his head or him mouthing "fuck no." Both are just as animated. *Way to be inconspicuous Jace. This guy is going to wait until close to sign these damn papers. What a prick.*

The damp microfiber towel in front of me we use to clean the bar acts as my distraction. *I need to keep my mind busy.* I will do anything to keep from looking desperate. I don't even fucking know this guy. The obsession of every little detail in front of me triggers a need to start cleaning the glasses. I must have been scrubbing mindlessly. I look down and the glass is crystal clear, aside from the white material inside. By the way those two salivated over this guy, he better be worth my anxiety and nervousness.

It was true, I hadn't had a boyfriend in, well, ever. Serious relationships never seemed to be worth the hassle. I just never let myself settle with someone I knew I would regret in the morning. Date after date had been a bit depressing. Sitting in the same restaurant every man in the city takes you to. It's obviously a little over your price range. They think if you're impressed with a thirty dollar salad you'll let him in and spread your legs. *Sure, I will, because honestly I have fucking needs too. Ha, do you see what I did there?*

Anyway, the time old question of "what's your favorite color?" can only go so far. Let's face it, neither one of us gives a fuck if I like red and you like orange. Let's get this one night stand over with and never talk to each other again.

"Hey!" My inner monologue is interrupted by Jace's whisper. Not a whisper really. More like a quiet shout or a loud breathy command. I look up from the squeaky sound from my glass as my towel rubs against it. He nods in the direction of the front glass doors. Immediately, my heart beats faster. *Why am I so nervous? This is just a guy. A supposedly hot guy nonetheless, but just a guy in the city. Nothing more. Fuck, my face feels hot and I feel like I'm going to throw up. Did I mention, this is another reason why I don't go on dates. Shit, am I sweating? Well great, now I feel like I am going to throw up, I'm nervous and I probably smell bad. Oh fuck, I didn't even think about my breath. This should help.* I pour a shot of peppermint schnapps and lean my head back. *Here goes fucking nothing.*

The doors swing open. The thudding sound of his boots on the hardwood floor vibrates along the bottoms of my feet and up my legs, stopping at my upper thighs.

"Bitch, turn around." Jace whisper commands once again. I guess I should do what he says. The nerves in my system mix with the minty shot. *Come on Thalia, where is that mask of confidence?* My face says calm and collected bartender; my insides, however, are on fire. My head is spinning. I don't do flirting or dating. I am *not* made for this.

"Hey, sweetheart," he begins. His smooth tone makes my heart beat faster and the hair on my arms stand on end. *Sweetheart, what the fuck? What is this, the fifties? Be calm, Thalia. Turn around, meet the new supplier. Just get him something to drink. It will all be over soon. He can't be as good as they said. No one is. Just turn the fuck around. Give him his drink and send him on his way to Janice.*

Reluctantly, I turn around and face the mysterious supplier.

Oh, fuck.

Suddenly, I don't mind the sweetheart comment. He's hot. Hotter than hot. His black, leather jacket sits snug around his arms, unzipped just enough to see his tightly fitted black shirt. I start to hear my mother's voice in my head. *"Stop staring, Thalia, that's rude. Now, fill this wine glass, would you?"* Yes, mother, of course.

I move my gaze up to his olive toned complexion. Well, from what I can tell anyway. Half of it is covered with a full beard connected to a mustache that's just as thick. *His eyes— those eyes really are like the ocean.* The way they contrast with his dark beard is—what do the kids these days say? Chef's kiss.

Oh. god. And he smells good too. The scent of sweet bourbon mixed with his cologne radiates off him. *Fuck, I am in trouble. Damn, I'm staring again.*

"You okay, sweetheart?" he asks. The use of the nickname again makes my heart stutter. His deep and slightly accented voice sounds very familiar with a bit of humor mixed in.

"Yeah, I'm just a bit out of it. It was a busy night." My voice is a little breathier than usual as my eyes scan over him.

"Yeah, where'd they all go?" He smirks as his hands gesture to the empty seats nearby. *Damn it.* I lean against the bar, in fear that

I would fall from my knees going weak. I wonder if he can tell my legs are turning into jelly.

"They just left." *I can smirk too.*

"Is that right?" His smirk turns into a full fledged smile across his handsome face. *Well, fuck. Now, the rest of me feels like jelly as well.*

"Yep." I nod, desperately trying to appear casual. "Is there anything I can get you?"

"Yeah," he pauses to think, as if to make me believe he doesn't already know what he wants. "How about bourbon?"

"Coming right up." *Shit, where is our bourbon? Oh, good. There you are, you bastard.* Still leaning against the bar, I begin pouring the brown liquid in the short clear glass, the splashing sound filling the tense silence between us. Satisfied with my work, I slide the glass closer to him.

"Thanks," he says while matching my gaze. *Oh, shit. Don't do that.* "So..." *Dear God, please don't expect me to have a conversation with this man. I can't remember words right now.* "What time does this place close? I mean I should probably know since we're doing business together."

"Three A.M. and you're not technically doing business with me. That would be Janice. I just work here."

"Well, Sweetheart," *there's that word again.* "You're going to be pouring the product. So, I'd say we *are* in business together." He brings the glass up to his lips just peeking out from his facial hair.

"I suppose so." I lean in closer. *Holy shit! Am I flirting? No, that's just my body trying to balance.*

"What do you do when you get off work?" His blue eyes shoot through me as he peers over his glass. *Why can't I think? What do I do when I get home? Do I even have hobbies? Damn, what is considered a hobby these days? Think, Thalia, think.*

"Hey, Thalia!" *Saved by Jace.* He yells from his side of the bar. He would say it was his normal voice. Anyone else would say yelling. "You got any plans *other* than your usual night time routine?"

"Routine? What is this routine of yours?" The mystery supplier's eyes widen at the question. *Oh, fuck. Jace, please don't.*

"Oh, yeah. Thalia has this set schedule when she gets home." Jace announces with his hands on his hips. *Well, this is fucking embarrassing.*

"Really? I'm intrigued. What's your name again?" He asks, setting down his glass.

"Jace, my name is Jace. And honey, I didn't mention my name yet. But I'm sure you'd remember if we both met."

"Something tells me I'd remember meeting you too." *There's that smirk again. Oh, God. I think I'm going to throw up.*

"Well, anyway. Every night Thalia gets off work, she stops at her favorite Thai place, goes home and listens to her favorite true crime podcast."

"Every night? You eat noodles every night?" His voice pitches up in question. His eyes dart toward me and my stomach turns with butterflies. *Never a good sign.*

"No, not every night. Just when our tips allow me to." I answer like I just broke my mother's favorite vase.

"Oh, that's damn near every night." Jace cuts in.

"Does this podcast have a new episode every night?" Our new supplier asks. He smiles while taking another drink of his bourbon.

"Not since last night." Oh God, my voice is cracking.

"You listen to the same ones over again...?" He asks while laughing. His eyebrows raise in what seems like curiosity. *Why do I feel judged? I don't even know this man.*

"Sometimes..." I reluctantly reply.

"It must be one *hell* of a podcast." He crosses his arms across his chest and leans back in his chair. "What's it called?"

"The Manhattan Murders Podcast." My voice gets quieter, while I look down towards the laces of my black boots.

"You don't say." He bends closer with his elbows on the bar and licks the bourbon off his lower lip. If he keeps raising his eyebrows at each one of my answers, I'm going to get suspicious.

"Janice!" Jace yells in her direction. *Oh, thank God.*

"I believe you both have met our new supplier." Janice's heels clicking once again toward our direction. "Janice Martinez." She extends out her hand for a professional handshake. His large tattooed hands engulf hers. *Damn, I wonder how they would feel...Now is not the time, Thalia.*

"Lee Reynolds," he says, accepting her hand. *Fuck. I knew he sounded familiar but I couldn't place his voice. Now, I know I am going to throw up. Are my eyes as wide as they feel? Shit. Shit. Shit.*

"Girl. You okay?" Jace whispers in my ear. This time, in what I would call a *normal* whisper volume.

"No. *Fuck.* I don't know." I am in panic mode. My body feels like I am going to fall over and pass out. Shit, I just made a fool out of myself in front of the man I listen to on a nightly basis. "That's one of the men in my headphones." I know I am trying to hide it, but my face shows everything.

"Bitch, you sure? Which One?"

"I listen to him just about every night. I fucking know who Lee Reynolds is. He's the producer. Yes, I am sure." My tone is sharper than I intend it to be.

"This is fucking perfect." He's no longer whispering, and it's not helping my situation.

"What's perfect?" Janice looks up from her conversation with Lee. *My Lee. Okay not my Lee. The Lee whose voice echoes throughout my earbuds on lonely nights. Fuck. This isn't really happening.*

"Just the new business plan. Excited for the new product. Another great opportunity to see your baby grow." Janice knows I'm lying. I'm sure they all can tell. I can feel my voice cracking again. I watch the smile on Lee's beautiful face get wider. *He just watched me fangirl over him, and I think I'm going to die from complete fucking embarrassment.*

"Uh huh. Well, Lee," she turns to face him, "I believe we have some papers to sign."

Chapter Five

THE PLAN

🎙️ALAN

"You with us, Son?" My eyes move up to the man in front of me. I was daydreaming again. He must have caught me in mid dissociation with my gaze on the black table in front of me. I focused on the painted wood as if I could make it move with the powers of my mind. Just call me Charles Xavier.

My boss's dull gray eyes focus on me while he stands at the front of the long conference table. We're all sitting and supposed to be listening in highback, black leather office chairs. I have a similar one in my studio. We all pretend to listen while he talks about some useless business plan. Whether I hear what he is talking about or not won't stop me from taking over his law firm one day. It pays to be sleeping with his daughter, even if it's not her I keep fucking in my mind.

I have been fantasizing about that long red hair– how it would look wrapped around my fist as she took me deeper into that pretty, little mouth. I can't stop thinking about how good her pale, tattoo covered thick thighs would feel wrapped around my waist or straddling my lap.

"Alan?" There it is again, his agonizing voice.

"Yes, sir. Sorry, I just have a lot on my mind this morning." That's one way to put it. I've not stopped thinking about my red headed siren, Thalia Smith, since Friday night.

I scrolled through her perfectly posed photos on her Instagram page quietly, while I sat in my large bed. Sunlight peaked in through the blinds and my eyes were still glued to the phone screen, careful not to double tap on each one. She has taught me so much just from the way she presents herself to her followers. Does she have any inclination as to what a picture like that can do to a man? A man like me? *She has no fucking idea.*

"All right, that's it for now." My father-in-law's voice jolts me back to life once again. I'm sure he could feel me jump in my large, leather office chair.

"Alan, are you doing okay?" *No. I am sexually frustrated. My mind is filled with visions of a pretty redhead in a variety of positions.* I'll admit, it's a bit concerning. A whole list of fantasies make their appearance in the front of my mind, and I would be a more than willing active participant.

"Yes, sir. Just didn't get a lot of sleep last night." My eyes gaze up at him through the steam flowing above the coffee cup in my hand.

"Have a busy weekend?" His question seems forced. I know he doesn't actually care what his least favorite son-in-law did over the weekend. We both continue our meaningless conversation in front of the conference room.

"Just a lot of research." *It isn't technically a lie.*

"Oh, that podcast of yours. How's that going?" His inquiry is the last thing he wants to discuss. *Sure, that's what we'll call it.*

"It's going well, getting more attention everyday."

"How does Ashley feel about that? Are you guys spending *any* time with each other?" *Who?* I pause. Maybe a little too long. *That's right. My wife and his daughter.*

His inclination that Ashley and I don't spend enough time to-gether is *my* fault, is well, hilarious. Frankly, I don't think she cares much for it either way. It keeps us separated and she gets to have her alone time. She has her Kindle, her books, and her nights out with her friends. I have my podcast and my only real friend who meets up with me every Friday night to focus on the latest episode. We have our own interests and that's what works for us.

"Oh, she doesn't seem to mind," I admit bluntly. His smug smile appears on his face along with a condescending pat on the back. *What the hell is that supposed to mean?*

"Well, good. Glad to hear it." He walks towards his office. *What a prick.* He isn't so bad *out* of the office.

Who am I kidding, the guy is a fucking cocky asshole. My hand digs my phone out of my dark gray slacks checking the time while walking to my own office.

"Hello, Mr. Jones." My secretary, Stacy, greets me after every morn-ing conference. She was hired by my sonofabitch father-in-law. The bastard isn't as cunning as he tries to make everyone believe. I know it is so he can salivate whenever she bends over in her tight black pencil skirts. I wouldn't be too surprised if he tried to do more than just that. She is the center of every man's attention as they walk by her small desk in front of my office. A bunch of beasts in three piece suits.

Her dark brown hair is pinned up. Only being held up by one of those clips I see my wife wearing from time to time. What do you call them? Claw clips maybe. She wears her large tortoise shell glasses that accentuate her big, beautiful brown eyes. The wolves of Wall Street basically drool over her and stare at her cleavage between her tight button down silk shirts that she seamlessly tucks into her skirts.

"Hello, Stacy." Trying my best to be polite in this place. She gets enough from the animals that work here. I give her a gentle smile and head in my office. Her cheeks blushing through the office windows. She seems sweet. Too sweet for a place like *this*.

This morning, my phone has become the hindrance of my occupation. After locking myself in my office, I mindlessly scroll through social media. Pictures of mutual connections fill the screen of my phone. Most of the accounts being other podcasts and true crime stories. Some of them include mysteries and cases that still have yet to be solved. Same shit posted everyday.

However, now I have someone new to look at. Maybe *look* isn't the right word. Gawk? No, that isn't it either. How about, study intensely until I know everything about her? Yes, that seems more fitting at this point. How does the song go? "I can't take my eyes off of you."

Her account in my list of followers with her name being at the top. Like the dedicated follower I am, I fixate on her face for what seems like minutes. While looking at her posed so perfectly, it feels like time has fucking frozen.

She shines under the glow of Edison bulbs, her face in a content expression with a slight upwards smile. Her picture shows her pouring what looks like bourbon in a glass. Her red hair is put up with long wavy pieces falling out just right. *Damn.* If you look close enough, you can see her black shirt hugging her tits just right. I bite my lower lip imagining what her smooth skin would feel like under my lips. *Thalia, you shouldn't pose like that. You could attract strange men. Strange men who stare at your pictures. Strange men who want to do more than just stare.* My breathing gets heavier and my skin tight. *New listener, what have you done to me?*

My unhealthy gape is interrupted by the sound of Stacey's voice through the intercom. "Mr. Jones, Mrs. Jones is on line one." Her voice is still sweet through the rough speakers of the office phone. *Focus, Alan. Your wife is on the phone.* "Thank you, Stacy. Put her through," I utter calmly.

Taking a second to breathe, I put on the act that I wasn't just lusting over a woman I've never met. "Alan Jones speaking," clearing my throat and turn on my professional attorney voice. You never know who could be listening. It always pays to be cautious in this business.

"Alan." The way she says my name is more so out of annoyance than a loving, compassionate wife.

"Ashley. Yes, dear..." My tone matches hers.

"I just wanted to let you know that I am leaving to go to my tennis lesson. I may go get drinks with the girls after. If you need anything, feel free to call. I may not answer right away." *Of course, tennis. Don't worry dear, I know you're fucking your tennis instructor. I have known for a while now. The way your eyes widen whenever he texts you, and the way you try to hide the screen on your phone gives away your dirty little secret. Don't worry, baby. I have my secrets too.*

"I'll be fine, Ashley. Go enjoy your lesson. Have a drink for me." I wonder if she can hear the smile in my voice as I look down at my phone, still staring at the woman unknowingly smiling back up at me.

"Thank you. I'll have a few for you." She laughs. "Don't forget, my book club is tomorrow night."

"How could I ever forget?" The more I scroll through Thalia's other posts, the less interested I am in what Ashley has to say.

"Okay," she lets out another small laugh. "I will be home later." *She won't. She'll say she's drunk and that she's staying with one of her friends.* It's become a weekly occurrence. I know where she really will be, opening her legs for another man while I think of burying *myself* between another woman's thighs.

"Okay. Enjoy your day." The phone clicks off as she hangs up first. A part of me is a bit relieved. The deep sigh I let out, as I exit out of Thalia's social media page, I admit is exaggerated. The lawyer in me goes back to what I should have been doing—looking through the long list of emails and tasks the boss man left for me. That *should* keep me from looking through Thalia's social media scrapbook.

I have been sucked in. I can shake my head at the thought but there isn't any denying it. Thalia is always on my mind. My overthinking makes me wonder what she's doing. Who she's doing it with. What her voice sound like, What she looks like when she laughs. What she would look like underneath me. How her voice would sound when she makes little moans, and how it'd change when she screams my name.

I have to know. I *have* to see her. I need to know first hand. I am officially obsessed, and I've created this unhealthy addiction to someone I have only seen in pictures. I do know one thing, however, she likes my voice, and I can use that to my advantage. *What woman wouldn't fall for my sophisticated words?*

I may not personally know her but I know her through everything she puts out for me to see. I know where she works, what she does, and what drinks are her specialties. I know with whom she spends her time. She lays it all out for everyone to see.

I can tell you where she stops after work, the route she takes, and the boots she wears while she's walking. *Such tall black boots with so many laces.* I can only imagine watching her slowly tie them up on her long legs. Imagining untying the long laces at the top of her thighs with my teeth makes my skin go hot. I picture her pale skin peeking through the tiny holes in her black fishnet stockings. What I wouldn't do to rub my hands down them—*tear* them. *Fuck, listener, what have you done to me?*

God knows how many people she has enticed. How many men she has lured into her web. My skin gets hotter and I loosen the tie around the collar of my shirt. I need to see her in person. I have to be near her and to hear her voice. From what she has already done to me, it's only fair. The craving to be in the same room with her is all I think about. There is no better time than tonight and Lee is always saying how I need to get out of the house. What better excuse to have than the one I do now?

I pick up the office receiver and my hands begin to shake as my plan begins to unfold in my mind. *Call Lee, suggest a spontaneous guys night, pick The Neon Rose Lounge as a spot for drinks, and meet Thalia.* What scares me is what I will do when we meet face to face. Will I mutter aimlessly like a babbling idiot? Will I sit and stare like a deer in headlights? Why am I acting like a teenager getting ready for their first date?

I dial Lee even as my mind is still unclear of my next steps. "Hey, asshole." He answers. "What do you want?" *Such a gentleman.*

"Hey, fucker. What are you doing tonight?"

"Not much planned. Just have to stop in at a new bar for a sec. I just signed a new client. I need to talk about inventory with the bar owner. Some of the new shipment is coming in. Why? You got something in mind?"

"Yeah. Ashley won't be home and I thought, what a better night than tonight to get some drinks with my good friend Lee." He can probably see the smile on my face through the receiver.

"Yeah? Ashley always goes out with her friends. What's so different about tonight? Finally taking me up on my offer?"

"Yeah. You've asked me enough. I figured I'd give into your constant bitching." I laugh.

"Whatever, asshole. Alright, I'll bite. You mind stopping in at this new bar? We could get a few drinks there first. Maybe try some of the new stuff that I've already shipped in." I hear the turn signal clicking in his Mustang through the pauses of his question.

"Yeah, sure. No problem. What's this place called? Is there a dress code? Anything I need to know before we make our way over there?" Questioning this evening's plans, I look down and give myself a once over in my business casual outfit I already have on.

"The Neon Rose Lounge. It's a fairly new place. Pretty casual. You know it?" *Fuck yes, I know it. What are the odds of that?* My heart is pounding through my buttoned down dress shirt.

"Yeah, I've heard of it."

"Good. I'll pick you up tonight around eight."

"Eight sounds good." My smile at this point is a permanent fixture on my face.

"Alright, sounds good. See you then." He hangs up the phone. Fuck, am I excited? Or am I nervous? *Keep it cool, Alan.*

Eight comes faster than expected. I have been sitting on my couch, waiting for Lee like he's my fucking prom date; my knee bounces in anticipation. I've not changed from work. My black button down shirt is still tucked into my charcoal gray slacks. My red hair is still perfectly in place from this morning. It seems as if my pomade works. It's messy in all of the right places – not a strand out of place. I haven't been out with Lee in years, and honestly, I have no idea what to expect.

Like an addict, I keep scrolling through Thalia's page. I could pick her out of a crowd if I needed to. Her bright red hair, brightly colored tattoos on her pale skin, and upturned smile are like a beacon guiding me towards her direction. Her profile would be impossible to miss among the waves of people in this city.

The lights from Lee's headlights shine through my large living room windows. My nervousness is tucked back under my mask as I put on a face of confidence. *Play it cool, Alan. This is all part of the plan.* My black pea coat hangs from the back of my large gray chair. As if in slow motion, it swings around my body. My arms slide in the silk lining. It fits perfectly over my toned arms. My phone fits snug in the inside pocket and my keys sit at the bottom of the pocket on the front of my coat. "Guys night has begun."

"What's up, you handsome bastard. Why are you all dressed up?" Lee asks as I open the passenger side door of his black Mustang.

"I just got home from work, and I didn't bother changing." He looks at me in disbelief all while his hands stay on the leather steering wheel. He belongs in his car, blending in with his black leather interior aside from his olive toned skin.

"You sure it isn't because you know the ladies love you in your business casual shit?" He laughs.

"What the hell do I care about that? I'm married." *If I can get Thalia to look at me, married or not, my night will be made.*

"Listen, even *you* deserve to have someone else look at you once in a while. Your wife is hot, but she's Ashley. You see her everyday. Plus, you know when she goes out and does whatever the hell she does with her friends, she's getting hit on by every guy there." He isn't wrong.

"Yeah, asshole. We're married. Seeing each other everyday is the whole fucking point." He doesn't answer and I don't comment about the rest of his statement. I know she does. I just don't give a shit anymore. *I don't know if I ever really have.*

Lee speeds out of my neighborhood and towards the city. The car ride out of my suburb goes quiet.

"So...guys night," he interrupts the silence.

"Guys night." I repeat, hoping it's an answer all on its own.

"What made you want to come out tonight?" *My obsession with meeting one of our new female followers. An addiction, you could call it, for a woman I have never met.*

"I just needed to get out of the house. Ashley is out for the night and I thought it was a perfect opportunity."

"*Right.*" The lights from the city get brighter the further away we drive from my house. I forget how much I miss the lights and the busy city. All the people and nonstop life even after I would normally go to sleep. The married life has changed me. Lee slows down the car next to a large parking garage behind his apartment.

"I thought we could take a taxi. A few drinks may turn into more than we planned."

"Right. Safety first." I nod agreeably.

"Always." His eyebrow cocks while turning to look at me. "You okay? You seem off or something." *Something is off. I have never thought about a woman like this before.*

"Yeah. Just a lot on my mind." It's only half a lie. Who knows how I will feel once I see her face to face.

"That's a bullshit answer. Whatever the fuck you're thinking about, you're going to forget. We're going to have a good night and forget about work, women, and whatever else you need to forget about for the night."

"Aren't we going to a bar that sells your product?" I cross my arms over my chest at the question.

"That's besides the fucking point. The point is, Alan, we're going to have a good fucking night."

"Right. Lead the way."

"I'll call a cab." I nod again in his direction. *This is really happening.* I smile like a giddy teenager at the thought.

Chapter Six

STARSTRUCK

THALIA

The room is dimly lit by my candle that sits on my nightstand. The small amount of wax in the jar makes the long burnt wick noticeable. A faint smell of what is supposed to be apple and cinnamon lingers in my room.

"Do you like that, Thalia? Do you like it when I'm this close to you? Do you like when my voice is only for you?" His deep breathy tone in my left ear is all I can hear while he hovers on top of me. His full lips barely touch the tips of my ear and my body breaks out in goosebumps. The hair from his thick beard brushes against my cheek and jaw line. He leaves a trail of soft kisses from the middle of my neck to the middle of my exposed chest.

He plants his tattooed arms on either side of my head and slowly pushes his hard dick inside me. A moan leaves my lips, and I watch as the shadow from the small flame hits all of the defined lines in his chest. My eyes trace over his tattoos that stand out under the orange flame.

"Fuck, Sweetheart." His breathy voice goes faster as he picks up speed. He moves my legs further apart as he comes closer, making it so his thighs are against mine. Another moan escapes my throat and my breath is just as quick as his. "That's it, Sweetheart. Just like that. *Ah*, fuck, you feel so *good*." His low guttural groan sends heat to my core.

My legs go clammy, and I can feel them start to slightly shake. My headboard is in rhythm with our synchronized breathing. *Oh, fuck*. My mind goes blank and all I can think about is this moment. My hand grips my black comforter as my body starts to relax and go tense all at once. I am so close to pure satisfaction, until–

My phone vibrates, shattering the illusion of him and the sound of his accented voice. *Of course*. The sound of my vibrator still buzzes on my bed just past my thigh.

"Yeah." My voice is breathy and short.

"Hey girl. What are you doing?" Jace asks, replacing Lee's voice on the other end of my phone. He is so lucky I love him.

"Oh you know, just practicing self care before work."

"Self care? Did you go running or something?"

"Jace, you know I don't run."

"Then why are you so out of breath?... Shit. New episode?" He laughs.

"Something like that."

"Girl, normal people don't answer the phone..." He pauses.

"I listen on my phone..."

"Just hit ignore, damn...or you could just talk to him."

"That sounds like a horrible idea. Whenever I see him, I feel like I am going to throw up."

"Better that than fucking him in your head by yourself." I guess he has a point.

"It's safer in my head. There isn't any chance of rejection." *It's so strange picturing him in my head and then seeing him sign paperwork in my place of work.*

"Bitch, shut the hell up. He stared at your tits as soon as he came in the door. Get yourself dressed and come into work. It gets lonely here by myself. Especially when Janice has to take inventory in the kitchen."

"You don't have to go in early every shift." *Now it's my turn to laugh.*

"My rent says otherwise." He has a point. "Wear something sexy. I think your producer is coming in." *My producer?*

"I'll see what I can find." I say, still with a laugh lingering in my tone.

"I know you've got something to show off those tits of yours. Hurry up. Love you, bitch." He clicks off before I have a chance to respond.

I throw the covers off my shaky legs. *Please don't let this be a foreshadowing of what's to come for the rest of the day.* My fingertips run along the covered hangers in my closet, more of a nook than a closet. I come to a stop, halting in the middle of the array of black clothes. My eyes focus in on what *may* be tonight's winner.

It's a black bodysuit with small silver stars and crescent moons throughout. It fits rather snugly on what Jace says are "all of the right places." The sleeves sit slightly off the shoulder, creating a kind of sweetheart neckline. *There's that word again.* Just the thought of that word sends a shiver down my spine, remembering Lee and what he called me last night. And this morning in my fantasy.

I grab a pair of light washed high-waisted jeans on a hanger not too far from where the bodysuit is hanging. These are always a favorite of mine. Jace says that my ass looks perfect in them. I always trust his opinion when it comes to what I wear. He would tell me otherwise, very bluntly I might add. *This should do.* My black lace up combat boots go on next. They are always a struggle to pull on, but they're my most comfortable shoes. They're my go to for long shifts at the bar. *These will be perfect for tonight's ensemble.* The thought comes to my mind as I grab them from the same spot I threw them last night.

The idea that I may be seeing Lee periodically has turned me into a panicked mess. One of the men I have grown accustomed to, only through my headphones and in my mind, now has a face. This makes everything a bit more complicated. I think about him hovering on top of me and seeing his face at the perfect angle and his olive skin glowing in candle light. The shadows hitting every defined line just right. *Concentrate, Thalia. You don't know if that's what he looks like. Now is not the time to fantasize. Get your shit together.*

Work has been slow, but that's normal for the middle of the week. The few regulars are spaced out around the bar with their heads permanently stuck in the downward position, staring at their phone screens. It is a wild night for me. I catch myself eyeing the door every so often and start to second guess if he's even coming in tonight. Did I really wear my "tits get you tips" bodysuit for nothing? Jace acknowledges my desperation. His facial expression is full of pity as he walks over to my side of the bar.

"Girl, you keep checking that door like it's going to come off the hinges."

"I'm honestly just regretting my outfit choices." He notices me shifting in my uncomfortable jeans. I should have just gone with my black jeans and a sweater. My boots make a squeaking sound underneath me as I lean my body up against the bar. The night is far from over and my feet are already sore.

"What? You think he ain't coming?" He asks, doing that thing where his voice raises at every question.

"I don't really care if he comes. I'm sure he has better things to do. Maybe other bars to supply." My arms cross instinctively on my chest. *Why does the idea of him not coming in disappoint me so much, and did I just get jealous?*

"Girl, you ain't fooling anyone. You look at him like he's your favorite bowl of noodles you get from that Thai restaurant. You really have no fucking clue do you?" His eyebrows lower.

"I really don't." I admit, lowering my arms to my waist. It's true. I am terrible at this. Dating is not my strong suit. I have no idea how to flirt, unless I'm drunk. Even then, it's still not good. More vulgar and sloppy than something to be admired.

"Well, bitch, I guess now it's your chance to find out." His eyes move to the front doors. He pauses and his dark brown eyes go wide. "Oh, look, he brought a friend. Damn. He's fucking fine as hell too." The doors swing open bringing in the cold, autumn breeze with them.

Lee is first as the two of them walk in. His voice echoes in the bar. "Come on, there is someone I want you to meet." His eyes meet mine. My cheeks get hotter as his face turns into that smirk he does. Still leaning up against the bar, I feel my knees start to go weak. Not but a few hours ago, I was imaging this man over top of me in dim candle light, and here he is in front of me. *Don't panic, just act natural.*

Jace's footsteps become quieter as he walks towards the other end of the bar. *Please don't leave me like this.* With pleading eyes, I do my best to beg him to stay with me. His smile is all of the confirmation that I need to know I am on my own.

Out of sheer nervousness and panic, I grab the closest glass I can see. Cleaning has always been there to hide my anxiety. His guest comes in shortly after, walking in the small space between Lee and the door. His long black coat falls past his waist to the middle of his thighs. The sleeves fit snug around his arms. His hair is a darker shade of auburn. He wears it short on the sides but not completely shaven, and a little curly on the top. Although it is a bit disheveled, I have a feeling it's the look he wanted. *Stop staring, Thalia. Nothing to see here. Oh, fuck. Here he comes.*

"Hey, Sweetheart. Cleaning glasses again?" Lee's Manhattan accent takes me back to this morning, making my insides feel like they're melting. His eyes peer up to mine, the vibrant color of them leaving me momentarily speechless. It's as if the world around me freezes. He has no idea what he does to me. *Maybe he does, and that's why he keeps his eyes glued to mine.*

In my peripherals, I can see his friend removing his black coat and hanging it on the back of the high backed bar stool. His button down shirt tightly fits what seem to be defined arms.

"Just trying to keep busy." Here I am, nervously stuttering. *Surprise, surprise.*

"I see. You keep scrubbing like that, you're going to rub a hole in the glass." Lee laughs.

"Just trying to be thorough." I do my best to smile through my awkwardness.

"I'd say you're being *very* thorough." His friend points out.

Another familiar voice.

My eyes widen. *I know exactly who you are.* My body leans onto the bar for more support. My once weak legs now feel numb. No, not numb, but instead the feeling you get when your feet fall asleep. Only this time, it's radiating up my thighs. *Oh, damn is it hot in here?*

"Oh, then I'd say I'm doing well at my job." I answer while glancing up towards his green eyes, more of a gaze than a glance really. *Those damn eyes are going to be the death of me. Am I flirting? If I am, I am doing a terrible job.* I see myself reflected in his thick black horn rimmed glasses. He hasn't turned away since he's sat down. I guess you could say that's a good thing. I don't think he's stopped looking in my direction and I don't think I've stopped looking at him either. It's like I'm one of those kids in that horror movie. You know what I'm talking about. The one with the clown. Just call me Beverly and him Pennywise.

"*Thalia.*" Lee interrupts my gaze. His voice stops my trance as it echoes in my ears.

"This is Alan." *I know exactly who he is.* Alan removes his black gloves and reaches his hand out towards mine. *What should I do? Have I ever shaken anyone's hand before?* My rag falls on the black tile behind the bar as I reach forward.

"Oh, shit." I bend over clumsily and reach down, hitting my head on the bar as I come back up. "Fuck." I curse, rubbing the back of my head.

"You okay, Sweetheart?" That's right, Lee is here too. They're *both* here. The men I listen to almost daily, dreamt about-and well, fantasize about–are standing in front of me.

"Yeah, just my normal grace." I answer, feeling my cheeks go red again.

"Alan Jones," He replies. "I'll keep my hands to myself this time." That voice, the one that I catch myself thinking about more than a normal person probably should, is real and it is in front of me.

"That may be the safer option." I smile, continuing to rub the back of my head. He looks at me above his frames. His full pink lips curve into a smirk. *Holy shit, he does it too.*

"I was telling Alan earlier that you're a big fan of the show." Lee once again breaks my stare. There is a bit of amusement in his voice. *He's enjoying this too much. Fucking asshole.*

"You're interested in true crime?" Alan's voice raises a little with excitement. *Oh shit, that was adorable.*

"Yeah. Ever since I was little. I used to watch those old shows while my mom was at work. Unsolved Mysteries. I've been hooked ever since."

"It's always nice to meet a fellow crime solver." He smiles. *He smiles and my insides melt. At this point they're like a melted snowman on the floor.*

"I wouldn't say that..." Okay, I am smiling a little too wide now. I have so many feelings going on in my head right now. A smile will have to do. "You want a drink?" I ask, trying to end this whole awkward flirting thing I was doing. *Okay, I know I'm flirting, I'm just really bad at it.*

"Yeah, of course. What would you recommend?" His stare from me breaks.

"Don't let him fool you, Thalia. He knows what he likes." Lee winks, and Alan shakes his head. *Am I missing something?* "He'll take an Old Fashioned." He adds. He pats Alan on the shoulder. "Don't let him leave without paying. This shit is expensive." He nudges his elbow into Alan's arm. Lee walks toward the back, probably to discuss inventory of his liquor bottles with Janice.

"I wouldn't dream of it." His hooded eyes look back up at me. *Fuck. Please don't leave me alone with this man. I have no trust in myself in what might happen.*

"Old Fashioned it is." I turn to face the bottles sitting on the mirrored shelf behind me. His eyes are on me while I reach for the Bourbon. He watches my every move as if he's counting every silver star and moon printed on my bodysuit. His stare continues as I turn back toward his direction. He observes my hands closely, his green orbs following them as I pour the bourbon, add the bitters, and the large ice cube in the small whiskey glass. He studies my every move, eyes missing nothing. He bites his bottom lip and looks up at me as I pour the brown liquid into the glass.

"It looks perfect." His deep voice makes the hair on the back of my neck stand up.

"I hope you like how it tastes." My response is timid and my voice is unitionally breathy. He lifts his glass to his pink full lips, the amber liquid sloshing over the large ice cube before tilting it back. I can't help but watch the muscles in his neck as he swallows. He gently places his glass on the bar, licking what is left on his lower lip.

"Tastes fucking perfect," he says in that voice I have grown to love so much.

"I'm glad you like it." *Why do I feel out of breath? Maybe it's these damn high waisted jeans. No, that can't be it.*

"Although, I knew I would."

"H-h-how did you know?" I ask, stammering my words.

"I watched your hands. I paid close attention to your movements. You know you're good at your craft. It's the small details that are the most important." He brings the glass up to his lips again. There is something about him—something I can't name. It fascinates me, and honestly, terrifies me at the same time. My heart races with every look in his bright green eyes.

"Is this your specialty?" My gaze is once again interrupted by his voice. *Stop staring, Thalia.*

"My specialty?" *What's a specialty?*

"The drink? Are you known for any others?" The glass is still in his hand, lingering near his mouth.

"I don't know if I'm known for many others. The Old Fashioned is just a house favorite. I make them a lot."

"Your practice has paid off. Look at that, not a smudge in sight." He slowly rotates the glass in his hand. The lights from above shine through, creating a warm glow from what is left of his drink. The glow around him is driving me like a moth to a lamp.

"How long have you been listening to the show?" He stops observing his glass and looks up at me. My breath catches from the weight of his eyes.

"Only a few months." My voice is low and close to a whisper. My mouth slightly parts as I watch him observe me.

"What do you think so far?" He leans in closer. His volume matches mine. His elbows lean against the bar.

"I-I-I like it. You and Lee make me laugh. True Crime has always been an interesting topic to me." I lean in on the bar further. "The way the 'sick fucks' do it." I reply using finger quotes. His smirk becomes a small smile. "Why do they do it? Who do they choose to do it to? What is their motive? It's all so intriguing to me."

His stare moves from my eyes down to my bright red lips then to my exposed cleavage. I may have not gotten many tips tonight, but if I get Alan Jones to look at my tits, I'd say a win is a win. He moves his eyes back up to meet mine. His green eyes are bright with flecks of copper around the edges. They shine like bright emeralds in the glow of the light.

"What was your favorite episode?" His elbows, still resting on the bar.

"I liked the latest one. The one about The Son of Sam. I've listened to it a few times." His eyebrows raise.

"Just out of curiosity, when do you like to listen? To the episode I mean. I've noticed everyone has their preferred time they like to tune in." He stares intently, waiting for my response.

"Usually after work. Multiple times a week. Depending on how my day went." My voice is slower and my breath has become heavier. *I think I just confessed to the man I fantasize about, that he's the topic of my fantasies.*

He sits up on the bar stool. *I see I've piqued his interest.*

"You guys get acquainted?" Lee's voice comes from behind Alan. My eyes trail from Alan's bright green eyes to Lee's deep blue ones.

Lee's eyes are like a silver bullet under the lights. If I was a mythical creature running through the woods, these men would be what causes my demise.

"You didn't tell me, Lee, that I'd be meeting our biggest fan." Alan crosses his arms around his chest.

"If I would have told you, I would have ruined the surprise." Lee admits as he leans against the back of Alan's chair.

Chapter Seven

Until Next Time

🎙️ALAN

Lee and I sit at the bar after my formal introduction to Thalia. We agreed to have a few drinks before calling it a night. I would consent to anything if it meant watching her at the bar. Even if it meant counting *every* one of those silver stars and moons on her shirt. She is glowing in her element, and I am mesmerized, which means I am *fucked*.

I watch her closely as she tends to the other patrons at the bar, assuming they're her regulars since she knows their names and their favorite drinks by heart. Goosebumps cover my skin as I observe the pristine way she pours liquor over ice cubes in the cocktail mixer. Hours could easily pass and I would happily stare at her, watching her mix whatever the fuck she puts in there. The way her tits look when she moves her arm up and down, shaking the mixer is intoxicating.

I bite my lower lip and watch her pour the drinks in their rightful glasses. Her red curls fall loosely down her back and half way down her arm. All I can think about is how she'd look bouncing up and down on my lap. I'm curious if they would move in rhythm with her perfectly round breasts. I want so badly to feel them—to feel every part of her.

My gaze is solely on her as she smiles up at the man in front of her. Her bright red lips curl half way up her pink cheeks. She bats her long black eye lashes in his direction. I'm unable to make out what she's telling him above the loud music but I imagine her that close to me. Remembering how she was only a few moments before. The show she is putting on has every man in the bar staring. She is the main attraction, and we are her drooling audience. *I wonder what kind of show she would put on if she had me alone in her bed. I crave so badly to be the only one in the room with her.*

"Can you believe we have broads like *that* listening to us talk every week?" Lee's question breaks my thoughts, ones a married man shouldn't be having.

"Absolutely fucking not." My eyes stay locked on her figure. She pours drink after drink for more than half of the male customers. Lee and I continue to observe her closely as she continues to flawlessly perform her show. Eyes from all the men in the room remain on her as she turns toward the mirrored shelves. I bite the inside of my cheek to check my composure. Being here is a bad idea, but I am so glad I came.

"So, what does Ashley have going on tonight?" Lee asks after he takes a sip from his drink. The ice hits the side of the glass as he moves it towards his lips. Suddenly, my trance is interrupted. Lee never liked Ashley and he isn't shy about letting me know. Not through words, necessarily, but in his own blunt way. His tone and his whole demeanor changes every time he brings her up.

"Who?" My gaze stays on Thalia with my glass in hand.

"Ahh I see. You guys get in a fight or something?"

"No. No fight, just the same boring shit everyday. Right now, as far as I know, she's just out with her friends. I think she said they were getting drinks or something after her tennis lesson."

"Oh, so she's fucking someone else is what you're telling me." He pauses and takes a drink. "You think it's the tennis instructor? Or maybe one of her friends?" He responds without looking up. He isn't wrong, I am sure of it. She spends a lot of time playing tennis, not returning until hours later.

It's the little things you start to notice. The over-explaining of where she's going, the excessive use of her phone notifications, the way she moves when I get closer to her. It feels like an uncomfortable reflex. The truth is, I care about Ashley, but not enough to do anything about it. Our marriage has been more out of convenience from the start. If our marriage was like any of the ones I've seen in the circles our families traveled in, I am certain history will repeat itself. I shrug and take a drink of my Old Fashioned.

"That's exactly what I think. Yet here I am." I set my glass down gently on the bar.

"When do you think she'll be home?" I look down at my phone to see that I haven't received any text messages.

"I don't have any idea." My attention goes back towards Thalia. She is like a portrait, and I am an art connoisseur looking for another piece to add to my collection. She glances every few minutes at me and Lee. I can't help but smile when I catch her. Each time she looks down at the bar or fidgets with the neckline of her shirt. She pulls it in a way that makes my eyes dart towards her chest. *A sly little vixen...*

"What do you think of Thalia?" Lee turns to ask. If only he knew that I was already trapped inside the web of a woman I had only seen a *glimpse* of. I am willing to do whatever I need to do just to keep seeing these small moments.

"I think she's..." There are so many things I can say. To make it short, I think she is the most interesting person I have ever seen. I could watch her for hours and happily not look away.

"Are you guys doing okay over here?" Thalia walks over from her other patrons. Again with her tattered rag, wiping down the bar. She leans over just the right way. Her exposed cleavage is enough to make me salivate. Her silver chain falls just past the neckline. The shine from the tiny "T" charm catches my attention. I imagine the charm dangling from her neck and catching it in my teeth while she rides on top of my lap.

I swallow hard when she looks up at me with her hazel eyes. My mind immediately goes to the fantasy bending her over and fucking her up against this bar, imagining how her beautiful face contorts when she comes on my dick. Such a beautiful vision of her staring at me in the reflection of the mirrored shelves behind her. *Fuck, she's only cleaning and all I can picture is how good she must feel.*

"We're doing great, Sweetheart." Lee winks as he brings his nearly empty glass to his lips.

"And you?" Her voice is low, and she sounds like she's out of breath. I can't tell if it was intentional but I don't want her to stop.

"Fantastic," I answer. "Do you think I could have one last drink for the night? The one you made earlier was *perfect*." Her red lips part only slightly, but it only makes me want to take them into mine.

She takes my glass, our fingertips brushing with the motion. *I shouldn't be here, but I don't want this to stop.*

Thalia turns to face the mirrored shelf once again, this time I can see her looking back at me. *There's something between us; I know she can feel it, too.*

She moves towards the bar in front of me, preparing my glass once again. Two shots of Bourbon slowly add to the mix. A few drops of the bitters splash on top of another large ice cube. She moves in closer, bending over perfectly. Showing off her fantastic tits. *Oh shit, Thalia.* She moves her fixed look to my glass as she slides it in front of me like she did before.

"One last drink for the road," she says as she leans in, pushing the glass closer towards the edge of the bar in front of me.

"If it's anything like what you made me tonight, I will be coming back for more." Her pale arms break out in small goosebumps at my whispered promise. She needs to remember me, and I will make sure she does.

"Let me know if you need anything else." Her eyes flash with something unreadable as she stands up and walks towards the front end of the bar.

"Don't worry, Sweetheart. We will," Lee calls out. He turns his head to watch her walk. "So, what the fuck was that about? Are you somehow Casanova now?"

"I have no clue what that was, but I'll be honest, I loved every fucking minute of it." Another smile covers my face and I hold my refilled glass up to my lips, tilting it back to enjoy the burn of alcohol as it slips past my throat.

"Welcome to the dark side, my friend." Lee moves his glass towards mine, hitting them together and making the ice clink against the sides. *Cheers, my friend.*

The night is hardly over. The time may only be ten or maybe eleven. If I were ten years younger, I would say that the night was still young. The truth is, I am in my thirties and other than staring at the beautiful bartender in front of me, I really have no interest in being here. Really in the city at all for that matter.

"You good to go?" Lee asks, scrolling on his phone through his list of text messages. He's probably texting an owner of another bar he supplies.

"Yeah, I probably better get home." I check my phone. Still nothing from the wife. No calls, no texts. I'm sure it will be just me for the night. No matter, some alone time will do me some good.

"You think Ashley will be there waiting?" He asks with a grin, still looking down at his phone.

"Probably not." I tip my glass back, drinking the remainder of the liquor. The small napkin that has acted as a coaster for my whiskey glass is replaced with a hundred dollar bill. Later, Thalia will notice the little message I carefully added to the napkin I laid on top of the bill. If our interaction wasn't memorable, *this* certainly will be.

"You think she was worth a hundred dollar tip?" Lee smirks.

"She was worth that and more." *One last look for the night.* Like clock work, I find her hazel eyes at the other end of the bar. She meet my gaze. Her normal look of bartender charm changes to one of surprise, and I can't tell if it's from curiosity or if she is enthralled by me like I am her. Maybe it's a little bit of both.

She stares as I grab my black coat from the back of the bar stool. My eyes move towards the glass, making sure she knows I am leaving her something...*special.* I give her a knowing smile as I swing my coat around my shoulders, sliding my arms through the black sleeves. I reach for my leather gloves and slide them back over my large hands, all while not interrupting our gaze.

"You got everything," Lee asks, disrupting our nonverbal conversation. He tips back his drink, ensuring there is nothing leftover in his glass. He slides on his leather jacket and zips it up halfway, still showing the collar of his shirt.

"Yeah." I follow him towards the glass door. "Right behind you."

"Hey, what did you say to Thalia? In your little note." Lee asks as we wait for the cab at the curb in front of the bar.

"Oh, you saw that. It wasn't much, just telling her how great she did tonight."

"I see. So, no number?" Lee lets out a short laugh.

"I'm married," I smirk as I turn my head to face the large windows of The Neon Rose. She picks up my glass and I watch as she reads my note through the windows of the cab. She'll know soon enough what it means.

Until next time, Listener.

THALIA

"Until next time, Listener. What do you think that means?" I ask Jace as he stands next to me behind the bar. He leans in closer, resting his chin on my shoulder. He stands a few inches taller than me. We both read over the note as he looks over my shoulder.

"I think it means that you have a new regular. See where it says 'next time'? I think that means next time he comes in for a drink." He slides it towards Janice all while laughing and swaying his hips. Jace doesn't know how to *not* put his whole body into his motions. I guess it's what the kids call "extra" these days. "What do you think, Janice? You think we have a creep going after our dear Thalia here?"

"I think it looks like he was just flirting with you, and you're just not used to it. Normally, you push guys away before they even order," Janice confirms as she hands the napkin back to me.

"You're sure?" My question is filled with disbelief. "Until next time, Listener." My attempt at his deep voice is almost comical. "This doesn't give you any suspicious vibes? I mean, the guy straightened a damp napkin before he left. Who the fuck does that? Hell, why not just give me his number?"

"Maybe, bitch, someone who is trying to write someone a message. Have you ever tried writing on wet paper? Hell, it'd look damn near like Swiss cheese. Not to mention, you're intimidating as hell." His face turns into a smile as he turns to face me. *Maybe Jace has a point. Maybe I am just overthinking everything.*

It's true, I haven't had that kind of interaction in a long time. I honestly don't think I have ever had one quite like the one I had tonight. *Whatever the fuck it was.* He knows I'm a fan, so maybe he and Lee are just trying to fuck with me. I'm sure it will be in their next episode.

"*Hey, Alan, you remember that broad that thought you were trying to hit on her?*" Lee would say in his deep, smooth, Manhattan accent. The one I always dream about.

"*Yeah, dumb bitch thought we'd go for her.*" Alan would answer in his deep, melodic voice. *Oh, fuck. I am fantasizing about them insulting me on their show? What kind of fucked up shit is that?*

"So, what are you about to do tonight?" Jace began. "Don't tell me, I already know."

Janice hands us our tips from the jar. Her heels click towards the light switch and in a mere moment, we all stand in the dimly lit bar before we all head towards the front doors.

"Until next time, Listener." Janice and Jace yell out as they get into their shared cab.

Chapter Eight

"It Supplies to Anywhere I Want it to, Sweetheart."

**LEE**

It has been days since Alan and I went to The Neon Rose. I haven't been back since. I keep imagining Thalia's perfect round ass bending over behind the bar.

I can't get the image out of my mind.

The way she looked up at me every time she leaned forward and slowly wiped the bartop down will be forever imprinted on my brain. I can't stop thinking about the way her tits spilled out of her fucking shirt. It had me drooling like the dog I know I am. She's a fucking tease, and I'm sure she knows how much I love what she does. How will I ever go back and be able to get my fucking work done?

Fuck, I would love to see her look at me like that again. She was so damn enticing. Just imagining those hazel eyes of hers looking up at me while her mouth is around my cock with my fingers entangled in her curls has my skin going hot.

I can't help but wonder what she is doing right now.

She's probably at her apartment, alone. Fuck, I hope to God she is alone. I picture her scrolling through her phone, adding photos of herself to her many social media pages. Maybe she's listening to another episode of our show. Thinking about it has my mind racing.

Maybe she's folding laundry, or cleaning her apartment. I bet she's doing whatever the hell women do, painting her nails or something like that. What do women call it, self care or some shit? Maybe there is a part of me that already knows what she does. My cock twitches at the thought.

I envision the way her face turns red when she looks up at me. I can make her cheeks flush like that again, and again. My cock fits firmly in my hand while I stand in my shower under the hot water. The image of the color coming to her pale skin is at the forefront of my mind.

I imagine her slender hands wrapped around the silver cocktail shaker. The way she holds a kitchen appliance has me fantasizing about them wrapped around my dick. I could watch the way she moves her hands for fucking hours. My eyes would follow them as they moved past her chest to her inner thighs, then, finally finding her clit. Who the hell am I kidding, I would gladly participate.

How inappropriate it would be if I fucked a subscriber to my podcast? I've fucked broads I met online, but this is different. It's not like picking up someone off one of those dating apps or sending them a message on Instagram. This girl listens to me talk on a daily basis. I could get her to listen closer to all of the things I would say. I would tell her so many things, so many fucked up dirty things.

My mind goes back to the fantasy of her alone, seeing myself standing in front of her bed as she sits naked with her back against her headboard. "Spread your legs for me, Sweetheart." I instruct in a low breathy voice. "Spread your legs so I can see what you do when you listen to me. I want you to show me what you do when you fuck yourself to the sound of my voice." Her long loose curls sitting just above her perfect pale breasts. Her hazel eyes stare into mine under her luscious eyelashes.

Her hands trace the middle of her chest and slowly move down to in between her perfect tattooed thick thighs. I watch as her black painted nails stop right where I want them to be.

"That's it, Sweetheart, just like that. Show me, Thalia. She slowly moves her fingers over her clit. "What do I do to you when you're alone?" A soft whimper escapes her lips as she begins to pick up speed. I move my hand at the base of my cock, gripping myself and moving slow at first and then speeding up, moving along with the fantasy.

"Fuck, Sweetheart." I moan softly. I picture her fingers moving from her clit to her needy pussy. She stares at me as she pushes one in at first. "Add another. I want to make sure that pussy is ready for me," I tell her. We watch each other closely as she does as I ask. "Good girl, Thalia. Just like that."

She lets out another small sound and her breathing picks up. "That's it, Sweetheart." I move my hand up and down my length faster and faster until the black tile in my shower resembles a Jackson Pollock painting. *Fuck, I need to see her.*

I stand under the hot water, tilting my head back and allowing the water to soak my coal colored hair. It drips onto my face when I turn towards the shower head. Small drops of water collect in my beard. They slowly fall to the black and silver tile. Bracing myself with my hand against the wall as I wash my thoughts of Thalia down the drain. The water slides down the back of my neck and down the tattoos on my back. Images of her enter my mind again.

I think of her here with me. The vision of water dripping down her soaked curls and over her breasts has my mind racing once again. There are so many things I would do to her perfect body in this shower. Thinking about water dripping off her tits onto her flat stomach makes my cock hard again. These fantasies of Thalia are fucking great, but I need the real thing. I need to see *her*.

The squeaking from the knobs almost echo in the bathroom when I turn off the water in the shower. My phone buzzes against my nightstand as I enter my room from my adjoining bathroom. I walk out of the shower and grip my black towel around my waist with one hand and check my phone with the other. Nothing too exciting, just another Instagram notification.

On second thought, that could be Thalia updating me and her other devoted followers on her current whereabouts.

Naturally, I click on the notification.

There are several direct messages from fans who watch the show, but I can get back to them tomorrow. They're most likely making suggestions for future episodes, nothing Alan can't handle. As if she's my new addiction, I begin looking on my feed to see if I can find any news on Thalia's plans for the night.

There it is.

After only a few seconds of scrolling, a new story update appears at the top of my phone screen. It looks like there are a few.

"You've been busy, Sweetheart. I knew you couldn't help yourself. I can always count on you to show me what I want to see." I say to the woman on the screen, as if she can hear me.

She begins by showing her followers her outfit choice for the evening. My eyes scan over her short black leather skirt, fishnets and boots. Her camera moves over to what would be a sad excuse for a shirt, but *fuck*, I'm not complaining.

The shirt is a red mesh material, making it easy for her black lace bra to stand out in the ensemble. It stops in the middle of her stomach, about an inch above where her skirt begins. The elastic hem of her fishnets barely meets the bottom of the red lace.

"You're killing me here, Sweetheart." Saying out loud again to myself as I continue to watch.

She shows her drink in the next story. It doesn't look like the glasses at The Neon Rose, where she works. *No, these ones are different.*

The shape around the rim is more square, and the red light from a nearby sign reflects off the glass. She must be out on the town.

"Where are you, Thalia?"

Needless to say, she answers me in another one of her stories. *It's almost too easy.*

It's another picture of her outfit just in new scenery. Her skirt looks shorter in this angle. The way it sits higher up her thigh has me basically fucking drooling. Her skirt contrasts against the crimson wallpaper. One of her hands leaning on the black porcelain sink and the other holding up her phone towards the mirror.

I *know* that bathroom, I've been there several times before. I toss my phone down on my black sheets and move towards my closet. It looks like I've got plans tonight.

The bar is dimly lit by the red neon signs and the outdated light fixtures on the ceiling. The building is mostly empty with black round tables and matching suede booths. There are only a few other patrons sitting in the high bar stools towards the end of the bar. Business seems slow, but it is the middle of the week so no surprise there. The bartender happily calls out my name when he spots me coming in the front door.

"Lee, what's up man." Mike from behind the bar waves me over. His long blonde hair hangs over his shoulders in waves. His black and white striped shirt glows purple under the black light above the bar. It hangs loosely over his thin torso. He's a skinny motherfucker and comes off cocky once in a while, but he's charming as hell. He takes out a glass and pours me a drink before I sit down. He knows what I like, probably a sign that I come in here a lot. Besides, this bar sells my product, along with a few others.

"What's up, man? How's the night going?" I ask, standing in between two bar stools.

"Slow as shit." His blonde mustache curls just slightly as he smiles. "What brings you in?" He gently slides my drink in front of me.

"Oh, you know, just making my rounds." I take a sip from the glass.

"So you had nothing to do tonight?" He laughs and takes a rag from behind the bar to begin cleaning a few whiskey glasses in front of him.

"Yeah, basically," I answer, voice muffled by the glass on my lips. He chuckles again and shakes his head. He grabs the clean glasses and stores them on the shelf under the bar.

I like Mike, his chill attitude is refreshing in this city. Maybe it's because he's easy going, or it's because he gets high as fuck before he comes into work. Either way, it works for him, and it makes him a pleasure to be around.

"Anything interesting happen tonight? *Anybody* interesting?" I ask, setting the glass gently on the black slate bar. *Way to be an inconspicuous asshole.*

"Hey, man everyone is interesting to me." Mike's smile goes wide. That was an understatement. I've seen Mike leave with all kinds of different people—men, women, non-binary, sometimes more than one at a time. As long as he's having a good time, Mike doesn't give a fuck.

"If you're thinking about yourself, you may want to direct your eyes in *that* direction." He looks toward the back of the room.

Jace's pink hair is easily recognizable anywhere. It glows bright under the red neon sign, with the word "SHOTS" reflecting off his purple sunglasses. He sits still in the booth, looking down at his phone screen. If he's here, Thalia must not be too far away.

I scan the area looking for her. My eyes come to a stop when I see her walking towards Jace. She's staring down at her phone, probably checking her views and likes on Instagram. By now, she must know that I've watched every one of her stories. I wonder if she would even notice that I'm in the same bar since she's always staring at her phone screen.

"Someone you know?" Mike teases. He must notice my continued gape at the redhead bombshell in the corner of the room. You couldn't pay me a million bucks to look away from that perfect body of hers.

"Yeah." I take another drink from my glass and set it gently on the table. I watch Thalia's every step in her black thigh high boots. The heels make a muffled sound on the dark red carpet. *What is it about thigh high boots that make men think worse thoughts than we already do?* The thoughts we already have should be deemed unethical, but when a broad puts on those boots, I instantly think about how I wish my face was in between them.

She picks up her nearly empty glass and tips back the rest of her drink. Her words are quiet under the loud music playing in the bar, but they aren't hard to figure out with her smile and her body moving towards my direction. *Fuck.* I turn and face Mike and take another sip of my drink.

"Yeah, she works at another bar I supply." My voice is steady, but on the inside I am nervous. *Nervous, I never get fucking nervous.*

"Well, you gonna talk to her?" He asks, refilling my glass. "Because here's your fucking chance." He leans in closer. His volume is nearly a whisper as she gets closer to the bar, and the muffled sound of her heels increases.

"Another rum and coke?" Mike asks, putting on his bartender charm. She hands him her empty glass and nods. *She's next to me, so fucking close that I could touch her. She smells fucking delicious. What is that, fucking cookies? God, I would love to taste her. I bet she would taste better than the baked goods she smells like. She would be like my own delicacy that I would happily eat over and over again.* I turn my head just past my right shoulder just so she can see that it's me.

"Hey, Sweetheart." My eyes meet up to hers while I lick bourbon off of my bottom lip.

"Lee?!" The pitch in her voice raises, and if you could believe it, her eyes lighten. Did my heart just skip a beat or did this drink give me indigestion? "What are you doing here?"

"Just doing his rounds," Mike chimes in, handing Thalia her drink. He smiles again, like it's a permanent fixture on his face.

"What he means is, that's *my* rum you're drinking." I smile, watching her take a sip. Her long, black nails wrap around the glass and once again I think about how nice they would be wrapped around my dick. Her full red lips cover the square rim of the glass. She licks the drops of rum off of the top of her lip. I wonder what else her tongue could do. My jeans tighten at the idea.

"Does Pour Decisions supply every bar in the city?" She asks slowly as she sets the glass down on the bar. Her eyes peek through her full eyelashes and hooded eyes.

"It supplies anywhere I want it to, Sweetheart." I follow suit and set my glass down next to hers. "What made you want to come out to a bar? Don't you get enough during work hours?" I move a step closer. My jeans, now touching her fishnets just below her skirt. If I move my knee in just the right way, her skirt would leave me even less to imagine.

"I could ask you the same question." She moves in towards me, barely leaving any space between us. The texture of her mesh sleeve brushes across the tattoos on my bare arms. If we were any closer, I would be inside of her. *That's not a bad idea.*

Thalia's chest moves faster under her sheer shirt. Her black bra stands out under the bright red mesh even through the dim lights. Seeing her chest raise, makes my skin hot. I pick up my glass and take another drink of my bourbon, leaving it nearly empty, before I set it down on the small, square napkin in front of me. Her eyes are on me through every movement I make. I'm not sure whose heartbeat is louder, hers or mine.

"Do you normally go out on the town wearing short skirts and fishnets?" I counter, slowly scanning down her body.

"I don't normally go out." She laughs, her hand still tightly wrapped around her glass as her lips meet the rim again. My eyes stop at those perfect lips, thinking of how they would feel going down my chest to my hips.

"What made you want to?" I ask, trying to create small talk the best I can.

"Jace." She turns towards him and smiles. He looks over and returns the smile before returning to his phone screen. "What are the chances I would get to see you while I was out on the town?" *Yeah, what are the fucking chances?*

"How *lucky* that I was out making my rounds," I smile. "I would have never gotten to see you." My hand moves just above her knee, my fingertips barely touching her thigh. Just lifting the hem of her skirt. Leaning in closer, my lips graze the side of her ear. My beard gently pushes her hair out of the path of my lips. I ask her just above a whisper, "Do you want to get out of here? I hear the drinks are too expensive and the music is too loud."

"Fuck yes, I do." Thalia answers in a volume similar to mine. She turns her head, nearly brushing her red lips against mine, our noses almost touching. "Let me grab my coat and tell Jace." I watch her walk over to her table and grab my glass, drinking what is left of the bourbon.

"Looks like you're done making your rounds," Mike comments, wiping the space of the bar in front of him. His smile still planted on his lips. Hell, it never went away.

"I guess so." I offer him a side smile of my own, and turn to face Thalia.

"Ready?" Thalia asks, meeting me at the bar. *You have no fucking idea, Sweetheart.*

Chapter Nine

A Dream Come True

THALIA

His black car sits out in front of the bar. The lights of the city reflect off the dark paint. I don't think I have ever seen a cleaner car in my life. In fact, I know I haven't. His hand brushes against my waist as he moves around me to open the passenger side door. *Do men still do that these days?* His fingertips gently touch my hip as he moves past me to the driver seat.

"Are you going to get in?" He asks while standing on the other side of the car. There is a soft tone to his voice and a smile to match. It's enough to melt the fishnets off my legs. I offer a nervous smile before sliding onto the leather passenger seat.

The dark lettering of his tattoos on his hands matches the color of the steering wheel and the leather seating. Silver rings shine brightly on both of his hands, reflecting every light we pass. I catch myself biting my lower lip at the sight of his hands gripping tightly around the steering wheel. *Way to be fucking inconspicuous, Thalia.* I try moving in the small seat, pressing my thighs together the best I can to try to hide my excitement. His eyes burn through the small holes in my fishnets as my skirt hikes up my thigh each time I move. Crossing my legs the best I can, trying not to expose myself.

"Nervous?" Lee asks, looking back at the road. *Fuck yeah, I'm nervous.*

"No... are you?" *Who the hell am I kidding? He has to know that I am. He already knows I listen to his show every night. Alone. After work.* His eyebrows raise in response to my answer, while his eyes stay focused on the road. I watch his lips curve into a small smile under his dark beard. He's content to leave me with my question *unanswered.*

"Most people don't drive in the city." I will say anything to break this awkward silence.

"I'm not most people, Sweetheart." He turns to look at me. *Fuck, that smirk will be the death of me.* His voice sounds just like it does on the show — low, smooth, and just a hint of that Manhattan accent. The soles of my boots squeak with every movement I make. Gripping my jacket closer, I hug it tight around my body.

"Are you cold?" He inquires. My eyes never leave his hands as he reaches over to turn the dials on the dash to turn up the heat. I stare at every move they make when the car shifts and changes gears. The way he grips the shift knob makes me wonder how they would feel going up my thighs. I bite my lower lip again at the thought of the red marks he could make around my pale skin.

"Thank you." The heat from the vents hits my face. *Damn, how far away is his house?*

"Not much farther now. The traffic in the city doesn't help though." He unknowingly answers my question. I smile and turn towards the window, forgetting about my skirt rising, I feel his eyes again on my thighs.

My jaw drops as his car slows down as we get close to what looks like the biggest parking garage I have ever seen. He drives up two levels of empty spaces. His car comes to a stop in a spot that has his name painted at the top of the space.

L. Reynolds.

I have only ever seen something like this in shopping malls and airports.

"Home sweet home," he says, putting the car in park. Still looking ahead and fidgeting with the hem of my shirt, I reach towards the handle in the passenger door —

"Don't you fucking *think* about it," he says in the same tone from earlier. Something about it still shakes my core. He turns to face me with a smile on his face. I nod as I wait for him to get out of his car. His arms go tense under his black jacket while he turns off the ignition.

"Who the fuck said chivalry was dead?" I say under my breath, clutching onto my black purse. *What the hell am I doing? I don't know this person. I should know better by how many episodes of his show that I've listened to. Sure, I guess I don't really listen to the content some of the time.* I shift in my seat and look down at my lap. "This is your fucking fault," I admit aloud.

"Everything alright?" Lee asks, opening my door. His hand is still on the handle.

"Of course." I manage to fake a smile on my red lips as I slide out of the passenger seat. His hard chest brushes against my back making the goosebumps on my arms stand out. The echo of the car door closing fills the parking garage. It makes me nearly jump out of my skin in my platform boots.

"Right this way, Sweetheart." He takes my hand in his, engulfing it with its size. He pulls me to his side and we quickly walk across the street and into the large building in front of us. If I told you I don't have the biggest smile on my face, I would be lying.

The doors to the lobby are huge tinted glass doors. Lee nods in the direction of the door man as we walk in. "Hello, Mr. Reynolds." It's like he reads from a script. His uniform is an all black suit in pristine condition. *What is this, The Plaza from Home Alone?* The look on Lee's face is far from welcoming. I guess he isn't much for conversation. He makes a quick line for a nearby elevator, pulling me along with his arm now wrapped around my waist.

"You have a lobby? Scratch that, a door man?" I ask probably louder than I should as soon as the elevator doors quietly shut.

"You don't?" He laughs as he turns his head just slightly to face me. The button labeled *PH* lights up yellow with one single touch.

"Who the hell are you?" I ask, only half joking.

"You want to find out, Sweetheart?" *You have no fucking idea how much I want that.* He gazes at me through hooded eyes. They trail from my lips down to my thighs.

"I thought that's why I came with you." My voice is now quiet and shaky. *Am I trying to flirt again? I really am doing a terrible job.* His lips turn into a sharp grin. He turns his head and looks forward towards the elevator doors.

The silver doors open to the sound of a quiet *ding*. "This is our floor." He continues to hold my hand as we walk out. We both come to a stop in front of the door to his apartment. He fishes his keys out of the side pocket of his leather jacket. I look down at his hands as he slides the key into the lock. The echo of the clicking sound from the lock resounds in the hall.

"After you." He opens the door, leaving enough space for me to get around him.

I look around his place and drop my purse by the entrance at the sheer shock of its size. "Holy shit! This is your apartment?" His apartment looks like it was designed to look like those places you only see in magazines. Everything from the furniture to the cabinets are in the modern black aesthetic. Aside from an empty whiskey glass on the dark wood end table, his place is pristine. There is no way he could have designed it. This has "hired designer" written all over it. He stands nearby with his arms crossed over his chest. *Damn, he's going to kill me with that sexy smirk he does.*

"This is home." He comes closer. "Let me take your coat." He grabs the back of the collar. Brushing my neck with the tips of knuckles, moving my hair out of the way. He slides it down my arms, leaving me in my red mesh shirt. "You want a drink?" He asks, hanging my jacket on the coat rack by the door.

"No, I think I had enough for the evening." *I want to remember this moment. On lonely nights, it will replay over and over in my mind.*

"Water?" He counters with a smile, now leaning in front of his opened fridge. He holds the bottle out in my direction.

"Yes, please," I answer walking towards his kitchen, the heels of my boots clicking on the black tile.

"Please? I like the sound of that. You want to beg for it, Sweetheart?" His voice deepens. He holds the bottle over my head teasingly. My heart beats faster, and I move in closer to his chest.

"Please." I look up at his full lips. *Is this really happening?* I have dreamed about this many times.

"Please what, sweetheart?" He sits the bottle of water down on the granite counter. *Please, what? I don't know. I never thought I would get this far. Please, can I have my water? No, that's not it. Please touch me. Do something. Say something, Thalia. Stop thinking and just do it.* My hands reach up his sculpted chest under his tight black tee shirt, slowly tracing over all of his defined lines. *Fuck, he's just like my fantasy. What the hell? Who the hell has a body like this? This can't be real. He's like one of those statues of those Greek gods. I know this isn't really happening to me right now. It's another one of my dreams and I'm going to wake up any minute in my bed with Artemis at my feet.*

"What do you want?" His question breaks me out of my trance. His blue eyes peer down to meet mine, searching for the answer that is surely reflected there.

"What do you want, Sweetheart?" He asks again. He places his fingers gently under my chin, lifting my head up to meet his gaze. *No, it's really happening.* My hands grip the bottom of his shirt.

"Do you want me?" My eyes go wide at his words, and I nod. "Use your words, Thalia."

"*Yes,*" I whisper, the word soft, but he hears it. I can hear his intake of breath at my response before he grabs my face in his hands.

"Oh," he says, almost breathless, "I *know* you do."

His eyes move to my mouth, biting his lower lip before kissing me. *Oh, damn I love how his lips feel against me.* I let my lips part, and I feel his tongue on mine. His mouth muffles the quiet moans slipping past my lips at his touch. I shudder as his hands move through my hair, getting wrapped in my curls. More goosebumps collect on my arms as I feel him harden against my outer thigh.

He grabs my waist and lifts me onto the kitchen counter, his lips still eagerly exploring me—seemingly unable to stray far from my skin. His fingertips move slowly from my waist to the hem of my red mesh shirt as if trying to memorize the lines of my body. Pulling off my shirt, he leaves me in just my lacy bra. I run my hands down his chest and remove the tight black fabric hiding what I've been waiting to see. *If he gets to look at me, I get to stare at him too.*

Intricate lines draw my eyes down the length of his perfect form, the light around us painting him as an angel. *Or a devil.*

"You like what you see?" He asks. *What? You can't see me salivating?*

"Hell yes, I do," I blurt out without thinking. *Shit, did I just say that out loud?* My hands immediately begin tracing each detail of the tattoo that runs from his chest down to the waistband of his jeans. If it distracts him from the words that fell from my mouth, he doesn't let on. Instead, he watches as my hands stop at the black metal button of his pants.

"Keep going, Sweetheart." He commands, and I look up at him. "Take off my fucking pants, Thalia." *You don't have to tell me twice.* My hands quickly move the small button through what seems like the tiniest hole possible. He keeps his eyes on me as I move the loosened denim down his toned thighs.

"That's a good fucking girl, Thalia." I can feel the heat under my skin and cheeks go bright red. *That was so fucking hot.* He smiles as he steps out of his jeans and stands in front of me in only his black boxer briefs and all of his tattooed glory. *Hot damn.*

He steps in closer between my thighs, baring more of me to him—his warmth. His eyes move from my lips to my neck. His hand grips the back of my hair while he claims my lips again. I willingly take another kiss from him and bite down on his lower lip. A groan rumbles between us making me crave more of him. *Please, make that sound again.* He removes his lips from mine and kisses me on my outer jaw down my neck. His fingertips gently feel around the other side to my back and stop when he finds the clasps of my bra. Within seconds, my black lace bra falls onto the tiles, leaving me exposed.

"Oh, fuck," he breathes, "I have been craving you for so long." He steps back and looks me up and down. *What the hell does that mean? How long has he known about me?*

"You have?" I ask. My voice is just as breathy as his.

"Oh, don't tell me you haven't noticed." He moves in towards me, lips landing on mine once again as he grips the tops of my thighs. "Every time I caught you staring," he admits, kissing in between the confession. "Every glance I make in your direction." He brushes me with his lips. "Every time I look at one of your *fucking* Instagram stories." His kisses land harder, and he moves his hands up to grab my breasts in the process. "*You make me want you so fucking much.*"

He moves his lips from mine, trailing kisses from the middle of my neck down to my breasts. Circling each nipple with his tongue first before softly biting each one, making me faintly moan his name.

"Oh, you like that?" He asks in a low tone. My eager whimpers have him moving further down my stomach, his kisses landing at the waistline of my skirt. *So close, but so far from where I want his touch.*

"I need to taste you, Thalia." His sea blue eyes look up at me through his thick lashes. "Right here, right now."

I nod, as if I suddenly don't know how to speak, my brain muddled from his intoxicating touch. His wicked mouth curves up from under his thick beard as he lowers himself to his knees. Rubbing his hands up the bottom of my calves up to my inner thighs. I shiver at his touch and the feel of my fishnets moving against my skin. My legs fall open at his exploration, my mind consumed with chasing the feeling he gives, and my already short skirt leaves nothing to the imagination. His hands grab the fabric near my inner thighs the closer he comes to my center. I can feel his hot breath on my skin as he moves in closer.

"Oh, fuck yes," he growls and rips my fishnets, leaving a big enough space to slowly move the tips of his fingers over the black lace material of my thong. His eyes are fierce, piercing mine as he moves the thin material aside. *Shit, that was...that was so hot, I can't even fucking think straight.*

He moves his fingers over the sensitive parts of me slowly, teasing me, making me want him even more. His eyes move back from his hands back up to me. "Is this what you want, Sweetheart?" He moves his fingers over my clit, making me wet just for him. Pressing harder to see my reaction. I moan again at his touch. He begins moving slowly in circular motions. "I can't hear you, Thalia," he teases.

"Y-yes, please," I answer in between my heavy breaths.

"That's my girl. I love it when you beg." He continues, moving a finger into my wet pussy. He looks up when I whimper louder for him. *"Oh, there she is."* His finger moves in and out faster while his thumb circles my clit effortlessly, slickened by my arousal. He braces his other hand on my inner thigh, squeezing harder.

"Relax, Sweetheart." He pulls out of me, only to add another finger. "You think you can take another one for me?" His gaze returns to my face, waiting for my response.

"Please, don't stop," I plead quietly. My toes curl inside my boots.

"What's that?" He asks. "I couldn't hear you, Sweetheart. I need you to be louder for me."

"Please," I beg louder.

"Please what? Tell me."

"Don't. Stop." I move my hands through his messy, black waves, words fragmented from the glorious agony.

"I couldn't stop if I tried."

I watch as his hands move away from where I had hoped they would stay forever, wringing pleasure from me. Instead, he advances closer, moving my legs further apart. His lips plant kisses on the sensitive space between my legs to my middle. He looks intently as if planning his next move. His tongue moves up and down, stopping at my clit. His eyes meet mine as he runs his tongue over my most sensitive area. My eyes roll back as his tongue moves in circles around my clit. My legs burn as I try to keep them from collapsing inward, encasing Lee with my thighs.

"Fuck, Lee," I let out beneath my breath. His hands squeeze my inner thighs as he moves his tongue faster.

"Oh, shit, Sweetheart," he pauses to look up at me, "keep talking like that. *I love it.*" He goes back down and continues what seems like his last meal and only stops when he feels my release go against his mouth. I can't help but stare at his gaze as my come glistens in his beard.

"Mmm," he growls before he stands up and wipes his face with his forearm. "You taste like fucking *heaven.*"

Fuck, she looks so perfect right now. Her loose red curls hang around her perfect tits with strands plastered to the sides of her cheeks. I watch her chest rise and fall with each breath she takes.

"Fuck, I love how you look right now," I tell her, standing in between her legs. My hands run down the top of her hips, I will never get used to the way she feels under my touch. They reach in between her legs, grabbing the remainder of her fishnets and pull them down to her ankles.

"Here's what we're going to do, Sweetheart..." I say while pulling down the elastic band of my black boxer briefs down my thighs. "I'm going to fuck you, just like this. You're going to wrap those pretty thighs around me." She nods as I step out of my boxers.

She stares up at me with those big, hazel eyes of hers, and I know just what she wants. *I want to hear her say it. I want her to beg and plead for my dick.* "What do you want, Sweetheart?" I ask, grabbing my cock in my hands. I stroke it slowly from the tip to the base, teasing her. She bites her bottom lip as she watches me. *Fuck, Thalia. You're driving me crazy.*

"Please," she asks again with heavy breaths.

"Please, what Thalia?" I demand again.

"Please. Fuck me, Lee," she pants.

"Fuck, I love that. Do you see how hard you make me?" I move myself closer, teasing her with my cock against her clit. The way she moves her hips closer to meet me makes it twitch. "Do you want this, Sweetheart?" I ask, moving her wet clit over my dick. I watch as her hazel eyes fill with lust. "Tell me you want it, Thalia." I move in even closer with my lips barely touching hers. "Tell me you want me to fuck that pretty pussy of yours."

"Yes, I want it, Lee." She grabs my dick and I push in deep, making both of us moan in unison.

"Ahh, shit, Thalia. Wrap your legs around me, Sweetheart." She feels just how I had imagined. So warm, wet and tight for me.

"Is this what you pictured?" I ask with my lips barely touching the shell of her ear. "Is *this* what you thought of when you fucked yourself to the sound of my voice?" I move my hips slowly, enjoying every flicker of emotion that passes across her face as my cock fills her. She interlocks her feet together, squeezing around my waist just like I asked—like the *good girl* she is. The tips of her black nails dig through my skin, making crescent moon shapes on my biceps.

"Y-yes," she answers. Her voice is muffled with her face buried in the crook of my neck.

"Tell me, Sweetheart." I say through heavy breathing. "Is this better?" Each word punctuated by the thrust of my cock, our slick skin melding together with our passion.

"Yes!" She moans. Her head tilts towards the white ceiling. "So much. *Better.*"

"Look at me," I tell her. "I want to see your face when you come on my dick." She does as I command. "That's my good girl." I praise as I move my hips faster, matching the rhythm of our breathing.

"Look at you, taking every inch of me." I groan, pushing deeper into her pussy. I can feel her tighten around my length. "Oh, fuck, you're close." I tease. I move in and out slowly. "Do you want to come, Thalia?" She answers with a single nod. "Answer me, Sweetheart. I want to hear that sweet voice of yours while my dick is inside of you."

"Yes, Lee. Make me come. *Please.*" She sounds so fucking good when she begs.

"Fuck, yeah you do." I respond by moving my hips faster and harder, keeping one of my hands next to her on the counter and the other one wrapped around her small waist. "I want you to remember this." I say in between thrusts. "I want you to think about this next time you're alone. Instead of making yourself come to the sound of my voice, I want you to remember how I fucked you on my kitchen counter after I kissed every part of you."

She runs her hands through my hair, pulling me closer. I can feel her coming down my length to my naked thighs, moaning my name while still clenching on to me.

"Ahh, *fuck* Thalia," I groan in her ear. "I can feel you dripping down cock." I move in deeper and faster until I chase my own release while still pushing myself deep inside her. I stop moving with my arms wrapped around her waist and her fingers entangle around my neck. "God, you're perfect." I tell her while still inside of her. *What the hell have I gotten myself into?*

Chapter Ten

"I Can't Take My Eyes Off of You."

ALAN

I stare at the dark ceiling. The only light coming in is from the street lights outside. They make little white lines on my bed, peeking in through the blinds. *Fuck, it's late, and I can't sleep.* My mind has been racing, and all I can think about is the look on Thalia's face when I caught her staring at the bar.

I smile thinking about her gaze. Her hazel eyes went wide when I captured her stare, piercing mine in the process. My mind goes to the fantasy of bending her over the bar, fucking her under the glow of the Edison bulbs. Her black shirt barely holding in her perfect tits, putting them on display for me. Thinking about her round ass in her tight jeans makes my dick hard under my sheets.

In the dark ambience of our bedroom, I turn to look at my wife on her side of the bed. She has her back to me while her face looks towards the blank white wall. Her bare shoulders are uncovered by our gray comforter. The sheets quietly rustle under the sound of me moving closer. I pull her close to me with my cock resting on the curve of her ass.

I kiss the side of her neck. My hands move up her arms, gently grazing my fingers up to her shoulders. She stirs in response, her sleepy, blue eyes flutter as she turns to look up at mine. I kiss her full pink lips, moving her around to face me and then pulling her on top of me. Her hands land on my chest and mine on her hips. By routine, I peel off whatever nightgown she has chosen for the night. Tonight it is her light blue silk gown. Her paid for sun kissed breasts are exposed for me. I stare at the picture of plastic made perfection and she situates herself on my length and moves her hips like she always does. She grinds just the right way, making me harder.

As if it is part of our intimate routine, her eyes close. She puts herself in her own perfect fantasy. I move my hand up between her breasts to the crook of her neck. It feels too comfortable resting there.

"*Fuck,*" I moan and she moves her hips faster. My eyes go heavy and I am transported to a fantasy of my own.

Ashley's blonde, loose waves evolve into bright red curls. Her sun kissed skin has become a milky white complexion. Her eyes, now hazel, look into mine as I dig my fingers into her pale thighs.

"Good girl," I moan and Ashley's hips continue grinding harder against me. Both of our breaths meet the same rhythm. She brings her face down to meet mine and presses her full lips to kiss mine. In my mind, they are a devious shade of red, dark as sin.

I bite down on Ashley's bottom lip hard, making her whimper. My hands go through the back of her hair. "Don't you fucking move," I tell her.

My lips graze her jaw and move to the middle of her neck, nipping and licking as I explore, leaving imprints of my teeth along her sensitive skin. She squeezes her pussy around me, making it hard for me to last much longer. She plants her hands on the pillows on either side of my head. I can feel her toes curl on the side of my legs. Ashley sits straight up, making my dick hit the perfect spot. She closes her eyes, only to go back to her own mind, and I go back to mine.

My hands go up to what I imagine would be Thalia's breasts. They're fucking amazing, fitting in the palm of my large hands. I sit up to meet them in my mouth. After rolling my tongue over each nipple, I gently bite down. Her breathing gets heavier, and I imagine her eyes rolling back as she bounces up and down.

"Just like that," I praise, matching her movements. She clamps down around me and collapses on my chest, pushing me back down. I remain on my back while her chest moves up and down against mine and her full lips softly touch mine. There is a brief moment in time where everything is perfect, ecstasy flowing through our veins.

I watch her as she slowly makes her escape to the adjoining bathroom. It is then that I'm transported back to reality when I see her red curls become the gold waves that fall down her naked back. As quickly as it began, the fantasy fades. The colorless life I've surrounded myself with coming back into focus.

I turn on my side and feel for my black framed glasses and my phone on my cherry wood night stand.

"Fuck, what have you done to me?" I ask aloud, scrolling through Thalia's Instagram page.

The black wheels of my chair slide on the protective plastic covering on the gray carpet. I stare down at my phone, her picture staring me in the face. *Does she not know the way she looks makes my heart feel like it's going to fall out of my fucking chest?* I wonder what she's doing right now. It's the middle of the week, she's probably working. *What time is it?* The late hour in the night shows in the lower right of my computer screen—just barely past eleven. My focus on the newest episode wavers. A half hour passes while I stare at my laptop, working on the intro for next week's episode. *Lee is going to kill me if I don't send it to him tonight.*

Our newest episode is on the "sick fuck" as Lee would call him, Joel Rifkin. He was sentenced to prison for two hundred and three years. It looked like they thought he may have killed seventeen people, nine of them being women. Who really fucking knows though. It may have been more.

He killed his first victim, we'll call her Susie, in 1989. According to the research I had made, she was a "prostitute" or a more politically correct term, sex worker. A lady of the night as my grandmother would call her. Words like "prostitute" were too dirty and too real for her to say.

Rifkin took her back to her place and bludgeoned her to death. He later dismembered her body. He put her teeth, fingertips and head in a paint can and disposed of her legs, arms, and her torso in the East River around New York City. They later found poor Susie's head on the seventeenth hole of a golf course in New Jersey of all the fucking places. Susie's skull wasn't identified until 2013. *Shit, that's a long time.* My focus changes from the computer to my phone. *Fuck, I can't concentrate.*

I scroll through Thalia's Instagram page again. Stopping at each picture, examining the photo. Wondering where she is, and who she is with. I look closely at what she is wearing, paying attention to the details. *It's the small details that matter.* My eyes move from Joel the Ripper on the monitor on my laptop, and then to my phone. Fuck it, I give up. *I need to get out of this house and get my mind off of her.* I shut the lid to my laptop and slide out of my large, leather chair. The room goes dark, and I walk towards the long hallway.

Ashley is asleep on the couch, clutching her Kindle that rests on her chest. The television is playing soft ambient sounds showing a picture of a fireplace. It looks like she is spending the rest of the night in. Like the good husband that I am, I spread the gray throw blanket across her lap. She won't miss me if I leave; she won't even notice.

I continue down the hallway to our room and with a flip of the switch, the light turns on. I search the closet for something more casual. Once I take off my slacks, I hang them neatly on the velvet hanger that I have specifically for my work clothes. The metal hook slides precisely next to the row of freshly ironed pants. Next, I neatly hang up my silk, black button up shirt. Buttoning up every button, making sure it stays snug on the hanger. It fits neatly next to the other button up shirts, hanging in a long row in my walk in closet–all in order by color.

My black tee shirt is hanging up exactly where I left it, sitting next to the other row of tee shirts that are also categorized by their color. It fits comfortably but clings tightly to my arms. I reach for a pair of dark gray sweats and pull them up over my thighs. They sit perfectly just below my hips. My white and black Nike tennis shoes mold perfectly around my feet. They are where they're supposed to be on my small white shelf in my closet, next to the few others that I own. Each a different color to match my different color coordinated outfits. My reflection stares back at me in the large mirror in my bathroom. A few strands of auburn curls hang just above my eyebrows.

Walking towards the front door, I notice Ashley still sleeping soundly on the couch. She hasn't stirred since I covered her up with her favorite blanket. I walk quietly through the front door and shut it slowly so I don't wake her. My run begins though the black iron gate that is attached to the iron fence which runs around our property. The gate squeaks loudly as I push it open. The brisk wind hits me when I turn towards the long sidewalk. With every gust of air, the hair on my arms stands up, and I push myself through the cold. I need to clear my head. *Anything I can do to distract myself from thoughts of Thalia.*

I shouldn't be having these thoughts, I *can't* be having these thoughts. I'm a married man. Fuck, I don't even know this woman. Her face flashes across my mind and clouds my vision. In my head I see her smiling up at me through the whiskey glass she hands me. *Damn, she's beautiful even through thick glass.* My legs keep pumping through the cold air.

She's just a listener, like the other thousands you already have. *Keep telling yourself that.*

Nothing special, just another listener.

My legs move faster around the corner. *Maybe if I push myself harder, I'll think about something else.* With more exertion, my breath gets heavier. The heavy breathing only makes my thoughts worse.

I imagine our heavy breaths syncing in tandem while she lies underneath me. She sweetly moans my name as I move inside her. *Fuck. She's just another listener, just another listener and nothing more.*

My legs move faster and harder and I come up on my property. *"Thalia, what have you done to me?"* I mentally ask myself while quietly walking back inside my house, my heaving breaths the only outward sign of my internal struggle.

Chapter Eleven

THE ALLEY

The sound of my leather gloves gripping on my steering wheel fills the interior of my car, breaking the silence of being alone. *Watching.* I am parked just far enough to be out of Thalia's view, but close enough that I can get a perfect view of her.

My car sits on the curb in front of another bar across from The Neon Rose, situated between two cabs. I move my hood up around my head and hide in the shadows. The street lights bounce off the pavement, reflecting on the smooth surface. Inside my car is silence. All of my attention on the woman I can't get enough of.

As expected, Thalia is working. Knowing exactly where she is and what she is doing at this very moment fills me with a sense of relief.

Another squeaking sound of the leather permeates the front end of the car as I shift in my black leather seat when I see her. Her bright red hair stands out in contrast to her white tee shirt. Who knew a simple item of clothing would look so fucking perfect on her. The loose fitting fabric hugs her tits in just the right way. The cropped hem exposes her pale flat stomach, showing the sunflower tattoo peeking out from her jeans. I would love to run my tongue down the length of the stem along her rib cage.

On anyone else, a cropped tee shirt isn't anything special, but when Thalia wears one—it's fucking amazing. Her body is perfection like Venus de Milo. Oh, how I would love to slide my hands up the space between the fabric and her skin. I stare while I bite my lower lip as it lifts just slightly as she reaches for one of the liquor bottles on the top shelf.

Her hands grip the silver cocktail mixer as she pours liquid in the short whiskey glass. She shoots the customer a smile and slides the glass in front of him. The corners of my mouth move up, just seeing her smile. I could watch her all day. His tattooed covered hand reaches for the glass with his fingers grazing over the top of her hand. The way he makes her jump makes me sit up in my seat and I watch this asshole closer.

His long, dark hair is pulled up away from his face and off his shoulders. His sad excuse of tattoos look like black blobs on his tanned neck. I've seen this guy come in before. Every Friday, as I've driven past the bar, I noticed he sits in front of Thalia and asks for the same drink. Normally, he's just full of one liners and uncomfortable stares. Today, he went too fucking far. He stares closely at Thalia with his mouth wide open. His jaw almost hitting the floor like one of those fucking cartoon characters, all while turning his head and following her as she moves to the other end of the bar. My hands grip the steering wheel tighter, making my fingers inside my gloves tense up. I can feel my blood start to boil and my mind goes dark.

I wait...

He comes out of the bar shortly after she denies him. His disappointment is short-lived when he reaches in his pocket and grabs his phone. The smug bastard plasters a cocky smile on his face. *He's acting like he didn't just try to touch what isn't his.*

My eyes trail him as he continues walking down the empty sidewalk. *Shit.* The cold air hits my face as I step out of my car. My shoes splash in the nearby puddles, the once brick streets long gone–erased with asphalt. He continues to move at what I assume to be his normal pace. *Why the fuck does he think he could touch her?* My mind is dark and all I can feel is anger and hate. I follow behind him, far enough that he can't hear my steps against the wet concrete.

"Hey, baby," the fucker says, with his phone plastered to the side of his face. "Yeah, I'm just leaving work now. Don't worry, I'll be home soon." I wonder if his wife, or whoever the fuck "baby" is to him at home knows he's been trying to sleep with the bartender at his local bar. *Like hell you will.* He hangs up and slides his phone into the large front pocket of his dark brown jacket. I pick up my pace, now very close behind his slender form. If he turns around now, he would see the outline of my dick in my pants.

"You work around here?" I ask from behind him with my hands in the pockets of my jacket. He stops.

"What was that?" He asks without turning around.

"I heard you on the phone. You told someone you were on your way home from work. Was it your wife?"

"Why the fuck is it any of your business?"

"You normally tell your wife you're at work while you're assaulting women in bars?"

"Listen, asshole…" He turns around with one hand in his pocket and the other now clutching his phone. His large, dark brown eyes look me up and down. His expression is almost humorous with his mouth open in shock as he notices my size. The fucker has to look up at me and it makes this all the more exciting.

Within seconds, I reach my arm out and grab his inked covered throat. His wide eyes now look like they would burst out of his sockets. I would fucking pay to see the jellied texture explode on his smug face. The thought of seeing them burst paints a large smile on my face.

"You didn't answer my question." I drag his limp body to a nearby ally between two buildings, and I throw him against the brick siding. I can hear him trying to catch his breath. "Are you ready to tell me who you were talking to?" The blue hue on his lips matches the lights on the sign of the bar across the street.

"I'm waiting," I tilt my head so that I can get a good look at him before I decide if he lives or dies, "but I'm losing my patience." He nods his head in a panic, and I loosen my grip.

"The bartender came onto *me*," he says in between his disgusting choking sounds.

"Did she?" I tighten my grip. "Is that what you're going to tell whoever you were talking to on the phone? You know, from my perspective, it looked like she didn't want anything to do with you. We could go ask her if you'd like? Or maybe we could see what the person on your phone has to say about all of this?" I grab the phone he still has clutched in his clammy hands. *Disgusting.* His eyes become swollen with tears. That is all the response I need. With one hand, I tap on the screen with my thumb, still gripping his throat with the other. I turn the screen towards him, allowing me to use his face to open up his phone. "Maybe she'd like to see what kind of man you *really* are."

His camera is through a ridiculously long list of apps on his phone."Oh, there you are." I select the icon, hit the record option and turn it in his direction.

The echoes of his head hitting the brick wall radiate through the alley. Slamming his head against the brick in front of me is pure justification for what he did. His eyes go heavy and his neck goes limp in my hand. "It's a pity really. She has to deal with men like you. Men that stare and try to touch her." I slam his head into the brick once again. The sound of his skull breaking reverberates through the small area. I let go of his throat and his body slides down the brick wall, leaving a trail of blood made by the crack in the back of his head.

I hit the stop record button on his phone and stare at his body slowly leaning further down the brick wall. My eyes move from the body in front of me to the recording. Listening to the sounds of his cranium hitting the side of the building coincide with the echo of his body hitting the hard floor beneath him. I throw it on his limp form when I'm done listening to the melodic sounds.

"What the fuck am I going to do with you now?" I question, crouching down, looking down at the lifeless body laying at my feet.

The handle on my switchblade feels cool in my hands as I reach in the side pocket of my pants. This knife has been my sense of security since the city is notorious for pushy assholes. Who knew I would be using it to make my mark. Moving the knife between my fingers, I look down at his limp body. "What to do with you..." I ponder, picking my front teeth with the blade. "Oh, I know..." his hand is small in comparison to mine. The sharp edge of the blade gently moves over each finger, allowing me to examine each of his fingertips. The blade on my knife is sharp enough to make a clean cut through the tips to get rid of his fingerprints.

Pushing the knife through his skin is the easy part. It takes some force, sawing through each finger, reminding me of Christmas dinner when I was a child. Slicing my knife through butter was a satisfying feeling, knowing it would be spread across the fresh baked bread sitting in front of me. The thought of the pure taste made me salivate until I made the first satisfying bite.

Cutting through the tendons is more of a task. The smooth slice stops once the metal hits the tissue. I add pressure to the blade and cut through the fatty layers. The sound of the knife scraping against the hard concrete resounds through the alley. I find myself sitting on the wet concrete, removing the man's appendages behind the large dark green dumpster, once again hidden in the shadows.

I store his severed fingers in the pocket of my jacket as I look over my work with full approval. His limp body continues to fall slowly down the slippery brick building. His body sits comfortably against the dark green dumpster. In this position he looks like a limp rag doll with the plastic fingers nibbled off by the family dog.

Next, I remove the hair tie that is holding his long, dark brown, and now bloody hair. With his blood caked hair plastered to the side of his face, he'll no longer be needing this. I place it in my pocket next to the ten unattached fingers. His hair falls, now covering his shoulders. His eyes are barely opened and vacant. With a vacant and empty stare, he looks towards the wall against the other building that stands just a few feet away. "I couldn't *stand* the way you stared at her." I whisper close to the dead man in front of me. Moving my knife in between my fingers, I lean in closer, my nose almost touching his.

My knife goes into his eye socket so easily. I move it around, creating a tiny slit, making the removal easier. Using my blade, I carefully remove the other eye. His dark brown eyes come out so easily, reminding me of removing a soft boiled egg from the hard shell. They're small in my hand and an awkward shape. Moving the pad of my thumb over the dark pupil. "You know, now that I think about it, I don't think she appreciated it either." His useless eyes go into the other pocket of my jacket. I kick his boot and walk in the direction towards the empty road.

Chapter Twelve

A Body Has Been Discovered

THALIA

My night comes to an end when I hear loud sirens in front of my apartment complex. The light from the day peeks in from my cheap, plastic blinds. *Shit, what time is it?* With my eyes barely open, I feel for my phone on my black nightstand next to my bed. The brightness from my phone screen temporarily blinds me, the multiple missed calls and texts from both Janice and Jace sharpening as my eyes adjust. I sit up under my comforter and lean my head up against my black wooden headboard. The blurred words becoming clear the more I scroll through the countless text messages from Jace alone.

Jace:

> Idk how many times I've tried calling your ass!

> Damn Thalia! Pick up your phone!

> Listen Bitch. If you don't answer your phone I'll come down to your apartment myself!

Well, shit. I guess I should call him. His phone only rings once until he picks up. "About fucking time, bitch." Jace answers.

"Good morning to you, too."

"What the fuck you mean, *good* morning? Don't you know what is going on?" I am clueless honestly. I just woke up. I don't even know what time it is. I haven't even stretched yet.

"No, I've been asleep."

"Apparently...listen. The Rose is closed until further notice."

"What the fuck? *Why*?"

"Maybe if you would have gotten your ass up and answered me earlier, you would know." He pauses. "The cops found some guy in the alley between The Rose and the little shop next to it. Janice said they told her that his fingers and his eyes were missing. Some really fucked up shit."

"Do they know who it was?" I sit straight up in my full size bed no longer resting against the headboard.

"They said they can't release any names yet. Not until the family is notified or some shit like that."

"Well, damn. Who do you think killed him, or who do you think was killed?" I ask.

"Bitch, I don't know?! Maybe a couple of those homeless guys that usually sit by the front of the bar. They probably went off on each other over beer or drugs. That's what usually happens outside of places like bars." *Jace's assumption just doesn't make sense. Something about the way he died doesn't add up.*

"Poor guy probably doesn't have a family. That's usually the type they go after..."

"*Who* goes after?"

"Or...you know...maybe it was a murderer."

"Who the fuck said it was a homicide?!"

"It just doesn't make sense. If he's missing body parts, it just doesn't sound like it would be two homeless guys fighting over beer and drugs. The guy had to have some kind of hate towards this person. Something must have pissed him off."

"Bitch, don't use your true crime shit on me. Just stay the fuck home. Hell, I'll come over and make sure you don't leave if you need me to."

"That doesn't sound too bad actually. We could order in. Maybe watch something on Netflix..."

"Yeah, whatever." He laughs. "I'll be over in a few hours."

Jace shows up a few hours later just as he planned with plastic grocery bags full of random snacks and a bottle of Tequila. The bright red words "THANK YOU" on the bag are bent, covering what it contains. This night is going to be my kind of night.

"Move, bitch." He laughs, pushing past me through the door. "Okay, I brought the essentials. All the fucking chips they have at that little convenience store just past your apartment. I also got some sour candy, that Bunch a' Crunch candy you like, *and* of course my Nerd Clusters." He sets the grocery bag on the counter in my small kitchen.

"I see you brought drinks." He places the large bottle next to the bag of snacks.

"Fuck yeah, I did." He searches my cabinet, and pulls out two black coffee mugs. He twists off the silver cap and pours the Tequila, filling the mugs half-way. "You got any sprite or juice?" He opens my partially full fridge. "Hell yes, there it is." He shimmies out of the way of the door and tops our drinks off with a remaining bottle of Starry I had sitting on the bottom shelf.

"I just ordered Chinese from that place you like. It should be here any minute."

"See this, this is why I love you." He takes each of the plastic packages out of the grocery bag and sets them next to our drinks. The takeout is at the apartment within minutes.

The two of us sit on the couch and search through my Netflix horror choices. Some are classic slasher films from the eighties, but most are current movie choices that haven't gotten many good reviews. With the amount of talking and drinking we are going to be doing tonight, the options could go either way. Jace's idea of small talk, however, turns into more of a game of twenty questions that he asks while using my remote to scroll through the many choices.

"What do you mean, he fucked you on his kitchen counter?!" Jace asks, shoving noodles in his mouth. His question is muffled with lo mein.

"Exactly what I said..." I pick up the steamed broccoli with the flimsy wooden chopsticks provided by the restaurant. Thinking about the night still sends goosebumps down my arms. The night ended just right. Waking up in his bed the next morning was the icing on the cake. However, the money on the end table next to me and a missing Lee, wasn't the morning greeting I expected.

"Okay bitch, *details*. I need fucking details. You left with him from the bar, then back to his place, which you say is huge. You asked for water and then...you fucked in the kitchen?!"

"Yeah, that basically sums it up." I answer by taking a bite of the broccoli I have been struggling with.

"I don't fucking believe it. That shit only happens in books."

"Then I must be living in one fucked up book, my friend." The smile on my face widens as my chopsticks grab a piece of the spicy chicken.

"How does it feel to be one of God's favorites?" He laughs, finally picking his movie, the third movie in the Friday the Thirteenth franchise.

"Why this one?" I ask, stuffing more food into my mouth.

"It's a classic. He hides in the woods like a fucking shadow." His explanation is almost funny as he grabs a handful of sour candy.

Chapter Thirteen

NEW MATERIAL

🎙️ALAN

Three, two, one. Lee's hand gestures towards my direction. Signaling me to enter this week's episode introduction. "Hello, ladies and gentlemen," I start. "Hello, you sick fucks," Lee adds, and I can't help but laugh. His additions always get me. I never know what he is going to say next.

"If you've never tuned in, this is the Manhattan Murders Podcast. Another beautiful day to talk about the murders in the city that never sleeps." I continue with the usual theme of my introduction.

"Yeah, we've all heard it before, Alan."

"Well, you never know, Lee. We may have some *new* listeners with us this week."

"Oh, some new sick fucks out there tuning in?" His voice turns up at the question.

"You never know, my friend." I shrug my shoulders for our viewing audience, and turn my head in Lee's direction.

"On that note, what can you tell us about today's episode?" He takes a drink from the clear glass sitting in front of him. This time it's full of the bourbon he brought with him. The ice cubes hit the sides of the glass as he tilts it up to his lips.

"Today, we're talking about a story that's a bit more recent than our last few episodes." I lift my black coffee mug to my lips. His eyes widened at my answer as if to act surprised. It's all for show of course, more or less for the viewing audience.

"Really? How recent are we talkin'?"

"We're talking about the early nineties, my friend."

"Shit, times were so different then."

"Hell yeah, they were. Full of landlines, none of this social media bullshit of taking pictures of what drink you got from Starbucks or what fucking sandwich you're eating." We both laugh into the microphone.

"Times were fucking simpler then. All we needed were are our fucking Game Boys and our bikes." Lee takes another drink of his bourbon.

"Well, Alan. Can you tell us what sick fuck was working his way though Manhattan in the nineties?"

"That, my friend, was none other than—"

"Holy shit!" Lee shouts. I look up from my mic. He stares at his phone clicking off the record option soon after.

"What's up?" I set my coffee mug next to my mic.

"Did you fucking see what happened?" His eyes are still scanning over his phone screen.

"No, asshole. I've been recording with you. Not looking at my phone..."

"Pick up your fucking phone, dipshit." His eyes look down to my phone sitting in front of me. My first instinct is to check TikTok. These days, that's where they show the news that people aren't afraid to hide. I stop at the first live video.

"Holy shit, holy shit, holy shit!" A loud woman yells. Her heavy accent comes in through the speakers. Her phone zooms to an alley between two brick buildings barricaded by caution tape. Her voice echoes on the other side of the studio, coming in from Lee's phone speakers.

"A fucking body?!" Her friend's voice chimes in after hers. His accent is just as thick. "What do you mean a fucking body?! Well, who the fuck is it?!" Her phone now zooms out and pans over to two officers. They're trying their best to calm the two bystanders down but are failing miserably.

"We can't tell you that." The male officer answers. His calm tone has a hint of irritation. The crease in between his dark brows deepens. You can tell he had been at the scene for what may have been hours.

"Well, why the fuck not?!" The woman asks. Her voice cracks and her eyes start to glisten. I almost feel sorry for her. *Almost.* I'm scanning around her as much as the camera in the phone allows.

"I can't tell you until everyone is notified, ma'am," he continues to try to keep his voice calm. A scream echoes in the distance and the phone pans over to a woman with long black hair and pale skin. Her body is facing what looks like a dark green dumpster. The phone camera shakes as it zooms in on the poor woman standing behind the caution tape. Her hands hold her tear covered face.

"Turn off the phone please. Show some respect." The other officer commands. The live ends abruptly.

"What the fuck?!" Lee says from across the studio still looking down at his screen.

"You think that's the family? Or someone that managed to get through the caution tape?" I stroke my chin in question.

"That's seriously what you have to fucking say?" He looks up. "A fucking body was found, who knows the fuck where."

"Before we freak out about this, remember this is New York City. Unfortunately, bodies are found all the time. Did anybody mention where?" Simultaneously, we both look down at our phones, searching for answers. Another live video comes up on Lee's phone when he re-opens TikTok.

This time it's a new set of bystanders. There are no voices except for the background noise of cars and the people standing around, also waiting for answers. He stares intently. "Fuck..." His eyes widen. "Fuck, this can't be happening." He slams the phone down on the desk and puts his face in his tattooed covered hands.

"What? What the hell is going on?" My voice gets louder the more worried I become. I stand up from my leather chair. The wheels sliding on the plastic cover. "Where is it!?" In my mind and judging by his reaction, I already have an idea and I hope to God it isn't there.

Lee reaches his arms out and hands me his phone with his screen facing up. I can only imagine what he sees. The camera pans to the alley that is filled with officers and the remaining caution tape. "This is just what we saw earlier," I say, interrupting the few moments of intense silence between me and Lee. My stare at the screen is intense.

"Keep fucking watching." His voice is muffled, his hand balled up into a fist covering his mouth. Whoever is controlling the camera pans over to the building to the left. A voice from behind the phone camera chimes in and breaks me out of my concentration.

"Hey, isn't that the place where we had drinks the other night?!" Her shrill voice echoes in my studio. She moves the camera and focuses on the brick building.

I know that building. It's that little boutique I saw in passing when Lee and I drove to the Neon Rose last week. It's simple and cute, somewhere my wife wouldn't be caught dead going.

Then it hits me.

The Neon Rose.

The camera moves to the right, showing the sign I remember being lit up. The letters are now a dull red set of bulbs swinging just slightly in the wind.

"No, no, no, no." The whispers to myself get louder. My heart begins to race and I hand Lee his phone and fall back in my chair. It almost slides from under my feet. Anywhere but there. *Fuck, Thalia. Should I message her? Should I call her? Fuck. What should I do? What should we do?*

"I need to call her...right? Right, I'll call her..." He looks over to me, as if answering my inner question. His knee bounces in anticipation. He stares at his phone. "I'm going to call her." He looks at me for reassurance.

"Well, fucking do it!" My voice raises, filled with anxiety.

I watch him scroll through his list of contacts. His phone *beeps* once he selects her name. He puts his phone on speaker so that I am able to hear. The time goes in slow motion as it rings and even longer as it rings a second time.

"Hello." Her sleepy voice comes over the speaker.

Suddenly, I am able to let go of my tense shoulders and breathe. A vision of waking up next to her comes to my mind. Picturing her red hair spread out over my pillow. Her sleepy body moves alongside mine when I put my arm around her waist, pulling her up against me.

"Fuck, Sweetheart. I am so happy to hear your voice," Lee talks into the speaker. His chair squeaks as he leans back.

Lee and I take the rest of the day off from recording. We sit in the living room on the overstuffed sectional and scroll through our phones. He sits on the end towards the wall, and I choose the opposite end near the space that opens to my spacious kitchen.

"What do you think about scrapping that episode?" I ask after a long pause, still looking down at my phone.

"What the fuck are you taking about, Alan?" His fingers scroll on what I assume is some social media page.

"What I mean is," I pause, sitting up. "What if we get rid of that whole episode and talk about what we saw today?" My eyes look at him over the rim of my glasses.

"Too fucking soon, man." He shakes his head.

"Why? The news is already talking about it. By this point, the family has been notified. Everyone in New York already knows the name of the victim." Just another one of those poor bastards that spend their time at bars. I'm assuming it's one of those guys who wait around until close to get numbers from unsuspecting women. Too bad this guy had a family at home.

With a few minutes of research, Lee and I learned of his condition when they found him. His fingers were cut off and his eyes were gouged out. Not only were they removed, they were *missing*. We've got another sick fuck on our hands walking around Manhattan. Who better to talk about it than the people who talk about New York killers weekly.

"We would get a ton of views and listeners. Hell, I bet we would get a bunch of new followers." I continue my argument. My voice stays the same tone and volume.

"The bastard just died last night and you want to do this week's episode on it?" *It isn't a no...*

"Maybe not this week. We'll take a timeout, do more research. We'll give our viewers some time to get a breather from Friday night's tragedy. It gives them a while and it'll give us a week to focus. People will have their heads locked into their phones and by then, their attention will be focused on other shit anyway. They'll forget about the whole thing. When we bring it up, it'll be like news to them." Lee looks up from his phone screen. *I caught his attention.*

"Damn it. You've got a point. But what about the family?"

"The victim's family? People still get shit from the families of victims from thirty years ago. Just another perk of this business."

"Fine, you asshole. I guess we'll cover it, but if I lose any business because of this, I'm out."

"You supply most of the bars in the city. I think you can afford to lose a few." I laugh looking down into my phone.

"Whatever, you prick. Shut the hell up before I change my mind." The corners of his mouth turn up into his beard.

"So, it's settled then." I stand up and walk towards the kitchen. A bowl of mint chocolate chip ice cream is calling my name.

Chapter Fourteen

A Night In

THALIA

I am going fucking stir crazy in this apartment. It has been days since I have left. The Neon Rose is still considered a crime scene until the police find more information about the body. *The body*. It's weird calling him a body. His name has been released, Ruben Ara. To us at the Neon Rose, he'll always be known as "the neck tattoo guy."

Thinking about him with a family makes my stomach turn. Watching his wife and kids crying on the news makes me angry. I want to yell through the screen and tell them how much of a skeeze he was. Just thinking about the ways his dark eyes followed my every move when he came into the bar still makes the hairs on my arm stand on end, still feeling his fingers graze the top of my hand when I handed him his last Old Fashioned. *His last*. I wonder if he knew it was going to be his last drink. His last trip to The Neon Rose. His last conversation with his "favorite bartender." I question how he felt when he knew that night was going to be it for him. Curiosity consumes my mind to know what his last thoughts were right before he knew he was going to die.

Stories around the city say he suffered from head trauma. And by around the city, I mean Jace. He keeps me informed while I refuse to leave my apartment. *A fucking killer walking around the city this close to my apartment? No, thank you.* I couldn't imagine how it would feel to have your head bashed into the side of a building. My bet is that it would fucking hurt until you just black out, and then you're just...gone. The terrifying feeling that you have your life in someone's grip, not knowing what will happen next. The thought of knowing that your life depends on someone else. Gently, I caress the back of my head at the notion.

The police found a trail of blood from a crack in his skull, after whoever it was smashed it against the brick. That's what killed him, the impact of the brick against his head. *Damn.* I have so many unanswered questions. Why did the killer choose him? What did it sound like when the killer smashed his head against the wall? Was there an echo throughout the alley? Wouldn't we have heard it next door? Why did he kill him the way that he did? Was there a real reason why he did what he did?

There had to be.

There was too much passion in it. It had to be more than just a guy wanting to get his rocks off on a random unsuspecting guy.

All of that happened while I was just a few feet away on the other side of a wall. While I was mixing and pouring drinks, he was getting thrown against the wall of the other building in the alley. I was cleaning whiskey glasses and he was getting his skull smashed in. As I cleaned the bar, his fingers were being removed. The same time Jace was mopping the hard wood floors, Ruben's eyes were getting plucked out by a man hiding in the shadows. To think, I walked right past his body on my way back to my apartment without a fucking clue. The thought sends shivers down my spine and goosebumps cover my arms.

I stare at the tiny screen of my television and watch the news. It's playing on every channel and it's displayed on every one of my social media feeds. The only thing I can do is watch and try to retain all of the information that my mind can hold. There is no use trying to block it out.

It's so close to home. I need to know more information. Why did the killer choose him? There had to be a reason. Maybe he was followed. Maybe it was just a bad time for poor Ruben and the killer just chose an unsuspecting patron leaving the bar at late hours. I have so many questions and no one can answer them. *I wonder if Alan has any ideas.*

Alan and Lee have been sending me messages since Ruben's body was discovered. Both of them make sure that I am safe inside my tiny box. Lee insists that I don't leave, and I haven't argued. Staying in my safe zone with Artemis is number one on my list. Never in a million years did I think I would be on a first name basis with the two guys I had been daydreaming about for months. I wonder what they're doing right now.

Is Alan staying at home, thinking about new episode ideas? I imagine him sitting in his studio, writing down lists of ideas with a large cup of coffee. Maybe a gray cat at his feet. I picture him in his office clothes. Maybe his black horn rimmed glasses are sliding down the bridge of his nose. I wonder what the rest of his house looks like. I bet it's huge with large windows. Maybe a large kitchen, similar to Lee's.

Lee.

I wonder what he's doing. Is he alone right now? Does he think about the night we had together as much as I do? Would he ever want to see me again? I could always ask him. *Maybe he would want to come see me?*

I glance around at my tiny apartment. It looks so small compared to his penthouse. The walls are a dingy white, stained by cigarette smoke from the previous renters. My kitchen is nowhere in comparison to his. I could only *dream* of my countertops holding me up like his sturdy granite ones did that night.

Moving the sheer curtains in front of my black loveseat, I peer out my tiny window into the view beyond. Lights twinkle in the distance, but it's pretty dark in the buildings next to mine with the exception of a few windows. I guess they had the same idea I had.

"Well, Artemis, it looks like another quiet night for the two of us." He looks up at me through his heavy lids as he lays in his white plush bed in the corner of the living room.

I look down at my phone and search through my notifications. No new messages from Alan, Lee, or Jace. An exaggerated sigh leaves my lips as I make another attempt to aimlessly scroll through my several social media feeds.

Nothing is scratching the surface of good entertainment. I need a laugh, a thrill or something. I need another feeling other than *numbness.*

With that, I reach for my earbuds from my purse. I press play, and Alan's voice echoes through the speakers.

ALAN

It's ten o'clock at night, and I am sitting in my car parked outside of Thalia's apartment. I have been parked here with my lights off for maybe a half hour. I check my phone. Ten o'clock and I have heard nothing from Ashley. *What a fucking surprise.* I look back up at Thalia's apartment. *Fuck. What am I doing? I'm making sure she is safe. You can never be too careful.* She puts her whole life on Instagram, even the view of the lights of the city from her apartment.

By simply watching her story, I can tell that she's just a few blocks from Time Square. With a bit of research I can pick out its general area. It's hidden in the shadows of the city and not the best neighborhood, might I add. I guess she's doing what she can on a bartender's wages.

I'm staring up into her window, watching as she opens her sheer curtains, and looks out every so often. She turns her head and surveys down either side of the long strip of road, as if to see if something drastic may happen. She's like a bored animal at a zoo trapped in her enclosure. She paces back and forth–out of boredom I assume–going from the kitchen to the few steps it takes to get to her couch. I see her slouch down and put the tiny speakers in her ears.

If someone were to break in, she wouldn't even notice.

I check the time again, ten-fifteen. Still nothing from my dear wife. *If she gets to have her fun, then fuck, I will too.*

I grip the steering wheel tightly, knowing what I am about to do is ridiculous, but there is something about her. I can't *help* myself.

Watching her isn't enough. My fingertips crave the feel of her pale skin. I want to hear what she hears. I want to see her up close, and there is a part of me that wants her to see *me*.

The sound of my car door reverberates through the empty street. I check around to the back of the building to determine just how to get in her place. I make my way around the back to a small door that I assume leads you to a set of stairs. To my surprise, the door is unlocked. *This might be easier than I thought.*

I climb the two flights of white tiled stairs. My steps echo through the tiny space made specifically for the narrow pathway. The pathway continues through a hallway filled with a number of other doors leading to other apartments. The dark brown carpet muffles the sound from the soles of my black dress shoes.

How the fuck will I know which one is hers? *Maybe you should have figured that out before you decided to be a fucking creep.* I look down to the end of the short hallway. My eyes peer towards the small sliver of space between the metal door and the carpet. *The light in her apartment is on.* Quietly walking past each one, looking to see if I can see small signs of soft yellow light.

The first two are black. No one is home, or maybe they're asleep.

I keep moving, noticing light shining beneath more doors but not enough to be *Thalia's. I'm guessing their light is coming from a small side table lamp. Thalia's apartment is lit by her overhead ceiling light fixture.*

Beaneath, the next to last in line of brown metal doors, the light is dimmed but it's on. *This is it. It has to be.*

I'm sweating with anticipation as I jiggle the door knob, hoping she still has her ear buds in. Her door opens. *Thalia, you can't be serious.* As an avid listener to our show, she must not be paying any attention to the content.

Carefully, I open the metal door, taking a step in the small apartment. She's right where she was when I got out of my car.

Her body lays across her small black loveseat. Her feet dangle off the arm rest with her pale ankles crossed. I notice her toenails are painted a deep shade of red, and I don't know why but it entices me even more.

I make my way in, carefully shutting and locking the door behind me. *You can never be too careful.* My focus moves to her cat, glancing up at me. He doesn't make a sound and nods back off to sleep. *I am so fucking grateful she doesn't own a dog.*

I make my best attempt to muffle my steps onto the hard tile in her kitchen. I've made it in. I'm standing in the corner of the kitchen with my hands in the pockets of my black slacks. While trying to control the rapid movements in my chest, my anxiety speeds up my breathing. *Holy shit, I'm in her apartment.* As a nervous habit, I roll up the sleeves of my white button up shirt past my wrists. *I'm so fucking close that I can almost smell her perfume of vanilla and what may be cookies. I've never wanted to taste someone so fucking bad.* I continue to keep my quiet composure on the outside while my inner thoughts berate my idiotic actions. *What the hell am I doing here? I'm officially overcome with obsession.* As I watch her from behind in a dark corner of the kitchen of her apartment, I know I've become a victim of my addiction.

Standing here, I am *just* out of the view of the window in front of her. I can see her long red hair pulled up messily on top of her head. Her reflection in the window in front of her is a beautiful vision. Her gray shorts are pulled up to the middle of her thighs. Her long black shirt sits loosely at her waist. She's almost breathtaking in her own element.

Her black fingernails move up and down her phone, scrolling through a playlist. I look closer, as well as I can through the reflection of the window. *Oh, fuck.* I instantly recognize the logo on what looks like the Spotify app.

The two white M's in Olde English font in the small black circle stand out over everything else.

My pants get tighter and I adjust myself in the dark corner I'm confined to. I watch her scroll through a list of our previously recorded episodes, picking from the list only after a few seconds. She drops her phone on the dingy gray carpet.

Teasing herself, she moves one of her hands to the waistband of her shorts and her other hand under her baggy black shirt. I can only imagine how amazing her full tits feel. *Fuck, Thalia.*

Her right hand moves slowly under the gray waistband, making her way under the light cotton fabric of her shorts. I stare intently at her reflection, keeping my eyes on her hands with anticipation to see where they will go next.

Her legs open just enough so I can get a perfect view. *Good girl, Listener.* She slides the gray fabric to the side and teases herself with her fingertips. She gently moves over her clit, rubbing it in *agonizingly* slow circles.

Watching her like this, all of the blood in my body flowing *lower,* and knowing she is listening to *my* voice is making me fucking crazy. *Fuck it.* I slowly unzip my pants while still trying to be as quiet as possible. First pulling myself out through the open space, then I work myself from the base to the top of the head with every heavy breath I hear coming from her direction — moving along with her movements.

Her quiet whimpers get louder, the private and vulnerable sound almost making me lose it. I watch her back arch against the armchair. Her shirt moves up, exposing her flat stomach.

"Oh, fuck." I hear her moan, and I move my hand faster at the sound of her words. *That's it.* She drags her hand out from under her shirt and trails it to her inner thigh. Her fingers squeeze her skin, creating tiny red marks. She moves the other hand down and puts two fingers in her perfect cunt, moving slowly then picking up speed. Her cries get louder and her breathing gets faster. Seeing the reflection of her face like this is the sexiest thing I've ever witnessed.

Her breath starts to slow down and the grip on her inner thigh loosens. Her arms fall to her sides and her thick thighs crash together inward. *That's my signal.* It's my time to get out before she notices that I have been jacking off to her next to her tiny fridge. I tuck my dick back into my pants and carefully adjust myself.

Before I leave, I notice a keychain sitting on the short white kitchen counter. Her single key is sitting near me on a stack of white napkins. I'm guessing they're from her favorite Thai place she loves so much. I notice the pen sitting on the other side of me. *This is too damn easy.* Within a matter of seconds, I color over her key on the white napkin and stuff the napkin in my pocket.

Next time I visit will be so much easier.

Chapter Fifteen

MORNING COFFEE

🎙️LEE

It has been a *week*.

A week of staring at her pictures.

A week of driving past her house like a fucking stalker, just to make sure she is home and safe.

A fucking week since the murder of that creep with the neck tattoos.

I knew who he was as soon as they showed his face on the news. I remember seeing him in the bar, always doing his best to win over Thalia. *My Thalia. Oh, fuck. what am I saying.*

I haven't stopped thinking about her since I brought her back to my house, and it fucking scares me. The memory of that night plays over and over again in my head. The way her mini skirt hugged her ass, sitting between her perfect thighs was enough to send me over the edge. Her smooth skin under my fingertips and the way she sounded when she came on my dick is all I think about. I miss her. *Fuck, I miss her.*

I told myself I wouldn't do this shit after my divorce. I'm not going to let some broad consume my thoughts again. I told myself my ex was the last person I would ever let put me through that shit again. I can't fucking do this. My knee bounces in agitation as I sit in this tiny little cafe just outside of the city. My hands clutch the black case on my phone as I wait here in these fucking uncomfortable wooden seats for Alan to arrive.

He isn't late. He was always on time; I'm just early. I needed to do something other than sit in my house and spiral into the thoughts consuming my mind. Thinking about what, you ask? Long fucking red hair barely covering the best pair of tits I have ever seen. I will distract myself anyway I can to keep from calling Thalia or jacking off in my shower for the hundredth time. *Oh good, the bastard shows up.* Just in time for me to try to come up with another topic in my head.

Alan climbs out of his silver Lexus. His long black coat pristine as ever moves just out of the way of the door when he shuts it. I think he would go fucking nuts if his coat wasn't smoothed out perfectly. He gets out of his car like he thinks he's a male model or some shit. He looks towards the front of the building and casually nods at the sight of me sitting in the window. Like a fucking gentleman, I nod back.

"What's up asshole?" Alan asks, pulling out the wooden chair in front of me.

"What do you mean, 'What's up?'" You asked to meet me out here, you fuck." I look up from behind my phone.

"Yeah, dick. We're here to talk about the newest episode." He laughs.

"I know. You sure you want to talk about what happened last week?" At this point, I am still not sold on the idea.

"Absolutely. It's still fresh in people's minds. It's the case people want answers to." He stares at me with his green eyes behind his glasses. His frames sit in the middle of the bridge of his nose.

"You don't think we'll have any kind of backlash from this? I meant what I said the other night. If I lose any business because of this shit..."

"Lee, we won't get backlash from doing an episode on what everyone is already talking about," he confidently informs me using air quotes around the word backlash. "I doubt you'll lose any business," he adds.

Looking down at the menu, he continues, "Now, let's not worry about the people who'll bitch about the idea, and think about the listeners who will *love* it." His eyes scan the options and picks an Americano, his usual choice.

"You know what you want?" He asks, setting down the one page menu on the small wooden table between us.

"Yea, black coffee," I answer, not even looking down at the menu.

"Black coffee? That's it?" He raises his eyebrows at the question.

"Yeah."

"You can just make black coffee at home."

"Fucker, I don't know what the hell all of this other shit is. Black coffee is what I'm comfortable with."

"Alright, order the fucking black coffee."

"Okay, just let me have my fucking black coffee in peace."

"Hey, I'm not stopping you." He smiles and crosses his arms around his chest.

"Are you guys ready to order?" A pretty little brunette comes up to our table and takes our order. Her bright red lips turn up in a fake smile while she waits. She looks at Alan first.

"An Americano, please." He hands her his menu and flashes her his winning smile. I swear she fucking melts right there. *Arrogant prick.*

"And for you sir?" She looks at me.

"Coffee. Black." I hand her my menu. "Thanks, Sweetheart." She smiles and turns towards the bar.

"Sweetheart?" Alan asks. His eyebrow raises again at the question.

"Yeah. It's a term of endearment. Broads like that kind of thing."

"Yeah. They do. Thalia likes that kind of thing." He smiles behind his phone.

"Shut the hell up, asshole."

"Here's your order." The waitress comes back to our table and gently sits both of our white mugs in front of us. "One Americano. One black coffee."Alan and I both nod in unison. She heads back in the same direction as before.

I pull out the tiny bottle of bourbon in the pocket of my leather jacket and pour about two shots in my small coffee cup.

"Black coffee?" Alan asks, taking a sip of his drink.

"Black fucking coffee." I answer, from behind the rim.

THE SHADOW

I stare at the prick's fingers that I stuffed in a clear plastic bag before picking it up, and examining them closer.

The memory replays in my mind.

The feeling of my switchblade sinking into his flesh, it giving beneath my weapon like butter before a hot knife, has goosebumps covering my arms. The thought is dark and *devious,* but it fuels the fire burning under my skin.

I need more.

The plastic is clouded with moisture from the rotting flesh it contains. The once tan skin now turning darker, tinted with gray. The few tattoos he had on his fingers are harder to make out, the bloating making the ink look like black blobs.

Maybe I should have thought about the trophy I picked up from that night. Perhaps I should have taken the fucker's phone instead. I would replay the sounds of him gasping for air every day. It would be a reminder of the day I got rid of the bastard that touched what didn't belong to him. My cock goes rigid at the thought and I adjust myself in my pants.

The asshole's eyes are staring at me from behind an empty jar I brought from my kitchen cabinet. I filled it with alcohol I had in my medicine cabinet, a homemade attempt at preserving my *prize.* The two eyeballs float from the bottom and stay around the middle of the tall mason jar.

"What am I to do with you?" My fingertips stroke my chin as I ponder out loud. I move the jar upside down to watch them flow through the clear liquid to the top of the silver metal lid, then back down to the bottom of the jar.

With one look at my fingers, I wonder what someone would have done with mine in this situation. I know one thing, they would have needed more than one of those fucking sandwich bags. While I stretch my fingers, I compare the length to the ones sitting in front of me on the table. Who am I kidding, there is no real juxtaposition.

The metal chair creaks as I stand up, planting my feet on the solid concrete underneath my shoes. The legs echo through the room as I push it under the white folding card table.

One day, this room will be filled with trophies—trophies that will remind me of the times that I saved Thalia. For now, there are only two, but deep down I hope–no, know–there will be more.

I will be the one to rid her of the people that stand in her way.

I will be the one that always keeps her safe.

Even if she doesn't know it.

My footsteps echo in the empty storage unit while I walk to my large metal shelf on the other end of the room and place the jar and clear bag right next to each other, placing an index card in front of them. *Ruben* written roughly in black pen. I wonder what name will be next to his. The thought leaves me curious as I leave the small space and slide down the red metal roll-up door, locking it up with my round, silver key.

Chapter Sixteen

HONEY, I'M HOME

🎙ALAN

The gold hands on the onyx face of my watch point to ten'0 clock, which seems pretty late for a book club meeting. The night sky shows through the open curtains in our living room. I peer out the window behind my glasses, and hold my clear whiskey glass up to my lips while the lights of her car shine in through the large windows. The ice in the glass clinks to the sides when I set it down on the counter.

Standing at the island in the middle of the kitchen, I'm in the same clothes I wore to the office. A pair of dark gray slacks, my white button up shirt, a black tie, and my black leather Silvano dress shoes. I haven't been home for long. My night has consisted of driving past Thalia's apartment just to make sure she has been home. To my satisfaction, she was sitting in the same spot she was when I left after my little visit the other night. It's better that she's somewhere safe, rather than out in the town with a killer on the loose.

Ashley doesn't know that; how would she know? She's rarely ever home, and when she is, she's in her own headspace. The topic of her loving husband rarely sits as a focus in her mind.

Today, however, she will see me.

I lean against the island and stare at the front door, waiting for her to come in.

"Long night of reading?" I say as she walks in the front door. It squeaks through the long hallway in the entryway. She gasps, holding her chest. *Maybe she wasn't expecting to see her husband in his own home.*

"Fuck, Alan. You scared me." Her blue eyes shoot daggers in my direction. I smile, lifting my glass up to my lips.

"My mistake." I admit while she hangs up her white pea coat in our coat closet. She kicks off her slide on canvas shoes and pushes them up against the closet door. *Why can't she just put them in her closet where they belong?*

I set my glass down, and she tries to ignore me but I move slowly towards her , meeting her in the entryway. Her arms grow rigid at her sides.

"What's the matter, baby?" Her eyes get wide when she feels my hands gently rubbing her stiff shoulders, fingers trailing up to her tan neck. Then, gripping the tufts of hair at the nape of her neck, making sure to intertwine fingers in her thick strands. "You know what would be perfect after a hard, long day?" I ask in almost a whisper just above the tip of her right ear.

She stands still and her breathing becomes shallow. Goose-bumps start to form on her arms.

"A nice glass of red wine with your husband." Little does she know, I can smell the liquor she already has on her breath.

"Okay," Ashley answers in a shaky whisper.

"Okay," I confirm.

I let go of her golden waves, and I move farther into the kitchen. "You know what really sounds good?" I ask, turning around from the bright white cabinets.

She sits on one of the tall matching wooden chairs at the island in the middle of our large kitchen. Slowly, she turns her head to face me, mouth pressed into a tight line.

"The wine we got from your parents. The one they gave us as our wedding present." I look down at the bottle, reading the label. "You remember, right, baby? The one from Napa Valley. 2012. Wasn't that one hell of a year?"

The bottle makes a popping sound as I pull out the cork. I begin pouring wine in the already prepared glass in front of me. It's a clear crystal glass she must've bought. The sweat from the cold glass slides down the smooth surface when I sit it down in front of her with a wide grin on my face. "So tell me, what was this month's book about?" Her shaky hands reach for the glass.

"Why do you want to know?" She asks softly, now looking up at me.

"No particular reason. Let's just say that I'm... *interested*." Now, I take a drink from my own glass.

"You're never interested in what I read." Her voice is a little stronger and more confident. She wraps her full pink lips around the rim of the glass. The small mark from her lipstick stays in place as she sets the glass gently back down on the counter.

"Well, I am certainly interested in this one. Considering your book club took what..." I pause, looking down at my watch, "five fucking hours. Damn. It must have been one *hell* of a book." My voice stays calm and I keep the smirk on my face. I pick up my whiskey glass and take another small sip of my bourbon.

"Sometimes we get caught up in conversation. Or sometimes we go out for drinks. You know that." Her blue eyes playfully look into mine.

"Oh, I know that, baby. You've told me a number of times. What I didn't know is that your tennis lesson and your book club were in the same building." She stares in my direction. Her soft features are now harsh.

"Did you track my phone?" She asks, picking up her glass again. Her lips wrap around the thin rim in the same spot as before. Visions of Thalia's lips fill my thoughts. I bite my lip to stop the fabric around my dick from getting tighter.

"Baby, I've been tracking your phone for *years*." I lean against the surface across her, holding my chin in my hand.

"How long have you known?" The tense feeling in the room makes the sound from her glass hitting the counter deafening.

"How long have I known what, Ashley? That you've been fucking your tennis instructor?" My voice holds the same calm tone it has this entire conversation. She crosses her arms over her chest at my suspicion.

This isn't news to me. I've had my suspicions for a few months, but I've never really put much thought into it. Now, though, it's all changed. On one hand, she has her rich and attractive husband that looks good in pictures. On the other, she has her side piece that she could have access to anytime she wanted. It's time I have the same thing. I'm not going to let her or my guilty conscience get in the way of having Thalia. *My listener.*

"Not your tennis instructor?" I raise my eyebrows with the question. "Let me see," I continue my interrogation. "Is it someone you met at the country club?" I pause, leaning in closer to her face. "Or maybe it's someone in your book club." I lean back, crossing my arms over my chest again. "Now, there is an idea," I smirk.

"It's none of your fucking business," she spits.

"See, that's where you're wrong. It *is* my fucking business. This, Ashley, makes it my *fucking* business." My voice gets louder and I point to the white gold band around my left ring finger.

She turns her head, refusing to look at me.

"Are you going to say anything about this?"

She moves her head just slightly to face me. "Oh, like you haven't been with anyone else!" *She's trying to hide the shakiness in her voice, but I can see the tears forming in her eyes.* She knows she's been caught, and I know that there is no going back from this.

"No, I didn't. But boy did I want to. I wanted to so fucking badly." I can feel my face getting hotter. "You know what kept me from bending her over?! *You!* Even though I knew deep down you were on top of some other guy's dick. Or who the fuck knows now?! Maybe, just maybe you had your head in between some bitch's thighs!" With one look at me, she stands up from her chair and takes her wine glass with her. "Ashley, we aren't fucking done with this conversation!" I walk after her.

"I am fucking done with this conversation, Alan!"

I grab her small wrist, making her turn to face me. Her full wine glass spills down the front of my white shirt. The sound of glass breaking fills the already loud silence between us. As I tilt my head down, I notice the dark red stain forming on the front of the white fabric. The heat from my face is now moving everywhere else in my body. I take a deep breath in an attempt to calm myself down.

"No," I say quieter, "you don't get to be done with this conversation. You know why?" She stands in front of me trying her best to be defiant. "Because I fucking *own* you. Thanks to our spoiled, rich fucking parents, I own you and everything in this damn house."

"You don't get to touch me!" she yells. I scoff as she tries her best to remove her wrist from my grip.

"Why not? Everybody else fucking does!" I pull her in closer. "I am going to make you touch me, Ashley. You... Ashley, you are going crave every fucking minute of it. You understand me?" I lean down with my mouth just above her ear. She struggles and is able to get out of my grasp. She runs towards the front door of our large house.

"Ashley!" I yell, stepping over the broken glass and begin to follow her out of the front door. "I don't have time for this!" She looks back when she hears the echoing of my footsteps. She runs as fast as she can in her light blue cashmere socks. "Baby, you're going to get your socks wet. I know how much you hate that."

The sounds of her running are snuffed out by the mud on the gravel driveway. My large strides are an advantage the closer we get to the wrought iron gate surrounding our property.

"Look at you." She turns to face me after she realizes the front gate is locked. Her blue eyes widen as I wrap my arms around her body tightly and throw her over my broad shoulders. We continue the walk back to the house in silence, only hearing the scuffs of my shoes on the wet grass.

"Put me down!" She yells as I carry her into our room. Her body bounces off of our bed after I let her fall off of my shoulders. She stares as I shut and lock the door. She sits herself onto her knees in her overpriced black leggings and cropped white sweatshirt. Her eyes peer up at me under her long sweeping bangs.

"What do you want me to do?" Her yelling turns into a compliance that I could get used to.

"You are going to beg, baby. You are going to beg for my forgiveness." I stand with my arms crossed and my back leaning on the door.

"How am I going to do that?"

"I want you to crawl. Fucking crawl on your hands and knees and ask for my forgiveness."

"You want me to crawl to you?" The disbelief in her voice is almost amusing.

"That's right, princess. You want forgiveness? Well, then you are going to do *exactly* as I say."

Without much more protest, my cheating wife sits at the end of the bed. She stands up and starts to walk in my direction.

"I said fucking crawl!"

Her shocked expression covers her face and she gets on her hands and knees.

"That's it, baby," I encourage her like I would a dog. She stops in front of me looking up towards my chest.

"Take off my belt." Her tiny hands scramble up my pants and find my waist, searching for the metal buckle, undoing the ends in a matter of seconds.

"Take out my dick," I command.

She unzips the black metal zipper and pulls my pants and gray boxer briefs down to my thighs.

"Show me how fucking sorry you are." She grips my dick and wraps her mouth around the head and moves down my length. "Fuck, Ashley."

She moves her head in a steady rhythm. "That's it, baby." Her rhythm moves faster and I steady myself by placing my hand on the back of her head. Her moans send vibrations down my cock, making my balance uneven.

"You know, baby, you've always been such a good little slut for me." I pause, taking in deep breaths. "But it just makes me wonder, who else?" Her head keeps moving and I am left without an answer. "You going to tell me, baby? Who else were you a slut for? Where else has my little whore been?"

She stops and my dick falls out of her mouth and hits my exposed thigh. Her eyes stare at me in disbelief, words unable to escape past her lips.

"Can you answer me baby, or is that mouth only good for *one* thing?" I ask her and look down at her swollen red lips. Her head fits perfectly in my hands. She stares up at me when I look into her big, beautiful blue eyes. With one quick twist of my wrist, I hear the crack from her neck. My wife's body falls backward with her gaze towards the ceiling.

I tuck my dick back into my boxer briefs and pull my slacks up my legs. While staring at her lifeless body, I clasp the silver buckle. The belt slides smoothly in the loops of my pants. "Well, baby. What am I going to do with you now?"

Chapter Seventeen

Our Marriage in Pieces

🎙️ALAN

Staring down at the plastic bags won't make this process any faster. My look fixates on the several plastic bags in front of me. I took the day off to drive to the local hardware store. There are more pressing matters here at home that are worse than a few clients trying to sue some landlord who won't fix their mold problems. I grip the handle of my coffee mug tightly and continue sipping the sweet bliss of the liquid caffeine. This will not be my only cup for the day; I'm going to be up all night trying to figure out how to get out of this mess I put myself in.

The bags in front of me are more important than the lukewarm coffee I've been sipping on for the last half hour. The sound of the plastic crinkling is louder than it should be. I pick up the three bags and a pair of kitchen scissors, taking them to my ensuite bathroom. Leaving my mug on the granite counter, I walk over my wife's lifeless body as she lies on the plush carpet. It's reminiscent of the way I have seen her lie on her side of the bed many times before. *Only this time she isn't asleep. She isn't coming back.*

The plastic bags are bulky and inconvenient, but for everything the clerk put in them, it makes sense. The bags fall on the marble with a loud thump in my large bedroom. I begin to empty out the flimsy bags and put them in order of how I will use them — planning out my actions if you will.

A plastic raincoat is first in my line of items. Next, a clear plastic tarp that will help in the disposal of Ashley's body without leaving too much of a mess. The now tiny, confined, wrapped square will soon be large enough to cover the whole bathtub.

I grab the medium-sized box next. The red box with the black outlined picture of the minisaw stands out under the clear plastic box. The tape on the box's opening tears off easier than I expected. I'm able to remove the saw from its box in one fluid motion. The black cord attached to the battery charger is neatly wrapped with plastic and a zip tie. I set the tool and rechargeable battery to the side and examine the long list of directions and warnings. Gently, I set the manual next to the minisaw. I cut the zip tie that binds the plastic-wrapped cords with the kitchen scissors. The long cord quickly falls out of the casing. I plug the rechargeable port into the outlet next to the large mirror in front of the white bathroom counter. *That should charge while I continue my prep for Ashley's body.*

The other bag contains a few normal household items you would use in home repairs. *There isn't anything normal about what I'm about to do. Just a necessity.* A package of latex gloves, a roll of duct tape, paper towels, and a bottle of bleach. I'm sure the employees think I was buying what I needed to finish a project I had started at home. They may have been staring at the tarp and minisaw with uncertainty but said nothing when I paid with cash.

My morning task begins right as I walk to my living room and shut my white curtains before turning off the lights in the living room and kitchen. *Nothing to see here.* I make my way back to the bathroom and focus on the items in front of me on the floor, stepping back from the bathroom counter. *Remove my clothes: check.*

My gray sweatpants fall to the marble, leaving me in my bright blue boxer briefs. I take off my black tee shirt. It falls on top of the pile. If I get that bitch's blood all over my clothes, I'll have to burn them. My arms slip through the clear plastic coat and I situate it on my sculpted form the best I can. *This will have to do.*

Next, I unwrap the clear tarp and lay it across the large bathtub, making sure to smooth over any creases or folded over edges. The tarp covers the bottom and the sides of the tub perfectly.

As I walk into our room, I stare at her body. She is still lying in the same spot with her neck facing upward. Her leggings hang a little looser on her slim hips than I remembered and the cropped sweatshirt she has on hangs a little lower at the middle of her ribcage.

"Baby, look at the mess you've gotten yourself into." I say walking towards her bare feet. My fingers move towards the waistband of her leggings and tuck them underneath. "We both knew this wasn't going to work. From the time I saw you in high school in that tight little cheerleading uniform. As bad I as I wanted to fuck you, I knew you would be just like everyone else."

"We were supposed to be the picture of perfection." The black fabric moves slowly down her legs, as I tug it down to her small ankles. "We were the couple everyone thought they wanted to be." I add as I fold them in a pristine stack and set them on our bed.

My blood begins to boil when I turn to face our wedding picture in a silver frame on her nightstand. "What a waste of money that night was."

Next, I move up to the waistband of her pale pink thong, carefully grabbing the delicate lace in my fingers. "As much as I loved these, Ashley, I knew they were never really for me." I fold and place them on top of the leggings. *Two pieces down, two more to go.*

Her sweatshirt is the most difficult.

"Arms up, baby," I quietly suggest before I gently fold her sculpted, tan arms through the sleeves. It's astonishing how the body bends and folds when it's no longer in use. Folding her arms through the sleeves is the easy part, but moving her abnormally broken neck through the headspace is like trying to play the game Operation. Only instead of a buzzing sound, it would be replaced with dislocation.

Her blonde hair passes through the opening with ease. Another successful removal. All that's left is her pale, pink lacy bra. The second half to the last matching set that I will ever see her wear.

Unhooking the metal clasps holding in her breasts is an easy task. I had undone them several times before. "I guess I'm not the only one who took this off of you, am I, baby?"

I pick up her lifeless body and sit her back up against my chest. Slowly sliding the pink, silk straps down her slender arms, I watch her bra drop to the floor.

"There you go, baby. All ready for our next step." Sitting her gently back down on the carpet, I add the bra to her stack of clothes.

You never truly know the concept of deadweight until you're holding your wife's lifeless body in your arms. Her body falls limp over my shoulder and I carry her over to our bathroom. I lay her down softly on the clear tarp in our porcelain bathtub, making sure to cradle her upturned head in my arm.

Aside from her contorted neck, she looks peaceful.

My eyes trace over her naked body at the same time I put on a pair of light blue latex gloves, snapping the band along my exposed wrist. It's almost pathetic how eager I am to use my electric mini saw.

"Oh good, it's charged." I grab the appliance and unplug the retractable cord from the white electric outlet. The battery makes a satisfying snapping sound when it slides under the saw's handle.

With my feet tucked under my thighs, my eyes scan over my masterpiece. It's a shame it will all be destroyed in a matter of hours.

"Where would you like me to start, Ashley?" I graze her body with the blade starting at her shaved pussy and moving down to her ankles. "How about we go in order?" I move towards the end of the tarp where her toes barely touch the edge, flipping the power switch forward to the on position. The sound of the mini saw isn't as loud as I expected it to be. The many years of watching nineteen eighties slasher movies had trained me to believe differently. Of course, those were gas powered.

The chain moves so fluidly around the blade. I stare with my mouth agape as it slides smoothly into her golden skin. "You know, baby, it's been too long since we've had time to ourselves like this. You know how the saying goes, saving the best for last."

Pools of blood pour from her left ankle. The red liquid sprays against her adjacent leg and splashes against the white surface of the tub. I push the saw through to her bone, listening as her ankle separates from her calf against the tarp.

"Sorry, I'll try to be more careful next time." I move to the other side of her body and line up the blade with the exact stroke of the last cut I made. "It's the fine details that matter." I inform the body lying in front of me, watching closely as more blood pours out from under the other ankle. Ashley's once tanned skin tone is now that of a sick child. The new hue of her flesh stands out in contrast to the crimson puddles collecting beneath her.

My fingers run up to her thighs. The feeling of skin against latex is not what I'm used to, but it's what I have to limit myself to tonight. I squeeze her flesh and place the blade of the mini chainsaw in the skin right above her knee. The blade slicing into the flesh is so fascinating; unlike anything I have ever seen before.

When you cut anything, it's such a simple concept. It's just as easy putting something between two sharp blades. The smooth slice is so simple and mundane. Cutting through skin, however, is complex. Watching the blade cut through the layers of tissue and muscle is so fascinating to me. The way the different tissues ooze out vastly different colors of reds, the varying yellows among the different layers of her skin. I could examine the precise cuts all night.

Hearing the blade hit the hard bone and listening to it crack sends a whole new sensation throughout my body. It's like ASMR that I could listen to for hours, lingering on the line of a new discovery and release.

After gently setting Ashley's femur on the hard surface of the bathtub, I lean over to reach the other side of her body. I repeat the process and slide the blade into the velvet texture of her skin, listening closely to the crack of splitting bones. The sound that radiates through the bathroom is a new melody of which I cannot get enough. I watch her blood paint the tarp and the white surface next to me. The sound of her blood splashing against my clear coat echoes in the acoustics of the bathroom, reminiscent of raindrops hitting an umbrella. I watch as the red drops slide down the plastic covering on my chest and my arms. Hitting me in the face and across my lips. The strong smell of copper overpowers the fumes of her expensive perfume. More of my money going down the drain along with Ashley's blood.

I stroke my chin and examine the project at hand. Ashley's body is almost completely dismembered.

All but one major piece.

My legs are wobbly as I walk on my kneeled knees right next to her bent neck running my fingers through her now tangled golden highlights. With careful consideration, I grab my mini saw and plan out where the perfect cut would be.

"Don't worry, Ashley. It will all be over soon." I press the power button near the bottom of the device and slide the moving blade through the tendons right below the flat surface of her chin. Her decapitation is easier than I would expect. Her head gracefully separates from her slender neck. Her wide, beautiful, blue eyes stare up at me as I turn off the mini saw in my hand.

The clear tarp that was once a blank canvas is now a beautiful picture. Different colors litter across my canvas, each speaking to a layer of life. Crimson for the blood that once flowed through her veins and shards of bone glisten in the gore, their brightness undeniable. Hues of amber colored tissue intertwine with the carnage, standing out against the white tub.

I continue my project by letting each limb separate from the bone. Each one of her sections a beautiful puzzle piece I would happily put back together and break apart once again.

She is my masterpiece.

Her once tanned large, round breasts are now bloodied. What were previously attached to my living and breathing wife, are now a part of a separated torso. My light blue latex gloves are painted with the blood and other various fluids of my wife. They're a struggle to peel from both of my hands. I bend down and rub my bare hands over her still chest, making sure to stop at her breasts.

Her tits feel like I remember, only this time, they are cold and covered with drops of her own crimson. I rub both of my thumbs over her nipples slowly and my cock stiffens in my boxer briefs.

Still on my knees, I lower myself to her hardened nipples. I take them in my mouth one last time, sucking on them gently and adding pressure with my teeth. With one hand, I pull out my cock while the other is still on Ashley's breast. My hand moves up and down my shaft, using her blood as a lubricant.

"Fuck, baby," I moan. I move my hand faster until I start to feel my balls tighten. I look down at the rest of her separated limbs. The sight alone sends a fresh coat of white, giving my work of art just what it needs. Looking down at what was once my wife, I notice what is now just a jigsaw puzzle of a woman. Like my nanny used to say, we must put away our toys when we are done with them.

I strategically move her pieces in a way that I can wrap her up and store her somewhere else useful. In this case, it's a few black trash bags I had under my kitchen sink. After I determine how much would fit in each bag, I pull out three large bags from the packaging.

One bag for her feet, calves, and thighs.

One bag for her torso.

The last bag is set aside for her arms, head, and her delicate hands.

I pull off the shiny band of her wedding ring and examine the diamond closely, wiping the few drops of blood from the clear cut between her forearm and her wrist.

"You know, it didn't take much effort picking out your wedding ring. White gold, thirty-five carat, white emerald-cut diamond. It was the most expensive thing I could find. Your eyes were always filled with dollar signs. I knew instantly you would say yes to my proposal. It's too bad it couldn't keep you from riding some other man's cock."

I tie up the plastic drawstrings of the final trash bag after staring at her blue eyes under long blood-stained lashes for the last time.

Chapter Eighteen

MY GIRL

THALIA

I am going to go fucking stir crazy if I have to stay in this apartment for much longer. I have done nothing but pace from my kitchen, to my living room, to my bedroom. I don't know how Artemis does it. *Oh, to be a house cat.*

The alley next to The Neon Rose is still under investigation; however, Janice has agreed that Jace and I can finally go back to work tomorrow—music to my fucking ears. This little vacation has been, well, boring. Not to mention, having gone about a week without a paycheck and tips has done a lot to my bank account. A lot in the *negative* sense. I have been living off of Cup of Noodles, coffee, and Pop Tarts.

I have had opportunities to go out with Jace, and to be honest, my mind wavers at the thought. The night life excites me while at the same time terrifies me. Maybe a night of work will bring back some normalcy into all of our lives. It's everything we can all hope for.

With a sense of excitement—maybe too much excitement—I scan through my closet. The only advantage of not leaving my apartment is I didn't have to do any laundry. I've been in the same gray cotton shorts and black tee shirt for who knows how long. My few pairs of jeans and many black shirts are still hanging up neatly as possible. My black, short skirt and a black cropped tee to match are laid out across my bed. My favorite platformed boots to fit the ensemble stand out on the dingy white carpet next to my closet. These will be just what I need to complete tonight's outfit.

I take a step back and look over all the pieces put together.

Perfect, cute but comfortable. It will look even better with my hair and makeup done. My leather jacket will complete the outfit. *It will be okay, I can do this.*

The next morning, I wake up to the sounds of thunder and heavy raindrops hitting my window panes. *I guess I will be taking an umbrella to work today.* I stretch my arms and legs under the many covers I have laying on top of me, accidently moving Artemis in the process. *Sorry, little guy.* His bright blue eyes shoot daggers at me. *Oh, what a terrible life you live.*

Without looking, I search my nightstand for my phone. These days, texts from Jace and Tiktok videos have been my only news source. I open my screen to Jace's *good morning* texts, just like I would have expected.

Jace:

Good morning, bitch. Get your ass up. You get to see me at work today.

A smile stretches on my face at the thought of working with Jace again.

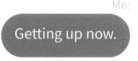

Me:

Getting up now.

I swing my legs over the side of my bed and make my way into the small kitchen. My spoiled cat waits by his food bowl for his breakfast. He barely lets it sit before he begins his attack on the dry pellets. He lets me pat his little white head between his pointy ears before I head back into my room.

I grab my phone and search through my apps. *There you are.* Spotify is always there when I need it. My "Daily Mix 1" plays in the background while I begin the task of putting on my makeup. My look is complete once I add my signature bright red lipstick. Next, I grab my curling iron and curl each section as well as I can while dancing to the music on my playlist. When I'm done, my loose, red waves fall down past my shoulders.

I slide my black skirt over my hips, having to jump in the process. Sometimes it's a blessing and a curse to have this ass. My cropped tee comes on next. The wrinkles are easy to smooth out as it falls just about an inch above the waistline of my skirt. I spot my boots in the middle of my closet and slide them up my calves. They sit just right below my kneecaps.

I pull my black leather jacket over my tee shirt and grab my leather purse. The black leather strap carelessly hangs over my shoulder. My umbrella is next on my list of necessities. Remembering how heavy the rainfall was this morning, I make sure to grab it off the small counter in the kitchen. My cat watches while I grab things in a rush, trying my best not to be late for my first day back to work. "Be a good boy for me," I tell Artemis as he lets me pet him on my way out. Quickly, I open the door and head down the short hallway towards the building's exit.

LEE

I've been sitting outside her apartment all morning. From where I am parked, I have a perfect view into her bedroom window. *Mental note, buy Thalia curtains you can't see through.* With a hint of reluctance, Janice decided to re-open The Neon Rose, which means she'll need more of my liquor to sell to her regular customers.

The idea that Thalia will be in the same place that guy was killed has me on fucking edge. There is no way I'm going to let her be there by herself today.

My grip tightens on my steering wheel when I see her walking out with her black umbrella. She holds it just barely over her head with one hand while the other holds her phone. My knee bounces in anticipation at the idea of getting to see her tonight. I've been distancing myself since the last time we'd seen each other, only texting her every now and then, but it's just small talk. Seeing her, it does *something* to me, and honestly, I don't fucking like where it's going.

I continue to watch her walk in the rain down the sidewalk as she heads towards the direction of the bar. *I can't let her walk alone.*

Damn it. While pulling my car out from my spot to get closer, I honk my horn, stopping her in her tracks. She quickly turns her head towards my driver's side window as I roll it down. My mischievous grin emerges from behind the receding glass.

"Lee?!" The way the pitch in her voice raises when she says it makes my smile widen.

"Hey, Sweetheart." I lean out of my lowered window.

"What are you doing close to my apartment?" Her question shouldn't bother me but it does. *Maybe because there is a killer on the loose. Or maybe because I can't stop thinking about you and it's making me crazy.* For now, I'll put those constant thoughts in the back of my mind.

"I was in the area and I saw you walking by yourself." *It was only half a lie.* "Would you like to ride with me to The Rose? I'm going there myself." My smile stays plastered on my face like I'm giddy fucking kid.

"Yeah, I'll take that ride." The not so subtle wink she gives makes my cheeks hurt from how wide I'm smiling. *Fuck, she's adorable.*

"Alright, Sweetheart. Hop in." I reach over and open the handle of the passenger side door. As she shakes the water off of her umbrella, I watch how her ass moves in her short skirt. I do my best to keep my thoughts to myself but I can't help the idea of fucking her in my car and making us both late for work. *Damn, it would be so fucking easy to slide that skirt of hers up to her waist. I wouldn't give a shit who saw her grinding those perfect hips of hers on my lap in the driver's seat.* That all ends when she climbs into the car and closes the door.

"You walk alone in the rain often?" *This is me, trying to make conversation. Whatever I can do to make this situation less awkward and to take away from the fact that I look like a stalker right now.* It feels like you can cut the tension between us with a fucking knife. *Leaving the apartment before she woke up the next morning probably wasn't one of my best ideas. God, she probably thinks I'm a jackass.*

"Yes. Normally, I don't mind the rain though."*I would love to see that perfect body of hers wet. Fuck, not letting her walk in the rain has its drawbacks.* She looks up at me with those beautiful eyes, her full lips parted. *What is it with women watching men drive?* Whatever it is, I don't mind her doing it.

"You think it's going to be busy tonight?" I keep my eyes on the slick road, desperately trying to keep my mind off the vulgar thoughts spiraling in my head. With Thalia being this close, it's hard to *think.*

"After being closed for about a week, absolutely. We're going to be slammed with our normal regulars. Well, most of our regulars." She wrings her hands at the thought. *My girl is anxious about tonight.* I can only imagine the thoughts that must be going through her head right now. *Wait a second. My girl? What the fuck am I saying? I can't mean that.* I mentally shake the thought and continue the short drive in silence.

The drive soon ends as I park my car in front of the bar. "You ready, Sweetheart?" I ask after I turn off the ignition.

Thalia briefly glances over at the alley between The Neon Rose and the boutique next door before we make our way inside the bar. I know she has mixed feelings about coming back to work—we all do, but life goes on. *Well, for most of us.* I do my best holding her little umbrella for us both. It mostly covers Thalia, but that's okay; I don't mind getting a little wet.

Both Jace and Janice look to the door at the sight of the two of us walking in together. By the way the two are smiling, it must be a sight to see–one that will have them speculating all night.

"Look at you two together," Janice announces. Her voice is heard over the music, and I see Thalia's cheeks getting redder by the second. *It's so fucking cute.*

"Oh, what's going on here?!" Jace's finger is pointing forward, aimed directly at us as he sways his hips at the same time.

"I was just in the neighborhood," I mutter, shutting the door behind Thalia and me.

"Whatever you say." Jace's hips sway again as he makes his way back towards the kitchen.

The night goes quicker than I would have expected. The Neon Rose is packed. People are crowding in, filling in at the bar, the tables, and even the small amount of floor space is filling up as they stand around chatting with one another. I listen to the customers gossip about the homicide of the man in the alley that was only a week ago. *Who knew a murder so close to the bar would make a killing in sales.*

Janice explains that most of them are her regulars, as if she's still trying to keep up her humble persona. She knows she's going to make one hell of a profit by the end of the night. I don't miss the smile on her face as the bar patrons continue to file in the doors. She must be happy to see her loyal customers once again. While The Neon Rose was closed, the three of them were thrown out of the routine they all had grown to know so well. Life may not be fully back to normal for these people, but it's closer to normal than what it had been.

I mostly stay around the back towards the kitchen. My attention is focused on the inventory of liquor bottles and recording how much more Janice will need for the rest of the month. Occasionally, I make glances at Thalia in her element. The way she puts on her bartender charm has me captivated. She looks like a fucking goddess under the glow of the lights. I can't help but smile when she catches me looking her way. The smile I get in return is the icing on the fucking cake.

"What's up, Red." My eyes quickly move from my drink in my hand to a skinny motherfucker sitting in front of Thalia. His hand strokes his chin and he watches her walk closer to his seat. His pathetic excuse for tattoos stands out on his pale arms. I scoff at his black, greasy hair slicked back and plastered against the top of his head. He successfully misses his lip ring when he bites his lower lip as she slowly walks up to the bar. The grip on the half empty whiskey glass is the only thing I have keeping my temper from taking over.

"Hey, what can I get you?" Her voice is sweet despite the asshole sitting in front of her. *He's not deserving of her sunshine.* She bends down and lowers her body against the bar. She places her chin in her hands, bats her eyelashes and all of that shit. My body gets hot with jealousy over this idiot. *Fucking jealousy?! I've never been fucking jealous over a broad before. Calm down, Lee. This whole act is all for tips.*

"What would you recommend?" His pale blue eyes trail down her whole body. *He's clearly fucking her with his eyes. If she suggests anything other than a fucking cocktail or a plate of nachos, I will lose my shit.*

"You look like a domestic beer guy," her eyes zero in on the fucker in front of her. "Am I right?"

"It's like you already know me." I quietly laugh at his response, head shaking in disbelief. *What a fucking idiot. Is that really the best he has?*

"I guess I do." Thalia stands straight up, and runs a glass under the beer tap. She slides it in front of him, winking at him in the process. *Oh, fuck no.*

I slam my glass down against the bar, getting the attention of the skinny weasel of a man. Honestly, I'm surprised it didn't break from the impact. His eyes shoot over in my direction, and I make sure to let him know—the scowl on my face clearly evident—how fucked he would be if he continued to talk to my girl. He looks over at me with fear in his eyes and immediately looks down at his beer.

With Thalia's back towards us, I walk over to the idiot. *I can't believe I'm doing this.* He stares at me with his wide eyes as my fist grabs the collar of his black v-neck tee shirt.

"What the fuck, man!?" The guy yells.

"You think it's okay to eyefuck someone else's girl?" I ask, practically growling in his ear.

"No, man. I was just trying to grab a drink." His eyes quickly look down at the beer in front of him.

"I think it's time to order your drinks somewhere else, asshole. You even *think* about looking in her direction, I won't fucking hesitate to kill you!" The loud volume from the speaker shuts off at the right time. *Of fucking course.* Two other men at the bar give me their unsure glances, but I don't give a shit. "You got a fucking problem?!" The two men look down at their half drunken beers.

I let go of his now wrinkled shirt and gently slap the scruffy five o'clock shadow on his cheek. *Well, maybe not too gently.* Without taking a sip of his beer, he leaves the bar. *Good, I needed another drink anyway.*

Oh fuck, I have an audience. Other patrons in the bar look in my general direction as I take small sips of the asshole's beer. *Damn, does everyone in this fucking place have nothing else to look at?* A wide-eyed expression covers Thalia's face as she nearly overflows the glass in her hand. *Fuck.* I watch how her cheeks go from pale to red. *I can't tell if she's turned on or surprised, but hell, I'll take both.*

I told myself I wouldn't do this, that I wouldn't get attached to another woman. Coming here tonight only solidifies that I *truly* fucked myself over. Every look, every stare, every smile, every conversation has me craving more. She's like a drug, and I keep relapsing like a fucking addict.

The night ends around three AM. I sit on the high barstool, watching Thalia and Jace clean up. I don't miss the concerning stares coming from Jace and Janice as I sit and wait for closing. They know I could have left hours ago. *To them, I look like a fucking stalker watching Thalia's every move. I don't give a shit about what they think. I need to make sure she's safe and this is the only way I'll know for sure.*

"Everything is accounted for," Janice announces as she tucks the cash into the register. Jace and Thalia both look over at her with relief written on their faces. The two stop cleaning and put their wet rags on the small shelf under the bar. After the long night, we're all ready to leave this place.

"You two doing anything after work?" Janice asks. Her large eyes look in between Thalia and me.

"No. I'm going home to sleep," Thalia answers before I can respond. *Are you sure about that, Sweetheart?*

"Umm, hmm." Janice looks down at her keys smirking knowingly. Jace turns his face away from Thalia to hide his silent laughter. *You're not fooling anyone.*

We walk out of the bar into the cold, wet night. Thalia grabs her umbrella from the brass hook behind her and does her best to hold it up for both of us. She smiles when I grab it and take over the task of keeping us dry. We both walk towards my car while Janice and Jace walk in the opposite direction, looking for a cab to share.

Once we reach my Mustang, I stop her before she can open the door on her side. It's adorable how her eyes light up. I smile as she moves just enough to stand between the passenger seat and the door.

"You're going to have to get used to someone doing nice things for you, Sweetheart." I tell her as I open the passenger door for her.

Shaking the rain off her umbrella, I watch her sit in the seat. I snap the strap and place it on the floor next to her feet. I turn to face her after I climb in the driver's seat. She immediately takes out her phone, and I start the ignition. Even her silhouette is fucking beautiful. The lights from the neon signs make an almost pink glowing outline around her unkempt curls. She looks like her own brilliant light in the passenger seat of my car, drawing me in closer. No matter how hard I try, I can't get enough of her.

I pull out of the spot in front of the bar and drive towards her apartment. We drive in silence until we reach our destination. I park my car and attempt to break the somewhat uncomfortable silence between us.

"You okay, Thalia?" My voice is low compared to my normal volume, mindful of how close we are inside my car. "I know today must have been a bit difficult."

"Yeah, I'm okay." She pauses. "Just glad to be back to a somewhat normal life."

"I'm glad I got to see you again." I lean in and place my hand on the middle of her thigh. I feel her body jump beneath my touch before she turns to face me in her seat.

"Yeah?" Her voice asks in a whisper. Her red lips turn up in that sweet smile I love so much. If only she knew how much she's been on my mind.

"Yeah." The console presses into my side as I close the gap between us, eager to kiss those beautiful lips of hers. Her mouth parts and my tongue slides in searching for hers. Sweetly, she returns the intimate touch, the feeling of her tongue against mine driving me crazy.

Pulling back slightly, I bite her bottom lip and grab her waist. She lets out a little whimper as I pull her on top of my lap. She takes her time situating herself in the small space of the car. I know she can feel me hardening inside my jeans. Her breathing picks up with every kiss I place on the contours of her neck.

"You're so fucking beautiful."

I admire her with my lips against her pale skin. "I haven't stopped thinking about you since the night we were together," I admit between kisses. "You are like my fucking drug, one that I can't get enough of. I've missed you so *fucking* much."

She leans down and kisses my lips again. I move my hands along the open space between her waist and the bottom of her shirt. Her little moans drive me crazy when I slip my hands underneath, fingertips trailing up sensitive skin. Unable to stop myself, I grab her perfect tits.

"I need to see all of you." I pull off her black shirt and throw it on the passenger seat. She grinds her clothed pussy against my erection as my arms reach around her ribcage and unclasp her bright blue bra. The straps slide down her arms and her bra settles right where her thighs straddle my lap. I rub my thumbs over her nipples before replacing them with my tongue. Her fingernails dig into my forearms through my leather jacket. She slides the sleeves down my arms and grabs my biceps.

"Tell me again, Lee," she says.

"Tell you what, Sweetheart?" I ask. *At this point, I would do anything she asked me to do.*

"Tell me you *missed* me. Tell me you can't stop thinking about me." She leans in and kisses my neck. Her hands trail down to the end of my shirt and she pulls it over my arms.

"Fuck, I've missed you." I tell her as she moves her hands over my tattoos. She traces her fingertips down each one until they reach the top of my pants. Her hands brush over my belt buckle. I stare down as she undoes the silver clasp. Her fingers deftly find the button of my jeans and she sits further back on my thighs to expertly unbutton my pants.

I move my hands from her waist to the front of her black skirt. I stare into her hazel eyes as I move the bottom of her skirt moves up her perfect hips.

"Take me out, Sweetheart." I watch as she tugs the waistband of my boxers down, my cock finally springing free. She thumbs the drop of precrum glistening on my tip, the feel of her soft hands almost making me come on the spot. "Fuck me, Thalia." I beg.

She moves the small fabric that covers her pretty pussy and slides down on my cock. Her eyes roll back as she moves her hips in just the right way, and the way her wet warmth envelops me has a gasp of my own escaping past my lips.

"God, you're fucking *perfect,* Thalia," I moan, grabbing her waist. I move my mouth up to meet hers. "You're so fucking perfect and you're *mine.*"

Chapter Nineteen

SOMEONE'S TRASH...

ALAN

The black trash bags that contain what's left of my wife loudly land in the dark green dumpster. I couldn't have found a better alley to make her final resting place.

"What do you think, baby?" I look down at the last black trash bag sitting next to my dark brown dress shoes. "Is this good enough for you?"

The last bag is a bit heavy, but I'm able to grab it by the red drawstrings and throw it in the dumpster with the others. "I know it's a little smaller than what you're used to."

The area has been cleared of any signs of the investigation since they found Ruben, or as Thalia would call him, the neck tattoo guy. The now *famous* alley in New York City is no longer considered a crime scene. The local businesses took notice and started refilling the dumpster with trash of their own.

Looking over the edge of the dumpster, I find an empty spot near the back corner that's a perfect fit for my *own* trash— my wife. She will be covered by the rubbish from businesses and the locals on the street in a matter of days. Before too long, her body will be emptied in the city dump along with the rest of the trash in the city.

After I dump my undesirables, I dust off my long coat and dark brown slacks before heading next door for a quick drink. It's been too long since I've seen my favorite bartender.

Thalia is a sight to see through the glass door. She stands with her back to the bar and her eyes focused on the large screen of her phone. I watch her delicate pale fingers scroll through what I assume is some social network app. Her black fingernails bring me back to the memory of watching her in her apartment.

What a lovely night that was.

I pull on the black metal handle and quietly walk in.

The bar stool in front of where she stands looks like a good spot to sit. My black coat hangs around its tall wooden back right before I slide into the seat.

"Hello, Listener," I say in the smooth voice I try to put on specifically for my episodes.

"Holy shit!" Thalia gasps. She turns around with her phone in one hand and the other clutching the loose white fabric of her band tee across her chest. "Alan?!"

"Anyone else call you that?" I ask, giving her my charming smile. "Are you listening to any other attractive podcast hosts?" I lean in closer and place my hands on the bar in front of me, lowering my tone. "Are you cheating on me and Lee?"

"Of course not." Her once startled face is now covered with a smile. *Fuck, I love it when she does that.* "What can I get you?" I listen to the panic tone leave her voice, and I watch her closely as her shoulders relax. *The fear in your voice has a nice ring to it.*

"Oh, I don't know. What was the drink you made me last time?" I move my hand to stroke my chin all while keeping my eyes focused on hers.

"I think it was an Old Fashion." She leans on the bar on her forearms in front of me. "You don't remember?" Her sweet voice is slow and soft. *Of course I remember. I would remember anything that you did for me.*

"That's right. I'll take one of those." Thalia nods and grabs a whiskey glass from under the bar.

"What are you doing out this way? I figured you would be at some sort of corporate office or something. What time is it anyway?" She asks. Her voice carries over the music in the speakers. I watch her closely as she adds the large ice cube in the small whiskey glass. Her hands are so meticulous as she adds in the different liquor in the cocktail. *Corporate office or something, how adorable.*

"It's just now six. I just left the office. I thought I would make my day better and see you." I cross my arms over my chest. She smiles while she moves the short glass in front of me.

"Has it gotten any better?" She inquires as she slides the glass in front of me.

"Absofuckinglutely," I answer with my glass up to my lips. The corners of her mouth move up, her smile is all I need to confirm that the trash I threw into the dumpster was a necessary step in the process of winning over my sweet, *sweet* listener.

"What are you doing after your shift?" I counter while I set the glass back down onto the bar. She stares as I lick the few drops that fall to my bottom lip.

"Going home, watching something on Netflix, and going to sleep with my cat." I can't look away from the beautiful smile still has on her alluring face.

"Would you like to grab a cup of coffee or something?"

"Yeah, I'd like that." Her long lashes flutter over her big hazel eyes.

"Yeah? What time do you get off?" I sit up in my seat. *Don't look so fucking desperate, Alan.*

"I get off around two A.M. Do you know of any place that serves coffee that late?"

"Thalia, we're in the city that never sleeps, I'm pretty sure we can find something." Instinctively, I cross my arms back over my chest and look at her over the black frames of my glasses.

"Pick me up around two fifteen?"

"Of course. I'll be here." I smile and tip the rest of my drink back before setting it down on the bar. "See you then, Listener." I stand up from behind my seat, keeping my eyes on her as I grab my jacket and walk out of The Neon Rose.

THALIA

I watch Alan leave the bar. *What the fuck was all of that about?* I stare in his direction until I can no longer see him in the view of the windows. I grab his whiskey glass and scrub it free of any of the remaining amber liquid and place it under the bar on the small wooden shelf in front of me.

"You trying to fuck both of them now?!" Jace asks, coming up from behind me.

"No. I don't know what that was about," I answer, still looking towards the front doors.

"Uhh huh...well if you do, will you tell me who is better?" He asks with his hand on his hip. "Lee looks like he would do a good job, but Alan has this... *thing* about him that makes him look like he would pay attention to every detail. Like he would make sure he knew exactly what to do simply by doing research or some shit." He smiles as if it's something he's been daydreaming about.

"I'm not going to fuck Alan, Jace." I laugh, shaking my head at the ridiculous thought. The last nights I've had with Lee are all that I had been thinking about. I never thought anyone could move that way in a Mustang. *Fuck, I'm biting my lip again. Way to be inconspicuous, Thalia.*

However, the thought about being with Alan has crossed my mind. No, no. I couldn't do that.

"Why the fuck not?" Both hands are on his hips now.

"Because, Alan and I are just going out for coffee. Maybe talk, like friends do. That's all Alan and I are. That and I already fucked his best friend. Multiple times. Just think how bad that would look." I grab the nearest rag and wipe up the spot where Alan had his whiskey glass.

"Who cares how it looks? The guy is sexy as hell, and it's not like you and Lee are official or whatever the fuck people call it these days." He leans his elbow on the bar, propping his head up using his hand.

"Well, I don't really know..." My voice quietly trails off.

"What the hell do you mean, you don't *really* know?"

"He told me that I was his, but didn't say much after that. I thought it was just something he said in the moment, you know?" I look up at Jace, questioning the whole situation.

"Wait...what the fuck you mean, he told you that you were his?"

"Just that. He used his sexy deep voice, leaned in and said, 'You're perfect and you're mine.'" I answer, using my best Lee impression.

"Fuck, that's hot. Damn it, Thalia, why the fuck do you get two sexy as hell men trying to sleep with you?" Jace laughs. "What's it like living my dream?"

"I didn't ask for this..." I look up smiling at my best friend.

"Yeah, bitch, but you aren't complaining either." He stands up and walks towards the other end of the bar.

Two A.M. comes faster than I would have expected. After counting down the drawer and wiping off the tables, it's time for Janice to lock up. Alan will be here in fifteen minutes to escort me to I assume a twenty-four hour diner to get coffee. My stomach growls. Okay, maybe I'll get a cheeseburger and fries too.

I walk into the bathroom in the corner of the bar and look in the small mirror above the white porcelain sink to do my best to prepare. I smooth out my somewhat wrinkled shirt and run my fingers through my loose waves. My hands reach into my black purse and fish out my bright red lipstick; touching up the corners of my mouth, spreading out the red paint on my lips. *This will have to do.*

"Are you ready for your date with Alan?" Jace asks, meeting me at the bathroom door.

"It's not a date. Just a cup of coffee between friends," I reply while walking past him, nudging his arm on the way out.

"Really, then why did you need to get all sexy in there?"

"I just touched up my makeup. Nothing sexy here." I gesture to all of me.

"You're not fooling anyone. You added your 'fuck me' red lipstick." He points to my lips.

"What?! I always wear this lipstick."

"Yeah, for tips. But now you're meeting Alan so... it's turned into you looking sexy for your date. Which turns into your 'please fuck me, Alan' lipstick."

"I promise you, Jace, it *isn't* a date." I walk to the front of the bar and watch Janice as she finishes counting down the register with Jace's words echoing in my head the whole time.

Chapter Twenty

DARK SIGNS

🎙ALAN

I sit in my car across the street from The Neon Rose so that I can watch Thalia. Her arms are folded across her chest, and her purse hangs on her shoulder overtop of her leather jacket. Strumming my fingers on my black steering wheel smiling, I watch Janice, Jace, and Thalia exit the bar.

I get out of my car quickly as if I am a giddy teenager about to pick up my date for prom and head towards her, picking up the pace as I watch her get closer to the sidewalk. Her bright red lips turn into a smile as the distance between us closes. *Your desperation is showing Alan.*

"Hey!" She yells as she sees me approaching the curb. *My heart just skipped a beat.*

"Hey, are you ready?" I ask, gazing a little too long at her full lips.

"Y-yeah, let's go." I grab her free hand to lead her across the street to my car. She nods at Jace and Janice before making the step out onto the road. They both return her gesture with smiles of their own and climb into their taxi.

I direct her to my silver Lexus and open her door. She keeps her smile and slides into the black leather seats. Like the gentleman I am, I shut her door after I notice her black combat boots are safely tucked in the car. Quickly, I walk to the other side and climb into my seat.

"So...coffee?" I ask and turn on the ignition.

"Yes. Coffee sounds good." She places her purse on her lap. "So where are you taking me?" Her voice is quiet.

"Just this little diner, not too far from here. They stay open pretty late and I figured you would be hungry after your shift." My focus stays on the road.

"Very," she pauses. "You're still in your work clothes." Her eyes scan my lap down to my dress shoes. My body grows hot at the way she runs her eyes down my form.

"Yeah, I wanted to look good for our date." My smile stays in place while my hands grip tightly around the steering wheel.

"This is a date?" The pitch in her voice goes up at the question. The shocked expression on her face is adorable.

"It's whatever you want it to be." I pause, pushing my foot down on the accelerator. "I would gladly go on a date with you." Another pause, as I let up. "Or, it could be just a night between friends who find each other extremely irresistible."

"A night between friends sounds good." I watch her out the corner of my eye fidgeting in her seat.

"So, you think I'm irresistible?" I laugh. Her smile is the only confirmation I need.

I come to a stop and park at the curb in front of the diner. She reaches for her door handle, but I put my hand on her thigh, stopping her.

"I'll get that for you." My voice is harsher than intended. I peer down at her from behind the lenses of my glasses. She pulls her hand away and places it in her lap. *She's already so obedient.*

I get out of the car and quickly move to her side to open her door, watching her slowly climb out. Like clockwork, my eyes move up the curves of her body. *Fuck, I could stare at the vision of her forever.*

My arms are covered in goosebumps and my hands start to get clammy. *Am I actually nervous? No. Nervous isn't what you would call this...I am in disbelief that she's actually here with me. Thalia Smith climbed in my car and agreed to come have coffee.* It's as if I'm one of her obsessed followers. *Why even hide the truth now?* She's always on my mind. Being near her is a constant desire that I can't rid myself from.

My attention comes back to me when the impact of the door shutting interrupts the quiet tension between us. She walks close to my side with her hands in the pockets of her jacket. I open one of the double doors and hold it open for the both of us. Biting my lower lip, I stare at her ass as she walks in the space between me and the glass door.

"I think this is one of those places where you seat yourself," she says, breaking the silence. I move my hand forward and motion for her to pick out our seat. It's a gentlemanly gesture, but I also want to use the small moment of unsupervised freedom to trace over her figure with my eyes.

I watch as she slides into the bright red cushion of the booth, placing her black leather purse next to her. She takes off her leather jacket, exposing her pale, slender arms. After setting my jacket to the side, I roll up my white sleeves. She sits with her hands on her lap, anxiously looking around the diner.

"Nervous?" I ask.

"A little," she admits. *Me too.*

"With me?" *Maybe she should be.* "I'm harmless." *Only to you, Listener.* She loosens her stiff shoulders and slouches back into the booth. *Perfect.* "Why don't we start with ordering something to drink?" She nods with the back of her head touching the booth. I offer my charming smile and a small wave to the waitress at the counter in front of the open kitchen window. She eagerly smiles and walks over to us. Her large hips sway from left to right as she holds tightly onto two menus.

"Hello, there!" She starts, seeming too happy to be working at two-thirty in the morning. She must be working really hard to earn her tip. "Can I get you anything to drink?"

"Coffee," I answer quickly.

"I'll take the same please." Thalia's quiet voice comes out behind the plastic covered menus. Her eyes scan the picture on the front page. "Actually, can I order a hamburger and fries as well? Oh, and a chocolate milkshake," she adds while handing back the menu. My eyebrows raise at her question.

"You know, I think I'll have the same." I say handing over my menu also. The waitress smiles, writes down our orders and heads towards the back.

"So..." Thalia starts.

"So...it's been a while since we've seen each other," I add. *It's only been a few days since I saw you with your legs spread on your couch.*

"Why did you want to meet for coffee tonight?"

"Why did you *agree* to meet me?" She smiles at the question. The waitress sets down the small white cups of coffee in front of us, leaving my question unanswered. "Maybe let's just start by getting to know each other," I suggest. I bring the small mug up to my lips.

"Yeah, we could start there." She fills her coffee with two of the creams the waitress provided in a white ceramic bowl in the middle of our table. She tears open two sugar packets and adds them into the mixture.

"Okay, we're getting somewhere. Now, I know how you like your coffee." I keep my eyes on her fingers stirring the metal spoon in the small white mug. "Ask me anything," I insist.

"Okay..." She pauses to think. "What made you so interested in true crime?" She picks up the white cup by the small handle on the side. She slowly moves it to her lips, blowing the hot liquid before taking a small sip.

"Good question to start with." I fold my arms across my chest and lean back in the booth. "Watching that show Unsolved Mysteries with my grandmother. The idea that the killer could still be out there was so intriguing to me. I pictured many ways the Feds could have caught them and what they could have done differently. I tried putting all of the small clues and details together to determine who the killer actually was. It's the small details that matter. Of course," I continue on with my answer, "we have much more of an advantage these days. Our technology has improved so much over the years. However," I pause while taking a drink from my cup, "these days, there are still so many cases that go unsolved. You never truly know anyone. The killer could be right in front of you and you would never know." *Careful, Alan.* Her gaze is hypnotizing and intoxicating. The way Thalia hangs on to my every word is like a *new* drug that I can't get enough of.

"Who do you think it is?" She leans forward. The volume of her voice is nearly a whisper. I can't help but smile at the hint of excitement and fear in her eyes.

"Who?" I ask as if I am playing dumb.

"You can't be serious. Don't fuck with me, Alan." The look on her face is almost humorous.

"Here you are, you two," our waitress announces while cheerfully bringing us our entrees. Thalia and I give her a polite nod and watch her walk away.

"I think it's nothing you should worry about." I lean in and match my volume to hers.

"I-I'm not worried." She grabs the giant hamburger in both of her hands. I stare as drops of grease make a small puddle on the plate next to her fries. She eagerly takes the hamburger into her mouth and clamps down through the bun and the patty. She wipes the bottom of her lip with the back of her hand, smearing some of her lipstick in the process. "I'm more interested to see who it is and why they went through all of the trouble with everything they did." *Even with grease running down her chin, she's still so fucking beautiful.*

"Why do you think he did what he did?" I ask while dipping a single fry in a blob of ketchup. "He?" *Choose your words carefully, Alan.*

"What makes you think it was a man?" I internally sigh at her question with a bit of relief.

"I guess there weren't any real witnesses that we know of. It could be either a man or a woman." *Nice.* I look at her as I take a bite off the end of my fry.

"That's what I'm saying!" She takes a drink of her milkshake by wrapping her mouth around the tip of her straw. *Oh, the places I would love to have your lips.*

"So, let me rephrase my question. Why do you think *they* did it?" I take another bite of the same fry.

"Well, it couldn't have been just some nonsense reason. It had to have been done with passion." The animated way she moves her arms in her explanation is addicting to watch. *My listener has turned into my little crime solver.* She swallows another bite of her hamburger and continues to tell me what she thinks of the mysterious killer in New York City.

"A random killer wouldn't just cleanly remove someone's eyes, let alone their fingers. They had to know what they were doing and there had to be a reason. People like that don't kill without a motive." *You have no idea.*

"Do you have any suspicions as to who it could be?" I ask. I wrap my hands around the cheeseburger in front of me. I picture her porcelain neck in my grip instead of the greasy buns. I continue my fantasy and imagine her exposed breasts and sounds of heavy breaths underneath me.

"No fucking idea," she says as she swallows another bite. My eyes focus on her throat closely until she goes in for another.

"Oh, come on, little crime solver. You don't have any clue?" I look up at her as I take a long drink from my straw.

"Like you said, it could be anyone." Her lips turn in another upturned smile.

Looking down at our empty plates, her eyes go from wide and animated to discouraged. She takes a sip of her now cold coffee and sits in silence. *It's okay, listener. I'm not ready to leave you either.* I could talk to Thalia for hours on end. Before she has a chance, I grab the check on the table between our empty plates. I pull my credit card out of my wallet and hand it to the waitress who is standing next to our table. Her rosy cheeks light up when I flash her my smile before she walks back to the register.

"Did you get enough to eat?" I ask. My head leans against my hand propped up by my elbow on the table.

"Yes, thank you." She looks up while glancing down at her phone screen.

"Please don't tell me you're ordering an Uber? Thalia, I can take you home." I reach my hand across the table and graze my fingers against her hand. She looks almost shocked at the feel of my touch. My nerve endings feel almost as if they're purely static electricity. *Did you feel that too?* She straightens in her seat.

"That's okay. I don't want to make you do that." She places her phone in her purse.

"Please cancel the ride. I really don't mind taking you home. What, you're just a few blocks away? Not to mention, there is a killer on the loose. I can't let you get in a car with someone you don't know." My knee bounces in anticipation. *I'm not ready to see you go.*

"Are you sure you don't mind?" She reaches back in her purse, scrolling on the screen.

"Of course. I can easily take you home." I rest my hand on my thigh to calm my bouncing knee. *Please just be with me a little longer.*

"You know, I really do appreciate this, Alan." *Say my name again.*

"Of course. What kind of gentleman would I be if I didn't offer you a ride home?" She gives me a small smile and we both reach for our jackets and check our booth to make sure everything is accounted for.

"Ready?" I ask as we both slide out of our booth. I walk up behind her, and wait for her to walk in front of me. She flinches just slightly as I reach out and touch the small of her back to lead her through the front doors of the diner. *What else can I make you do?*

I quickly move to her side, making sure I open her door before she can. She nods with her adorable small smile and clutches the strap of her purse before sliding into the passenger seat. Like a desperate idiot, I climb intO my seat and shut the car door. *Now that I have you here, what the fuck do I do?*

"Okay, where do you live?" *I already know.* I turn on the ignition and place my hands on the wheel.

"Turn that way." She directs, pointing left.

Chapter Twenty-One

"I'M NOT READY TO BE ALONE"

 THALIA

Alan's silver Lexus comes to a stop while we both sit in silence. The tension between us is thick as we wait for one of us to start talking. He has to notice the way I fidget with my keys and look down towards my lap. *He notices everything.*

"Thank you for agreeing to meet with me after work." His deep voice startles me through the cloud of silence between us. His words sound like we just had an office meeting, not something just shy of a date.

"Thank you for inviting me." I look up with the most innocent smile I can muster up. The charming smile he gives me in return could melt off the black jeans I'm wearing. He grips his fingers around the leather steering wheel until I hear the small sound of skin up against the rubber texture. *Is he just as nervous as I am?* I reach for the plastic handle in an attempt to leave his car.

"Well," I say, interrupting the few seconds of quiet, "it's late and I probably should be getting inside. I'm sure you have work early in the morning."

"At least let me walk you to your door." He removes his key from the ignition, turning the car off completely. With the same smile, I nod in his direction. *What choice do I really have at this point?*

He presses his heavy hand on my thigh as a signal to wait for his chivalrous attempt to open my door. My hand freezes at my side, and I watch him make his way around to my side of the car. The sound of my door opening echoes in the empty streets.

"Lead the way," he insists with the smile that he still wears on his face.

We both walk up to the metal door on the side of the building. It opens to the stairs that would eventually lead to a hall of many apartments. This door is supposed to be locked, but none of the residents ever lock it when they leave. Alan follows close behind while we walk up the white tiled stairs. His dress shoes tap along the hard, cold surface. *I wonder what his place looks like. Is it anything like Lee's place? I bet Alan lives in a large mansion in the middle of a gated community. I bet he has maids and cooks that cater to his every whim.*

What would Lee think if he knew Alan was walking me home? Would he be upset if he knew someone else was walking with me up to my apartment or would he be happy knowing that I'm being safe?

The memory of the other night in his car clouds my vision. *Did he really tell me that I am "his?" What does that mean for us? Am I his? Or is that just something he tells every woman he's with? Are we together or am I just reading too much into what he said? Honestly, with my history, it's probably the second one. What does that mean for me and Alan?*

When I look at him and he looks back at me, it's just different. It's like I'm being sucked into a fucking trance, and I can't do anything but stare back. His bright green eyes are the true cause of my hypnosis.

We stop when we come to the long hallway of brown metal doors. With Alan trailing close behind, the doors look like they will go on forever.

"You're apartment 6C, right?" He asks while looking over my shoulder.

"What?" *How the fuck does he know that?* I turn my head to look at him behind me. I wonder if he notices the red creeping into my cheeks.

"I can see your key."

Of course. The *6C* is engraved in the middle of the square-shaped silver key I'm holding in my hand. *Nothing weird about that. Calm down, Thalia.*

The once charming smile he has worn is now replaced with that sexy smirk he does. Either way, my jeans are fucked.

"Right." I continue to lead him straight to the direction of my door. My mind floods with nervous thoughts, ones that come a little *too* late. *I am taking someone I barely know to where I live. I am showing Alan Jones where I live. The host of my favorite podcast, a man that I think about when I'm alone, is going to know where I live.*

My keys jingle in my hand with every step I take. *Five more doors, four more doors...two more doors...here it is. Fuck, what should I do?*

"Well," I ramble nervously, "here we are." I lean my back against the door and look up at him.

"Here we are." His green eyes shoot into my core. His large body is so close to mine, the heat of him undeniable.

"Thank you for walking me home." *Fuck, did my voice just crack? He just smiled. Yep, it definitely cracked.*

"Anytime. I would gladly do it again." He places his large hand on my door next to my head. His casual dominance has my knees weakening.

"What if I called you, and I was standing on the stairs all alone at one in the morning?" *What the fuck am I doing? Is this my attempt at flirting? I am acting like a smitten teenager.* Alan looks down at his watch.

"Well, right now it's getting close to four A.M. and here I am. If it were any other night and you told me you needed me, I would drive as fast as I could from wherever the hell I was, just so I knew you would get home safe."

There is something in the way he leans in closer and the way the pitch changes in his voice tells me he isn't kidding. Alarms are screaming in my head that I should be scared right now. *This isn't some rom-com movie, this is real life. Tell him to leave, Thalia. You've only met this guy like what, twice? Use what you learned from his fucking show and don't be an idiot.*

"It's good to know I'll always be safe." I swallow a deep knot in my throat, putting on the most confident mask that I can muster.

"You'll *always* be safe around me." The volume of his voice is barely above a whisper. I nod and turn to face the door, Alan's warm breath brushing the back of my neck as he watches me slide the key in the lock. Time seems to freeze as my brain weighs the outcomes of our interaction—of all the questions still swirling in my mind.

I turn the knob and use my hip to push open the door wondering if he'll follow me in. *Or would he be a gentleman as always and wait for an invitation?* He leans his tall figure against the frame of the entryway with his arms across his chest. "Have a good night, Thalia."

He smiles and turns to walk in the opposite direction.

🎙️ALAN

"Hey, Alan..." I hear the quiver in her voice as she calls out to me. *Yes, my Listener.* Stopping, I turn around in the empty hallway of doors attempting nonchalance. If I'm not careful, I might look too desperate.

"Would you like to come in for, umm, I don't know...more coffee." She peeks her head around the archway of her door. Her body is cast in shadow from the light in her living room that I am all too familiar with.

My lips turn into the smirk that I know she loves and step further into her view. I check the hands on my watch again and pretend to look at the time on the face.

"I know it's late, and we just had coffee. You probably need to get home." She wrings her hands nervously. "I-I'm just not ready to be alone right now."

I wonder if she knows how bad I want this, just to be alone with her a little bit longer. *I'm not ready to leave.*

"I'll stay as long as you want, and when you want me to leave, say the word and I'm gone." I shove my hands in the pockets of my slacks.

"You sure I'm not keeping you out too late?" She asks while standing in the doorway.

"You're perfectly fine." She smiles up at me and leads me into her small apartment.

"Well, this is it." She motions to her space. *I've seen this all before.* I nod.

"It's cozy." It isn't a lie. It is lived in, and when I am standing in her space, *while she knows*, it is comforting and welcoming. It is vastly different from what I am used to–a facade of the perfect life.

"You want to sit down?" She asks, looking towards her couch.

"Yeah, I'd like that." I nod, imitating the words she used earlier this evening. I remove my jacket and lie it across her small counter. Attempting to calm my nerves, I roll up my sleeves and walk to her on the couch.

We sit close and I loosen my tie, leaning my thigh up against hers. *I know she wants me as much as I want her. I just need to prove it to the both of us.* I shift my weight so that I can face her and cross my arms across my chest, watching her closely as I try to guess her next move. Glancing over her shoulders, I notice the small black case that contains her wireless earbuds on the end table next to the arm of the couch. I try my best to keep a straight face as memories flood through me of the last time I saw her on this very couch.

She moves to face me, her knees touching mine from the close proximity. Her eyes drift from mine and land on my lips. She slides her body closer as if needing to eliminate all the space between us. My arms fall fluidly by my sides. One deep breath would have our chests brushing against each other, our rapid heartbeats close enough to sync up.

"Thalia, if you come any closer to me..." I whisper against her cheek. She seems to take my words as a challenge, her lips almost grazing mine. *You have no idea how badly I fucking want you.* "If you kiss me, there isn't any coming back from me. I won't be able to stop myself."

She moves in further and presses her full lips to mine. *Listener, you have no idea what you've just done.*

Leaning into her, my lips plant forcefully against hers. Unable to resist the urge to taste her—all of her—my tongue finds the opening between her parted lips to search for hers. *God, she tastes so fucking good—a mix of whiskey and obsession.*

I suck her lower lip into my mouth, needing to devour her, and pull her on top of my lap. The *very* center of her is positioned over my hardened cock. The warmth of her makes me ache as her thick thighs pin me down to her couch. There's no other place I'd rather be.

I move my hands to the nape of her neck, my fingertips tangling in the strands of her fiery hair as I pull her in closer so I can kiss her again. The soft sounds escaping past her lips spur me on as I chase every little thing she does. It's an addiction I'll never give up.

"I have been waiting so *fucking* long just to kiss you," I admit between heavy breathing. She kisses me again and moans quietly against my mouth. Pausing our session, I turn my head to look at her sheer curtains, remembering how easily I could see into her living room the night I came to visit. *I won't let anyone see what I am about to do to you.*

I pick her up by cradling her round ass and move us towards her bedroom. She wraps her thighs around my waist and keeps her arms around my neck. Her lips trail up the side of my neck, a sensual promise of what's to come as I move us both down the short hallway. Lust has my patience waning and I slam the back of her body into the wall uncaring if anyone outside these walls can hear us. With the help of the flat surface, I'm able to keep her stable. I lick the small space in between her collarbone and up her slender neck.

"Alan, I-I need you," she whines, hips rocking against me. Not wanting to take her up against a wall for our first time, I pick her up and move into the direction of her room directly across from where we're positioned.

Stepping into her dark bedroom, I sit us both down at the end of her bed. She continues to straddle my lap, her legs pinning mine to her bed. I move my hands to the bottom of her shirt and pull it over her red waves. Grabbing the back of her neck, I kiss along her jawline. My fingers gently run down her back until I find the metal clips that hold her bra shut. "Please, Alan," She begs. *Fuck, I love that.*

"How bad do you want me?" I ask while slowly removing the first clasp. I feel her body shudder as the band loosens. "Tell me, Thalia."

"So fucking bad." She almost whimpers. I can't help the smile that forms on my face as I unhook the second one.

"Oh, Listener. You're going to have to do better than that." I stop at the third and final clasp.

"Please, fuck me, Alan." Her breathy plea nearly sends me over the edge. I notice her tense body relax as I unhook the last metal hook. Her bright pink bra falls on the white carpet in front of her bed.

"Fuck, Thalia," I say barely above a whisper, looking over her exposed chest. I lean forward and leave trails of kisses from her collarbone down her breast. I stop at her rose colored nipples and circle each one with my tongue. She lets out a small whimper as I bite down with little pressure. I stop when I feel her hands move to the buttons of my white shirt. She plants kisses on my neck as she undoes each button. She slides the material off of my shoulders and my shirt falls behind me on the bed.

She squeals as I grab her waist and lay her on her back. My hands trail down her amazing curves and land on the waistband of her jeans. Within a matter of seconds, I undo the metal button and pull the denim down her thighs. I pause and take a moment just to admire her exposed body.

"Thalia, you're fucking beautiful," I admit as she stares up at me, eyes half lidded in want. She is everything I had imagined and so much more.

I stand up and begin to unclasp the metal buckle from my black leather belt, my erection straining behind my pants. Without speaking, Thalia moves towards the edge of the bed and replaces my hands with hers. The warmth of her touch has a hiss escaping past my clenched teeth.

As she looks up at me, she pulls my belt out of the loops of my pants and tosses it to the side of her bed. Her delicate hands search for the button just as I did for her. Once unbuttoned, she slides them as far as they'll go before I use my feet to move them the rest of the way down my ankles. Her eyes, clouded with lust, scan over my body.

I lean over her perfect form and stare down at the bright red rose tattoo starting from her ankle, climbing to the top of her thigh. I move in closer and run my tongue flat along the stem. Her breathing picks up the closer I get to where she wants me most. I stop and smile at the way her sexually frustrated body reacts. Goosebumps cover her skin as I graze my lips further up her smooth skin, exploring the length of her body until I get close to her full lips. Her small sweet moans are like music to my fucking ears the closer my tongue makes its way to her hips.

I move my hand down to her hips and pull the straps of her lacy, pink thong down her legs. My mouth lands at the crease of her neck and peppers kisses to the top of her jaw, stopping just below her ear. I place my hand where the small piece of pink fabric once was and gently rub her clit with the pad of my thumb.

"Is this what you do?" I ask as I look down into her hazel eyes. I scan over her perfect curves, highlighted by the moonlight peeking in through the lines of the plastic blinds. "Is this what you do while you think of *me*?" I move my hand lower and slide two of my fingers inside her already drenched pussy. Her wet warmth grips me and I watch her eyes roll back as I add pressure to her clit with my thumb, pumping my fingers faster.

"Y-yes," she moans with her back flat against the bed. I slide my fingers in and out faster just so I can hear her say that again. Her hands grip the black comforter underneath us.

"When?" I ask while still moving my fingers in and out of her. "When was the last time you fucked yourself to the thought of me?"

"When we were closed," she manages to answer through loud moans. "We were closed, and I was home alone." Her grip loosens from her comforter and those delicate fingers wrap around my arms instead. *Fuck, yes.*

"I want you, Thalia. I've never wanted anything *so bad*," I growl, finally removing my fingers, unable to hold onto my control. She pushes herself up onto her forearms, and watches as I slide my boxer briefs down my hips. Standing there in the dim light, every barrier between us has been removed, both of our bodies on display for the other.

I hover over her naked body and line my dick up with her tight cunt. I let out a guttural moan when I push myself further into her. She spreads her legs wider and allows me more access. Her tightness parts before me as I push my hips against her.

"That's a good fucking girl." I groan while I put my hands on either side of her head and move my hips faster. Bending my head down, I plant more kisses in the crease of her neck. I leave my mark by grazing her skin gently with the tips of my teeth.

"Alan!" She pants against my ear.

"Say that again. Say my fucking name again." She arches her hips and presses her clit up against me as I move in and out of her faster and harder. "Tell me who I am, Thalia."

"A-Alan." Her words are hardly audible under her heavy breaths. She wraps her legs around my waist and pins my body to hers. "Make me come, Alan."

"Is that what you want, Thalia?" I grab the back of her neck and tug on the tufts of her hair to pull her in closer. She wraps her arms around me and holds me as close as she can.

"Yes!" She moans. "Fuck me and make me come." I feel my dick throb inside of her.

"I don't want you to hold back," I command. "I want you to tell me when you're close." I feel her forehead on my chin when she nods.

I rock my hips forward and her mouth opens in a silent scream and I know. She grips my bicep and bites my shoulder as her pussy flutters around my dick.

"*There it is.*" I roll my hips harder and listen to her breathy whimpers. "I want you to scream my name like you do when you're alone. Show me what you sound like when you rub your clit to the thought of me fucking you."

"Fuck, Alan!" Her legs squeeze tighter around my waist, bruises sure to mar my skin tomorrow. I feel her release all down my cock, and I soon find mine inside her. Hot, sticky come paints her pussy, marking it as mine. The thought has me smiling against her skin.

She lets her legs fall against the bed. I gently kiss the top of her forehead and hold her close against my chest. *I could stay inside you forever.* I feel the aftershocks of her body while she keeps her arms wrapped around mine. I fall into another deep kiss and feel her nails dig into my biceps.

"God, Thalia, you're everything to me." *I wonder if she really knows what that means for her.* I roll to the side of her and stare at my perfect view. She lets out a huge sigh and turns to face me.

"Thank you for staying with me tonight." Her eyes that were once full of lust are now starting to close.

"You'll never have to worry about being alone, Listener."

Chapter Twenty-Two

MENTAL CHECKLIST

🎙️ALAN

Carefully, I attempt to climb out of Thalia's bed while trying not to wake her. She looks so peaceful in the early morning light shining through the small gaps between her plastic blinds.

She turns her body towards mine and sleeps against my chest. It feels so natural with her resting her head in the crook of my neck. I hold her as long as I can before I know I have to leave. She's such a heavy sleeper, barely stirring as I slide my body from under her slender frame and climb out of her full-sized bed.

I grab my clothes and put them on all while continuing to watch her sleep. My eyes catch on the way her exposed chest moves up and down with every breath she takes. *I need to touch her again.*

I reach my hand down and trail my fingers in between her perfect tits. I can feel her heart beat faster and faster with my touch. Slowly, my fingertips move down to her inner thigh, stopping myself before I get any closer to her most sensitive area. I watch as goosebumps begin to form on her porcelain skin. I cover her naked body under her comforter and kiss the top of her forehead before I walk out of her bedroom. I would have loved to stay longer. Honestly, it takes everything I have not to spend the morning lying next to her, pleasing her, hearing her say my name again, but there are some things that I have to take care of.

My drive home is silent. The thoughts in my head would have drowned out any music I would have picked out anyway. My mental checklist is overwhelming and the order in which I complete my tasks is critical.

First, I need to double check the cleanliness of the house. I had already vacuumed the carpet in our bedroom. *My* bedroom. It wouldn't hurt to run the vacuum again so I can make sure all of Ashley's blonde strands are no longer visible. I want to go over the light gray marble in the bathroom with bleach and scrub the drops of blood that I may have not seen before. Eventually I will replace it, erasing the stain of our relationship and the evidence entirely.

My next step on the list is to call the police and file a missing persons report. Everyone always suspects the husband, so I need to do whatever I can to persuade them otherwise. It's been three days since I saw my wife. *That's the truth to the story.*

I'll tell the police, "She's had days where she's stayed with friends, but she's never been gone this long." *What will Thalia say if she finds out my wife is missing? Did she even know that I was married? Shit, have I mentioned Ashley in any of my episodes? What will she think if she finds out that we fucked the same night I threw my dead wife's body inside a dumpster? That's a problem for another day. I can handle her anger. I would love to see what she looks like angry, or how she fucks.*

The house looks so much bigger without Ashley's presence. *Good. The lingering smell of infidelity is gone, although I can detect a scent of copper in the master bathroom.* I walk straight to *my bedroom* and remove my clothes. My black sweatpants and a light gray tee shirt are my go-to in outfit choices from the large walk in closet. My portion has always stayed open across from Ashley's.

Rows of pastel sweaters and dresses stare at me as if they're personifying a feeling of guilt. *Guilt for what? Murdering the spoiled, unfaithful bitch, or fucking the most beautiful woman I've ever seen after disposing of Ashley's body?*

"I wonder if there is another entitled, cheating bitch that would want all of this useless shit." I turn off the light and head to the hallway closet to retrieve the vacuum.

The vacuum runs effortlessly over the carpet about ten more times. I pour the dust and whatever remnants I have of Ashley's existence into an empty black trash bag. Next, I move on to the marble and scrub over the same spot more times than I can count. My thorough cleaning causes tiny tears in my blue latex gloves. After I have finished with my obsessive cleaning, I throw the half empty bottle of bleach and the contaminated rags in the bag with the dust and tie it off. It sits securely by the back door.

Next on the list—perhaps the most important—begins when I grab my phone from the nightstand next to my bed.

The phone rings in my ear, a sound that isn't usually ominous, but now...

"Yes, hello. I need to file a report of a missing person...my wife. Her name? Ashley Jones. It's been three days since I last saw her. What was she wearing? Last I know of..." My mind scans through the memories of when I saw her last alive. The last outfit she wore. Of course I remember. It's the small details that matter. *I stood in my bedroom. Our bedroom and pulled her black leggings down her toned legs. I folded her slender arms through the loose sleeves of her cropped white sweatshirt.* I must be precise with this description. "Black leggings, and a short white sweatshirt...Yes, thank you...I understand." The officer on the other end quickly hangs up the other end. *Just another missing person in New York City. That was easier than expected. Check.*

I take the pile of clothes that I stacked from that night into the kitchen and throw it down onto the floor and begin to search through the drawer that contains a collection of nonsensical items we have gathered over the years. In this case, the book of matches that stands out above the blank tablets of paper and random pens. I grab the matches with one hand and the bottle of wine her parents gave us that hasn't been moved from the counter with the other. *The irony in this is immaculate. This will be a good substitute for gasoline.*

I throw her clothes in the porcelain tub and dump a good portion of wine on the evidence. The match lights nicely and makes a bright red flame on her white sweatshirt. The memory of my wife goes up in flames while I take sips from our wedding present. The warm liquid goes down my throat as the flashbacks from that night turn to ash.

THE SHADOW

Her expensive diamond ring shines perfectly next to my previous trophies on the shelf in front of me. I write Ashley's name on a blank index card and place it in the space meant just for her. Standing back, I look at the small collection in front of me. I stroke my chin and map out the spaces on the shelf.

Strategically, I sit a digital recording of that night next to her outlandish wedding ring—the positives of having a wealthy lifestyle and security cameras.

The fear in her eyes catches my attention when I replay it a number of times on my laptop. The sound of her voice makes my hair stand still. I love listening to the change of the pitch in her voice. It was so fucking primal, and I can't help the way it affects my body. The way she looks when she knows that night may have been her last. Her expression sends a signal to my nerve endings. The hair on my arms stands on end when I look closer in her big, blue eyes. *Baby, I could watch you over and over again.*

The white gold band gives a nice contrast to the cloudy sandwich bag and the not so empty spaghetti jar on the shelf. I wipe off the white diamonds on the fabric of my black sleeve. I never really paid attention to the way it shined when it was on her hand. The lack of attention we showed each other really played a role in my lapse of clarity. It really is a beautiful piece of jewelry. The fluorescent light shines off of the emerald cut spotlighting the other pieces in my collection.

The fingers in the clear plastic bag are beginning to turn a darker shade of gray accented with spots of dark green. I know I will have to eventually get rid of the evidence, but until then...

I grab the clear, plastic sandwich bag and slide it in the small pocket of my zip-up hoodie. *At least I still have you.* I pick up the jar and examine the eyes that move along with the alcohol preserving what was inside.

Chapter Twenty-Three

OBSESSION

THE SHADOW

I park my car in the shadows across from The Neon Rose and I watch. This new routine of mine has become more of an obsession than a safety precaution for Thalia. I come here every night around closing time, and keep my eyes focused on the pretty, unsuspecting redhead while she helps close up.

Mentally, I've been a mess since our night together. She's all I can think about. The perfect body of hers and the way she moves her hips is something I will never be able to forget. My pants get tighter at the thought.

Her melodic sounds replay over and over again in my mind. *Fuck.* I wished I would have recorded the way she said my name when she came on my dick. I would play back the harmonies we made together so that everything else was tuned out and her moans were all I could hear.

Many text messages from Lee about upcoming podcast episodes have been overlooked. Thalia has clouded my mind and pushed out any information I had on the past serial killers of Manhattan. *She's my main focus now.* My work ethic, as my boss would describe it, has gone "out the window." *If he only knew what I had been up to.*

My stare only worsens as she wipes down the bar. The outline of her tits looks amazing pressed against the black surface. What I wouldn't do to have those perfect tits in my face as fuck her in front of her co-workers. I adjust my dick in my black sweatpants at the thought of claiming what's mine. Memories of the night we spent together plague me. Missing her and her body so fucking much is almost physically painful.

I watch Thalia, Janice, and Jace walk through the front door. The three of them have their ritualistic goodbyes, all of which I notice from afar. Thalia and Jace go in for a long hug and when they're finally finished, Thalia walks on the narrow sidewalk towards her apartment while Janice waves down a cab.

This night is different.

Janice waves to Jace and climbs into her cab alone and Jace walks around to the back of the bar. *Interesting.* Instead of following my little crime solver, someone else has caught my attention.

I fidget with my keys in my pocket and contemplate my next move. I would love to watch my listener from the perfect view outside of her apartment windows, her sheer curtains painting her body in an immaculate silhouette. There is something about watching her undress from a distance that drives me fucking *insane.* On the other hand, the odd way Jace is acting just feels...off. *Fuck it. I'll be back tomorrow to drool over her body.*

I get out of my car and carefully shut the door behind me making sure I don't create an echo loud enough for Jace to hear. Allowing myself to walk close behind to see the outline of his figure, I am sure to stay far enough back that I can still hide in the shadows.

I catch up to him, spotting him standing under a single lamp post at the other end of the alley. The same alley I killed the asshole who tried to touch Thalia. *No one fucking learns, do they?*

My shadow stands in a spot that is enough of a distance away where he can't see *me* but where I am able to get a perfect view of *him*. I zero in on his hands scrolling through his phone. He puts his phone against his ear and suspiciously looks around the area he thinks is empty.

Jace stands in the same spot for several minutes, shivering with his hand in his pockets. His head raises when he notices a black car with tinted windows drive by slowly before stopping altogether. He reluctantly walks up to the mystery car and taps on the blacked out windows. He continues to look around, raising my suspicion more. Slowly, I walk closer, while still staying in the darkness of the alley.

"Yeah, just the one bag today." His body continues to shiver under the light. His eyes avert to his surroundings and then back down to the car. The mysterious driver takes his money and exchanges it for a small sandwich bag of white powder. He stuffs the small bag into the pocket of his light denim jacket and nods to the man in the passenger seat.

Is that fucking cocaine?! Absolutely fucking not. There is no way he is bringing that shit around Thalia. If he gets caught with that, that's his fucking problem. If he got caught with Thalia around, that's another fucking story. There is no way I am visiting my girl in jail.

After watching the car drive further away, Jace takes out the tiny bag and examines the contaminants. He moves it around in a way a scientist would to get a better view of contents in a test tube. He shoves it back in his pocket and heads on his way into the dark and empty alley. I follow far behind, shaking my head at his dumb fucking choices.

JACE

Damn, it's cold outside.

I grip my coat closed across my chest as much as I can. The frigid wind is a bitch even when I walk through the alley between The Neon Rose and the small boutique that you see those little old ladies go into from time to time. It's kind of an interesting spot to put a clothing store – next to a bar. But what the hell, everyone is looking for a dollar these days. Maybe they thought they would get more business in this part of town.

It's weird walking through this alley. It seems so much colder than it did before the night of the murder of the guy with the dumbass neck tattoos. The small space sends a whole feeling of uneasiness through me. I stop myself before I reach the dark green dumpster just a few feet ahead of me. *That's where they found him*. God, I would've hated to be him that night.

Quickly, I turn around at the sound of footsteps against the wet concrete behind me. *Fuck no. I need to get the hell out of here.* I do my best to try to make my way around the dumpster before who or whatever the hell behind me catches up.

"Jace, right?" I hear just a few feet behind me. *Fuck.*

"Uhh, who the fuck is asking?" I ask with my hands on my hips. *How the hell does this fucker know who the hell I am, and why the hell did he follow me?*

"Sorry," I hear laughter in his tone. "I'm Alan, Lee's friend. You remember, don't you? I left with Thalia the other night." He pulls down his black hood and walks closer. *Why is he here so late? Isn't it a little bit weird to just be walking around here at this time of night?*

"Sorry, I thought I saw you walking around back. Just making sure everything is okay." He takes another step.

"I'm fine." I laugh nervously. "Just about to hail a cab home." I stuff my hands into my pockets and turn towards the sidewalk. It's getting late, and I need to take this shit home before I get caught with it. *I cannot go to jail.*

"Nonsense, I can take you home." Alan continues to close the distance between us. "My car is just across the street." He points at his silver Lexus. *Rich motherfucker.*

"No, that's okay. I don't mind waiting." *Bitch, I don't know you.* I walk closer to the curb, trying to create distance between us.

"You sure?" He asks, still trying to close in the space. "I could save you a few bucks." *Damn, he's got a point. No, Jace. This is how you get murdered.*

"No, I'm good." I turn to face the road.

"Please, I insist."

I must have blacked out because now I am God knows where and my head hurts like a fucking bitch. My eyelids slowly flutter open and the pounding in my head gets worse every time I turn my head.

I try to move my body but my wrists are tied together behind my back. *What the fuck? Are these zip ties?* I 'm tied to what feels like one of those metal folding chairs, and each ankle is tied to the front legs of the chair.

My blurry vision comes in spots. I can barely tell what's in front of me, and I'm blinded by a bright lamp. Between blinks, bits and pieces of the room become clear.

The room is cold, and mostly empty, but whoever the fuck tied me up put me in front of some kind of metal shelf. I squint to try to make out the items on separate rows. Each one has someone's name next to it on an index card. *What the hell? Is that a jar of...eyes? This is some kind of fucked up Saw shit. I need to get the fuck out of here.*

Through my pounding headache, I look around the room the best I can to come up with a plan to escape. I subtly move my body to try to get a look at every angle. The metal chair creaks from under me. *Shit.*

"Jace. You're awake." I hear his voice behind me. His tone is different from the last few times I had seen him at the bar. It's more menacing and it sends an uncomfortable shiver down my spine. He's sitting in a metal chair of his own. *How long have I been here? How long has he sat there just watching me? What the hell was he doing while he was waiting for me to regain consciousness?* I move my whole head to watch Alan get up from his chair and kneel in front of me. He has that fucking metal bar in his large hands. *Where did he get that?* His green eyes look into mine and he smirks. *Fucking smirks. Bitch, is this funny to you?*

"Yeah. You mind telling me what the fuck this is all about?" I give a small laugh and look down at the chair I'm tied to. *Try to act cool, Jace. He has a metal bar in his hand.*

"Oh, that." He smiles. "Just a precaution really."

"Precaution? For what may I ask." I raise my voice.

"Well, for me," he pauses, "yourself...and well, Thalia." He takes the metal bar and passes it between each of his hands.

"Thalia? What the fuck does she have to do with all of this?"

"It has *everything* to do with Thalia. All of this does." He uses the potential weapon in his hand as he motions to the room around them. *This fucker is crazy.*

"Okay, what does it have to do with me?" I ask, raising my eyebrows.

"Well, you see...I found what you had in your pocket over there." He points to my jacket with his metal bar. I try my best to look towards the same place he threw my jacket. I wince from the continuous pain in my head. A tiny bag sits on top of my jacket's side pocket. *Shit. How the fuck did he know what I was doing? Is that why he was following me?*

"Oh that...that's mine. Thalia ain't got nothing to do with that. She doesn't do that kind of thing." I pause and wince at the bright light bouncing off the metal bar he continues to pass back and forward to each of his hands. "Are you some kind of cop or something?"

"Or something. Lawyer, actually." He stands up, and I notice how large this man really is. *Fuck. I'm going to prison.* "Do you know what could happen to you if you get caught with that in your possession?" He asks, turning around with his back towards me.

I don't answer. I'm suddenly feeling like a child in trouble with my parents. He turns around with his hand gripping the end of the metal bar. "What happens is you and whoever you're with will get in a bunch of fucking trouble." He smiles down at me. Not like a normal smile that I had seen when he looked at Thalia. More like one that sends a chill through my spine. *Fuck, I really need to get out of here.* "I can't risk *my* listener getting charged with something like that." *Your listener...?*

"I wasn't going to– I mean, I– that's just for me. Thalia wouldn't do any of that. I can't get her to do any of that shit. I mean, she's one of those rare good girls you hear about." I manage to stammer. My body shakes the closer he gets to my chair. I swear I can hear it vibrate against the concrete underneath me from my body shaking out of fear.

"I know she is." I watch closely as his bright green eyes almost turn black. *What a fucking psycho.* "And I know you won't go near her with this shit." He takes a few steps closer, waving the metal bar in the air like some kind of baton.

"Oh, good..." I sigh.

WHACK. Shit!

"What the fuck?!" My pounding in my head gets worse and my body and the chair I'm tied to falls against the cold, concrete floor. With my cheeks on the cold surface, I look up and see him gazing down at me. My head pulses from the impact.

"You see, I can't just take your word for it." He kneels down to match my level. "You guys are always together..." *There's that terrifying smile again.*

"I can throw it away. I-I-I can flush it," I stutter.

"Oh, don't worry, I can take care of that." He nods towards my jacket. My eyes follow his movement, but a sharp *ZING* brings my attention back to him.

He hits the metal bar on the concrete again, creating an echo throughout the tiny space. The sound makes me flinch. With one hand, he picks me up by the back of the chair and sets it back in the original position. I look down at where I was and notice the drops of blood from the impact of my head hitting the hard floor. My awareness barely comes in spotty while he stands in the position he once was before he grips the bar in his hand like a fucking baseball bat. He takes a step closer to my chair. He raises his arms and takes his stance.

"W–wait!" I manage a scream. He pauses. *Thank God.* "You don't want to do that..." He looks at me with a bit of concern. *Maybe I'm getting to him.* His eyes follow my tears running down from my swollen eyes down past my chin.

"What I mean is, you don't want to hurt me. T-Thalia would be upset if anything happened to me. Y-you wouldn't want to do that. I mean, you wouldn't want to do anything to upset her. I'm her best friend. I'm her only family. I'm all she's got left." He drags his weapon against the concrete. It creates another metallic scraping sound that echoes through the room.

"See, Jace." *There's that fucking smile again. It will forever haunt me in my nightmares.* He picks up the metal bar with both hands, resuming the baseball stance. "There's where you're wrong."

He walks closer and brings the bar closer to my head. I flinch as he runs the cold metal across my cheek. He looks closely at the end of the metal rod as he catches each of my tears.

"Thalia will never be alone," his voice lowers and he moves the bar to my other cheek. "She'll always have someone watching and making sure she's safe." He steps back and strokes his chin. "After tonight, I just can't trust that you won't put her in harm's way."

I watch Alan walk over to the metal shelf. He places his blood and tear-stained bar in the middle of the shelf and moves what looks like a tripod with a phone attached a few feet in front of me. *Wait...is that my phone?* It's set up as if it is already recording. *What the hell?*

He grabs the same bar that he threw on the floor just seconds before, moves up, takes the bar in both hands, raising his arms above his head.

"P-please! Don't do this!" I scream. *WHACK!*

 THE SHADOW

Jace's body spasms with the impact of the last hit. I circle around his body while it seizes. I watch how both of his eyelids flutter, his long, black lashes brushing his cheeks, leaving his lids open, as he takes his last breath. The pool of blood gets larger, creating a puddle around his head and neck. I examine his face as his eyelids slow and life starts to leave his large brown eyes.

After placing the metal bar down on the shelf once again, I grab a pair of latex gloves I had so conveniently brought in earlier. I slide the gloves over my large hands, snapping the stretchy material over my wrists as if it's my new regimen. The sound is loud through the small storage unit.

"What should I do with you?" I circle around to his limp wrists and cut off the zip tie that holds them together. His arms fall flat on top of each other. I go down to his feet and cut each zip tie around his ankles. The broken zip ties are thrown to the side and his body slides easily off of the metal folding chair.

I examine his lifeless body on the floor as one would admire a painting. The way he's fallen is truly a work of art, arms and legs bent unnaturally. The harsh light from the lamp shines off of his silver nose ring. The pool of blood ripples with each step I take toward his fresh corpse. I gently move in closer and carefully remove the metal hoop from his right nostril.

"Look at that, Jace, not a drop of blood." I observe the piece of jewelry, and hold it up closer to the ceiling. *Where am I going to put you?*

"This won't do," I comment while looking down towards Jace. "Your space, it's too empty." I grab his phone that still sits on the tripod and set it next to the small ring. "This will sit here only for the time being."

I walk over towards his jacket, grab the clear sandwich bag, and set it down with the other items I've gathered over the past couple weeks. Stepping back, I admire my museum of trophies I've collected. A smile paints on my face as I look over the menagerie with a feeling of achievement.

"Now, Jace," I say, breaking my own silence. I turn my head and stare down at his eyes that were once full of fear. "What am I going to do with *you*?"

Chapter Twenty-Four

RIGHT UNDER YOUR NOSE

🎙️ALAN

L ike your stereotypical stalker, I'm sitting in my car with the bill of my black baseball cap covering half of my face. Thalia's apartment window is in perfect view. Her amazing curves are barely hidden by the sheer curtains in her window. My vehicle is close enough to keep my eye on her magnificent form, but far enough away that she won't be able to notice.

Normally, I would be more than happy to follow her on the short distance to where she works, only to make sure that she's staying safe. This time though, I have an agenda.

My eyes zero in on her body as she walks cluelessly down the sidewalk. *That's how I need her to be–completely clueless.* Her tight jeans frame her ass in just the right way that makes my mouth water. I wonder if she can feel when my green eyes trail over her pale skin in the small space between her jacket and the waistband of her jeans.

She clutches the handle of her umbrella with one hand and her phone with the other. Even from where I am parked, I can clearly make out the frown on her face as she looks down at the screen. I can imagine what she must be thinking. It had only been two days since I took Jace to my storage unit and killed him, but two days without talking to your best friend can feel like a fucking lifetime, especially to Thalia. I hate seeing her like this, but I did what I had to do.

I've seen her talking to Jace constantly through texting or through several calls throughout the day. *How can someone talk to another human being so much? I mean, hell, they even work together.* She must be wondering why she hasn't heard from him or why he isn't replying to any of her messages. I've had his phone this whole time, and I hadn't thought to reply back. I can feel the tiniest pull on my cold heart strings. It almost makes me feel bad for killing him. *Jace was in the way. He would have put her at risk.*

Once I notice her figure goes out of focus, I climb out of my seat, staring down at my blue jeans and plain gray tee shirt I bought from a local consignment shop. I adjust my black baseball cap on my unruly curls and shut the car door behind me. *This is unlike the business casual I'm used to wearing, but it will have to do if I want to go unnoticed.* I pop open my trunk and stare at the large roll of carpet padding which now contains Jace's body tightly wound up in the center.

After a night of planning and glaring down at Jace's lifeless body in my mostly empty storage unit, I came up with an idea to hide him in plain sight. It's only temporary. Just until I can set him up in his final destination.

I taped Jace's slender body in the middle of a large roll of carpet padding that I bought from a hardware store close to the storage unit I'd been renting. I made several even rows of duct tape across his body starting by covering his eyes and ending at the tips of his black and white Vans. Making sure I smoothed out each piece and they were secure and stuck to the carpet padding. The last thing

I wanted was his dead body sliding out of what would soon be compacted layers of tan material.

Taking one end of the carpet, I slowly rolled up the heavy material as if I was storing an old unused rug. I was careful not to go too fast, knowing the duct tape around his body could tear and come off his lean form if I moved too quickly. I cautiously carried his carpeted coffin to my trunk, surprised that it fit snugly in the small space.

Today, I look down at the large piece of carpet, sighing and wondering how in the hell I'm going to carry it upstairs to Thalia's apartment. Picking up the large roll, I cradle Jace's dead weight in my arms as if he were a newborn.

"Need any help with that?" I hear from behind. *Fuck.* I take a deep breath and turn around to face the good samaritan. My mask of an award winning smile falls over my face before I play the part of the apartment maintenance crew.

"All good here. Thank you." I nod and look down at the large amount of carpet in my arms.

"Oh nonsense." He smiles and shuts the trunk of my car. "It seems like you've got your hands full." He continues and states the obvious. "You taking that to the apartments?" He gestures with his pale, wrinkly fingers to Thalia's building in front of us.

"Yeah. Just doing a carpet replacement in one of the units." I shift my weight, hoping he notices. *You think we could stop talking? I have a body to hide and my arms are fucking burning from the literal dead weight.*

"Well..." He pauses. "It's about fucking time." He huskily laughs. *He must be one of Thalia's elderly neighbors.* "I'll get the door for you." He starts walking towards the building, managing to step his white New Balance tennis shoes in every puddle we both come across. The tiny splashes hit the sides of my cheap carpenter jeans. He looks back every so often and I paint the picture of a fake smile on my pale face.

With soggy shoes, we reach the brown metal door that leads to the white tiled stairs I'm all too familiar with. He heaves out a large groan and opens the door wide enough for both of us to walk through.

"There you go. That should do ya." His smile stays plastered on his face as he walks past me up the narrow stairs.

"Thank you." I say after him, nodding and smiling when he looks at me and turns back around.

"No problem, young man. Don't work too hard." He continues up the stairs to the long hallway of rooms. Sliding his hand along the smooth metal railing. *Poor old man doesn't realize he has just become my accomplice.*

I look around the small area, still holding on to Jace. Stuffing him into the small nook Thalia calls her closet seems unrealistic, but if it came down to it, I would do what I must. I imagine stuffing the large roll of carpet behind her long row of black tee shirts. *The only way that plan would work out is if I propped Jace up with her black boots. I'm sure she'll be needing those soon. That plan won't do.*

I continue to scan the small space, looking for anything to hide a large roll of carpet and it to be considered normal. Then I see it. Under the stairs, the door to the small closet with the sign reading "Maintenance," like it's standing out under a figurative spotlight. *Fucking perfect.*

I jiggle the door handle and to my advantage, it's unlocked. *Does no one lock their fucking doors anymore?* I sidestep myself and Jace into another small room and notice a pile of dingy looking carpet in the corner next to a variety of items. A small arrangement of extra door knobs, screws, paint cans and a large tool box.

A rush of relief goes through me.

I gently stand him next to the other carpet remnants and move the heavy paint cans next to the bottom near Jace's feet to make sure the carpet stays put. *Don't worry, Jace, I will be back for you. This is not your final haven.*

Satisfied, I brush my hands against my pants and make my way out of the supply closet. I look around the small hallway before stepping out. The heavy door squeaks as I pull it shut enough to hear a small clicking sound. I may not be able to lock it, but I will do everything I can to keep Jace secure and unnoticed.

Continuing to walk out of the apartment complex with my hands in the pockets of my death-soiled carpenter jeans, I have a new feeling of confidence. *This could work.* I walk towards my car and start planning out the next item on my to-do list.

I think I should pay the police a visit. By now they should have leads on Ashley's disappearance. Everyone suspects the husband, so playing the part of the worried spouse will be a challenge, *even for me.* It's what I have to do to keep them from getting suspicious.

The police station is busy today. *It's New York City, it's always busy.* I stare at the detective while I sit in the black plastic seat across from him with my arms folded across my chest. His chair groans loudly over the commotion of people outside the office I was kindly escorted to. Detective Myers sits at his desk in front of me, frantically going through the stack of papers on his desk.

"Detective Myers." I read his name plate on his desk aloud. He looks up from the pile of paperwork he has been scanning through.

"Mr. Jones." His thick accent is noticeable in his tiny office. He looks up and offers a kind smile. The nice gesture is unexpected when I see the dark circles under his eyes and the hot cup of coffee on his desk. From the workload I'm sure he's been going through, it's more than what I deserve. *He doesn't know that. As far as he knows, I am the worrying, doting husband.* With a long sigh, he stops rummaging through the loose papers.

"In the case of your missing wife, I assure you we are doing everything that we can." *Just going to get right to it then.* He takes the stack of papers in his hands and lines them up neatly. "Unfortunately, we don't have much that we can go by." *Perfect.*

I keep my eyes on his as he goes through the papers he just neatly lined up.

"You said the last thing she told you was that she was going to her book club." He looks up at me with his dark brown eyes through his thick lenses.

"Yes. That's correct." I nod. "That's been about one week ago now." I peer up at the ceiling as if I am mentally adding the days in my head.

"Mr. Jones," he says my name in the most comforting way a busy detective knows how. "Without her cell phone, identification, or her wallet—hell, even a body, there is no way for us to go on." He pauses and lets out another loud sigh. "Have you tried contacting any of the ladies—" He clears his throat. "I'm sorry, I'm *assuming* ladies in her book club." The worry in his middle aged voice makes me smile.

"You think I haven't tried to contact any of her friends?" I ask, this time adding a little more harshness to the tone. *Play the part, Alan.* The black plastic chair creaks underneath me while I sit up higher against its backing.

"I think you did everything that you could. These, unfortunately, are the questions we have to ask." His sympathetic smile is proof that he's falling for this shitty routine. "You think that she may...not want to be found?" He picks up the paper cup of coffee. The hot steam gets lost in his bushy gray mustache. *Damn, baby. Everyone knew you were a fucking cheat.*

"I'm sorry, Detective, I don't follow." I lean my elbows against the tops of my thighs. My face successfully becomes a facade with worry and concern. Wearing his sympathetic smile, he gently sets his coffee on his desk. His fingers intertwine and he places his hands in the middle of the small surface.

"Unfortunately, we have cases like this all the time." He moves his glasses further up the bridge of his nose. "Do you think Mrs. Jones could have run away?" I continue to keep my act of confusion. "Did Ashley have any affairs that you know of, Mr. Jones?" *Yes.*

"Not that I am aware of, Detective." *Keep playing dumb.* He leans back in his chair with his arms folded.

"I think you may not know that much about your wife, Mr. Jones." He pauses, running his large hands over his tired face. "With no leads and no evidence of foul play, there isn't much we can do except try to continue our search." His eyes look through the glass windows in his office as he sits straight up in his chair. "If you want my honest opinion, Mr. Jones, I don't think it will do you much good."

I stroke my chin, moving my fingers over my mouth to hide my smirk.

"What do you mean by that?" I mirror the Detective and sit straight up in the chair.

His body comes closer in as he leans his elbows on his desk once more. He lowers his volume to almost a whisper. "I think, if your wife still has her wallet and her cell, she's not willingly going to come home anytime soon."

"And you're absolutely sure about this? Why would my wife just leave?" I raise my voice, feigning anger.

"I don't know. Did you guys have any recent altercations you can think of?" He nervously asks. He's doing his best but there is a reason why he is a detective and not a marriage counselor. *You could say that.*

"Nothing that would grant her just leaving our marriage." My voice wavers.

"Give it time, Mr. Jones. We'll keep doing our part for the time being. Who knows, maybe she'll come back home." He takes another sip from his coffee.

"Thank you for your time, Detective." He nods as if it's part of his job description. Another task required by the police force. The legs from the plastic chair scrape across the floor as I stand to leave his small office. The smirk I was trying to hide now covers my face as I walk out of the office door. *Check.*

Chapter Twenty-Five

INTUITION

 **THALIA**

"Thalia!" Janice's loud voice breaks my stare from my phone screen. My eyes glance back down at the unanswered message I left for Jace: *Where the hell are you?!*

"Girl, you okay?!" She breaks me out of a worry-filled dissociation again.

"Yeah...hey, have you heard anything from Jace?" I ask while sliding my phone into the back pocket of my jeans.

"No. Not since after our shift a couple of nights ago." She looks down and writes something down on her paperwork clipped to her clipboard. "Why?" She asks, still not looking up.

"I haven't either. We haven't talked in a couple days either. It just feels like something is up. We don't go days without talking. It's also not like him to miss work. He's usually in here before me."

With a fresh new feeling of worry, I cross my arms across my chest. Janice sets the plastic clipboard on the bar and grabs her phone out of the side pocket of her dress pants. I nervously watch her scroll through her list of contacts. She presses the call button, letting out a long sigh and puts the phone up to her ear.

"Straight to voicemail." She confirms as she presses end.

"Something isn't right." My voice wavers with panic.

"Maybe he's just having an off day. Like, I don't know...maybe he missed his alarm or something."

"He hasn't answered any of my messages in the past *three* days." I grab my phone out of my pocket and show her all my unanswered texts.

"Maybe...maybe he's feeling under the weather."

"No, that isn't it. He would call me and bitch about how sick he is." She laughs at the notion and nods her head in agreement. *This just doesn't feel right. Something is seriously wrong.*

"Don't worry, chica. I'm sure he'll come in those doors. He's probably just running a little late." *We've already established it's not like him to be late.* She picks up her clipboard and gives me a sweet smile. Her heels click on the hard floor as she walks towards the kitchen. I grab one of the rags from under the bar and begin cleaning a few glasses. *Anything to keep my mind occupied. I feel like I am going insane.*

As the night goes on, I catch myself staring at the front door. *Jace, you have to come in. Please fucking walk in those doors.* Through my peripherals I see Janice's face clouded with worry, joining me in checking the doors. *I'm not the only one. She has to feel it, too.* My phone is still a loss of answers as I scroll through the many texts in the thread. *Still nothing.*

Something is seriously wrong, I know it.

The shift ends and Jace hasn't graced my worried presence. I wonder if I keep staring at the dark street in front of me, something would happen; like he would magically walk in these doors, panicking because he slept in, or lost track of the time. I guess I can only continue to hope.

"Money is all accounted for." The sound of the register sliding closed wakes me from my overwhelming thoughts. A fake smile is the best I can come up with for my sympathetic boss. *Who the hell am I kidding?* I grab my purse and jacket on the brass hook behind me and walk out from behind the bar.

"He's going to turn up. Don't you worry your pretty little head. I bet he's sitting in bed, surrounded by tissues and cold medicine. He's probably just too exhausted to answer his phone." She opens the glass door and we both walk out of The Neon Rose together.

It's fucking two am and I should be asleep in my own bed, but here I am sitting in my car, watching Thalia walk out of The Neon Rose. She doesn't see my black Mustang across from the bar in the shadows of the other buildings. *Wasn't it lucky that I was already out, exploring the night life that is New York City?*

I keep my stare with a greasy Philly cheesesteak in hand as she walks down the long stretch of sidewalk alone. *Where the hell is that Jace kid? He's always tagging along everywhere she goes. It's too fucking late for her to be walking by herself.* While still hanging on to my greasy sandwich, I take my phone out of my side pocket with my free hand and send her a quick text.

I continue to stuff my face with the best fucking Philly cheesesteak in the city, and watch her stare down at the light coming from her phone.

My attention stays on my screen, waiting to watch it light up with her message in my hand.

Thalia:

> Hey, Lee

Me:

> What are you up to tonight?

I type while stuffing my mouth with another bite, licking off the liquid cheese that slides down my lower lip.

Thalia:

> On my way home.

I watch the three dots appear on my end of the conversation. *What is it, Sweetheart?*

Thalia:

> Do you want to come over? I mean, if you're not too busy. I just don't want to be alone tonight.

She stops in her tracks on the sidewalk and stares down at her phone as if she's waiting for my response. *Absolutely, Sweetheart.*

Me:

> I would love to see you. Just give me a sec, and I'll head over to your place.

I put the greasy sandwich in the brown paper bag, already dripping from its unhealthy juices. Grease from the dripping steak covers my tattoos when I wipe my beard with the back of my arm. *Perfect, just the way I like it.*

My eyes stay on her as she continues her walk on her route towards her apartment. Waiting until her body is no longer in clear focus, I start my car and back out of my space in the shadows. My car moves slowly and far enough behind her. *If she sees my Mustang, I'm fucked and she'll think I'm a fucking stalker. I'm not a stalker, just highly fucking interested in her safety.*

My focus doesn't divert from Thalia's form as she stops in front of her apartment complex. She glances down at her phone and stuffs it back into the pocket of her jacket. *I'm almost there, Sweetheart.* I pull into the small parking garage that faces the front side of the building.

The grease on my fingers slides down my screen with my quick text. It takes only a matter of a few seconds for her reply. My phone vibrates on my leg when I wipe off the juices from my sandwich on my pants.

Thalia:

I'll meet you in the parking garage.

She responds and like a fucking smitten teenage girl, I can't help but smile. It's been too long since I got to see my girl. *My girl.*

Quickly, I turn off the ignition and wait a few seconds before I see her walking towards my car. I step out of the driver's seat and wipe the rest of the philly grease down my jeans and shut the car door, leaving the remainder of the sandwich in the passenger seat. Her red lips turn up into a small smile the closer she walks to my car. *I wonder if she can see my smile hiding under my beard and how fucking pathetic I look.* She hugs her leather jacket around her body. Her boots click on the concrete floor the closer she walks. We both meet in the middle of the garage.

"Hey, Lee." Her sweet smile stays frozen on her face while she continues to hug her jacket close. *Something's wrong.* I see the worry all over her face.

"Hey, Sweetheart." I bring her into my chest and wrap my arms around her and kiss the top of her head. "What's wrong?" I ask with her head tucked into the crook of my neck.

"Can we talk about it inside?" Her small voice is muffled against my jacket.

"Of course." I answer. She takes my hand and leads me to the side of her building.

# ALAN

My knuckles turn white under my black leather gloves as I grip my steering wheel. *What the fuck is he doing here?* I watch the two of them while I'm parked a few rows back in Thalia's parking garage. They can't see me as Lee's whole body practically covers her when he brings her into his chest. My body vibrates with rage when I see the two of them walk towards her apartment building. *What the fuck is this?* I bite my lip until it bleeds when I see his fingers intertwined with hers. *Calm down, Alan. Nothing has happened until you see it for yourself.* I take a long breath to relax my nerves. *Ten, nine, eight, seven...*

I continue to count back from ten before finally making my way out of the driver's seat. Quietly, I shut the driver's side door, making sure it doesn't echo throughout the garage.

I stuff my hands in my coat pockets and begin following Lee and Thalia, keeping myself hidden by standing in the shadows of the tall concrete pillars and large cars. I watch her eyes light up with every glance he gives her. *She looked at me like that.* Inside my pockets, my hands ball into tight fists. I close my eyes and take another deep breath. *Calm down.*

Still watching from the darkness, I lean my shoulders against one of the concrete columns in the parking garage and watch the two of them make their way into the side entrance of the apartment complex. My fist releases and feels for the metal ridges of the key I had made. The pads of my fingers run along the cold edges as I watch Thalia and Lee disappear into the door to her complex.

The soles of my dress shoes click against the concrete as I pick up my pace towards the building. They echo loudly the closer I get to the large exit of the parking garage. *Pace yourself, Alan. Don't give yourself away. Lee isn't going anywhere anytime soon.*

The thought of him on the same couch I was on just a few nights before has my blood boiling. The image of her grinding against his lap while he kisses her makes the hair on the nape of my neck stand at attention. *Don't jump to conclusions. Take another breath and collect yourself.*

Before I know it, I'm standing right under her window. I can't help myself, and I look up through her sheer black curtains. The light in her unit is on. *They're already inside. Just wait.* I pause before I decide on whether or not I should start making my way around the building to the door that leads the white tiled stairs.

THALIA

I pull Lee inside my small apartment. *What is he thinking? I know my small space isn't much compared to his home.* He catches me staring while taking off his leather jacket and lays on the back of my couch. Those thoughts vanish when I realize he isn't looking around my apartment, he's only looking at *me*.

"You okay, Sweetheart?" His eyes narrow like he's trying to read my face like his car manual. I shake my head and slide my arms out of my jacket.

"Not really.," I admit while laying my jacket on top of his. He moves in close and sits down on my black couch that in no way measures up to his. My small couch becomes unbalanced by the weight of Lee's size when he sits down. I join him on the slightly raised side of the couch. He crosses his arms around his chest and raises his eyebrows, looking at me as if he demands an explanation.

"What is it, Thalia?" His gentle voice doesn't match what I've heard from him before. *Is he worried about me? Is it wrong if that makes me smile?*

"It's Jace." I turn to face him. "I haven't heard from him in a few days." Lee's eyes scan my body up and down as if he's studying me. It's a whole new side to him. He nods.

"I thought you guys were always together and you guys talk all of the time. Why the hell won't he talk to you?" He continues to study my face and waits for my response.

"I have no fucking idea, and that's why I'm freaking out." My voice gets louder and I move closer to him, filling in the small space that was between us. "It's not like him to just stop talking to me. Even if he was angry with me, it's not like him to just cut me off. I have mentally run through every possibility in my head and nothing adds up. Something *has* to be wrong." I can't stop the turning in my stomach as tears start to well in my eyes. Before I realize it, one falls down my cheek.

"Listen, Sweetheart. He'll turn up." He wipes my tears off my cheeks with the pads of his thumbs. "We'll find him. Whatever it fucking takes, we'll find him." His confidence bring me a semblance of comfort as he pulls me into his chest and I rest my head on his shoulder.

Thalia's body vibrates against my chest. I can feel her hot tears fall on my neck. She feels so small in my arms while I kiss the top of her head without breaking our embrace. With glossed over eyes, she looks up at me as I take her head in my hands and kiss her red lips. *I may be a man of few fucking words, but I know other ways that I can comfort my girl.* I bring her in for another kiss, this time pulling her in deeper. I love the feel of her full lips when she kisses me back and wraps her arms around my neck. I pull her on top of my lap and she moves her thighs in just the right fucking way. She sits herself perfectly on my hard dick under my jeans.

I kiss the middle of her neck and grab her waist. "You're fucking mine, Thalia." I say with my teeth almost grazing against the edge of her jaw. Her breath picks up with my mouth so close to her skin. My hands move up to the middle of her back and bring her in closer. "Do you like that, Sweetheart? Do you like that when I tell you who the fuck you belong to?" I ask with my lips almost touching hers.

"Yes," she answers.

"I like the sound of that." I grab her perfect round ass and she wraps her thighs tightly around my waist. "Wrap your legs around me, beautiful." I stand up, still holding Thalia and walk us into her bedroom.

🎙ALAN

I lean up against a large lamp post in front of her apartment building. My hands rest in the pockets of my slacks while I watch Lee and Thalia basically fuck fully clothed on her couch. I stare down at the onyx face on my watch until I notice the light from the tiny lamp in her living room shut off. *They're going into her bedroom. You know exactly what is going to happen next.*

Memories of my night with her flash back to me in the front of my mind. The way her cheeks flushed when I fucked her until she screamed my name clouds my vision. *Now, she's doing that with him.* I slide my hand back into my pocket and continue to walk around to the side of the building. *What the fuck am I doing?*

My fingers continue to graze the edges of the metal key with each step towards the door. Instinctively, I jiggle the handle. *Locked for a change. Finally, I get to put it to good use.* I slide the key into the lock. My heart skips a beat when I hear the clicking sound of the lock turning over.

The cold, metal surface of the doorknob slides against the palm of my hand and I step inside the long, narrow staircase. I walk quietly on to the white tiled stairs, minimizing the evidence of my presence. I don't want these small sounds to echo throughout the building. I shut the metal door gently and let the soft click echo through the long hallway. Slowly, I walk along the carpeted floor.

 **LEE**

I set us both down at the edge of her bed with her thighs still wrapped around my waist. I look her over and move my hand underneath her tee shirt. Gently moving my fingertips over her smooth skin, the light fabric of her tee shirt comes off her body so easily. I toss the flimsy shirt to the side of her bed. She kisses me softly and pulls off my black tee shirt. I don't know where she threw the damn thing, but fuck, I don't care.

She runs her fingers down the tattoos on my chest and stops at the top of my jeans. "Tell me what you want, Sweetheart. You know how much I like it when you use your words." She stops searching for the metal button on my jeans.

"I want you to fuck me, Lee." Her breathy admission is all I need as I move my hands down her perfect curves.

"Fuck, Thalia. I love it when you talk like that." My girl likes it when she gets a little praise. "How do you want me to fuck you, beautiful?" With her cheeks flushed, she stares at me with no answer. "You want to ride my dick until I come, baby?"

She answers with only a single nod.

I pick her up off my lap and unbutton her jeans. She doesn't move from my stare when I gaze into those big beautiful hazel eyes of hers. Her skin feels so smooth under my touch while I slowly pull the denim down her thighs. She steps out of her jeans once they gather at her ankles. I could stare at her perfect body for-fucking-ever. She has me practically drooling when she stands in front of me only wearing a red bra and a lace thong to match.

Thalia slowly moves her body closer to mine and runs her hands up my thighs. She steps in between my open legs and moves her hands to undo the button on my jeans. She looks up at me like she's going to devour me as she unfastens my jeans. I arch my back and watch her undress me just as I undressed her. She stares at my cock as it springs free.

"Come here, Sweetheart," I command. Like the good girl she is, she crawls up the bed and situates herself on my lap. "You're fucking perfect, you know that?" A sweet smile covers her face. I pull her in by the back of her neck and kiss her full lips. My other hand moves down in between her legs and slides the red lace to the side to press my thumb over her swollen clit, moving it in circles just so I can hear the sweet sounds of her moans that I love so fucking much.

"Oh, fuck, Lee." Her words are like a drug with her lips so close to my ear.

"You like that, Sweetheart?" I ask. Her body tenses on top of mine. "I think you might like this too, baby." I push two of my fingers in her sweet pussy.

"Yeah, I like that too." She admits between shallow breaths.

"Fuck, Thalia. You're so fucking wet for me. Sit on my dick, Sweetheart." I move my hand from under her and she slides down on my hard cock.

🎙️ALAN

The closer I get to Thalia's apartment, the more I can feel my body going numb. A million thoughts fill my mind with each step I take. *He's probably touching her right now and she's loving every minute of it.*

No, she wouldn't do that to me. *She can't do that to me.* My fingertips brush up against every door I pass on the way to her unit.

I stop when I see her door, apartment number 6C. The gold plaque is barely hanging on the loose nail, just as it was the last time I was here. *Last time I was here, I had my dick buried inside her.*

My thoughts fill with rage and I pull the key out of the pocket of my slacks. Doing my best to hesitate entering her unit, letting out a long sigh before I jiggle the handle. *You already know what's going on. What good is this going to do?*

"I need to see it for myself," I say out loud. I grab the doorknob and smirk at the locked door. "About fucking time."

I slide my key inside the lock and quietly walk into her tiny kitchen. A smile stretches across my face when I look at the tiny corner next to the fridge that I am all too familiar with. *I wonder if Lee knows my DNA is all over her apartment, even in her kitchen.*

I walk further into her space and look over her living room. Her cat lies sleeping on his white, plush bed.

"Such a quiet little guy." He doesn't move as I pat his head and sit on her black couch. "You know, your mom had me over not too long ago." I say, still smiling looking down at his sleepy face.

I look down at my watch as if I'm waiting for one of my business meetings to start.

"Well, there is no reason to delay the inevitable." My conversation with Thalia's cat ends, and I stand up from the couch.

My heartbeat picks up faster the closer I walk to the small corner next to the white door to her room. My hand runs across the spot on the wall that I once had Thalia pinned against. *Right here. Right here is where you begged me to fuck you.*

My memories get interrupted by her soft whimpers. *They're practically next to you fucking in her room.* Reluctantly, I turn just slightly and look in through the small opening between her door and the cheap molding around the doorway, slowly widening it as I move the tip of my shoe in the tiny space.

They're both in there. *This can't be fucking happening.* I knew that it was. *But I didn't want to believe it.* My skin gets hotter the more I stand in the hallway while I practice the act of voyeurism. Like a reflex, my hands ball into a fist once again. The tips of my nails digging into my palms being the only thing keeping me together and refraining from entering the room.

The way she moves her hips on Lee is so fucking hypnotizing. I stare at the curve of her ass as she takes every bit of him. He lays there on her bed with his hands behind his head and he stares up at her like she's a fucking goddess. *I wonder if he knows his goddess was fucking his best friend not too long ago in that same spot.*

Lee moves his hands around her back and unhooks her red bra. It falls around her thighs that are straddling his lap. He takes her round breasts in his hands and pulls on her perfect nipples. I bite my lip, picturing myself biting down on her breasts just as I had done before. He sits up and kisses down her chest. He stops at each one of her nipples and takes them in his mouth. Their intimate show has me watching them with my arms across my chest and my blood boiling beneath my skin.

Thalia arches her back and places her hands behind her on his extended legs. He moves his lips past her breasts and up to her neck. I wonder what he whispers in her ear that makes her moan in the most addicting way. He pulls her in closer to his chest.

My body heats with rage and I close in the small space between the door with the pointed end of my dress shoe. My soft steps continue on the dingy gray carpet in her short hallway.

While looking over her living room, I wonder if Lee knows how Thalia straddled my lap in here on her couch. I move my gaze to the direction of the small, dark corner in her kitchen. *Or if he knows I stroked my dick to the view of her fucking herself to the sound of my voice.* I start to make my way out of the apartment, not before giving her cat one last pat on his head.

Chapter Twenty-Six

DISTRACTION

🎙ALAN

"Fuuuuuuck!" I scream in my car, a deathgrip on the steering wheel. My body vibrates in my seat with anger. "FUUUUUUCK!" I scream louder. This time while punching the middle of the wheel, signaling the horn to go off in the parking garage. I ignore the painful effects it has on my throat. What she did was worse than any physical pain she could have caused.

"I did everything I could to make you mine!" I yell at Thalia as if she were sitting in my passenger seat. My eyes burn from the tears I try to hold in. "You weren't supposed to be like her! You were supposed to be mine and mine alone!"

My body shakes and I try to take a few breaths. I run my hands over my face. I look down at my lap and watch how my tears fall onto my coat. *You knew this was going to happen when you followed them into her apartment.* The agonizing voice echoes in my mind.

"Yes, but I wanted it so badly not to be true. I just want her to want me like I want her," I answer my thoughts aloud. I stare at the key to her apartment with hate, anger, love, and sadness all at once. I put the key in the middle of my fist and squeeze as hard as I can. Craving to feel anything other than what I feel right now. The metal ridges are hard against my skin, but it isn't enough. I pull out my car key from my coat pocket and push it into the ignition and let out another defeated sigh.

My drive home is the longest it has ever felt.

The sunrise starts to peak over the horizon as I sit in silence through the long stretch of road in the middle of the busy city. My body feels numb and tired. I go through the deadening motions of driving when I pass through the large buildings and bright lights.

While I endure the many minutes of dissociation, I manage to find my way home. My body drags as I make my way inside my house and throw my jacket on the back of the couch and kick off my shoes in the middle of the living room floor.

Today, I couldn't give a shit about their rightful place. *Nothing fucking matters anymore.* My aching head pounds against the tense silence in my large house. *I need a drink. Maybe you'll disappear from my thoughts. At least just for today.* I grab a smoky gray whiskey glass from a long row of identical glasses in one of the cabinets. I reach for my bourbon from my liquor cabinet and generously pour until it reaches near the rim. While closing my eyes and with overly shaky hands, I put the glass to my lips. The warm amber liquid slides down my throat and all I can think about is her.

She was so beautiful when I first saw her behind the bar. Visions of her face keep flooding my thoughts. Her large piercing hazel eyes met mine and it was as if we were frozen in time. Her gaze stayed on me when she watched me drink the first drink she made me the night we met. The memory of her tripping over her words during our first conversation causes my mouth to turn up in a slight smile. My eyes gloss over with my hot tears, and I tip the glass back, making the liquor flow quicker to the back of my throat. *Fuck, I love you, and I don't think I ever truly loved anyone else.* I grip my glass and pour in more bourbon, filling it to the rim again. "I need you to go away. Why won't you go away?" My sobs echo through the empty house.

With each drink, she stays in my mind, embedded in my brain like a fucking computer virus. I lean my forearms on the granite countertop with my head in my hands. Just her face comes to mind and I rub my eyes to try to black it out. With each moment, my palms digging into my eyes, my vision goes dark, but my memories of her become more clear.

I recall all of her sweet smiles, ones I've caught from when she glanced up at me. The first time I held her small, delicate hand in mine as we crossed the street from The Neon Rose to my car. I smile at the memory of how excited she looked when I called her my "little crime solver" at the diner. It fades when I remember what soon came after, *"I'm not ready to be alone right now."* I hear Thalia's voice repeat inside in the torture chamber that is my thoughts. *Oh, please not this one. Anything but this one.*

I grab my drink with my shaky hand again and engulf what it contains as if I have been dying of dehydration, pouring more bourbon into the glass for the third time.

Oh, God, that fucking night. Why did I have to go in there with you? Why did you let me be alone with you if you knew you were going to shatter me to fucking pieces? My body continues to vibrate with a plethora of different emotions. Sadness and anger is at the forefront of my mind.

"If you kiss me, there isn't any coming back from me. I won't be able to stop myself." I play the somber flashback in my head like my mind is a projector, replaying the events from the night on a large screen

in front of me. Blankly, I stare ahead towards my empty living room. I am the only one who came to watch the sad son of a bitch fall for the hot, edgy bartender.

A tale as fucking old as time.

My blank stare continues while I go over in my head, what I said to her that night. *"I've waited so long just to fucking kiss you."* Why *did you kiss me, Thalia? That fucking kiss that made me fall harder for you!*

I throw the now empty glass against the backsplash above the kitchen. It shatters and leaves shards and tiny splashes of bourbon in the sink, on the counter, and across the kitchen floor. My mind falls back to that same night.

"I need you, Alan." Goosebumps cover my arms while I still hear her moans in my mind.

I stand up and run my hands down my face now saturated with tears. Without warning, my body on autopilot, I find myself walking to my bedroom. I start searching for something—anything that will help me feel something other than pain. I grab the baseball bat I have had since I was a kid. It sits in the corner of my bedroom like it's figuratively lit up under a fucking spotlight. My hands run down the smooth wooden handle and grip around the smaller end. With my eyes filled with a mix of rage and tears, I walk towards the kitchen.

As I stand in the middle of the large space, I look around the freshly painted cabinets. "Oh, God, I wish you were here!" I scream. My loud voice bounces off of the surface of the cabinets and the walls. "Why won't my thoughts of you go away?!"

I pick up the bat and with every memory of her, I swing.

The bat smacks into the half empty bottle of bourbon that sits on the kitchen with the thought of her pale, smooth skin that felt like silk underneath my fingertips. The glass cracks under my feet, and I don't flinch when the sharp edges cut into my skin through my gray socks. *The way my heart breaks is worse than the shattered fragments digging into my flesh.* My feet leave bloody footprints when I move to another part of the kitchen.

"Fuck, Thalia. You're more beautiful than I had imagined." Hot tears continue to fall down my chin onto the kitchen tile.

The once happy memory of her exposed breasts is replaced by the loud sound of wood crashing into each other. The top row of newly remodeled cabinets are shattered. Several pieces of wood fragments collect in the same scattered piles of the shards of glass.

I take a few steps to the right and look at the top row of cabinets that have been untouched.

"I want you, Thalia. I've never wanted anything so bad." Another memory I wish would dissolve turns into the few remaining pristine cabinets into a broken mess of wood and crystal.

With every painful memory of every time she screamed my name and begged me to make her come, I splinter any piece of wood and break all of the glass or ceramic that remains.

Standing in the middle of my spacious kitchen, now filled with shattered remnants of what was a beautiful picture of home design, I find myself just like the broken glass at my feet. I drop the bat and I fall to my knees with my head in my hands. More pieces of glass digging into my kneecaps. No amount of pain will ever match the mental torture that Thalia has caused.

"FUUUUUUUCK!" I scream again, the agony inside me too much to contain. The realization has set in the louder my sobs become. She has broken me.

THE SHADOW

I drive past The Neon Rose and see her pouring drinks like she does every night. My heartbeat speeds up when I see her smiling at the patron in front of her. *Even my heart isn't ready to let you go.* She hands him a drink she just made him without a fucking care in the world. She has no inclination that she just ruined me and all of the future plans I had for us. My stare out of my car window is evident as I keep driving. *Tonight isn't for you.*

I continue the drive until I notice a smaller building with a row of people in a line waiting to get in. *This is another bar that Lee supplies.* He keeps all of his clients in close distance to each other. How lucky for him, this one happens to be close to The Neon Rose. *Maybe he's just as intrigued in her as I am.*

Just thinking about his name makes me strangle the leather steering wheel with rage. A man who I once considered my brother is now my adversary. I bite my lip until I taste blood and my thoughts clear of all emotion. My lips turn up into a smirk when I notice the small space across from the club and I parallel park.

My car idly sits in silence. I let out a long sigh and pull my dark hood up over my head. A mental task list of sorts forms in my mind while looking over the bar and the long line in front of the door to the small club. *If Lee is here, I need to find a new way in. My plan will only work if I can remain unseen.*

My eyes scan over to the crowd of people in the long line. The men standing next to their dates are looking desperate in similar outfits of distressed jeans and flannel shirts. It's like they're photocopies of what their dates asked them to be. *Pathetic.* They're positioned behind their dates – or who they wish were their dates – with looks of impatience and overeagerness. Their eyes move down their skin-tight clothing as it clings to each of their curves. With each glance, I wonder how easy it would be to replace Thalia with one of these desperate looking women.

I look around to the side of the building and notice a small alley, similar to one I familiarized with in between Thalia's bar and the small boutique next door. I zero in on a man coming out of a small door next to a large dark green dumpster. *He must be one of the employees. There's my way in.*

The echo the door creates while it shuts is muffled by the loud noise from the crowds in front of the bars and restaurants on either side of the narrow street.

I stuff my hands in the pockets of my black zip up sweatshirt and look both ways before crossing the busy street. *Safety first.* I manage to walk through the empty alley unnoticed. The pink light from inside of the club shines under the small slot at the bottom of the door. It creates a soft neon glow on the wet and dirty concrete. I try my hand at jiggling the gold, metal door handle. *Too fucking easy.*

Making my way in through the back way of the club, I manage to get past one of the employees as I hide my face under my hood and look down towards the dark, stained carpet. *I made it in.* I walk through the short hallway, past the bathrooms and the kitchen until I've walked into the small open space of the club. The bar is near the back of the building, unlike The Neon Rose.

My senses are assaulted as I make my way through the crowded room full of barely dressed women and the smell of overpowering perfume. *Play the part, Alan.* Reluctantly, I sigh and remove my hood. I walk through the thin spaces between groups of people towards the long bar in the back of the building, continuing to push myself past many groups of people who reek of intoxication and sadness. *This is fucking pathetic.* Only a few more steps and I'm there.

I find an empty space at the end of the bar and watch as the bartender eyes me up and down. Without any sign of hesitation, he gives me a wink. My mask of contemptment conceals my expression as I try to hide my disgust. His eagerness is annoying as hell.

"Hey, handsome. Are you here alone tonight?" His dark mustache moves up covering his small smile. *Remember, play the part, Alan.*

"Yeah." I parrot his smile. "I just needed to get out. Rough week at the office."

"I get that." His eager look stays on his face. "You want anything to drink?" He stands with his hands on his hips and waits for my response.

"Yeah." *Keep it up, Alan.* "I'll take a bourbon and coke."

"Coming right up." He grabs the glass and adds a few ice cubes. I watch his hands move as he pours in the two shots of bourbon and fills the rest with coke. *His technique is sloppy.* He slides the drink in front of me. "Here you go, handsome." His mustache moves up again over his smirking lips.

"Thank you." With a curt nod, I pick up the glass and notice the splashes of bourbon around my glass. I wipe the excess drips from my cocktail on my jeans as he walks towards the other end of the bar. *Thalia would have made a better drink.*

I study the people sitting at the bar with my drink in hand. *Who will be the lucky lady to make me forget that image of seeing her ride my best friend?* The women here are not my ideal. They all look like clones with masks full of makeup. The sad excuse for outfits they wear made of flimsy fabric covers their obviously fake tits. Most of the hems of their skirts sit right in the middle of their thighs, showing off their long legs. I notice some of the women wearing their jeans skin tight as if they painted the denim directly on their flesh. They all sit at the tables with their phones attached to their hands. Some women scroll mindlessly while others take numerous pictures of themselves and their drinks.

Standing with my back touching the bar, I try to hide my look of disgust. I let out a long sigh and put the glass up to my lips. More of the bourbon burns my throat as I take a long drink.

The men in the club are just as ridiculous. Some stare at the women while they stand like lost puppies across the room. Others peacock themselves and bravely walk up to the set of clones they've had their eyes on only in hope to sink their dicks into what might as well be silicone robots. *This is fucking hopeless.*

I turn towards the bar and set down my half-empty whiskey glass. *Maybe I should call it a night. None of these women come even close to Thalia.* The thought is soon overlooked when I turn my head towards the other end of the bar. *Then again, maybe I shouldn't be too hasty.*

I see her long dark, purple hair fall straight down her exposed back. She looks towards the front of the bar and picks up her full glass. I can't help but smirk as I notice her short, black fingernails.

I'll imagine Thalia, while her black tips are wrapped around my dick later. She keeps my attention as she brings her drink to her full, black lips. She wraps her lips around the rim of the glass and I think of the many places on me that I would like them to be. She turns her head just slightly and notices my pleasing demeanor. Her small sweet smile catches my attention and she grabs her small black purse. Without breaking eye contact, she walks towards me at the other end of the bar. *You'll do.*

Her hips sway as she walks in her tight light-washed jeans. Her loose fitting black silk shirt barely hangs on her slender shoulders by a small silver chain. It hangs down her large chest like a fancy handkerchief. *Is that even a fucking shirt or just piece of overpriced fabric.* She stops next to me and sets her glass next to mine.

"Are you lost?" she asks loudly over the music blaring through the speakers. My smile widens at the question.

"If I am, would you mind showing me around?" I catch on to the small smile she tries to hide. She picks up her glass and brings it up to her lips again. I watch them closely. Her black lipstick sticks to the rim of the clear glass. I mirror her movements and pick up my glass, drinking the remainder of my poorly made bourbon and coke.

"Well, that depends," she answers.

"Really? Depends on what?" I ask, setting down my glass. My charming smile is still stretched across my face.

"It depends on how well this night goes." She scans my body with her large, almond shaped, brown eyes. *Oh, I think this night will go very well.*

My body leans back in the driver seat of my Lexus as my hands trace the curves along her slender body. She leans down and pushes her large breasts against my chest as her thighs straddle my lap. I grab her hair on the nape of her neck and bring her in close to kiss her full lips, the black lipstick already smearing. She lets out a soft moan when I gently bite down on her bottom lip. Her hips move in just the right way as she grinds on my hard dick under my jeans. My large hands move up under her shirt and fit one of her full tits in each one. Goosebumps cover her pale skin with the gentle kisses I trail from the middle of her neck down to her collar bone.

"I don't know your name," she says through her heavy breathing.

"I never gave it." I pull her in so that her lips come back to meet mine.

"Don't you want to know mine?" She asks after kissing me back.

"Tonight, I don't fucking care what your name is. Stop talking, beautiful, and lie back in the passenger seat for me."

The look in her eyes is almost sad. The poor thing tries to hide her disappointment with a small smile. *I'm sorry, pretty girl. Tonight isn't about you.*

She turns her body with her back to me as she tries to awkwardly get off my lap. Before she can successfully pivot herself around in the seat, I roughly grab the back of her head and slam it hard into the passenger window. Her body falls limp on the smooth leather surface. I stare at the small drops of blood on the glass and how they correspond to the ones on her forehead. *Oh fuck, I can't wait to see how you taste.* Her body slumps down in the passenger seat. Her chest moves slowly up and down while her heavy eyelids close.

Good. She's still alive.

I watch her body as it slouches against the back of the metal folding chair. Gently, I tied both of her ankles to the front legs of the chair with long, thick, black zip ties. She barely moved when I tighten the thick plastic on each ankle. Her limp arms made it easy to secure her in place when they fell behind her. I taped them with the same duct tape I had used to attach Jace's body to the roll of carpet. *He's still stored in the supply closet at Thalia's apartment complex. He will be taken care of soon.*

She stirs in her seat and her heavy lids start to open. Sitting across from her, I watch with my arms folded across my chest.

"There she is," I say softly. "You hit your head pretty hard. I didn't think you were going to make it." Her eyes go wide, and she frantically looks around my storage unit.

"Where the *fuck* am I?" She asks with tears already spilling down her cheeks. *The tears don't normally come this soon. This one will be easy to break.*

"It doesn't matter. You're not going to make it out alive anyway." I calmly explain. She bites her lower lip and lets out a small cry. My focus zeros in on her white canine as it pierces her skin. A small drop of blood falls just past the black lipstick that I smeared across her lips mere hours ago. My chair creaks when I stand and I walk closer to her tied up body. I run my finger under her bottom lip and lick her blood off my finger. She stares up at my tongue as it covers my fingertip.

"Tastes fucking delectable." I crouch down and whisper just above the tip of her ear. I can't help the smug look on my face while she shifts her thighs in her chair. *Even when she knows she's going to die, she's still willing to try to fuck anything that's in front of her.* I stand up and walk back towards my chair.

The bottom of her chair scrapes the concrete as she tries to move against her restraints. I sit back down, and pay close attention to the terrified woman in front of me, mentally dissecting her every move. She's fascinating really. I study how her small, trembling body reacts to its new surroundings. *I wonder what she'll do next.* She opens her mouth and screams. *Of course. Why do they always scream?*

"Help! Someone! I'm in here!" Her voice is a big contrast from earlier this evening. Her smokey sensual tone has turned into a shrill scream mixed with violent sobbing. She tries her best to move her chair, scraping the bottom of the legs along the concrete to create the most noise possible. She stops her annoying screeching when she notices my long sigh.

"Are you done?" I ask. She stares at me. Her whole body vibrates as she silently sobs on the metal seat. Large tears fall on her flushed cheeks.

I stand up out of my chair and turn around to face my shelf—an arrangement of a few basic tools as well as the trophies I've collected. I've kept a jar of eyes from the creep at the bar that tried to touch Thalia and his bloody hair tie *or whatever women call these fucking things,* Jace's nose ring and his small bag of cocaine. Ashley's wedding ring stands out, shining under the harsh lighting.

My eyes continue to trail over the many different shelves.

"Oh, there it is." I say in a playful tone and grab my switchblade. I turn around and face her, spinning the tip of the knife on my finger. Staring into her eyes, I walk towards her chair.

She screams at full volume again.

I crouch to meet her at eye level and observe the scared little girl in front of me as her face turns a deeper shade of red the louder she gets. Her lip trembles and she stops. I closely line my face up with hers, the tips of our noses nearly touching.

"Scream all you want. I love it," I admit. "No one can hear you. There is no one around for miles." She moves her body in hopes of getting further away from me. *There is no getting away from me. You're all mine now.*

"Where do you think you're going to go?"

She turns her head and looks around the room as if she's trying to conjure up an escape plan. It's pathetic really. The look of defeat covers her face when she notices the padlock on the closed roll-up door.

"Why did you agree to get into my car?" I ask, still spinning the tip of the knife on my index finger. "Didn't anyone tell you not to get in a car with a stranger?"

"I-I-I..." She stammers.

"Look at you," I shake my head. "Now at a loss for words." I run the blade of my knife across my bottom lip. "You know, you look pretty when you're like this." Her tears and sweat make several of her dark purple strands stick to the side of her cheeks. I glide the tip of the blade along a few of her thin fibers.

"I don't want to hurt your pretty face," I whisper next to her ear. I gently move my blade from the top of her neck to the neckline of her shirt. I watch more tears fall down her cheeks.

"Just sit back, beautiful. It'll all be over soon."

The sharp blade presses down hard on her shirt starting at the neckline. It cuts smoothly through the silk threads. I pay close attention to the goosebumps and the beads of sweat that form in the middle of her chest. Her body shivers and her chest heaves as I move the blade along her skin beneath the opened flaps of the silk fabric. The way her body tenses from the sharp blade entering the skin, allows the knife to glide down, just above her tits with ease.

What's left of her shirt hangs loosely off her body. My eyes stare at the trail of blood I left between her tits, ending just below her rib cage. I lick my lower lip at the sight of my mark contrasting against her pale skin.

"Tonight, you're mine, and baby, we're going to play." Roughly, I grab her chin and kiss her swollen lips.

"Why me?" She asks through quiet sobs.

"Because, you're the next best thing." I close my switchblade and slide it into the pocket of my black jeans. Her sad eyes look up at me as I stand up and I walk back towards the shelf. I grab the tripod I had set up for Jace and set it next to the empty metal chair.

"What are you going to do to me?" she asks with her trembling voice.

"Whatever the hell I want." I grab her small, black purse I sat next to the metal shelf when I first brought her here.

"What are you doing with my stuff?" She questions angrily. I let out a small laugh and hunt for her phone. *Even when she's about to die, she's still worried about the material things. Just like Ashley. Fucking typical.*

"Here it is." I grab her phone from the tiny bag. She shifts in her seat the closer I get to her body. "Smile for me, baby." Her chin is small in my hand as I hold her head up to her phone. "Good, girl." I praise and watch how the phone opens up.

Her phone fits securely into the tripod sat in front of her. In what seems like minutes of silence, I search through her many apps until I can find her camera. I hit the record button and step out of the way.

"Why are you recording me?" She quietly asks.

"Because when you're dead, I want to replay the sounds you make right before you meet your end," I answer. Standing behind the tripod, I adjust the height, making sure my face will be out of view.

"Someone will come for me. They'll notice I'm no longer at the club. There were witnesses. People saw me walk out with you to your car!" She cries.

"If someone noticed or even cared that you were gone, they would have said something by now. No one is coming." I look at her from behind the tripod and revel in her trembling body. The long red line that goes down her chest continues to entice my mind.

"You wear my mark so fucking well." I walk closer to her chair and take the switchblade from my pocket. The clicking sound of the knife opening echoes in the small storage space. Keeping my eyes on her, I lean in close and run the tip along her pale skin. "I think it would look so much better with a few more."

Before I begin running the sharp edge of the cold blade along her pale skin, I look up at her terrified face. *Keep it that way. I love the way you look right now.* I study her reactions as the blade pushes deep into her skin. Her body jumps at the feeling of the serrated edge carving into her sternum. She bites her lower lip again and her tears fall out of her heavy lids. Thick clots of red stream out in tandem with my knife as it cuts into her chest in slow motion.

I stop once the end of my new mark lines up with the first one. "Oh, pretty girl, you look like a fucking work of art."

I stand back with my hand stroking my chin and admire the new canvas in front of me. She lets out small whimpers while I walk back to my chair and sit down on the cold metal surface. My stare is permanently on the blood streaming down her snow white chest as I pinch the blade between my fingers.

"What else are you going to do to me?"

"Terrible, awful things." I look down at her exposed skin and notice how her many tears have mixed with her blood.

"P-please. Just let me go," she begs and I ponder the thought. *We could make this so much more enjoyable.*

"Oh, I like that idea." I stand up behind the tripod stop the recording.

"You're going to let me go?" It's almost adorable the way the pitch raises in her voice at the question.

"I'm going to give you a head start." Slowly, I walk towards her chair. "I'll let you run. If you can get out before I catch you, you're a free woman." I crouch down behind her and cut her wrists free from the silver duct tape binding them together. Next, I sit on my knees and cut the zip ties around her ankles.

"What happens if you catch me?"

"You better hope that doesn't fucking happen."

I examine her closely while she stands up from her chair. She rubs the tacky surface of her arms left over from the tape. Reluctantly, she stares at me closely when I walk over to the padlock attached to the door. Her eyes pierce through me like lasers when the lock comes loose. Being the tease that I am, I pull up the large door slowly. Her body stiffens when she sees the small crack between the concrete and the door get larger.

"Once this door is open, you run," I calmly instruct. "If I catch you, then you're back to being my pretty little plaything." Her gaze holds on the door the higher it moves off the ground. I watch her closely, as if the gears are turning in her head. I wonder what she's planning. Does she think she'll make it out alive? *She won't be able to escape. I'll make sure that she doesn't.* What if she does? What will happen then? *The poor thing won't even make it past the gate. Not in the state that she is now.* "I must say that it's a little disappointing how you're so eager to leave."

The loud sound of the door sliding up echoes in the public storage facility. She looks at me and to the open space dumbfounded.

"Well?" I ask. "I would start running if I were you."

Her heels make loud clicking sounds on the concrete as she runs out of the unit. The countdown begins when I hear her shoes scuff along the long pathway of loose gravel. *This will be fun.*

"TEN!" My loud voice carries over her heavy panting. "NINE!"

I slowly turn around and look out of the small building.

"EIGHT!" I continue to yell as I step out onto the gravel.

"SEVEN." I start making larger steps in the direction of the sounds of her breathing and the crunching of loose gravel beneath her tall heels.

"SIX!" My steps turn into quick jogs. Adrenaline pumping into my veins as I pick up speed around the corners of the facility.

"YOU BETTER HOPE I CAN'T FIND YOU, PRETTY GIRL!" My loud voice booms through the rows of other storage units. I smile wildly and stop my pace when I hear the rattling of a metal chain linked fence. *I know exactly where you are.*

"FIVE!" My heart picks up as I start running towards the locked fence around the property. *There you are.*

The look of sheer panic on her face when she twists her body around at her waist triggers my rush of adrenaline. I stand back and watch as she unsuccessfully tries to climb her way out. The front of her pointed heel gets caught in one of the links and she slides down the middle of the fence. I laugh as her body retreats into itself the closer I get. The poor thing sits awkwardly on the damp gravel. She looks defeated. *Good. Now it's my turn.*

"Four." The volume of my voice lowers and I walk closer, taking smaller steps. She moves back further into the gate, as if she's trying to meld with the metal.

"Three." Her tired cries become louder with every one of my steps.

"Two." I count. She looks defeated, whaling with her head in her hands.

"One," I stop and scan over the broken girl in front of me. "Oh, don't look sad, baby. You did so well. Come on, a deal is a deal." I crouch down and look into her wide, tear filled and terrified eyes. "Let's go play."

She screams so fucking loudly when I stand. *Will she ever stop?* I pull her along the gravel by the tufts of her long hair.

Her slender body goes limp after I throw her in the storage unit on the concrete floor. Once I see her body hit the hard surface, I turn around and slide down the red door. She lets out another small sob when she hears the clicking sound of the padlock closing.

I pick up her body and tie her to the metal folding chair just as I had before. *She knows she lost.* "Oh, pretty girl. Don't be sad." I do my best to comfort her while replacing the old zip ties I had cut from her ankles with new ones. She flinches as I run my fingers up her calves.

"Why are you doing this to me?" She pleads for an answer. Her body tenses with the tightening of the zip ties around the small parts of her limbs.

"Why does anyone do anything, pretty girl?" I ask, leaning on my knees behind her chair. "I needed a distraction and there you were. Just there for the taking. Like a shiny new toy for me to play with." My eyes stay on hers while I stand up and walk backwards over to my chair. Her eyes never leave me. She watches as I sit down and press my elbows on my thighs.

"What am I distracting you from?" She asks between her loud cries. "Was it an old girlfriend? Couldn't we have just fucked and then never talked again like normal people?"

"Pretty girl, haven't you realized? I'm not normal."

"Well, no fucking shit!" she almost screams. Another smile paints my face as I put my arms across my chest.

I shift my body in the chair when I feel my phone vibrating in the back pocket of my jeans. *What the fuck is this about?*

Thalia:

Hey, Alan

No. Not her. Not now. She can't do this to me. Not right now. I'm in the middle of something. Just when I was about to forget her.

"Fuck!" I scream. My pretty hostage startles as the loud exclamation bounces off the solid walls. *Don't answer her.*

Hello, Listener

Shit. I stand up and shove my phone back into my pocket, angrily pacing around the small space between my chair and the terrified girl in front of me.

"She can't do this to me," I say. "She thinks she can have us both. She thinks she can fuck us both and that everything will just be okay." I pause and take a long sigh. *Maybe she does care.* "If she cared, she wouldn't have been riding his dick." I answer my own thoughts aloud. *Maybe she feels guilty. Maybe she didn't know you cared so much.* "I told her what she meant to me. She knows how much she means to me," answering my own thoughts again. "What do you think?" I ask the confused and tormented girl in front of me.

"What...?" Her voice shakes.

"Do you think she loves me?" I impatiently wait for her answer.

"Uhhh..." she stammers.

"Only one way to find out."

I feel her eyes on me again while she watches me walk over to the array of basic tools sitting on my shelf. I gently drag my fingers over the different handles. The cold metal feels so heavy in my hand. My body vibrates with anticipation when I feel the buzzing of the phone in my pocket for a second time.

Thalia:

I miss you

"Fuck!" I scream again and I throw the phone down on the concrete floor. *She misses me. She loves me.* "She doesn't miss me. She's just alone without Lee."

The adrenaline rushes through me and I quickly walk over to the chair across from the tripod. She winces in pain as I rip the duct tape from her small wrists. I feel the fear running through her vibrating the metal chair on the hard floor. "What do you think?" I ask again, looking into her terror filled eyes. She looks down at my large hands gripping the pliers in my hand. Her much smaller hands trembling on her lap.

"What are you doing?!" She cries as I grab one of her hands, isolating one of her fingers. She stares with her mouth agape as the flat surface of the jaw of the pliers slides under the tip of her short fingernail.

"What do you think, pretty girl?" I ask, still looking down at her black fingernail. "She loves me?"

She screams in agony as I pull on the tip and watch the nail detach from the tip of her index finger before moving to the next digit.

"She loves me not?" She screams again. Her body shakes violently in the chair. I move the pliers to her ring finger. "She loves me?"

"Please don't do this!" She cries loudly. She screams again when I pull hard on the handle. "Just stop! Please!" She begs. I set down the pliers and gently grab her face between both of my hands.

"Shhh. Pretty girl. Only one more." Grabbing the tool again, I slide it beneath her pinkie nail. I pull and she lets out another scream. "She loves me." With much relief, I stand up as she cries behind me. A loud metallic sound fills the small space between us as the pliers fall from my hands and land on the floor. I grab my phone out of my pocket and type out a quick text message to Thalia.

I slide my phone back into the back pocket of my jeans and turn around and look at the mess I made in front of me. She babies her injured hand in the other. Her face is covered in sweat, tears, and smeared black makeup.

"You look perfect. So ruined and so broken." I remove her phone from the tripod and walk it closer to her to unlock it. The screen opens again before I set the phone in the tripod and find the camera app to start the recording all over.

"You asked me earlier what my name was. My name is Alan, pretty girl." I press record and take the switchblade out of my pocket. She panics as she watches me walk closer towards her chair. For just a moment, I stand behind her shaking body. With one hand, I move her neck so her head faces the camera. With the other I press the blade up to her porcelain skin. Her blood reflects off the mirrored edge of the knife the deeper I press into her neck. I watch and listen as she gasps for air. Flowing like my own personal fountain, crimson floods down her pale chest. Her limp body falls forward and her blood splashes on the concrete as if it were rain on the sidewalk. I move towards the tripod and end the recording. The cotton of my black shirt becomes useful as I wipe off the fingerprints on her phone case and place it neatly inside her small black purse.

"I've got the perfect place for you, pretty girl," I tell the lifeless body in front of me.

Chapter Twenty-Seven

DISPOSABLE

ALAN

L ife drains from her eyes while she slumps over in the folding chair. I slowly walk around her slender body, trying to determine my next move. Her blood on my switchblade still drips from the sharp metal. I crouch down behind her chair and cut off the tight zip ties around her ankles. Her lifeless body falls hard on the clear tarp I had laid out for her. The impact of the small drop creates a loud sound in the little storage space.

The scratches on the small of her back trace over the curvatures of her spine. They're most likely caused by the loose gravel when I drug her slender body. *Another touch of my handy work.* The several raised marks down her flesh add a touch of character to her smooth skin. Her body rolls over nicely on the tarp. The large brown eyes looking up at me were once full of life, but now look heavy, tired, and clouded with death.

I smooth out her long purple hair as well as I can with my fingers until I can no longer feel a tangled mess. "You never really deserved this pain," I reassure her quietly. My blade cuts through the ends of her locks smoothly and I hold the lock of hair in my hands, running my thumb over the shiny strands. The tarp creases below my knees while I stand up from the hard floor.

"There is a perfect spot on my shelf that I have picked out for you." I tell the body behind me. "Don't worry, pretty girl. I'll never forget our night."

My wide eyes scan over her body. The way that her blood stops in the middle of her stomach excites me in a way that would concern most men. I've come to the realization, however, that I am one of a kind.

"I'll clean you up, pretty girl," I promise her with my lips nearly touching the side of her face. I kneel next to her body and lap up the pool of crimson collecting near her abdomen. My tongue moves along the trail of liquid scarlet, slowly up between her breasts. I keep running the flat of my tongue up her body until I reach the gash I made in her slender neck. I lick the the few drops that fall off my bottom lip. The copper tinge on my tongue sends a shiver up my spine.

My focus changes its course to the cuts I made on her earlier. Goosebumps cover my skin as the tips of my fingers touch the raised, red surface.

"Even as a warm corpse, your body still looks so fucking beautiful with my marks."

She feels nice cradled in my arms, her form fitting perfectly in mine with her feet dangling off my forearm and her neck resting on my other bicep.

I comfortably put her body in the passenger seat as if she were asleep. The seat belt wraps loosely around her leaning body. Her blood continues to stream down between her breasts. The strap of the seatbelt barely sits on her slightly exposed chest.

"Sorry, pretty girl. I did the best I could with your shirt." The thin, black fabric I cut earlier still lays gently on her large, fake breasts.

Her shiny, black, leather purse sits next to her feet on the floor in the car. It falls lopsided next to her black heels. Her phone fits snugly inside with her screen face up. I make sure to take glances every so often. *Still no messages for my pretty girl.*

"Sorry, there's no one looking for you." I move my exposed arms through the sleeves of my black zip up sweatshirt and settle myself into the driver seat. "You ready?" I ask her as if she's going to give me an answer, nodding at her silent response, and turn on the car.

The drive is long and quiet. As is to be expected with a dead girl and her killer in the same car. Every now and then, out of the corner of my eye, I notice the shadows casting down from the lights of the city hitting her very pale face. She looks almost peaceful. "Almost there, pretty girl."

I take glances at the familiar alley between The Neon Rose and the small boutique and then back again at the lifeless girl in my passenger seat.

"The sun will be up soon. I better get you settled. You'll have a big day in the morning." I turn off the car and unlatch the loose seat belt around her lap and grab the small purse on the floor. The leather strap slides conveniently on my shoulder. It settles in the creases between the black cotton of my sweatshirt. "Stay right there, pretty girl. I'll get your door."

I scoop up her body just as I had done earlier at the storage unit and quietly shut the passenger side door with my hip. The two of us both watch for cars and we quickly cross the street. I set her body against the large dumpster that I had been acquainted with two times before.

"I know it's not much, but you won't be here too much longer." I smooth down her frizzy, dark purple hair as it hangs on her delicate shoulders. Next, I fish out her phone from her tiny purse and rub down the case with my cotton shirt. "You know the drill, baby. Say cheese." She complies as I grab her hair from the top of her head and move her face in view of her screen. Her phone opens up, allowing me to open her gallery and play the last video I took of the show we made.

"You did so well." I praise the beautiful corpse before setting the small purse on her lap.

The light of my phone shines brightly on my nightstand. I should be asleep, but my mind is overrun with thoughts. I reluctantly look over at the screen. *It's late. Only one person would send me anything this time of night.* I roll over on what used to be my side of the bed and check the screen. *Fuck. You knew it would be her.*

"Why the fuck did it have to be her?" I ask myself out loud.

Thalia:

Hey, Alan.

I grip my black phone case and stare down at the message like it's going to self-destruct any minute. *Don't answer her, asshole.* My fingertips glide over the keyboard on the screen.

Me:

Hello, Listener.

Thalia:

Alan. I want to see you.

Me:

Anything for you

Chapter Twenty-Eight

SEDUCE AND DESTROY

ALAN

M y eyes stare down at my phone. Her text message invades my thoughts like a fucking parasite. I run the pads of my thumb over her words.

Thalia:

> I miss you, Alan. I want to see you.

My car sits idle in front of her apartment complex. *Am I really doing this? There's no coming back from this if I go in there.* I drum my fingers on the leather surface of my steering wheel, refocusing my gaze to the window of her apartment. Letting out a loud sigh, I reluctantly turn off the ignition. *I can't believe I'm fucking doing this.* I send her a quick message before I step out of my car.

Me:

> I'm here, Listener.

The car door closing echoes in the mostly empty street. The lights from the street lamps reflect off the slick road. *This is it, Alan. No turning back.* My phone buzzes in my pocket as I make my first step across the damp cement.

Come on up. I'll meet you at the door.

It is almost pathetic how much I smile as I shove the phone back into the side pocket of my slacks. *Look at how eager you are to see her. As if nothing ever fucking happened.*

My heartbeat gets louder in my head the closer I step to the door that leads to the hallway full of units. Nervous thoughts fill my head, and my hands go clammy with each step. I can't tell if it's my cold sweat or the raindrops that leave wet streaks down my thighs when I rub my palms on the smooth fabric. I notice the cold, wet, metal doorknob only a few inches in front of me. There is a part of me that wants to resist touching the cold surface. *Do you really want to put yourself through this again?* I wonder to myself in my internal monologue of uncertainty. Unfortunately, my precariousness is interrupted by the small opening coming from the door.

"Alan."

I love the way she says my name when she sounds out of breath. She must have ran through the hallway and down the stairs to meet me. *How sweet.* The corners of her freshly painted red lips turn up into an innocent smile. I pair her smile with the one I know she loves so much. *That red lipstick is going to look so fucking good smeared all over your lips.*

"Listener." *God, I love the way cheeks flush red when I call her that. I think what I will miss the most is remembering how her body responds to me.*

"You're here." She looks me up and down while she states the obvious.

"Of course I am," I answer matter of factly, crossing my arms around my chest. "You asked to see me."

I watch as she melts at my charming smile spreading across my face. Eagerly, she opens the door wide enough for the both of us to easily fit through. The heavy door shuts loudly behind us. Both of our steps are muffled on the dingy, dark brown carpet.

"Lead the way," I tell her, my arm outstretched in the direction of the stairs. As she focuses on the path ahead, I look quickly towards the small supply closet just a few feet from us. *I wonder if the door is still conveniently unlocked. Of course it is, no one locks the doors around here. Don't worry, Jace. Your time will come.*

I stare at her figure in front of me while we both slowly climb up the single flight of stairs. She's wearing the same gray shorts she wore when I made my first visit. They ride up her pale thighs in just the right way. Allowing me to see more of the tattooed roses on the long, green stem twisting and turning up the contours of her leg. My line of sight moves to her tight, black shirt. The hem sits right above the waistband of her shorts. A sliver of her pale skin shows through the small space.

She's already making my mouth water. My thoughts become riddled with memories of when we were last together. I can't help but picture the look on her face when she screamed my name while she came on my dick. Fuck, she already has me getting harder in my black slacks. I run my hands along the cold, metal banister just to keep myself from wrapping my arms around her waist, feeling her smooth skin against mine, and fucking her here on the stairs.

My dirty thoughts become worse as we reach the second metal door that leads to the long row of apartments. She turns back to look at me and grabs my hand to lead me down the hallway. I smirk at the look of lust that fills her large, hazel eyes. She looks forward and her bare feet glide along the brown carpet to her unit. *So fucking eager to let me tear her apart.*

Her large door squeaks loudly in the hallway when she pushes it open. I shut it softly behind us when we both step into her small kitchen. The lock clicks loudly when I turn the deadbolt to the locking position. As if from muscle memory, I remove my jacket and set it on the small counter next to me like it's a new routine I've created for myself. Her cat, Artemis, rubs his furry, white body along my calf.

"Hey, little guy. I didn't think I would see you again," I answer by petting his head between his pointy ears. The sounds of his purrs waver as he moves in and out of my legs.

"He seems to like you," Thalia notices with her hands on her hips and her head tilted to the side. She gives me one of her sweet smiles. *Fuck. One more thing I'm going to miss.*

"Yeah. It seems I'm a cat person." I admit. "We met the last time I came over." Her smile widens at my flirtatious wink. *More times than you know.* I stand up and slide the sleeves to my white dress shirt up my arms. I lean against the counter with both of my hands in my pockets. I wonder what she plans to do next. Her eyes scan up and down my form.

"Why did you ask me here, Thalia," I ask, moving closer to her.

"I-I wanted to see you." Her small voice stammers just like the day we met. *This may be easier than I thought. I love how small she looks. Easy for me to take and even easier for me to devour. Just how she fucking devoured me.*

"Really? Just wanted to see me. And why is that?" I question, while lowering my voice. Mimicking the voice I put on every episode. The same voice I *know* will bring her to her knees. She stands mostly still as I start making my way over to her. My body closes in on hers to the point that we are almost touching. Her breath is warm on my skin between the few opened buttons around the collar of my shirt. She completely freezes as I move my finger gently under her chin so that her eyes look into mine.

"I've missed you, Alan." Her soft voice still quivers when she says my name. *I love that.* I bite my lip at the visual in front of me.

"Oh, yeah. Show me, Listener. How much did you *really* miss me?"

My lips collide with hers. I bite down on her lower lip, *hard*. Her body caves into mine and her whimpers are muffled on my mouth as my tongue searches for hers. I move my fingers from under her chin, and tangle them into the middle of her messy waves. Her delicate hands grip my forearms. She lets out a heavy sigh when I move my lips from hers. My hand moves easily through the ends of her red locks. She grabs my hand and leads me to her dark bedroom just a few feet away.

She looks back at me, just as she did in the hallway, and continues to lead me until we reach the side of her bed. *This is where I held her last. It all seems so long ago now, even though it's been only about a week. Is this what she said to him when she brought him in here only a few days ago? Was she so eager to fuck what was right in front of her?* My brooding thoughts get interrupted as I notice her eyes peer down at her black comforter and then back to me.

"Sit down, Alan," she commands with pure seduction in her tone.

In an instant, I do what she says and sit where she instructs. She faces me and slowly straddles my lap. The thin gray fabric of her shorts moves further up her thighs and gathers around where I want to be most. She moves her fingers through the top of my red waves and moves my face to meet hers.

"Have you thought about me as much as I have thought about you?" She asks before biting her lower lip. *Did you think of me, while you were taking in all of him?*

"You have no idea how much you are on my mind," I confess. *Why did that hurt so much to admit out loud?*

She kisses my lips and her hands move from my hair to the white buttons on my shirt. One by one, the tips of her fingers graze my chest. She slides the material off my shoulders once she reaches the bottom row of buttons. My shirt settles around me on her bed. She moves her hands over my skin as if she's never touched my body before. Goosebumps form on my biceps beneath the smooth touch of her hands.

While I take in the sight before me, I run my hands up her pale arms, stopping when I reach the thin, black straps of her tight shirt. They slide nicely down her skin. The top half of her shirt falls down her chest and leaves her breasts exposed. *You're making this too easy for me.* Like a beacon, my hands immediately feel her perfect breasts. I run my tongue along her nipples and bite down, gently at first, and apply more pressure with my teeth like I know she loves.

"Oh, Alan," she moans my name so sweetly. *It will sound better when she's screaming it.* As I continue to cup her perfect tits, I kiss down the crook of her neck.

"Thalia, take off your fucking shorts." I say with my lips still moving down her neck to her chest. "I want to see all of you."

She moves down my lap in a way that grinds on my clothed, hard dick. I watch her thumbs hook in the waistband of her cotton shorts. The flimsy fabric falls gracefully down her thighs. She stands in front of me, naked, like a flawless vision. *Destroying you will be the hardest thing I will ever have to do.*

"Come here," I command, sitting up and kicking off my shoes. I remove my belt and gaze down at her perfect body. As quickly as I am able, I undo the black button on my slacks and slide them down my legs. My dark gray boxer briefs soon follow and add to the pile of unwanted clothes on her carpet.

She moves in what seems like slow motion but I don't mind watching her figure the closer she gets.

"Lay down for me, Alan." Her voice is filled with pure lust. My head leans back against my arms and I stare while she straddles my lap on my extended legs. I let out a low groan as she grinds her wet slit against the shaft of my dick.

"Fuck, I can feel how wet you are for me." I move my hands to her small waist. "Fuck me, Thaila."

She moves her hips and quickly situates her tight pussy down my cock.

"That's it. Fuck me. Show me how much you've thought about me since I saw you last." Her hips move up and down in just the right way. My grip tightens on her waist and makes red marks on her porcelain skin. *God, I love seeing my marks on you. It will look better when they're carved into your snow white flesh.*

"Alan," her soft voice whimpers. She leans her body down and places her hands flat on my chest.

"You like that, Listener?" I whisper next to her ear. "You like riding my dick, don't you?" I move my hands from her waist to her round ass.

"Yes," She answers through quick breaths.

"Yes, who?" I roughly ask, slapping her ass hard after demanding an answer.

"Yes, Alan." She screams loudly in my ear. *There it is.*

"Fuck, I love it when you say my name." I grip her flesh harder as she continues to move her hips.

"Look at me, Thalia." She looks up and bites her lower lip again. "You're with me tonight. I want you to remember every part." Her moans next to my ear makes my dick instantly harder.

"This is what's going to happen. I want you to use me. Use me to make yourself come. After that, I'm going to flip you over on your back and I'm going to fill that pretty pussy of yours." I watch her eyes roll back at my words. "Do you want that, Thalia? You want to be my toy?" I ask. She moves her hips faster, and I can feel her cunt tightening around my cock.

"Yeah, you like that, don't you?" I listen to all of her sweet sounds when I grip her ass hard the faster she moves. "Are you my little whore, listener?"

"Yes," she nods as she says with her loud moans. *I love the way her face contorts as she gets closer to pure satisfaction.* Her delicate hands grip my shoulders and I continue to watch her face as I feel her cum drip down my length. I feel how her pussy spasms on my dick, making me jump in the process. She lays her body on my chest. Her fast heartbeat vibrates throughout my body.

"My turn." I flip her sex induced comatose body on her back.

I look her over while kneeling at the foot of her bed. Her pale skin is covered in goosebumps and small beads of sweat. She stares up at me with hooded eyes.

"Tonight, you're mine. I have all of you and I don't plan on letting you go anytime soon." She nods, not realizing what she's agreeing to.

"My little whore," I whisper with my lips against the skin on her thigh. "My toy that I can play with."

I run my fingers up her leg until I reach her inner thigh. I barely touch the small space between her inner thigh and her cunt. Her eyes follow my hands the closer I move to her clit. She stares intently at my hand and then back at me.

"I've watched you so carefully, Listener," I admit, getting closer to her most sensitive areas. "I know all of your favorite spots," my thumb stops on the bundle of nerves. *With my hand here, I can make you bend. I can break you. I can make you beg for more. Or I can give into you, like I have so much already. I don't want to give in to you, Listener. I want to break you into pieces so you know the pain I felt. I want your heart to shatter for me just as mine did for you.*

"I know what makes you tick." I run my tongue along the bottom of my lip and work her clit with my thumb in slow circles. She slightly arches her back but keeps her eyes on me. Her sweet whimpers almost echo in her quiet room. "I know what makes you break." I press my thumb harder against her sensitive skin. Her sweet sounds disappear as her canines almost pierce her sensitive skin.

"I know what makes you come undone." I move two of my fingers into her pussy.

"I know you better than you fucking know yourself," I say moving my fingers in and out slowly. Her whine is almost addicting when I remove them.

I move my body over hers.

"You're mine, Thalia." I tell her again as I line my dick up with her tight cunt. "Your mind." I say pushing myself into her. "Your body." Another push. We both moan in unison. "Your fucking soul." I look down into her now wide hazel eyes. "I fucking *own* you, Listener, and you love it. Don't you?" She nods in agreement the best way she can with my body pinning her to the bed. "My whore loves to be owned." She wraps her thighs around my waist.

"Yes," she admits. Her hands grab ahold of my biceps. Now, it's her turn to leave her marks.

"Fucking use me, Alan," she moans.

"Gladly." I move my hips faster and faster. "Tell me how it feels, Thalia." My breathing gets faster. "How does it feel to be used by me?" I ask with my lips now close to her neck near the bright blue vein that contrasts under her pale skin. *With one bite, I could spill your blood underneath me.* I feel myself getting harder at the breathtaking mental image of her laying in a pool of her own crimson.

"So, fucking *good*," she screams in my ear.

"Fuck, that's my good girl." I feel her as her body comes apart again with me inside her. My head tilts back as I fill her full of me and claim her one last time. She wraps her arms around my back, and I lay my body on top of hers.

I take in all of this moment, knowing that it will all be different tomorrow. I'm about to break the one thing I've ever loved, and she has no idea.

She looks peaceful as she sleeps on her back with her hair spread out over her pillows. Her round tits peek out from under her comforter. I take it all in as I did the last time she invited me into her apartment. My eyes don't leave her chest while it moves up and down as she breathes. I pull my slacks over my legs and quietly buckle my belt. She stirs in her sleep when I slide my arms through my white sleeves.

"What are you dreaming about?" I ask the sleeping woman in front of me. I move my hands up to the small white buttons on my shirt through the small holes as if they're tiny keys.

I stand over her fragile body on the bed after slipping on my leather dress shoes, memorizing every part of her. The small imperfections of her tattoos, her perfect curves, and even each tiny scar that stands out on her alabaster skin.

"Don't worry, Thalia. I'll be back." I kiss her temple and begin my preparations. "That was just the beginning, Listener."

Oh, how much fun we will have.

Just as I suspected, the small supply closet under the stairs is unlocked. *No one around here fucking locks their doors.* I shake my head at their careless actions. The door makes a loud squeak as it opens. The large roll of carpeted Jace is just where I left it–propped up against other random remnants of old pieces of carpet. The closer I walk to the large roll, I notice the harsh smell of death that seeps through the layers of thick material. *Fuck, Jace, you're starting to smell.* The paint cans helping prop up his corpse slide smoothly on the hard floor. I hold out my arms quickly to catch his limp body as it falls forward. *At least he's protected by a layer of padding.*

Luckily it's still dark as I carry Jace to the trunk of my car. *We shouldn't be interrupted by any good samaritans this time.* Jace's bendable body fits nicely in the trunk. His form folds evenly with the layers of padding that hold tightly around his corpse. I give him a once over before closing the door. His neon pink hair stands out in the opening between his head and the layer of carpet touching his back. My lips form into a smirk as I close the trunk. *You're going to be the perfect gift for Thalia.*

I park my silver Lexus in front of my storage unit along the loose gravel. The soles of my shoes scuff through the tiny rocks. My round key fits smoothly through the padlock on the red rollup door to the unit. The cold, dark space lights up with the yellow, harsh light with a quick flip of a switch on the battery operated lamp.

I slide one of the metal chairs front and center in the middle of the small unit's space. *Jace's body may need more reinforcements this time.* I grab his corpse from my trunk and throw it over my shoulder. His foul scent almost makes me gag. The cadaver bounces in between the layers of carpet as I throw him down on the hard floor. I take my time in unrolling the carpet that encases his rank corpse. The carpet easily lays flat on the surface. He is just barely secured by the duct tape I had added for an extra sense of certainty that he would stay stable in the large roll of fabric. The ends of the silver adhesive are lifted from the moist carpet and areas of his clammy, cold, skin. I survey the body in front of me.

"Where should I start?" I ask his lifeless body.

I begin by peeling one of the many strips of tape along his long, slender figure. The long sound of tape peeling off carpet echoes in the small area. It's muffled at first and then gets louder as it peels off some of his cold, dead flesh. A thin layer of dark gray and brown skin comes off his forehead and on to the sticky underside of the tape.

The removal of the duct tape takes longer than I had planned, but it is a necessary step. I set his body in the metal chair.

"Look familiar, Jace?" His body is barely stable without any restraints. "Now, don't you go anywhere." I say smugly as I turn to look at the white folding card table behind him I had already set up.

Before I had finally decided to drive to Thalia's house last night, I made a quick stop here. I previously laid out a pile of several black, industrial zip ties, my switchblade, the mini saw I used on Ashley, the same clear raincoat, a new tarp, a new roll of silver duct tape, a black silk sleeping mask I snagged from Ashley's piles of lingerie in her dresser, and an unopened package of black trash bags. *It's always good to be prepared.*

"Can you believe I bought most of this at a hardware store not too far from here?" I ask Jace. I signal to all of the items in front of me. "It's amazing that people won't bat an eye when you pay for everything with cash."

Jace's limp body leans forward in the metal chair and falls onto the hard floor. "Whoa, where do you think you're going?" A shit eating grin stretches across my face as I turn around with a handful of zipties.

I pull his body up on the chair and move his wrists behind him. The zipties easily wrap around his slender wrists. His ankles sit perfectly against the leg of the chair.

"You're being so cooperative this evening, Jace." I wrap another zip tie around the tight denim on his ankle. "Only one more," I reassure his body while looking up at his cold, dead eyes.

His other ankle is just as easily strapped onto the other leg of the chair. I stand up and give him a friendly pat on the back. Walking back to the table behind us, I grab the sleeping mask and stuff it into the deep pocket of my slacks. Afterwards, I look over at the new roll of duct tape in front of me. *Only one more piece will make this more believable.*

The small strip of duct tape rips easily enough and I place it over his mouth. Other than the random patches of his skin that have been removed with the old duct tape, he looks like he's back to his old self. *Minus the breathing part.*

"You know, Jace. This wasn't going to be your final resting place." I admit while sliding the metal chair he's attached to. I move him just a few feet from where he was the last time we talked. "You're just the perfect addition to Thalia's punishment." I set an empty folding chair next to his and look over the room. "It's set up just the way I planned." I look in his general direction, slide my hands into my slacks and head towards the exit.

"See you soon, Jace." I add as I pull down the door and secure the lock.

Chapter Twenty-Nine

"Pain in the Core of Pleasure"

 **THALIA**

"Listener, wake up." Alan says sweetly next to my ear. He leans in and kisses the top of my head.

"What time is it?" I ask with blurry vision. The kind of vision you get when you're still half asleep. His smile is something nice to wake up to. He lets out a small laugh as I stretch my whole body in my bed.

"Don't worry about that. I want to show you something." He leaves a trail of kisses down my neck. I turn my head and watch his green eyes light up. *I don't think I could ever say no to him.*

"Let me get dressed," I say as I sit up against my headboard. He smiles and throws my gray shorts and my black tank top next to me on the bed. I nod my head at his gesture and slide my shirt over my shoulders. He watches me close as I swing both of my legs down from my bed and slide my cotton shorts up my thighs.

"What do you want to show me?" It's a little pathetic how excited I am.

"It's a surprise. I'll show you when we get there." He makes that smirk and it's as if my insides instantly melt.

"Where are we going?" Curiosity fills my mind as I make my way over to my closet and slide on my slip on Vans.

"Don't you know anything about surprises?" His smirk widens to his charming smile. My hair is a tangled mess of after sex curls and my makeup must be smeared all over my face but Alan stands with his arms across his chest looking at me with approval.

"You ready?" He asks, still with his charming smile still stretching across his face.

"Yeah, let me just grab my phone..." I watch how his whole aura changes. The color leaves from his cheeks and his face goes pale. Alan grabs my waist and pulls me into his chest before I can get to my nightstand.

"No need. We won't be gone that long." He whispers softly in my ear. *I never go anywhere without my phone. Anyone who knows me knows that.*

"Alan, I need my phone." My smiling facade isn't fooling him. He has to know that I'll be a nervous wreck without it.

"Thalia, it's late. No one is going to send you any messages and you won't have any notifications at this hour." He turns my body to face his. His body is pressed up against my chest and I can feel my heart racing. He looks down at the expensive looking watch on his wrist.

"If anything happens, I'll have mine we can use. I promise, you're safe with me. You won't need it." Alan grabs my hand and holds it against his chest. "Have I ever given you a reason not to trust me?"

I shake my head and offer an uncertain smile. *Deep breaths, Thalia. It's only a phone and he said we won't be gone long. It's Alan. I know him.* He waits for my uncertainty to subside and his whole persona goes back to how I know him. *My Alan.* With one unsure smile I turn on a switch and he is back to the way I know him best.

He takes my hand in his and leads me quickly out the front door, through the long hallway, and down the stairs. He moves in such long strides that we almost run through the cold drizzle 0f raindrops outside towards his car.

Like the gentleman he is, he eagerly opens my door, and I climb in. His eyes never leave me as I settle in my seat and he politely shuts my door behind me. My eyes follow his shadowed figure, walking around to his side of the car. His eyes meet mine as soon as he sits down. I've never seen this side of him before. His smile is infectious as he acts like an excited kid on Christmas morning.

"Put this on." He playfully hands me a black, silk sleeping mask.

"What's this?" I ask while trying to be equally as playful.

"What's it look like?" His tone stays the same. "What would a surprise be without a blind fold?" *Touché.* "Don't take it off. That's for me to do later." He gives me a wink before I slide it over my eyes. He waits to start the car until the mask is comfortably sitting over my eyes. My vision goes dark and that's when I hear the ignition start.

ALAN

It's almost funny how trusting Thalia is right now. The car slightly shakes while she sits in the passenger seat with her knee bouncing in anticipation. *I can't wait to witness the look on your face when you see what I have in store for you.*

"Are you excited?" I ask with humor in my voice. I keep my eyes focused on the road in front of me. *I know I am.*

"A little bit and a little nervous," she admits. Like a natural habit, she turns her head to face me when she talks.

"Nervous?" She reluctantly nods her head. "You're with me, remember. Nothing to be worried about." *You should be nervous, Listener. You should be running away from me, but you've fallen for my act. Stupid girl, you should have run away from me that night after we went to the diner. You should have looked the other way when I caught your gaze at The Neon Rose. I thought I was a measly insect caught in your web, but it is you who has fallen into mine.* My hands grip around the steering wheel until I can see my knuckles whiten. She smiles and does her best to keep her attention ahead.

"Not one for surprises, are you?" She shakes her head while still trying to maintain the act that she isn't full of unknowing anxiety. *I can see right through you.*

"Where are you taking me?" She slides her clammy palms up and down the uncovered skin on her thighs.

"What would a surprise be if I told you?" Out of the corner of my eye, I notice the wide smile that forms on her lips while she continues to face the uncertain path in front of her.

I notice her body tensing up when she hears the soft sound of gravel under the wheels. She stops moving her palms down her exposed skin and fidgets with the loose cotton of her shorts. Without any words, she questions my next move. She turns her head to face me when she feels the engine turn off.

"We're here," I announce playfully as I remove the keys from the ignition. Her hands grip the door handle as if she's trying to keep herself inside. I move my warm hand on the smooth skin of her upper thigh covered in goosebumps.

"Don't worry, Thalia. You're safe with me. I'll hold your hand and guide you inside." Her tight grip loosens and I watch as the muscles in her arms relax. "Good girl."

Her tight shoulders release and automatically rest against the back of the chair. *It's amazing how one phrase makes her practically melt.* I watch her become putty at my words. Slowly, I get out of my seat and shut the car door. *I love knowing how the anticipation of tonight eats away at her.* She startles when I slowly open her door, but willingly reaches for my hand, and I pull her into my chest. *If you were smart, you would start running.*

"You're alright. Just a few more steps." My voice is a guide towards the small storage unit that will soon be her hell on earth.

"I hope you didn't go through a lot of trouble in setting up this...whatever *this* is." Her laughter is loud in the small concrete space. *You have no fucking idea.*

"For you, it was worth it." Her smile is like red paint spread across her face and I can't wait to see how she looks when it dramatically changes shape. "Stay right here. I just need to unlock the door." She nods her head and does her best to keep balance after I let go of her hand.

I slide the small key in the space in the padlock and I push up the large, red rollup door to the storage unit. The body in the middle of the room is still strapped to the metal chair like the perfect gift I've prepared for my guest. Jace sits in the same position I left him in earlier. His body has slumped down a little but he's still secured to the chair. *Perfect.*

"Okay, ready?" Thalia's head turns like a confused dog while she listens for my footsteps on the concrete floor. I walk towards her and guide her by grabbing her shoulders, leading further inside.

"As I'll ever be, I guess. Where the hell did you take me that has a door that you have to slide up?" *So many fucking questions.*

"It's just a space I rented for this occasion. I thought we could do a bit of role playing." I bend down so my lips just barely touch the tip of her ear. My smile widens at the redness forming in her cheeks. *You have no fucking idea what awaits you.*

"Are you going to take off my mask?" You *keep trying to act so innocent with that sweet voice of yours, but I know who you really are.*

"Not yet." I kiss the top of her head and lead her to the empty chair next to our guest. Reluctantly, she sits down once her skin touches the cold, metal chair. Immediately, she comments on his smell. *Fuck.*

"Oh, shit. What the hell is that?!" Her nose turns up in disgust. *Nothing, just the rotting corpse of your dead best friend.*

"Oh, I'm sure it's nothing. Probably just a dead animal outside or something." *Or something.* "Have you ever been tied up before?" I ask with my lips still next to her ear.

"Once or twice." She smiles flirtatiously, and my body fills with rage and jealousy. I bite my lip until I can taste copper to help contain my anger. At this point, it's the only thing that urges me to keep playing this part in our uncomfortable foreplay. *Hold it back, play the part.*

"Really, Listener?" I pause. "This time, it might be a little different."

I stare down at her breasts and I watch how they move up and down. Her rapid heartbeat is almost noticeable as it vibrates in her chest under her milky white skin.

"Oh, Thalia. This is going to be so much fun. Sit still in this chair for me." She nods without saying a word. The souls of my shoes echo again through the unit as I walk back to the table behind us. I survey over the tools in front of me and I grab three zip ties. My heart almost stops when I turn behind to look at her in her chair. So willing to obey me, unknowing, and so *fucking* trusting. It beats faster as I walk up close and kneel behind her. *I'm doing this. I'm really fucking doing this.* Gently, I grab both of her wrists and run the smooth surface of the plastic zip tie up her skin from her small wrists to up to her forearm. Her arms shudder at my touch.

"If this is too tight, let me know." I stare at the back of her head as she nods again and I wrap the zip tie around both wrists and secure them in place. "Comfortable?" I ask, trying to sound like I care. *I can't let myself care about how you feel if I want to break you like you broke me.* My uncertain thoughts are pushed to the back of my mind when I hear her soft voice.

"Yes," she nearly whispers.

"Good." I kiss her cold skin right above the zip tie. Next, I move to her ankles, restraining each one to both of the legs of the chair. She jumps as I run my hands up her bare calves. More goosebumps form at the feel of my palm on her skin. Memories of earlier come to the forefront of my mind, and I can feel my dick straining against the fabric that keeps it in. *That's not what tonight is about.* Scolding myself and adjusting myself before I slowly stand up and walk around to the front of her.

"You look so good like this. Exactly where I want you." She runs her tongue over her lower lip at my words and releases a small whimper as her thighs shift in her seat. *You poor thing. You have no idea what you've gotten yourself into.* "This is going to be a night you'll never forget. Just a little fuck toy and her master." *She looks so helpless right now. I wonder how long it will take her to scream.*

The longer I stand watching her so helpless, the more her shoulders tense. She practically jumps in her seat when she hears the door of the storage unit come down at full force.

"Relax." I laugh and lock the padlock, securing us both in the small space. "You're in good hands."

I walk slowly to the white card table behind her chair and look over the array of tools. My switchblade stands out under the harsh lighting. I move my fingers over the smooth black handle.

She startles in her seat as I unlatch my trusty switchblade causing her chair to scrape on the concrete. It's a harsh, new sound that reverberates in the small space. I can't help but let out another small laugh. My vision fixates on the sharp edge and the point as I stand in front of white table. The reflection of her behind me bounces off the metal surface as if it tells me my next move. My fingertip slowly runs down the edge from the tip of the blade to near the top of the handle. The blade closes with one click of a button and I slide it into my pocket. *No better time than now to tell her how much she broke me.*

Mentally, I go over my next steps as if I'm reading over a check-list. I move to the front of the room and set up the tripod I had previously used for Jace and the girl I picked up from the bar the other night. My phone fits in the rightful space. *This image will be for my eyes only.* I can only imagine how many times I will replay tonight's scene of just the two of us. The tripod is set up in just the right way so we are both in view of my camera. Once my phone is ready, I eagerly hit record. *Perfect.*

"Tell me what you're thinking," I say, breaking the tense silence in the room.

"I honestly don't know what to think." She laughs. *I love the way you laugh while in the state you're in. Just wait until you see what I have planned.* I keep my gaze on her smeared, bright red lips. They're a nice contrast to the black blindfold covering her eyes.

"Tell me, Listener, when you were a child did your parents ever tell you not to play with knives?" I ask, walking closer to her chair. I spin the tip on my index finger as she anxiously shakes her head.

"What do you mean?" It's cute the way her voice shakes at her question.

"Have you ever been enticed by the blade, so much that you graze your skin with the sharp edge...just to feel...something?"

"No. I can't say that I have." Her voice still shakes. *I like watching the way you squirm.* Her chair creaks as she sits up straight and the muscles in her calves flex. I examine her body—how it tenses in her seat as I move towards her tied up body.

I feel the cold surface on my knees through the fabric of my slacks as I kneel in front of her. I look up at her as if she's a deity to worship. In a way I am. I am worshiping the time we had together, preserving the moments with her that will stay in my mind. The way she made my heart fucking jump out of my chest, only to be contained by the buttons on my shirt. Honoring the times she looked at me like I was a fucking delicacy she would devour and run her tongue over every last bit.

I start removing her shoes and throw them to the side. Like a natural reflex, she moves her head down as I move my hands up her skin from her feet to the tops of her thighs. I feel her tense muscles release the closer I get to the hem of her shorts.

"There you go. Relax for me." I lightly press kisses on her skin and slide my hands back down her legs. I replace one hand with the smooth, flat side of the blade.

"When I was a child, my mother always told me to never play with knives. Sure, it was in her nature that she wanted to keep me safe. Even in her materialistic stupor, she had the motherly instincts of a spider, but she had good intentions. Her waspy lifestyle led her to believe that her child needed to act and look a certain way to keep up the appearance that we were a normal and wealthy family. Wealthy, yes, but even as a child, I was never what you would call normal." I continue to glide the flat surface of the blade up her shin.

"Unfortunately for her, and the rest of my superficial family, I had become interested in blades of all kinds. She and my father were appalled by my new found love of weaponry. I would stare at the shiny metal and how it looked under the sheath.

When I became a teenager, I would buy them and sneak them into my bedroom when they were away at some sort of town meeting or fencing lesson. I had a collection. I never used them. Well, not often anyway." I keep my slow pace of sliding the flat side of the blade up past her knee and onto her lower thigh as I continue with my story.

"I never used my knives on anyone or anything. I just appreciated the way the sharp edge cut so easily through the pads of my fingers. It was so fascinating how easily I could control the pain it caused and the depth of the cut along my skin." The tip of my switchblade sits just slightly under the opening of her cotton shorts. I pay close attention to the way the goosebumps quickly form again along her skin. The flat metal surface of the knife makes her shift slightly in her seat.

"Usually, they were stored away out of fear that I would get caught. Once my mother found the collection hidden in the one place I thought she would never look, my underwear drawer. You know what she did? She removed them. How would it look if her baby boy had nicks and cuts all over him from the knives he was so attached to?" I look up at Thalia while her breathing becomes heavier. I watch her chest move quickly as I carry on with the history of my fascination.

"Has anyone marked you before?" I ask, moving the knife gently into the opening between her pale skin and the gray fabric.

"What do you mean?" She asks, trying to stay as still as possible.

"Just what I said. Has anyone marked you as their own?" I turn the knife on the sharpened edge and glide it back down her leg.

"You mean has someone fucking carved their name into me?" Her voice raises and she jolts in her seat.

"Precisely." I come to a stop at her ankle, right where the stem of her rose tattoo starts.

"No." Her voice is no longer shaky. It's almost a command, like she's reprimanding a child or a fucking pet. *She's not in the position to tell me no. I'm not the one strapped to a chair.*

"Relax, Thalia. What's wrong? You don't want people knowing you belong to me?" I ask, now spinning the tip of the blade on my index finger.

"It's not that...I-I-" My blood starts to get hot as she stumbles over her words.

"You, what?" I move the knife through my fingers, and I stare at the reflective blade, allowing the small weapon to go under and over each one. Her red hair reflects off the blade in different angles.

"I've just never had anything like that before..." The panic in her voice raises.

"So you've been tied up before but you've never played with knives? Interesting. Don't worry, Thalia. It won't be so bad. It's not near as bad as I'm sure this tattoo felt. Sure, it hurts but the pain goes away, and I'll be here to clean you up." I look up and notice her cheeks flush again.

"What do you think people are going to say if they see your name carved into my skin?" Her nervous laugh is almost adorable. It's cute how she tries her best to hide her real feelings of fear and anxiousness, but I can sense how she feels. I know exactly why she's trying to hide any evidence of me. I just want to hear her say it. *Say the fucking words, Thalia. Just admit what you did.*

"Who said it has to be my name? It can be something meaningful between us. Don't worry, I can make my mark hidden. No one would be able to see it. Well, unless they see you naked." I laugh at the ridiculous notion. *I'm the last person who will see all of you. I will make sure of that.*

"Why do you care what anyone thinks about us?" I tap the flat side of the blade on her shin, and I wait for her answer. She flinches under the cold knife. Her kneecap jolts when the sharp tip hits the bone.

"It's not that I care what people think..." Her answer trails off and I am becoming exceedingly impatient.

"Oh, no. It's not what just *anyone* thinks... is it?" I stop my knife from hitting her skin. I move the blade and run the tip along my bottom lip. "You're worried about a specific *someone* finding out about me. You're worried that a certain *someone* will find out you agreed to go with me to that diner, that you've invited me into your home multiple times, and that you begged me so sweetly to make you come." Her bottom lip quivers and I watch the tears fall down her cheeks from under her blind fold. "Isn't that right, Listener?" I wait for her answer.

"But I wonder who it is. Who else could you be talking to?" Another pause.

"No, that's not what we need to be asking, because fuck, that could be anyone." I softly slide my fingertips up the long stem of her tattoo. "Who else could be taking up your sweet, valuable time? Who else's voice makes you so fucking deliciously wet? Who, baby? Can you tell me what other deep voice makes you spread your legs so fucking easily?"

I grip the middle of her inner thigh squeezing one of the inked roses on her skin. Her body shakes in the chair when my hold becomes tighter.

"That's it, isn't it?" *Enough with the fucking unanswered questions. Just shake your head and sob.* "ISN'T IT, THALIA?! FUCKING ANSWER THE QUESTION!" My causal tone turns goes loud. Her tears fall from her cheeks to her lap. "Are you fucking Lee?!" She shakes her head quickly. "You're not fucking him?! Don't lie to me. Fucking admit it, Thalia!" Her chair continues to shake when her body jumps at the loud volume of my voice.

"Yes!" she cries.

"How long? Tell me, how long have you been with him?!" I ask, looking up at her, trying to keep the hot tears from falling down my face. "I swear to God, Thalia. If you were with him before you brought me back to your place..." I do my best to mask my heavy emotions, but they're at the forefront of my mind. *Hold it in, Alan. Keep it together.* I can't help the raised amplification of my tone in the small space.

"A few weeks." She answers through her pathetic sobs.

"Weeks?! What the fuck, Thalia! What was I to you then? Did I even fucking mean anything to you, or was I just there for you to use when you couldn't see him? Was I just a fucking convenience for you?!" Another question unanswered. *Just sit there and fucking cry. Crying isn't going to get you out of this.*

"Did you think you could fuck both of us and everything would be okay? Did you think you wouldn't have to eventually choose between us? You can't possibly think we weren't going to find out you were riding both of our dicks!" My loud voice bounces off the walls in the small space.

"I didn't think we were anything serious! It was just sex!" She cries.

Just sex?

"Just sex? Are you fucking serious? Damn it, Thalia, you know what you and I have is more than just sex! I see the way you look at me. You fucking understand me like no one else does! We have something more than that, and I know you fucking feel it too!

"I did everything so I could have you! Fuck! How could you not see that?!" My emotions take the best of me and the tears I try to hold in fall down my face.

"Is that what you plan on telling him too, or just me? Would you tell Lee that it's just sex?" She lowers her head as if she can see the black and white squares on her Vans. *Silence is the loudest answer.*

"You know, I never thought I would have to compete with my best friend, the one person that I would have considered a brother.

Hell, he's the only real family I have left." I tap the flat surface of the blade on her ankle. "I guess, there is a first time for everything."

I press the sharp edge of my switchblade to her skin. I bite down on my lower lip when the tip of my knife carves deep into the green ink in her ankle. The crimson looks magnificent seeping into the bright color.

"Ahhh! What the fuck, Alan?!" She screams.

"Oh, that's it, Thalia. You know I like when you scream my name. Scream for me, baby." I mock. My knife digs deeper into her skin and further up the tattoo. "You think you could make that noise for me again?"

"Fuck!" She cries out in pain instead of the pleasurable screams I'd grown to crave. I think I crave this even more. No, I know I do.

"Oh, yes, baby. Just like that. Do you scream like that when you're with him?" I pause for an answer but she only lets out another strangled cry. "Is that a no?" I mock again as her cries get louder. I carve deep into the long stem up her calf.

"Tell me, Listener. Did you beg him to make you come, or was it when you were only with me? Did you rub that pretty clit when you thought about the both of us?"

I continue to taunt her while the blade goes deeper into her tattoo. Her screams get louder as her head rolls back towards the ceiling.

"You know, I'm glad you finally admitted what you did. If you would have lied to me, I would have made this night so much more painful," I explain calmly through her ear piercing screeching. I watch intently as the knife carves into her shin. Her body shakes in her chair from the pain. "Careful, you don't want me coloring outside of the lines." I look up while I continue to carve her skin like I've watched my father carve up the turkey every Thanksgiving. I notice her red cheeks, beads of sweat falling down her forehead, and her black makeup mixing with her smeared red lipstick. *God, I love how shattered you look right now.*

"When I saw both of you in your parking garage together, I knew deep down something was going on. Something told me not to follow you into your apartment." I don't give her time to respond and I continue engraving her skin, now closer to her thigh.

"But did I listen? Absolutely fucking not." More of her blood pours from her leg the deeper I move the edge of the blade into her skin. Her loud sobs are like a fucking melody in my ears. Thalia's tissue between the layers of snow white skin reflect off of the blade. I stare intently at her blood spilling between the opened space.

"Don't move, I could cut an artery. I wouldn't want you to bleed out before you see your surprise." I tease. "There. Perfect. You look so fucking good with my mark engraved into your flesh."

I stop carving once I reach the end of the stem, right where the top red rose begins. I slide the sharp edge of the blade in the middle of my tongue. Her blood mixed with the cold metal feel of the blade tastes euphoric. She continues crying quietly to herself, and I rest my knees in the small puddles of her blood on the hard floor. My dick gets harder in my slacks as I stare at the work of art in front of me.

I lean further into the puddles of crimson, and move my lips to the bottom of the tattoo on her ankle. I look up at my new masterpiece and my eyes fixate on the black makeup running down her cheeks while my tongue runs up the stem of her bloody tattoo. Like a man dying of thirst, I lap up the blood that falls out of her fresh wound. Her head falls back and she lets out a quiet whimper when I continue to move up the long line of green and red.

Without swallowing I collect all of her blood in my mouth. Once reaching the top of the stem, I squeeze her cheeks and force her parted lips to open, spitting all of her blood into her mouth. I feel her flinch when I grip the back of her hair and pull her in for a forced kiss. Both of our tongues search for one another through her pool of blood that stays in her mouth. I force her lips closed with my forefinger and my thumb after we finish our passionate blood filled kiss.

"Swallow." I watch her throat as she swallows a combination of her blood and our spit. "That's my good little whore." I praise and mockingly tap her cheek.

I catch myself in the view of the camera as I walk over to the tripod. My white button up shirt and my dark gray slacks are both stained with her blood. Watching myself intently through the phone, I clean the blood off the lenses on my glasses. *This is who I am now.* A small smirk forms on my face and I end the recording.

"What do you say we have a break?" I grab my phone and scroll through the series of apps.

"What are you going to do to me?" She asks, breaking the intense few minutes of silence. Her voice is shaky and broken. *Fuck, I love how you sound right now. So fragile and so easy to destroy. Just like you fucking destroyed me.*

"That depends on how much of a good girl you're going to be tonight." Her head leans forward and I wonder how her tear filled eyes look under her mask. "Are you going to be a good girl for me,

Thalia?" She nods her head, and I can hear the sobs she makes under her panting.

"That's what I like to hear." I walk closer to her chair and kneel in front of her, rubbing the palms of my hands down her exposed thighs again. She winces at the feel of my fingers brushing over parts of her fresh wound near the hem of her cotton shorts. "Are you ready to see your surprise?" I'm so close, my nose almost touches hers.

She nods reluctantly.

"I need your words, Thalia." My grip tightens on her skin. She hisses when my thumb digs deeper into the gash on her inner thigh.

"Yes." Her voice still shakes and I fucking love every bit of it.

"Yes, *who*, Listener?"

"Yes, Alan."

"Fuck, Thalia. Even now, I still love the way you say my name." I lean in closer now with my forehead touching hers. "You know, now that I think about it, I don't think you're ready for your surprise."

"Please, Alan."

"Oh, Thalia, you know I love it when you ask so nicely."

"Will you let me go after you show me?" *She asks so innocently, but it's all an act. It's always been a fucking act.*

"No, baby. You're not going anywhere. You're mine now." Her shaky voice turns into more sobs, and I can't get enough. "This is the last place you're going to see, and I'm going to be the man who gets to watch life leave those beautiful eyes of yours." Her whole body vibrates in her chair matching the rhythm of her loud cries.

"Shhh, Thalia. Don't worry. I'm going to make it so fucking worth it." I rub my hands down her arms.

"Please, just let me go," she pleads.

"Now, you know I can't do that."

"Why? Why can't you just let me go. I won't tell anyone you brought me here."

"Oh, I know you won't. Because when I'm done with you, those full, pretty red lips of yours will be of no use." I pull her head in close and I force her lips on mine.

"No more of your sweet sounds to escape them." Another forceful kiss. "No more of your breathtaking kisses." I force another kiss while trying to hold in more of my tears. I bite her bottom lip until I can taste more of her blood. *I have to do this. There is no backing out now. She broke me into a million fucking pieces and I need to do the same to her.*

LEE

My sheets gather under me while I toss and turn in my bed. *What the fuck?* I can't sleep, and I stare up at my tall ceilings. I turn my head to look out the large windows in my room and stare down at the lights from the city underneath me. My mind floods with thoughts of the other night with Thalia. She looked so good the way she moved her hips on my lap. *The way she grinds her clit against my dick in just the right way makes it hard to fucking think straight.* I remember how great her tits looked when she moved in perfect rhythm. I can still hear her sexy moans from those red full lips of hers. *I would love to have them on every inch of my body.* My dick gets hard under my sheets when I reminisce about the sweet memory. *Damn it!* I need to see her right the fuck now.

I reach for my phone on my nightstand next to my bed. The bright numbers on the screen nearly blind me. Two A.M. on a Sunday night. The Neon Rose is closed on Sundays. *She should still be awake, right?*

Hey, Sweetheart

I send her a quick text and wait impatiently for what seems like a few minutes for her response. *Staring at my phone isn't going to make her respond any quicker.* I send her another text.

Are you up, Beautiful?

A few more minutes pass and she doesn't respond. I continue to impatiently wait for a text back. *Fuck it.*

I climb out of my bed and grab a pair of black, drawstring sweatpants from my closet floor. My black tee shirt that sat in the same pile of clothes goes on next. *If she won't answer her phone, I'll just go to her apartment. She seems to like my surprise visits.*

I grab my phone and keys and slide them into my side pocket, before quickly pulling on my black Converse high tops. The door shuts loudly behind me. At this point, I don't give a shit about the other people in this place. *I need to see my girl.*

The drive to her apartment feels like a fucking eternity. For the first time in my life, the fast-paced life in New York City has a feeling of slow motion. I speed my way into her small parking garage and practically jog to her building when I get out of my car. I am lucky enough to be let in by another resident coming in for the night. He holds the door open for me like I live in the building.

Lucky me. I nod like the fucking gentleman that I am, and continue my way up the stairs that lead to the hallway.

I walk through the long hall until I reach apartment door *6C*. It seems like a perpetual trek as I pass through the long row of identical doors. It's as if time stays at its slow pace with each step closer to her unit. My body gets hot, making the hair on my arms stand tall. I turn the door knob, half expecting it to be locked. It squeaks loudly into her unit then shuts softly behind me. *She must be asleep; all the lights are off.*

Quietly, I walk back down the tiny hallway towards her bedroom. *That's weird.* Her bedroom door is wide open. *She must be dead to the world if she didn't hear me come in.*

"Sweetheart, are you asleep?" I ask the dark bed in front of me. The shadows from the lights outside bounce off her black sheets. *Wait...are these sheets fucking empty?* I throw her loose sheets from her bed. *What the fuck? Where the hell would she be?*

I notice a small light shining from her nightstand. *Is that her phone? Why the hell wouldn't she have her phone?* I stare down at the locked screen, noticing a few notifications popping up from her social media accounts . Her passcode is ingrained in my memory. I've watched her countlessly enter it on the nights we were together. I scan over the notifications and look over the missed text messages I sent and all of her others. *It's not disturbing her privacy when I'm trying to fucking find her.*

The messages we've sent each other make me smile. *This girl has made me sentimental.* I move over to her other messages. A few from Janice that are mostly about work. Several messages that have gone unanswered to Jace. *What a prick.* Several to Alan. *Why the hell does she need to talk to Alan so fucking much?* My blood boils as I read through their conversation.

"Are you fucking kidding me, Thalia?!" I yell like she's in the room with me and continue to scroll down to the last message from their conversation.

Alan:

> I'm here, Listener.

Thalia:

> Come on up. I'll meet you at the door.

Why was Alan here, and why the hell did she let him in?

I know one thing, I'm getting my fucking answers.

⟨🎙⟩ALAN

Her body shivers in the cold chair. *Probably from the loss of blood and the lack of heat flowing through the small area*

"Are you sure you're ready for your surprise, baby?" I ask, holding her head in my hands. She nods the best she can and continues to cry. Her tears fall down her cheeks and land in my palms.

"Okay. I want to warn you though, surprise might not be the right word." Her head falls forward when I move to stand up. "Maybe *reunion* would be a better description."

"Wh- What do you mean?" she asks with a shaky voice. My heels click along the hard concrete as I walk back over to the tripod holding my phone.

"You'll see." I press the record button. *I cannot miss the opportunity to document this.* I walk back over to her shaking, broken, and bloody body.

"I'm going to give you a countdown." I say walking back behind her. Thalia's body trembles as I put my hands close to the thin silk strap wrapped around the top of her head.

"You ready, baby?" She reluctantly nods her head. "Okay. Three." I move my fingers through her tangled curls. "Two." My fingers stop at the smooth surface of the silk strap. "One." I quickly pull the mask up over her eyes.

Her breathing picks up as if she has been gagged instead of blind folded. She's like a mouse in a trap as she looks around the room. She stops when she notices her best friend strapped to the chair next to her. "Jace?" She cries quietly. I watch with my arms across my chest as the nonresponsive Jace sits in the chair with his head bowed.

"I'm sorry, Listener. He's been at a loss of words lately," I laugh. *She doesn't quite get the joke.*

"What did you do to him?" *More fucking tears.* "Did you fucking drug him?" She asks louder. *How can she not see he's fucking dead?*

"Oh, baby. He's not drugged."

"What do you mean?" She asks. *Still not comprehending, I see.*

I walk over to the slumped over corpse in the chair. The black zip ties around his wrist begin to sink further into his rotting flesh.

"Well, Thalia, let's see. If he isn't responding to your pathetic little cries, and hasn't been drugged, what do you think happened?" *More cries.* "Thalia. Stop crying and use your fucking words!"

"Did you kill him?!" Her cries turn into loud screams. *There's my girl.*

"What the fuck do you think?" I yell back and remove my switch-blade from my pocket. With one push of a button, the blade quickly unlatches from its sheath. With what seems like all of the force that I have, I stab Jace's leg through the rancid denim on his outer thigh. The clotted blood that leaks from the open cut is immaculate. The dark red fluid flows like thick oil on his jeans. The look she gives her dead best friend is full of disgust and sadness. I watch intently as she turns her head and vomits on the floor next to her chair.

"Oh, don't be like that. I thought you would be so excited to see him." I sit down on my knees in front of Jace and slice open the black zip ties around each ankle. His body begins to slide off the metal chair, only being propped up by his arms wrapped around the back of the chair. Thalia screams as his lifeless, dark brown eyes look up at her while half of his body slides down the seat. "They always scream." I inform her nonchalantly moving to the back of the metal backing.

"They?" She asks quietly.

"Oh, she fucking speaks." I look over at her tear and makeup smeared face.

"What do you mean, they?"

"The people I've killed." I squat down behind Jace and slide the sharp blade through the zip tie that holds his wrists together. His limp arms fall to his sides. A loud sound of his dead weight falls onto the hard floor below him.

"You've killed... people?" Her voice continues to shake.

"Of course. Do you really think Jace is the only one?" I stand up and grab my folded plastic tarp and charged mini saw from the table behind us. She watches as I scan over the number of items strategically placed in a long row.

"Why?"

"Why what, Thalia?" I ask pulling the body laying on the floor in front of her feet.

"Why did you kill?" She looks at me while I spread out the clear tarp on the floor.

"For you, baby." I admit while smoothing over the wrinkles in the plastic.

"I never asked you to kill anyone," she cries.

"Oh, I know." I look up at her while on my knees. "Call it an offering, or a gift if you will." I stand up and move Jace's body over the tarp.

"Who did you kill, for me I mean?" *More fucking questions.* I walk over to my phone and press the option to stop recording.

 **LEE**

I've never driven to Alan's house quicker than in all the years I've known him. The lights from the large city buildings shine through my dark tinted windows as I drive through the many cars on the busy road. My blood feels like it's boiling with every shift I make. *She let him touch her. She fucking let him touch her! After I told her how I felt, she fucking let him touch her. I knew I should have never let another broad get under my skin.* My thoughts repeat the same phrases over and over until I reach his gated community.

Alan's house is dark aside from the light coming from above the oven in the kitchen.

"Alan, what the fuck?!" I yell as I park my car and slam my door. *As if the motherfucker can hear me.* I walk up to the front door and jiggle the locked handle. Luckily for me, Alan gave me a spare key when he first moved into this place.

My hands shake as I slide the key in the lock.

"You better be here, you asshole!" I yell while walking in the doorway. I follow it up with the loud slam of the front door. I look around the fucker's empty house and I get stopped in my tracks when I notice his kitchen. His cabinets are completely shattered. I mean, there is wood and shards of glass all over the tile.

"What the hell happened, Alan!?" I yell again and continue to search his house. *Leaving a mess like this, this isn't him.* "Ashley! Where the fuck is your husband?" *No sign of her either.*

I stomp through the house like a madman, searching his bedroom first.

"If I catch you fucking my girl, I'll..."

His bedroom door opens to his bed already pristinely made with no signs of wrinkles in the comforter. *What a psycho.* I search everywhere in this wing of his house. Nothing but a destroyed kitchen and empty rooms. There is only one more place to check.

The fucking studio.

THALIA

His eyes shoot daggers into mine as he stalks back towards my chair. My body shakes from the intense amount of pain from the large gash he made in my leg. The burning pain of my large wound, or *mark* as Alan calls it, stays constant against the cold, metal chair. My arms and legs are nearly frozen by the lack of heat in Alan's storage unit. I wait for his response and my earlier question goes unanswered.

"Who have you killed for me, Alan?"

He continues to look up at me while he kneels next to Jace's unmoving body.

"Well, Jace of course." His eyes scan down my form while he removes Jace's Vans. I can feel the bile start to climb up my throat after hearing the matter of fact tone in his voice. "I started with Ruban Ara."

"Who?" I ask through my loud sobs.

"Ruben Ara." Alan looks up at me. "He tried to touch you, Thalia." He throws Jace's shoe to the side and my thoughts start to connect.

"You killed him because he hit on me?" My cries turn into yells.

"Look at you, Listener. Finally fucking paying attention. "

He looks down at Jace and removes his other shoe. He tugs hard on the sole and throws it out of the way.

"You killed him, removed his eyes and his fingers, and set him up in the alley because he wanted to sleep with me? Do you realize how ridiculous that is?" The volume of my tone gets louder, filling the tense space in between us. He lets out a small laugh and pulls off one of Jace's black socks. *How is this at all funny?*

"How long ago did you kill Jace?" I look down at Jace's golden brown skin now a shade of dark gray.

"How long has he been missing?" He throws the socks to the side near the shoes. *How can this be so easy for you?* "I killed him the night you thought he was ignoring your calls and your texts. Wrapped him up in that roll of carpet over there." He points to a large pile of stained, tan carpet in the corner of the unit. "After that, I stored him in the maintenance closet of your apartment complex." The hot bile that I was once able to swallow fills up my throat. More vomit adds to the pile next to my chair. "And before you ask why, he was going to give you drugs, Thalia. There was no way I was going to visit you in prison." He gently lays Jace's feet down on the tarp.

He clears his throat and pulls at the waistband of Jace's jeans. "I first used this saw on Ashley's body." He looks up at me, pausing his thought process to notice my reaction. "Cutting into her flesh was something unexplainable." The look on his face is comparable to a man reminiscing over a happy memory. *What the fuck?!*

"Who's Ashley, Alan?" My throat goes dry. *Jace was one victim too many.*

"She was my wife, *Thalia*," he answers, adding an emphasis on my name. "She doesn't matter. She never really mattered. Our marriage was more of financial convenience." He pauses while sliding the denim down Jace's thighs. "She was in my way of getting where I wanted to be with you."

"You killed your wife?" I feel the tears start to form in my eyes.

"Yes, I did. I killed her so I could have *you*." His face contorts into a new expression from him, one that I've never seen before. I notice the bright green eyes that have hooked me in so many times have become glossy.

He clears his throat and starts to move the bottom of Jace's tee shirt up his chest.

"Anyone else?"

"One more, baby." He stands up and walks to his phone, propped up on the black tripod.

"You killed four people?" My dry heaves mix with heavy cries.

"All for you, Listener. *Everything* I do is for you."

I watch him scroll through his phone as if he just told me about the weather forecast, not his admission to murder. He opens up his phone to the local news source.

"Just in time. It looks like they found her just where I put her." Alan turns his phone around and shows me the screen. Police surround the alley next to The Neon Rose. Her body is mostly surrounded by law enforcement, and I'm only able to see her pale slender arm in the small space between people. "Let's see what they have to say, shall we?" He turns up the volume and the woman's voice on the evening news grows louder.

"Police are reporting a new body discovered just outside The Neon Rose Lounge." Her voice trails off, and I focus on Alan. He turns the phone screen towards himself and stares intently. He rubs his chin while looking at the scene as if he's taking in constructive criticism from their news report. "Police have no suspects at this time but are calling the killer The Shadow. The vic-" The news reporter's voice cuts off as he locks the screen.

"The Shadow. That's interesting." He props the phone back into the tripod.

"Why her?" Reluctantly I ask. *Do I really want to know the answer to this question?*

"Because she wasn't you." I watch as his green eyes go glossy once again.

ALAN

Aside from Jace's boxers, all of his clothes have been removed. This will make the separation of his limbs so much easier for disposal. I reach for my charged mini saw and place the blade against the gray colored skin on his ankles. Thalia stops the incision by asking more of her emotionally charged questions. *What now?*

"Stop!" She yells before I press the on button on the device. "What are you going to do to him?" She stares down and I can't help the wide smile that moves across my face.

"Well, Thalia. What do you *think* I am going to do to him?" I let out a loud sigh and wait for her response.

I am left with nothing but silence.

"I'm going to play, and you're going to watch." I stand on my knees and lean in closer to her trembling body so that my forehead touches hers. "I'm going to watch your heart break just as you broke mine. I'm going to make you feel what I feel as I cut your best friend's body in to tiny fucking pieces just like you did to me." I move back to the other side of the lifeless corpse in between Thalia and I.

I stare down at the blade as it cuts through Jace's tender flesh and his bone. His blood does not flow as easily as Ashley's did. His coagulated crimson spills slower out of the large separation between his ankle and his leg. The blade slices so freely through the tender, decomposing skin. I brace myself as it hits his brittle bone and watch as it satisfyingly separates on the tarp below him.

"Next ankle." I look up at Thalia's wide hazel tear filled eyes with her mouth agape. "Keep looking at me like that with your mouth wide open, I'll be more than happy to stuff it full." I give her a wink and watch her neck as she swallows. I lean over Jace and slide the blade through his other ankle. Thalia's face contorts into disgust as she looks at another set of his limbs separate.

Her eyes are still filled with shock as I graze the blade of the mini saw up his thigh. Her chest rises and falls with every heavy breath she takes. She winces as she watches the blade stop at his pelvis.

"Closing your eyes won't make this process go any faster." I turn on the mini saw and wait for her to peel them open. "Open your eyes, Thalia."

"No. I can't watch you do this anymore." Her cries are growing tiresome.

"OPEN YOUR FUCKING EYES!" I yell, and she nearly jumps out of her seat. "There's a good girl."

I move the blade into his hip joint and stare down at the dark red blood covered layers of skin tissue, separating from each other.

"Oh, baby. I wish you could see this. It's like a work of art. So many intricate parts holding him together, just easily breaking off. It's nothing like you've ever seen before. I mean, I have of course..."

"How long are you going to make me watch you do this?" She sounds so broken and I love every way that her voice quavers.

"I guess that depends on how long you're strapped to that chair." I move the blade of my saw up Jace's body, gently sliding the blade on his skin. "If you're wanting to speed up this process..." My blade stops just under Jace's chin. I start the saw and the small chain moves through the flesh at the top of his neck. I stare intently as his blood flows over the blade and runs down the serrated bone. His head rolls back on the tarp. His neck, torso and arms are all that I have left to remove in the human jigsaw that lays in front of me.

I look over his body. Thalia's gagging sounds fill the concrete room we are contained to. Jace's head fits perfectly in the palm of my hand. His lifeless brown eyes roll back towards the ceiling.

"It's fascinating, really." I begin. "There are tiny bits of copper mixed in with his dark brown irises." Her gags turn into screams when I toss his head onto her exposed lap.

I walk slowly through his long halls and notice the light on and the door wide open to the studio. *Everything in his house is dark except for this room.*

"Alan?!" I yell down the empty hall. *No answer.*

"Hey, I think you and I need to talk about a few things." I say in a calmer tone while keeping my slow stride down the hallway until I reach the empty studio. Everything is kept in the same place as it usually is. The only question is, why the hell is the door open and where the hell is Alan?

I continue to look around the empty room for anything that can give me answers as to where the two of them are. *Why the hell is the light on, why has he been talking to my girl, and why the fuck doesn't Thalia have her cell?* While Still looking around the empty room, I notice my desk is cleaned off and prepared for our next episode. *If he's been fucking Thalia, there isn't going to be another episode.*

"Wait a second. What the fuck is this?" I ask aloud. *No one is here to answer me.* Alan's desk is cleared except for one piece of paper. The top of the paper, reading STOROVOX INVOICE FOR STORAGE UNIT in big letters.

"This isn't for the podcast. Why the fuck would he need a storage unit? His house is big enough to keep all of his shit here." *This isn't like Alan. Why hasn't he filed this away, and why is it in the studio?*

"None of this makes fucking sense." I stare down at the address in the top left corner of the invoice. *If he doesn't have her here, and she isn't at her apartment, then maybe...* My thoughts trail off. It's a stretch, but at this point, it's the only clue I've got.

"If you're here, I will fucking find you." I grip the piece of paper, making it ball up in my hand.

My mind races and the only thing I care about is finding my girl. The address to the storage unit is at the forefront of my mind. My strides get longer and I practically sprint out of the lit studio and towards the front door. I turn on the car, type the address into my phone, and quickly speed out of the long driveway.

"Why the hell would he take her to a fucking storage unit?" I ask myself, trying to connect the dots.

The directions to the facility take me down a long and dark country road.

"What in Deliverance is this shit?" I shine my brights down the long stretch and I see nothing but trees on either side of me. "It's like I'm living in a fucking horror movie."

My speed increases as I press harder on the gas, moving as fast I can along the long empty road.

ALAN

Fuck, her ear piercing screams are getting to me. Maybe I should just kill her and get it over with. *No, I'm not ready to see her go.* Thalia stares down at Jace's head in her lap, with a constant shrill tone to her voice. I watch her eyes widen with fear and sadness as the back of his head fits perfectly in between her thighs.

"Screaming isn't going to magically make his head roll off your lap." I walk around her chair to the back of the table and look over the materials. "Ahh, there they are." I say with a shit eating grin while I grab the new package of black trash bags.

The look of shock doesn't leave her face. Her extreme reactions are a new form of entertainment I could watch reruns of over and over again. I open the new package and continue to stare as her face changes from disgust to panic.

"Oh, don't you think that's enough, Listener? I mean, don't you think at this point, you're being a little *dramatic*?" I interrupt her loud, pathetic noises, kneeling down with a brand new trash bag next to the partially disassembled body in front of me.

"I had to cut Ashley's body into smaller pieces." I explain, gently placing Jace's ankle into the first trash bag. "Maybe, since the decomposition process has started to take over, Jace's body will be more flexible."

I add another portion of his leg in the black trash bag, staring down at the remaining torso and arms laying in front of me.

"Maybe..." I stroke my chin, trying to piece together his human puzzle. "He is small enough, I could always throw all of him in one bag. What do you think?" I ask Thalia and watch more of her vomit fall down the front of her chin. Drops of her bile fall on top of Jace's pink buzzed hair. "Such a messy girl you are." She looks at me with fear in her eyes. *Good.*

My hand grabs the back of his head, missing the drips of Thalia's vomit.

"Poor Jace. If he had made better life choices, his head wouldn't be in my hands right now." The bloody gaping hole under his chin looks almost inviting. Thalia's eyes are on me while I examine her friend's decapitated head.

"What the hell are you doing?" Her loud question almost breaks me out of my gaze. *Almost.* She watches me closely push my hand deep inside.

To my surprise, my large hand is a comfortable fit inside Jace's severed head. The cold, clotting blood feels like a protective slime that covers all of my hand. I strategically move my hand so my thumb sits nicely along his jawbone. My fingertips press deep into his skin tissue above his lips. His mouth moves in sync with my movements.

"It's time to say goodbye, Thalia." His lids half open look up at her large, tear filled hazel ones. I move his mouth open and shut as I mimic his voice.

"Please, don't make me do this," she pleads. She does her best to hold down more bile that gathers in her throat.

"Listener, don't be rude. This is going to be the last time you'll see your best friend. Is that any way to act?" I turn my wrist to face me, adding more to my new ventriloquist act. Her eyes close and she shakes her head. "Open your eyes and tell him goodbye."

"Goodbye, Jace."

"Goodbye, Thalia," my decapitated head hand puppet responds. She cries and watches me pull off his head from my hand and drop it into the black trash bag.

"Now, baby, that wasn't so hard," I tease, stepping over his remains while scanning my eyes over her body. Even like this, she looks mouth watering. Her breasts stand out under her tight shirt perfectly.

"I was thinking, I love what I've done to your leg, but since I'm not the only man in your life who loves these tits so fucking much, maybe we need to add more." I reach for my switchblade still in my pocket and release the blade. Her shocked expression will never get tiresome.

"I need you to sit still for me, okay? I'm going to love every minute of watching you bleed again for me." I stare into her eyes as I carve more into her pale skin. My blade cuts deep into the top of her chest and she screams, so beautifully, in agony.

"There we go, baby. Two M's to match the name of our podcast logo. Since you like fucking both of us so much." I look up at her as I run my tongue over the bleeding letters.

Chapter Thirty

"Your Knight in Shining Fucking Armor"

LEE

My heart beats faster as I pull through the open chain linked fence. Rows of red, pulled down doors seem never ending. I drive around until I can find any clue or create any idea of what I need to do next. It seems like a half hour until I see Alan's silver Lexus. A small sliver of light shines from under the door. They have to be in there.

"There you are, you fuck." I say under my breath.

Quietly as I can, I park behind his car. *Now, what the hell am I supposed to do? I can't just get out of the car without a plan. He wouldn't be stupid enough to leave the door unlocked. How the hell would I go in? Just knock politely and hope he answers? Honestly that might be my only fucking choice.* With the only terrible scheme I could muster up, I reluctantly get out of the car and quietly shut my door.

The eerie silence in the area is deafening. The hair on my arms stands on end as I continue to make my way to the storage unit. With each step, my blood boils more and more. *She fucking let him touch her!* The thought repeats once again in my head. I bang on the door loudly with what feels like all of my rage coursing through my body. No one answers, but I can hear Alan's voice and the sounds Thalia makes that I am all too familiar with.

"Alan! You better not be fucking my girl!" I yell and pound on the door once again.

Alan's voice stops, and I can hear his footsteps get closer. I can tell they're his by the way the soles hit the concrete. *Alan and his expensive fucking dress shoes.*

My body shakes with anger and anticipation as I wait for him to open the door. The lock from the inside clicks open and my heartbeat picks up more than I thought was ever possible. I stare down and watch as he slowly pulls it up.

"Oh, Lee. How nice of you to join us." A smirk covers his face but all I can focus on are his clothes. His pants are soaked in blood and his white shirt is slightly open with even more drops of blood covering his chest and sleeves. He continues to smirk while he digs under his fingernails with the tip of a bloody switchblade.

"Lee! Turn around! Get back in your car and leave! He's fucking crazy! He's killed everyone!" Thalia screams. I watch her body practically vibrate in the metal chair she's strapped in. *Why the fuck is she strapped to a chair?*

"I AM NOT FUCKING CRAZY!" He turns his head and yells back at her.

"What the hell did you do to her, Alan?" My eyes quickly notice her bloody body, starting with the large gash going up nearly the entire length of her leg.

"I just updated the body modification she's already had done to herself." His voice abnormally switches in an instant back to his normal tone.

"Why the fuck did you do that?"

"She needs to know, Lee. She needs to know how bad I feel knowing that I love her, and she think she can fuck us both." His tone changes again, this time with his voice cracking. I stare in shock as his eyes begin filling up with tears. *I've never seen him like this before.*

"What about Ashley, Alan? Where is your wife?"

"Oh, she's been missing for some time now." He spins the tip of the blade on the pad of his index finger.

"Did you do something to her?" He gives a wide creepy smile, letting his mouth stretch across his face.

"Won't you come in?" He moves out of the space between us. He stares as I walk into the small space.

"What the fuck, Alan?!" My loud voice echoes in the unit. The sight in front of me makes me want to vomit. I scan over the room of carnage and gore. *It looks like someone already has.*

Quickly, I cover my nose and mouth the best I can with the collar of my shirt.

"Who's body is this?!" Pieces of a torso with a few limbs still attached are in a fucking bloody mess on top of a clear tarp. I notice a miniature saw sits upward on top of the rechargeable battery attachment. Drops of blood still dripping off the chain and blade into the puddles on the plastic tarp.

"Lee, you need to get the hell out of here. Don't worry about me. Just run to the police. Don't look back," Thalia quietly cries. I look closer at her body and notice the two bloody M's on her chest.

"Thalia, what did he do to you?" I step closer, trying not to step in the gory mess in front of me.

"Just get out of here, okay?" she pleads. I can't stand to look at her like this.

"I can't just leave you here. I'm going to find a way to get you out."

"What are you two love birds talking about?" Alan walks towards the both of us. The look in his eyes sends a shiver down my spine. "Oh, Lee, you're thinking of taking her away. But I worked so hard at getting her here. Would you like that, Thalia? You want to leave and go home?" He mocks. She turns her head and nervously watches him walk around to the back of her chair.

"I suppose it's okay." He squats down and cuts the middle of the constraint holding her wrists in place. She flinches as he runs the flat side of the blade up the back of her forearms. Menacingly, he stares at me and moves the blade down to the black zip ties holding her ankles in place.

"Aren't you so happy he decided to show up after I left everything out for him to find? Your phone in your apartment, my empty house, and the invoice I left on the desk. All clues so your knight in shining fucking armor could see what I've done to you." His eyes look into mine once he trails his switchblade down her ankles above the black zip ties holding her to the chair.

She lets out her first loud scream as he cuts one of the tendons in her ankles right above the zip tie holding her to the chair. He cuts her restraints right after he gets what he wants from her – the sound of her breaking into smaller and smaller pieces of herself.

"Just one more, Listener." I cringe at another sound of his knife going into her other tendon right before she screams again. "What are you waiting for? He's right there. Get up and walk to him." He mocks and cuts the other zip tie off her ankle. I stare in a permanent state of shock as she falls on the gorey mess in front of her.

"What, you didn't catch her? WHAT KIND OF FUCKING HERO ARE YOU!?" He screams. In shock, I continue to watch her struggle to get up off the bloody corpse in front of me.

"Who's body is this?" *Do I really want to fucking know?*

"Oh, that-that was Jace." He looks down and watches Thalia sob over her bestfriend's lifeless cadaver.

"You're a sick fuck, Alan."

"Yeah. I guess I am." He shrugs.

"Come on, Sweetheart. I need to get you to a hospital." She reaches over what is left of Jace's body as I pull her up through the mess of vomit and bloody limbs. Her heart beats fast on my chest and I hold her close. "I'm so relieved I found you. I had no idea where you were." I kiss the top of her head and try to stop the tears from swelling in my eyes.

"I'm sorry, Lee. I'm so sorry." Her cries are muffled against my shirt.

"It's okay, Thalia. Let's just get you out of here." I stand up on the tarp, doing my best not to drop her.

"Well, isn't this a lovely sentiment?" Alan interrupts. His loud claps echo through the small, concrete space. "You, my listener, really put on another great performance. I almost believed this one as much as I believed that you actually gave a shit about either one of us." He stops until he's front and center. "Do you think that I'm just going to let him take you out of here? I worked so hard at getting you here and planning this surprise for you."

"You said you would let me go." She continues to cry.

"Oh, baby. I'm never going to let you go."

"Just leave her alone, Alan." I try my best to keep my voice stable.

"After all I did for you, and you chose him. I DID ALL OF THIS FOR YOU! I KILLED ALL OF THESE PEOPLE FOR YOU!" His calm voice turns into loud cries as he looks over at Thalia's shivering body. The look of defeat moves over her disheveled form. *I need to get her the fuck out of here.* The calm and collected version of Alan that I once knew has long gone. The blood, Thalia's and Jace's blood he wears on his once stain free buisness casual atire, mixes with his tears and sweat that stream down his face.

"Let's just take her out of here. She's lost a lot of blood. She needs a doctor."

"I'm not ready to see her go." He shakes his head. "You can't take Thalia from me. Not again."

"Let's just all get out of here. Get a doctor to look at you both. You and I can have a drink and talk this out." I start to walk around Alan, still carrying Thalia limply in my arms. He watches us both carefully the closer I make my way over to the door.

"Please don't do this, Thalia." He looks down at the concrete floor with his fists clenched. "Please don't leave me." I watch him sidestep a few short steps to the closest wall. "Do you have any idea how it feels to want someone so badly, and you can't do anything about it?" He pauses. "How the thoughts of that person consume your mind constantly?"

I pay close attention to his hands as they reach for something propped up against the wall.

"Of course you wouldn't." I can hear the words catch in his throat. "Thoughts of you have made me do so many things that I would have never done before I met you." He smiles to himself. "I feel like a whole new man now." He grips the mysterious object in his hand. *I know what I have to do.*

"Thalia, Sweetheart. I need you to go to the car." I whisper next to her ear. "I don't care if you have to fucking drag yourself over there. Just go and don't look back."

"I can't leave you," she cries. *Please don't cry, Thalia. I don't want my last memory of you to be like this.*

"Just fucking listen to me. I'm going to let you go, okay? Reach into my pocket, grab my keys and get the hell out of here. Don't fucking look back." This time I can't stop my tears. I kiss the top of her head as she grabs the keys to my car.

"I'll meet you there, Thalia. Just get in the car, and don't look back." I kiss her one last time and watch her as she falls to the gravel. Within a split second, all I can see is Alan swinging a long metal bar. I feel a crushing pain on the side of my head. My vision goes dark and I fall to the ground.

 # THALIA

"LEE!" I scream as I watch him fall on the hard gravel. I drag my worn and weak body over to his. "Please, don't die! Please, stay with me." Heavy breathing interrupts my sobs. "You're going to be okay. It'll all be fine. Please, don't die." My pleas are loud cries. I continue to cover his black shirt with more of the tears I didn't think I had left. "Please don't leave me, too. You have to wake up. Please, Lee, just wake up."

"We have to get out of here, Thalia." Alan reaches down for my arm.

"No. I can't leave him here." Lee's body lay still. "You killed him. *Why did you kill him?"*

"He tried to take you from me. You were made for *me*, Listener. I won't let anyone else have you." Seeing his face covered in tears, and with his forced smile is almost terrifying. "Please, Thalia. I need you."

"You killed him." I shake my head and watch more tears fall on his chest.

"I killed him for you. I would kill anyone so I can have you."

Chapter Thirty-One

My Little Bird in Her Cage

**THALIA**

Two Months Later

It's cold in here. It's always cold. I catch myself staring down at the large pink scar that wraps around my leg to my upper thigh. Alan says that once he thinks I'm better, he'll tell them to let me come home. *To his home.* He says he'll schedule a time with the best artist in the city to fix my tattoo. The raised skin along the malformed line still feels foreign on my fingertips.

Alan comes to visit me every day. He sits with me on my bed in my assigned room. He holds me every day until visiting hours are over. He lets me cry against his chest. He kisses the top of my head and runs his hand down the small of my back. My body and mind are desperate traitors and I cling to him for the only source of comfort I have. He's all I have left.

My nightmares over the past few months have only worsened. I wake up in pools of cold sweat in late hours of the night. Nurses come to my rescue when they hear my screams. My doctor says once my body gets used to my new medication, the dreams will get less and less. I don't know what is worse, continuous nights of watching the memory of Lee dying and my best friend's bloody corpse in my mind or nights of dark, empty, nothingness.

Another medication to make the pain go away. One for my physical pain, a few for my newfound depression, and several others for mental stabilization. I have become a walking pharmaceutical zombie.

With one look at my scars and another at the wealthy man who claims to be my boyfriend, it was obvious to them I was admitted for my clinical depression. There was no mention of the new sorrowful outlook on life that was caused by the boyfriend being a serial killer. The few warning glances from Alan were a strong indication I was not going to challenge that claim. However, I haven't determined which would be worse – sitting alone in this mental rehab center, or the chance of death and being free from this place.

# ALAN

I visit Thalia every evening after work. I smile at every nurse I walk past on my way to her room. They eagerly smile back at the man who pays for Thalia's treatment.

Thalia's room is always cold. Every night, she stays under the thick, black comforter I brought in for her. She sits up in her bed as if she's been waiting all day for my visit. Her now fading red hair hangs around her shoulders. It frames her pale, slender face. She's like my weak little bird trapped in her cage.

If she isn't dissociating and staring at the painted-over white brick walls, her stare is focused on one of the several books I provided.

Every night, she tells me about her day in the facility and what she's read. It's always the same, but I will never get tired of our time together. I stare at Thalia intently as her words seep into my mind the way warm bourbon enters my bloodstream. Afterwards, I hold her while she cries into my chest. Like any guilty pleasure, I look most forward to this part of every visit. She lets me cling onto her until I'm forced to let her go.

Eight o'clock comes too soon and I have to prepare us both for our night to end. It's the same routine we have after each visit. Thalia's eyes continue to overflow with pleading tears when I make my attempt to climb out of her bed.

"Please don't go." Her wide hazel eyes look into mine like they do every night.

"Listener, you know I have to." I would stay here forever with her if the nurses let me.

"Please, just tell them I'm better. Take me home." Her tears now fall fast down her pink cheeks. *Home. My home. Soon to be our home.*

"You're not ready." I kiss her lips and lay her down in her bed and cover up her weak body. "I'll be back tomorrow. I love you." She gives a small upturned smile through her silent cries. *One day she'll say it back.*

A part of my heart aches as I walk out of her room and quietly shut her door. "Goodbye, Mr. Jones. See you tomorrow evening." I give a small wave to the nurses and walk towards my car.

······|||·····||||||··|·🎤·||··|||||||·····|||·····

Artemis greets me at my door and rubs his white fur along my dark brown slacks.

"I just visited mommy. She's got a little while to go, but she'll be home soon." I pet our cat between his ears. He purrs with approval and follows me close behind as I walk towards the newly remodeled kitchen to fill his empty food bowl.

I walk over to the black restocked cabinet with dishes that I know Thalia will love when she officially moves in and take out a black mug to make myself a cup of coffee.

My hot mug nearly burns my lips as I take my first sip. Scrolling through my phone while I take in the caffeine and open up social media. Pictures of a mysterious fire to the local storage facility flood my news feed.

It's a pity really, Jace and Ashley have been missing these past couple of months and the police still don't have any leads. While I take another sip of my hot coffee, I continue to scroll through the many posts on my social media pages. There are several images of the units going up in flames. The fire is on everyone's mind this evening. It makes me question if our police force even really knows what they're doing when they search for clues and other forms of evidence. You know, it's the small details that matter. *Maybe they were all incinerated.* I smile while setting my mug down on the new granite, wondering how the jar of Ruben Ara's eyes look in the red and orange light.

Chapter Thirty-Two

WAKE UP

LEE

Fuck, my head is killing me.

That annoying beeping sound is a constant ringing in my ears. My vision goes from dark to blurry. All I see is bright fluorescent overhead lighting. Moving my head and the rest of my body seems nearly impossible.

My arm is hooked up to an IV with God knows what pumping into my veins. I stare at the number of machines wired to the sticky pads on my chest.

"I'm in a fucking hospital," I mumble to myself as I rub my eyes and my blurry vision starts to get clearer. My realization is confirmed when I watch an older man walk into my room.

His long white coat hangs just past his knees. Thick rimmed glasses fall slowly down his long nose before he pushes them up with the bottom of his pen. He looks down at his plastic clipboard and then to me. His thin lips turn into a tight smile.

"Hello, Mr. Reynolds. Welcome back to the land of the living."

ACKNOWLEDGEMENTS

Who would have thought writing my first novel would have taken so much time and effort not only for me, the author, but for the many people that have helped me through the crazy journey that is Hello, Listener. I know, personally while growing up and dreaming up the idea of becoming an author, I never would have thought one single book would take so much time and effort between all parties. Those who have been on this journey with me have had the pleasure of sitting with me through this wild ride, and for that I am eternally grateful.

I want to first thank The Man Upstairs, for giving me the ability, patience, and the motivation to write such a heavy book.

Next, I would like to thank my husband. Thank you, my love for always believing in me and pushing me to keep writing. There were many times where imposter syndrome almost got the best of me and you were always there to tell me to keep writing and to finish the story. From the time my writing journey first began in August of 2023 until now, you have been patient through the many nights of staying up while I wrote "one more chapter," or "one more line." Your love and support means so much to me. I love you, Handsome.

I would like to also thank my best friend, Paige. Thank you for always listening to all of my crazy and depraved ideas that became a part of this novel. You eagerly read each chapter even when they were filled with the many grammatical and spelling errors. Your anticipation to find out what crazy thing Alan was going to do next, helped drive me to keep going. You were there to make sure I wouldn't give up and that I needed to keep believing in myself. I love you so much for that!

Many people have asked where I got the inspiration for Alan, Lee, and the Manhattan Murders Podcast. To simply put it, I was inspired by my favorite horror movie podcast, The Sloppy Horror Podcast. Mark and Christian were a big inspiration for my main characters, Alan and Lee. I want to thank them both. Without their new episodes every Monday, and their hilarious TikTok videos, Hello, Listener would have not been possible. Thank you both, and I hope you enjoy the read!

While writing Hello, Listener, I had the opportunity to meet so many amazing people who have helped me along the way. Those who I have met online in the book and horror communities have been so supportive and helpful along the way! You all have been so great. It means so much!

To my beta readers: Brittany, Kourtney, Lilliana, and Amanda, you all were awesome! All of your suggestions and comments were not only helpful but hilarious. They were exactly what this book needed. Thank you all so very much. I look forward to working with you in the future!

To my Editor: Lo. Thank you for sticking with me through this process! We both know what an adventure it was. It means so much that you stayed even through some of the difficult issues that occurred! You're amazing!

Last but definitely not least, I want to thank my good friend Lauren (L.Clara.) You have been such a big help to this baby author! Without you and your advice, I would have been extremely clueless. You have been such an amazing friend for all of this and I just love you for it!

Thank you to everyone who gave Hello, Listener a chance. It has been such an indescribable experience and I am excited to continue this dream of being a writer. *Holy crap, I'm a writer!*

About the Author

So, About the Author page... What can I say about myself. I'll be quite honest, I have no idea how or what to say about myself. So here it goes. Be gentle, I'm new at this writing stuff.

Who is Lorien Ray? Well, I guess you could say that I am an introverted (as if you couldn't tell) author from the Midwest. When I'm not obsessing over horror, fantasy, and dark romance novels or when I'm not attached to my laptop, I'm watching anime with my two boys or horror movies with my husband and best friend.

I first became obsessed with writing when my eighth grade teacher required my class to write different forms of poetry. I fell in love with the idea of expressing myself through symbolism and figurative writing. Later on, I discovered Stephen King and Edgar

Allan Poe. After reading King's Salem's Lot and Poe's The Raven, I knew I wanted to follow in their footsteps.

It took me many years and many attempts to dive in and have the courage to complete a full fledged book. With all of the ideas I have cooking up inside my head, there isn't any going back now.

I'll even make it easy for you.

Made in United States
Troutdale, OR
11/23/2024

25197023R00196